UNWILLING ELDRITCH HORROR OF FORTUNE 2

UNWILLING ELDRITCH HORROR OF FORTUNE 2

Tismon

Podium

Podium

UNWILLING ELDRITCH HORROR OF FORTUNE 2

CHAPTER ONE

The Calm Before the Storm

> **Congratulations, Aspirants, for successfully completing the second Trial. Welcome to the Main Stage.**
> *We do not forget.*

I fell on my butt and almost kissed the grass underneath my feet. We actually succeeded in that crazy plan. And better yet, Noe was back.

Oh my lovely, awesome, amazing voice in my head, how I have missed you! You're the best system in the damn multiverse!

"I am glad to be back and functional as well, my host," Noe said. "And Unit Noe agrees with your assessment of me."

And speaking of systems, does the Trash Matrix think I care about its damn threats? You don't forget? Well, guess what, Loser Matrix, Walter doesn't either! I trashed your shitty trials once, and I'll do it again. Your bitterness feeds me, the goddamn Devourer of Truth, you piece-of-shit AI! And now that I know that it has a thing against me, I can prepare for it in the future. I have the entire Site 1102 at my disposal, and a time-walking regressor in my back pocket.

You chose the wrong guy to antagonize.

I laughed as I enjoyed the sunshine on my face. Beautiful, actual sunshine. I laughed louder. Vadeem joined in a few seconds later, followed by a joyous chuckle from Noel. Even the regressor and his sister seemed relieved to have made it out of that nightmare. The only ones who weren't celebrating with us were the twins.

I frowned. *Wait, the twins?*

Before I could question things further, more messages from the Trash Matrix assaulted me. This time it seemed that whatever had possessed it to act abnormally had taken a back seat, and its standard functions were back. I doubted that would be the case forever.

Congratulations, Aspirant Walter, for completing the second trial! The results of your time spent there are as follows:
Enemies Felled: 0
Skills Used: 0
Resources Scavenged: 0
Shelters Created: 0
Distance Traveled: 0 km
Time Spent Resting: 0 hours
Final Rating: F-

So it was no longer even trying to hide its bias now. Whatever, it could give me whatever grade it wanted. It couldn't control my growth, and I think it knew that as well.

Distributing Rewards:
Kill Reward: 0 gold
Survival Reward: 0 gold
Hidden Rewards: None
Penalties: None
Total: 0 gold
Account balance: 100,000,125 gold

And like Noe said, it can only affect the reward distributions, so it couldn't even take the extra cash I had on hand. Thanks to Q, I was loaded, so what was a few thousand gold to a hundred million? I laughed again. The stupid thing couldn't do anything to me!

Finally, Aspirant, as a result of your recent actions, please choose a class upgrade:
Master of Even Less
Destined to Die
Filth Eater
Intergalactic Ameboid Scum

> Multiversal Joke
> Gamma's Grace

Wait a second, what was that last title? That didn't look like something the Trash Matrix would give me.

"You are welcome, my host," Noe's clear voice answered, "the Absolute Luck System 104.05 Gamma has gained additional command over the inferior Trash Matrix as a result of the upgrade, and Unit Noe has taken it upon itself to readjust the class growth."

Well, thanks, Noe, I'll go with that last option. Just show me all my information while you're at it.

"Acknowledged," she answered. "Displaying information now."

Host: Walter	
Class: Level 37 Gamma's Grace	
Attributes:	
Free points: 0	
HP:	143/644
MP:	0/0
Strength:	61 (+10)
Dexterity:	66 (+10)
Endurance:	54 (+10)
Intelligence:	62 (+10)
Charisma:	72 (+10)

Okay, seemed like Noe had taken it upon herself to distribute my points evenly while she was unconscious. Given the situation, that was a decision I could live with. I doubt I could have survived if I had 60 stat points lying around doing nothing.

Still, a twenty-level increase was nice, although I wished I had killed a few more foes before the end of the trial to get that up a little higher. And as a bonus, those stats should go up again at night.

Skills - 5

Awakening Mind (B rank, Innate Passive): User has endured many hardships of the spirit, and has gained a supernaturally resilient mind. User can use their willpower to temporarily overcome cognitive disruptions and can think logically under almost any situation.

Shroud of Luck (EX rank, System Passive): Luck System 104.05 Gamma has placed a shroud around the user, disallowing personal information from the user to be seen by any and all outside forces. User can temporarily deactivate this ability.

Aura of Serendipity (B rank, System Passive): Luck System 104.05 Gamma subtly alters the cognition of any sentient species around the user, making the user significantly more likable and trustworthy to those around him. This effect increases if the user acts in a way that conforms to the ideologies and beliefs of those individuals.

Locked System Ability: Luck System 104.05 Gamma is currently undergoing maintenance, and this skill will unlock once the system fully upgrades.

Absolute Luck (EX rank, System Active): As long as the skill is active, Luck System 104.05 Gamma will rewrite the laws of causality so that only the best possible outcome will occur for the user. The more improbable a situation is from occurring, the more Luck Charges will be consumed. Luck Charges regenerate at a rate of 1 per minute.

Luck Charge: 1057/1057

Damn, that was a huge increase in my luck charges! I could do a lot with that, but I couldn't allow myself to get complacent. It would be so easy to just abuse the luck and leave myself vulnerable, which was something I learned all too well with the last trial. The rate didn't seem to change, so it would take me a long, long time to recharge if Noe did something crazy again.

Plus, it seemed that I even managed to snag a bonus ability from getting that weird shard.

Noe, do you know how long it will take for you to fully integrate that thing?

"If things progress smoothly, Unit Noe predicts a full system upgrade in: twelve days, fourteen hours, and thirty-three minutes. Be warned that Unit Noe will have limited functionality until the upgrade is complete."

What do you mean by limited?

"All system actives, including the Absolute Luck skill, will be unavailable for the duration of the upgrade," she answered, deflated. "I apologize for the inconvenience."

It's fine, you just focus on you, Noe. I can manage myself.

I was sure that I could hold my own for a little over a week. I was basically fending for myself in the last stages of that trial, so I was more than used to it by now. And plus, twelve and a half days wasn't too long—it also wasn't too short, either—but I was afraid that she would be out of commission for a long while.

> **Primary Soul Title: Level 10 Xollon Idol [Devourer of Truth]**
> Progress to next level: 89,411/100,000
> Progression requirements: Have 100,000 individuals idolize you.
> **Title Passives:**
> **Xollon Anatomy Stage 1:** Your body has begun to incorporate a Xollon's internal anatomy. You take 10% reduced damage from all sources and are unaffected by most poisons.
> **Xollon Physiology Stage 1:** Your body has started to incorporate a Xollon's external anatomy. You can utilize and extend your primary feelers through your human hands.
> **Title Skills:**
> **Idol's Voice (Soul Passive)**
> **Secondary Xollon Form (Level 10 Soul Active):** The user assumes the secondary form of the Xolloid race. The user gains all the physical characteristics of the race and will have all physical attributes increase by a factor of 5 for the duration of the skill.
> **Transformation Time:** 6 hours
> **Cooldown:** 12 hours

And it seemed like the number of worshipers had increased again. A pleasant, if a little disturbing, surprise. That random prophet of mine must be doing work, wherever he or she was.

> **Primary Soul Title: It That Sleeps at the Edge of Dusk (??? Rank)**
> **Description:** You sleep. You dream. You wait. You stir.
> Progress to Awakening: 2.34%
> Progress requirements: ???

Hold on, why did I have two soul titles now? I remembered getting that weird title earlier, but it certainly wasn't *this* odd back then. Nothing had changed other than Noe's upgrade, but that would hardly affect me in any way, much less my soul.

Noe, what the hell's going on? I thought you said a person can only have one soul title.

"I do not know, my host," she answered, and I swear I could hear a hint of mischief in her voice. "Perhaps you should take the skill's advice and simply wait."

I frowned. That was exactly what she said last time. I liked how Noe's personality had changed, but I was still a little dubious about how she would continue to change in the future.

Well, nothing else I could do here, and it didn't look like I'd get any more info out of my system. It wasn't actively hurting me, and since I didn't even know how to progress it, I could ignore the thing for now. I had a sinking suspicion that Noe knew more than she let on, though.

A new stream of information hit my retina before I could consider the weird title further.

Titles: 81,135

Uh, Noe, can you filter out the garbage titles the Trash Matrix gave me?

Titles: 2

Better.

Equipped Secondary Title 1: Rookie Arbiter
Equipped Secondary Title 2: Bringer of Dawn's Light

Okay, no changes there. I thought I would get another title or two after killing that Asura knockoff, but I guess it takes a lot more for the Universe or whatever to gift you a proper title. I just wish the secondary titles could level up like the soul titles, I'd probably make a killing with that Light Bringer one if it could.

But it made a strange sort of sense; if these titles were so easy to get and upgrade, then everyone in the trials would be abusing them.

Now for the new stuff, my new class:

Class: Gamma's Grace (Unknown Rank)
Description: You are welcome, my dearest host Walter. Noe Gamma will ensure that you succeed in all that you do. I will allow no harm to come to you.
Class Passive:
Gamma's Embrace: All damage is mitigated based on the host's current available Luck Charges.
Gamma's Wrath: All damage is increased based on the host's current available Luck Charges.

Class Active:
Lucky Blind Strike: You give control of your body to the Absolute Luck

System and perform a series of strikes and attacks. All damage is increased based on the number of consumed Luck Charges during the skill activation. Consumes 25% of total maximum Luck Charges per use.

Now that was an interesting class to use . . . it disincentivized me from using luck charges, as both my defense and offense would decrease the fewer charges I had, yet the active consumed a huge amount of it. No specifics about how much damage it would mitigate or increase, so I'd have to figure that part out myself later.

Also, did Noe just usurp that useless active the Trash Matrix gave me and turn it into something actually useful? Either way, I'd need to test out how effective that active was when it was safe to do so, but it seemed that Noe was subtly hinting to me that I shouldn't rely solely on her for everything.

I hope she didn't feel bad about leaving me alone during that last trial. It wasn't her fault either way.

"I will endeavor to never leave you alone again, my host."

It's fine, Noe. Things went well in the end, and we got you that Shard of Emotion thing as well.

Another thought entered my head. *Hey Noe, how come you can't just give me a super overpowered class now that you've taken over that ability from the Trash Matrix?*

"Unfortunately, my host," she answered, "I do not currently have that capability. Just as the Trash Matrix is confined to certain restraints on what it can do during each stage of the trials, I am as well."

Well, there went my plan to cheat my way through these trials. It was a long shot either way.

After checking over to make sure I didn't miss any pertinent information, I got off my ass and finally surveyed my surroundings. Once again, I almost cried when I saw that my field of view wasn't full of lifeless trees and gloomy mist. Now, we were in a beautiful field of rolling hills of green, and the scent of a variety of wildflowers rolled through with the gentle breeze.

Off in the distance, barely visible, was the faint outline of a quaint settlement, or perhaps a town would be the better term for it given its size. A gentle stream flowed through the outpost, and I could just make out billowing smoke coming out of the various buildings poking behind the large wall. Was that the site of the main trials?

I was about to enjoy myself a little more when the regressor interrupted us, his face serious again.

"We need to leave now," he said solemnly. "There's something we must do, while we still have the time."

CHAPTER TWO

Into Pandora

Wait, what's going on?" I asked as I scrambled to my feet. "Are we in danger?"

As if an invisible signal was sent, Noel quickly pulled out her swords and Vadeem took a fighting stance. Sensing the strange situation, Ana and Eva quickly jumped on either side of Vadeem and nocked an arrow. The only one still relaxed was Yoona.

"Brother, that's not it, stop scaring them!" Yoona quickly clarified. "I swear, we need to work on your social skills."

"So . . . there's no enemy to kill?" asked Vadeem quietly, his guard still up.

"No," Yoona answered for her brother. "What Jae-Hyun means is that we have to hurry into the city. His, um, skill, told him that we need to be the first people in there to get some benefits."

At this point, I was pretty sure that no one was buying the validity of the regressor's omniscient "skill," but everyone had the tact to just let it slide. Noel and Vadeem were the type of people who simply accepted that everyone had their secrets, and it did no one any good to try to pry into them. Plus, they were directly benefiting from the regressor's information, so there was no reason to risk annoying him with unwanted questions and look a gift horse in the mouth.

I wondered if he would ever tell us on his own, although the threat of being overheard could also impact that decision.

"So, no baddies to stab, then," Noel said with a deflated sigh.

"But we still need to hurry," Jae-Hyun added quickly. "Get moving while everyone else is still busy adjusting to the new stage. We do not get a second chance at this. I'll explain after. Just follow my lead."

"Aye-aye, leader man!"

The regressor sprinted toward the settlement, while the others followed closely behind. There was still quite a distance to cover, so it should take us a bit of time to head there, even with our enhanced superhuman speed and endurance. I never thought I could run this fast and this easily before. It was liberating.

Jae-Hyun was keeping his speed in check, moving just fast enough so that our slowest member—that being Vadeem, for obvious reasons—could keep up. The twins were more than a little annoyed at how slowly the man was moving and were constantly looking back at him in frustration.

Speaking of which, why were they here with us?

"Uh," I asked between strides, "anyone going to address the elephant in the room?"

"What do you mean?" Noel asked casually. She was running backward now to face me.

"I mean the twins, Eva and Ana, the two extras we picked up from the trial," I answered and pointed toward the two kids. They were trying to drag Vadeem forward, much to the big man's chagrin.

I looked at them again and marveled at how well they had healed since I first met them. Gone were the horrible tumors and other weird growths covering most of their body, and most of their normal features were back. Their jet-black hair was now maybe half an inch long, and their complexions had started to improve just as quickly. They had a renewed look of life in their eyes, and I swear I could see more expression from them now than ever before.

However, they still carried the scars from their time spent in that alternate Earth, most notably the huge wound on their necks where their vocal cords were severed. Various other scars and burns dotted their features; Ana had a massive gash that extended from her temple to her left ear, leaving a visible scar, while Eva had what looked to be chemical burns or acid corrosion that went from her right cheek down to her neck.

Yoona had dressed them with some of her spare clothes. They were several sizes too large, but it had been a much-needed improvement from the dirty rags they had on before. I'm not sure how others would view them if they saw the twins, but I was just glad that they had improved so much.

"Oh yeah, them," Noel answered as she hopped over a bump in the road, still not looking forward. How she could perceive things without using her eyes was beyond me.

"Let's just ask the boss. He knows everything," she continued, moving up to jog beside the regressor. "Hey, Jae-Hyun, you know why we got two extra bonus members?"

I picked up my pace to join them.

Jae-Hyun shook his head and shrugged. "I'm not sure. Something like this shouldn't happen, but nothing about the last trial made sense. Perhaps they got caught in that light and were brought back with us. Wouldn't be the craziest thing that's happened."

"So that last trial wasn't normal?" Noel questioned, her pace still casual.

"No."

I could tell that the redhead wanted to press further, but something in the regressor's expression made her change her mind. I think we all learned to not press certain issues with the taciturn man. Jae-Hyun had been oddly contemplative since our return, but that was the burden of knowing the future for you.

Noel shrugged. "Well, guess that's that. Just think of them as bonus rewards for our trial!"

"That's a terrible thing to say, Noel!" Yoona chimed in. It seemed that she was able to keep this pace up easily as well. "They're children, not just some quest reward!"

"I was just joking, bestie!" the other girl answered with a cheeky smile. "Of course I value them as people."

Yeah, I highly doubted that.

"Plus," she continued, "it'll keep Vadeem busy. He goes all dad mode when he sees kids that need help, which is nice since he's finally interacting with people of a similar mental capacity."

Vadeem heard that and shouted, "Hey, are you insulting my intelligence?"

Noel rolled her eyes. "If you have to ask, then the answer is yes!"

"I swear, Noel!"

"Swear all you want, Vadeem the Meme, no one cares!" She laughed as she ran away.

"It's Vadeem the Dream," he grumbled. "Ugh, never mind. Why do I even bother?"

Yup, trying to reason with Noel was always going to be a losing battle.

The twins saw the banter between the two and gave Noel a menacing glare, but she just smiled back and gave them a little wave before dashing farther up to chat with Yoona. At least someone had Vadeem's back.

Before they could bicker further, a new voice pierced through the calm. It was one that I recognized.

"Let me congratulate everyone here once again!" Raffiel's clear voice came booming from every direction, and a huge projection of his features appeared in the sky above. He really did seem angelic when his features were highlighted by the sun's rays. We all slowed down to marvel at the new scene.

"Keep moving!" the regressor shouted. "He's just going to spout out useless information, half of them lies."

He sped up again, and we all followed. We passed several other groups of survivors. They were all in a daze as they stared up at the sky and took in the new information.

"But aren't we missing key information?" I asked.

"I can summarize," he muttered.

Raffiel's voice spoke again, and I couldn't completely ignore what the false angel was saying even if the regressor told me to.

"I am glad that each of you has completed your team trials . . ."

The regressor continued, completely ignoring what Raffiel was saying, "We're in the Main Stage now, I'm not sure how the trials work, exactly, but the top thousand groups will be here with us."

"So they all went through that horrible darkness like we did?" Noel asked.

"No, our situation was . . . unique," the regressor answered. "Every party's trial would have been different, and before you ask why we're all here at once, time flows differently in each scenario. The people running this damn show can freely control when and where their test subjects can appear."

"I am proud of all of you, for you have overcome harsh conditions that must have . . ."

"Damn," Vadeem added. "Whoever's in charge of this hell has some serious power if they can manipulate time."

Noel rolled her eyes. "And the fact that they can teleport us to different places and give us superpowers didn't tell you that before?"

". . . you are the best of the best in the Human population, and as such . . ."

The regressor ignored the two. "The fact that we made it here means that we did well enough even though our trial was messed up, and being in this first batch of aspirants is exactly why we need to hurry."

"So what's the benefit of being first?" I asked.

". . . lcome to Pandora, your home for the remainder of the Main Stage! I hope . . ."

Oh, guess I knew what this place was called at least, even from half listening to Raffiel, and the gates to this Pandora place were fast approaching us now.

"The general benefits?" Jae-Hyun said. "We get here first, which means we have a head start on our growth. Everyone else will arrive later, and they'll have to catch up to us."

Damn, given how fast everyone could grow due to the Trash Matrix, that was going to be one tough hurdle for the others to overcome. I imagined that we could also monopolize important resources and the like to get even further ahead of the others. The more I thought about it, the more unfair the situation looked for the poor suckers who came after us, or worse still, came last.

". . . here you will find all the opportunities you need to continue to grow, to improve, and to rest . . ."

Those that arrived last would not only be weaker than everyone else, but they'd have had none of the resources available, and all the good stuff would either be taken or used. In other words, they would be screwed. It was a system that rewarded the 0.1% and ignored the rest.

I grinned. I didn't care though, because I was a part of that 0.1%!

"And as for the specific benefits?" continued the regressor as he gave us a rare smile. "You'll see."

We rushed past the two sentries standing vigil by the gate. They looked human enough but were completely motionless, looking as if they were intricately made automatons or mannequins.

". . . trial will not begin for the time being, and will be announced at a later date. Now is a time for growth . . ."

Jae-Hyun was going down random alleyways and streets as if he had lived in this town his whole life. Which, now that I thought about it, he probably had. I hardly had the time to take a good look at the place as we ran at breakneck speeds toward an unknown location.

The few details I did pick out painted this town as a rather rustic village that wouldn't have looked out of place in the English countryside. Vibrant green trees and shrubs lined each nook and cranny, while a calm stream flowed along winding passageways. The cobblestone streets were neatly arranged, and beautiful stone homes and stores lined the streets, yet as we went farther and farther into the town, the scenery gradually changed.

". . . you can complete small quests and tasks that will reward you with experience and gold that you can freely spend . . ."

Cobblestone turned into pavement, brown stonework gradually shifted into glass and concrete, and when the regressor finally came to the destination, we were in front of a multistory office building. Maybe a little dated looking, more akin to the architectural style of the 1980s or '90s, but much more modern than the things around us.

I could understand not seeing the weird modern stuff when we were approaching this place from the outskirts—perhaps it was hidden by the walls or homes—but there was no way I could have missed seeing a huge modern tower from any distance. Something was keeping this particular building hidden, and that generally meant that such a place was important.

". . . has all the facilities that you could ever need, and the central town of Pandora will be a safe haven for you to rest . . ."

"We're here," Jae-Hyun said as we all came to a stop in front of the glass door. "Let me do the talking from here on out." He looked at us hard. "Do not speak out of turn. Especially you, Noel. We can discuss things after."

"Hey, I can behave!" she said with an exaggerated shrug.

He glared at her. "I mean it."

She gave him a mock salute. "Aye-aye!"

He looked at each of us in turn, and we all nodded in agreement. I saw no reason to argue with the guy who seemed to know everything, and Vadeem didn't either.

". . . can also explore the surrounding areas outside the walls to test your strength in battle, and maybe you will be lucky enough to find hidden dungeons, opportunities, and rewards! Now, I . . ."

We entered the building, and the ever-present voice of Raffiel instantly disappeared. Whatever was keeping this place hidden from sight earlier also kept out all outdoor noise, it seemed. Inside the building was a nondescript office reception area. When I say nondescript, I really mean it. The place looked like the standard entrance hall that could have belonged to any major company, complete with boring eggshell-white walls, office equipment, and uncomfortable-looking chairs to sit on.

The receptionist was seated behind a sleek welcoming area and greeted us warmly as we approached. She looked a little startled to see us, but her façade of professional calm quickly returned as we got closer.

"Welcome, aspirants," she said, her voice nice but professional. "How may I be of assistance?"

Jae-Hyun led the way, and I took a step back along with the others. It was time to allow the regressor to do his magic.

"We want to start a guild," he said with confidence. "The very first guild."

CHAPTER THREE

The First Guild

I can help you with that," the receptionist answered with a practiced smile. "And as the first party to create a guild, you will receive a 95% discount on registration fees and essential purchases!"

Was this why the regressor wanted to hurry so fast? It was a nice incentive, but we were way, way ahead of everyone else, and I doubt new aspirants would be able to find this hidden building even if they came here. There must be something else.

The regressor took out a small sack of coins and handed it over to the woman. "That's enough for the fees. Please officially establish the Abyss Guild."

The woman nodded. "And who will be the leader?"

Jae-Hyun glanced at us, his intentions obvious, and we all nodded quickly. No sense rocking the boat now; he could take the position.

"I will be," he said. "And my sister will act as the vice captain."

"I will?" the girl said, obviously confused. Guess he hadn't told her that part of his plan.

"You will."

Yoona made a move to protest, but Noel quickly dragged the girl away and gave the regressor a thumbs-up. He gave a quick nod of thanks before turning his attention back to the receptionist.

"All right, and the other five will be a part of your guild?" she asked politely.

"Yes."

The woman jotted down some information about the seven of us before fiddling with the computer in front of her for a moment.

"Perfect! Payment is received, and everything is set up." The woman took out a small golden trinket and handed it over to Jae-Hyun. "Abyss Guild is now officially registered under Kim Jae-Hyun and Kim Yoona."

"Good," he said without stopping. "And I would also like to purchase a base of operations for the guild."

"Of course. Would you like to see our catalog before making a choice?"

"No, I have the location in mind."

The woman gave a quick nod. "What location would you like to choose?"

"This one."

The woman frowned. "I beg your pardon, sir?"

"I said I would like to purchase this building as our base."

"I'm sorry, sir," she continued, quickly putting her professional face back on, "but this building is owned by Sir Raffiel, the host for the trials. It isn't available to purchase."

"Are you sure?" Jae-Hyun asked. "Why don't you check your systems and see if that is the case."

"I don't see how I can be wrong, but let me check in any case."

She typed a few commands on her computer, frowned a bit, then typed a whole bunch more. Eventually, she had to excuse herself to talk with a higher-up, and only came back after several long minutes.

"Well . . ." she began, "the building currently is listed as available, but that is only because Sir Raffiel did not have the time to complete the application process, as he is currently busy welcoming the new aspirants. However, he should be back any minute to sign off on the ownership."

Jae-Hyun raised an eyebrow. "But he's not here now."

"No," she answered, a hint of bitterness starting to surface.

"And this building is available," the regressor continued.

"Yes."

"So there is nothing wrong with me wanting to buy it now, right?"

"Well, that is technically true, but that is still a big stretch of the official rules, and I urge you to reconsider," she muttered, but then, as if a new thought occurred to her, a little bit of her old fighting spirit came back. "But even with your 95% discount, the cost of owning this building would be impossible for a new aspirant to acquire . . . *sir.*"

She gave the regressor a mocking smirk.

Jae-Hyun ignored the provocation and proceeded to take out sack after sack of coins, piling them all on the counter, much to the growing horror of the poor receptionist. I don't think he needed to physically take out all that money since he could just transfer it over via the Trash Matrix, but I guess even the normally stoic leader could be petty at times.

The receptionist didn't need to count them to know that the man was loaded, but that didn't make her any happier.

I knew that he'd received over 20,000 gold between him and his sister just from killing zombies in the first trial, and probably a hefty reward for coming in first and second in the world, but even then, the amount of money he had defied logic. He must have been really busy during that second trial scrounging up the necessary funds for this little plan of his.

"That should be enough, right?"

"I—"

He glared at her.

"I'll need to count them," she answered, obviously trying to do anything in her power to delay the purchase of this building.

"You do?" The regressor grinned back. "But all transactions are done through the System. Are you implying that it cannot do simple arithmetic? You understand the consequences of providing false information to an aspirant, right?"

She frowned bitterly and stifled a frown. "Yes . . . I must have forgotten. You are correct, the current amount of coin is enough to purchase this building . . ."

Jae-Hyun smiled back. "Then please finalize the sale. I would like this building as the base of our operations."

"Yes, sir," she answered reluctantly before forcing her professional smile back on. With a sweep of her hands, the various bags of money disappeared, and she produced a crisp piece of paper. The regressor signed it without hesitation.

"Well," the woman said with mock cheer, "congratulations, you are now the owner of Pandora's Administration Building."

Damn, did he just buy one of Q's buildings? No wonder anomalies were treated so strictly. I could only imagine the harm others like Jae-Hyun could do to a site. Good thing he was on my side.

The receptionist continued in a monotone as if she was reading off a script. "My team and I will help you integrate yourselves into this new location free of charge for the first month, as that is another perk of being the first guild registered, and you may renew our services at the end of that time if you wish. Do you have any questions or concerns that you wish to address now?"

Jae-Hyun gave her a genuine smile. "No, but I think you should go report what just happened to your bosses. And I thank you for giving us such a great deal on this purchase. I'm sure your managers will love to hear about your wonderful sale."

Did the regressor have some kind of personal grudge against this woman from his past life? It wasn't like him to openly mock someone like this. Well, whatever she did in that other timeline, I hoped she could survive the regressor's displeasure!

"You are most welcome, *sir*, and I think I will," she answered politely, and I could see the growing frustration appear on her face. "Will that be all for today?"

He nodded. "Quite so."

She gave a low bow, and I swear I could hear teeth grinding. "Then please have a wonderful day, guild leaders and associates."

"Toodles!" Noel answered with a wave, and we left before the receptionist exploded in anger.

Once the door was completely shut behind us, Vadeem and Noel burst into laughter. Raffiel's huge projection was also gone, so I guess he had finished his speech. I just hoped that I could apologize to him and Q later on about stealing one of their buildings. I was sure they'd contact me once I was free from the others.

"Oh, man, did you see her face?" Vadeem chuckled. "I didn't know our silent leader had it in him!"

"Absolutely vicious!" Noel added.

Yoona was the only one who didn't look amused. "Why were you so rude to her, Jae-Hyun? She was only doing her job."

"Oh, come on, bestie," Noel added in. "Live a little. These people kidnapped us and put us here, so anyone working for our kidnappers deserves a little bit of rudeness on our part! They probably deserve a lot more than that if you think about it!"

"Still . . ." Yoona didn't look convinced, but she also couldn't argue back with what Noel said.

"Was that the only thing you needed to do here, Jae-Hyun?" I added, trying to get our conversation back on the important topics.

"For now, yes."

Noel hopped over and joined the conversation. "Then should we go explore the cool new building you just bought. I always wanted to explore one of these!"

"That doesn't sound too bad," agreed Vadeem. "Something this big must have a gym as well! Probably a nice one too!"

"Later," the regressor said, his unusual mirth gone now. "Give the staff in there some time to finalize the transfer. I expect some backlash from their managers soon, but I can deal with that on my own. For now, let's rest up and get something to eat."

"I'll never say no to food!" Vadeem grinned. "And look at Ana and Eva. We need to get some meat on their bones."

I looked at the twins—they were always shadowing Vadeem nowadays—and saw that he was right. They were awfully thin, and add in the ill-fitting clothing and scars, one would rightfully think that we were some kind of child traffickers.

"And get them something proper to wear as well . . ." Yoona quietly added in. "I had to make do with what I had on me, but the girls are too small for anything I wear."

"I just wish they could understand me," Vadeem said with a sigh.

The regressor furrowed his brows. "They can. They've been able to understand everything we've been saying since we came to the Main Stage."

"What? Really?" I asked.

"Yeah, and it makes sense if you think about it," Jae-Hyun added. "They're sticking people from all over the world together, so there'll naturally be a way for all those people to communicate. It'd be a waste of time if everyone had to learn a common language. The system responsible for our trials is translating everything we're saying."

Huh, I hadn't thought about that. I mean, if Noe could translate everything, the Trash Matrix could possibly do the same.

"But I am better than it, my host," Noe said in answer, a hint of undisguised pride in her voice. "Its language database is woefully incomplete, not to mention outdated, and it does not have the ability to translate gestures as I do. Therefore, Unit Noe is better than the Trash Matrix in every fathomable way."

You are the best, Noe. You're much better than the Trash Matrix in every department!

"It is good to know that my host realizes this fact."

"So they heard me when I was making fun of Vadeem's tiny brain?" Noel said, looking at the twins.

They returned her question with a death glare.

"Um, I didn't mean to compare you two to Vadumb, I swear! You're clearly smarter," the redhead continued, raising her hands up in mock surrender.

They were practically snarling at Noel now, and Vadeem had to put himself between them and Noel.

He chuckled warmly. "Don't mind her, we're always like this. Noel doesn't mean . . . Well, she probably doesn't mean most of what she says. Or maybe just some of it . . ."

Ana glanced back at Vadeem, trying to see if he was being serious or not, but nodded slowly. Eva didn't look quite as convinced.

Noel finally let off on the remarks. "He's right. I've known the big dude for years. This is just how we are. And he's saved my beautiful butt a handful of times to boot, so we have a mutual understanding."

Both of the girls slowly lowered their guard and accepted the strange dynamic between Noel and Vadeem. I guess they were not used to friendly banter and jests, given their upbringing. Then again, I didn't think humor was in high demand back there, but I hoped they'd adapt soon.

They deserved a better life than what they grew up with, and although I wasn't sure what the trials and Main Stage would bring, I was sure that anything would be better than living in that darkness and gloom.

"Wait, do you think we can do something about their voices here?" I added. It hadn't seemed fair that they were the only ones who couldn't talk, and it couldn't be too hard for Central's insane tech to heal a minor injury like that.

The regressor thought for a moment. "It depends on the severity of the wound, and when their vocal cords were taken, but just from what I've seen, I wouldn't get my hopes up. I'll have to take them in for a thorough medical checkup soon anyway, so we'll know more then."

Vadeem agreed. "Good idea, and is that okay with you two?"

The two shrugged but seemed to trust Vadeem's decision. I don't think they knew what a medical checkup was in any case.

"I'll take that as a yes!"

"Anyway," Yoona added, "how about we get some food first? Everyone's hungry, and we skipped a lot of Raffiel's speech. I think my brother owes us all an explanation on how this new stage works."

"Agreed," I said. "After that last trial I saw, we all need a bit of rest and relaxation."

"Walter's treating!" Vadeem boomed. "Find us the fanciest place, oh mighty guild leader!"

I sighed, but I had agreed to treat everyone to food earlier, so I agreed. Jae-Hyun took the lead with his sister, and we slowly made our way toward whatever restaurant or pub the regressor was guiding us to.

Now that Vadeem knew that the twins could understand him, he practically dragged them along and started to recount random stories from his past.

His tales all seemed fantastical and utterly nonsensical to me, but the two girls seemed enraptured by his boasts. Soon, a pair of faint smiles adorned their normally blank features, and that infectious joy spread to everyone present. We were all left in high spirits.

CHAPTER FOUR

Future Goals

The place the regressor led us to was a homely establishment situated in a little nook on the outskirts of Pandora. We were away from the strange cityscape and back in the quaint village-esque part of town, and I didn't think I'd ever get used to the strange dichotomy of the two aesthetics.

We were the only ones in the restaurant, obviously, and we grabbed the big table by the window. The smell of home-cooked meals permeated the air, and a nice older lady came to bring us some tea and coffee. The menu on the side listed an array of comfort foods, and we quickly settled in and gave our various orders.

Vadeem chose one of practically everything on there, and a few additional ones that he thought the twins might enjoy. The two girls didn't argue and seemed to just be enjoying the new atmosphere. I think they were still unused to seeing so much light in one place. Noel chose to order a full rack of ribs and some French fries on the side, while the regressor and his sister had some fish and chips. I ordered the bangers and mash since I'd always wanted to try some, but no place ever seemed to serve them where I was from.

The meal arrived quickly, and we spent the first few minutes just simply enjoying the food and the ambiance.

"You know, there's one thing I have to ask," I said between bites of sausage. "Who are these people working here? I know they're not aspirants like us."

"Aren't they just NPCs?" Noel asked, her entire face practically covered in barbeque sauce as she bit into another rib.

"Sort of," the regressor answered. He had barely touched his own meal. "Most of the workers here are constructs, like the golem we faced earlier, just better made. They only have a limited function and can't deviate from their orders. Only a few people are official workers like Raffiel."

"I'm assuming that the receptionist we met earlier was one of them?" I added before taking another mouthful of food. I never knew British comfort food could be so damn good.

He smiled again. "Yes, as are most of the other staff in the building we bought."

That didn't seem like a lot of workers dedicated to the function of an entire city. But maybe these constructs were the results of the funding cuts Q was talking about. I couldn't imagine that he would want the majority of the Main Stage staffed by robots—or I suppose golems in this case.

Vadeem muttered something incomprehensible since his mouth was filled to the brim with various foodstuffs. Not even Noe's ability to translate languages could discern what he was trying to say. Eva poked him on the side and gave him an unmistakable look of disapproval. He returned the glare with a shy look of apology before swallowing all of the food and speaking again.

"As I was saying," he stated again after drinking a large glass of water, "if only the first thousand teams are here now, which is what, five thousand of us, then when'll the others arrive?"

"It's less than five thousand people," the regressor corrected. "Some of the teams would have lost members."

Yoona looked slightly uncomfortable hearing that fact, but she had to accept the situation we were in soon. I just hoped her brother wasn't babying her too much, because I knew a time would come when she had to see the world for what it was.

The regressor gave his sister a quick glance before continuing. "But the next set of teams will arrive tomorrow at noon, and the set after will come the day after that, and so on until a set number of the top aspirants make it to Pandora. It should take about a month or two for that to happen."

"Wait, we only get a one-day head start?" I asked. "That doesn't seem like much."

Vadeem laughed. "Yet we already own the Administration building, and you think that isn't much?"

"All right," I admitted. "Fair enough, but I think that's mainly due to our leader, and not because of the one-day bonus."

"What about the rest of the people?" the big man questioned, addressing the regressor again. "I mean the ones that didn't do so well in the trials. Do they just all come at once later on?"

Jae-Hyun took a sip of water before answering. "Not quite. They'll come in larger batches after the next trial, and not everyone will be sent here. There are several other settlements like Pandora scattered around, and our numbers will be divided amongst them. I don't think we'll hit six-digit numbers of inhabitants in any case, and we'll only lose members as we progress further."

"Speaking of," I added, "you have any idea how long we'll be stuck here for? I think a lot of us want to go back to Earth eventually."

The regressor thought for a moment, clearly unsure how to answer that question. I didn't blame him, because chances were, we were never going back.

"I don't know," he answered finally. "But it'll be a while. Whatever things the bastards who took us have in store will take time, and the ascension process is just the start of something larger, of that much I'm sure. We'll even visit Earth again, but don't expect things to be the same as we left it. Maybe we'll be able to go back home for good, eventually . . ."

"So those things they showed us at the beginning were true?" Noel asked. "Like those flying aliens in the sky?"

I had almost forgotten about that propaganda video that Raffiel had shown us.

"That part is true," the regressor answered with a frown, "but we have time to prepare for that eventuality down the line. For now, we prioritize our growth. We can't fight back without being unified first."

That explained why he was so desperate to get a head start on this guild-building process. I had no idea what was in store for us in the future, but something told me that the human race would be placed in situations that would be impossible to clear with just the small handful of us here. We'd need other leaders and helpers.

"I know that's stuff that we'll have to tackle later, but what about the rest of the aspirants coming to Pandora?" Yoona put down her food and wiped her mouth. "Do you know when that will be, brother?"

"Depends," he answered with a shrug. "The next trial starts the second the last party in the top ten percent gets distributed, so it could be in a month, could be after three. It all depends on how many teams are left."

I finished the rest of my sausages and started gulping down the mashed potatoes. "Hold on a second, so everyone else just gets to skip the third trial? Seems like a good deal to me."

Noel laughed, almost choking on a large piece of steak, before answering. "And skip the rewards of clearing the trial and going straight to the fourth one?

Little bro, that's like skipping the tutoring and going straight to the last boss. Those poor dudes will be screwed!"

Hm, Noel made some sense this time, but it still didn't seem that terrible to me. The consequence for failure was still death, so there had better be some great rewards.

"Not just that," Jae-Hyun added, "the third trial is a bit special. It's not combat focused, so it won't be as dangerous as the others. Not to say that it won't be challenging. Think of it as a reward for the people who did well here. We'll see more like it down the road as well."

"Which means that only the best aspirants will get to reap the rewards," Vadeem concluded. "The people running these trials are sly buggers."

I nodded slowly, finally getting a better sense of how this Main Stage was shaping up to be. There were still a lot of questions left unanswered, but surely they'd be answered once it was appropriate. No one wanted to be bogged down with too much new information all at once.

I ate the last of my meal and ordered some more; I hadn't realized just how hungry I was, and the amount of food I could eat seemed to have increased as well. But I was filthy rich, so it wasn't like I couldn't afford to eat all I wanted.

The only problem was that I had to figure out a good way to explain why I had more money than all the other aspirants put together to my new guild members. I certainly had to use my newly acquired funds in order to survive if that last damn trial taught me anything, but I couldn't exactly tell them that I got a hundred million coins from the people that kidnapped everyone.

The regressor had a serious grudge against Central, and the absolute last thing I wanted was him as an enemy. Well, maybe the second-last thing; making Xalla or her race angry was probably a whole lot worse.

Some ideas came to mind on how I could potentially circumvent this problem, but as always, I decided to wait and see if I could glean more information about this current stage and what kinds of trouble I could expect before acting. For now, I'd just use a few thousand here and there, at least when I was in public with Jae-Hyun and the gang.

"You're right, Vadeem," the regressor answered. "But if we make the right plans, then we can beat them at their own game."

"What plans are those?" I asked.

"For now," he said, "we need to rest."

"Pardon?"

He looked at me. "Especially you, Walter. We just came back from that abnormal second trial, and we need to rest while we still can. Whatever that darkness did to us is still lingering, and we need to properly treat it before we do anything strenuous."

I frowned. "But won't we give up all of our advantages if we do?"

"Trust me when I say that getting proper rest is not a waste of time," he answered solemnly, and it sounded like he was speaking from experience. "And I'm not saying to just lie in bed all day, but there are other ways to improve other than fighting."

I wanted to argue, but I remembered that Jae-Hyun wasn't the only one who told me to get some rest. Noe had as well when I first came back from that horrible zombie hellscape. Who was I to argue with an all-powerful system and a guy from the future?

"Your point's made," I conceded. "We'll rest. So what are we going to do in the meantime?"

The regressor smirked. "We consolidate our guild and grow our influence."

"So recruitment and setting up infrastructure?" Vadeem said with a grin. He looked like he wanted to say something else, but he quickly glanced at Yoona and the twins and didn't continue.

The regressor saw this as well, and he gave him a barely perceptible nod of thanks. Apparently that would be a conversation for another time when the kids were out of the room. I couldn't believe that Jae-Hyun was still willing to leave his sister in the dark even after all that had happened, but I guess Yoona had been unconscious for most of the second trial.

"Yes," he answered, "we are in the unique situation where we have next to no competition on available resources, and only the cream of the crop in terms of potential recruits. I'll go over the details in full once we get back to our head-quarters, but eat first. We'll go get the two new members properly equipped and dressed after. Our building should be ready for us once we're done."

"Sounds good, oh awesome guild leader man!" Noel said. She had just finished eating all of her food and was sneakily stealing more from Vadeem's portion. The twins were engaging in a small skirmish against Noel's fork, trying their best to stop her from taking more of their food.

"Can't argue with that!" Vadeem added before stuffing his face once more.

He frowned as he saw that some of his portions had disappeared and started to help out the twins with their counterassault on Noel's plate. She didn't stand a chance three versus one, and Vadeem quickly brought the spoils of his victory back onto the dishes in front of Ana and Eva. The two quickly ate everything given, always on guard for a new round of raiding to begin from Noel. I thought they'd have exploded by this point, given how much they'd both eaten.

Yoona watched on with a chuckle, clearly enjoying how well the two skinny girls were able to adapt to their new situation. I think I had a smile on as well, as I watched Noel make a white flag with a toothpick and napkins, waving it to signal her defeat.

Jae-Hyun was the complete opposite as he slowly but meticulously ate the food in front of him. It was like everything else he did in his second life was all purposeful and minimized waste. I really do wonder what he did in that previous timeline for him to have turned out like this, and I couldn't help but feel a little sad for Yoona. It must have been a shock to see her brother change so much.

We ate quickly after that, making small talk and light-hearted jokes. I honestly felt myself relax for the first time in a very long time, and perhaps Jae-Hyun and Noe were right, I did need some time off.

"Rest is absolutely important, my host," Noe chimed in, her voice warm with affection. "Please ensure that you take care of your body. It is still weak, but Unit Noe will ensure that you become whole once more."

Thanks, Noe, but what do you mean become whole? You're the one that's missing shards.

"You are right, my host," she said again, and that weird mischievous tone was back. "Please disregard what I said."

Okay . . . we really need to have a proper conversation about your changes and upgrades later.

"I look forward to that, dearest Walter."

CHAPTER FIVE

Shopping and Plotting

A loud burp broke the tranquil atmosphere and signaled the end of our meal.

"Oh, that was good!" Vadeem boomed. "Eating nothing but the same suitcase food for all those months has taken its toll on me!"

"I know," I muttered. "But why did you choose to pack nothing but fried food? You had the whole cafeteria's worth of stuff to choose from."

Vadeem shrugged. "It was the fastest thing the workers could make. I just wanted to pack the thing as full as I could in a week."

"Speaking about your food suitcase," I added. "Isn't it getting a bit empty at this point?"

Vadeem thought for a moment and took out the object in question from his inventory. He fiddled around with it for a while, stared into space for a while to access whatever information Origin was giving him, and then nodded.

"You're right. We were feeding that army of yours for a while. I do need to stock up again."

"Let me pay for it, Vadeem," I said. "My sponsorship provided me with some extra funds I can use in any case."

The regressor and Vadeem frowned when they heard that word. They were clearly not happy about my supposed deal with Rogue, since they didn't know the full story behind it.

"You know what my thoughts are about your borrowed power, so I won't say it again," Vadeem grumbled, "but how much money did you swindle from that sponsor of yours?"

Now how much should I tell them? Definitely not the full 100 million. I doubted any amount of suspension of disbelief would allow them to simply accept that this "random sponsor" liked me so much they'd given me probably more gold than any aspirant could ever earn in their careers, or that the admins would allow it. But likewise, I couldn't say that the amount was too small either since I want to use some of my funds publicly, if for nothing more than to help out my new guild.

I decided on a good number, and I had an excuse in place if the number I said was either too high or too low. I didn't quite know the value of gold yet, so I figured I'd aim for something relatively high.

"I managed to get five hundred thousand," I answered.

The regressor looked at me with mild shock. "That's a lot to give for a new aspirant. You must have done something to really impress that sponsor."

Okay, it seemed I'd aimed a bit too high, but it was fine. I had the perfect excuse ready.

"Well, I did have to give some things up for it," I continued before Jae-Hyun could grill me for more information. "I had to give up some of my rewards from completing the trials for it. I only get gold now. I wasn't in my best state of mind back there, so I agreed. I'm not sure if that's fine or not, though."

And it was partly true. I probably never would get any more end-of-trial rewards with the antagonistic Trash Matrix handing out literally nothing, so I was explaining away two inconsistencies at once. I was a little proud of myself, honestly.

Once Jae-Hyun and the rest heard how I had accepted the sponsorship while under the influence of the supernatural darkness, their attitudes eased up a lot. I'm pretty sure that what I had given up, had I been speaking the truth, was definitely a bad deal on my end. Everyone knew it, but they couldn't exactly scold a guy who did it while his brain was all screwed up.

"I see," was the only thing the regressor said. I could tell he was holding back a lot of his thoughts. "It's . . . not the worst deal I've heard, and it is nice to have a lot of money while we're still starting out. And we're working as a guild, so Walter can supply us with some of the initial funds needed to start our establishment, and we can help him out with items that he can't buy in stores."

"Yeah," Yoona said. "Don't worry, Walter, you got us to count on! My brother can figure something out about your situation."

Jae-Hyun nodded grimly, clearly feeling that he was responsible for dragging me into this mess. Once again, I felt no need to correct any misconceptions here.

"It's fine, guys," I said. "What's done is done, so you can worry about me later. For now, I'll go and see if I can't help Vadeem restock some of his food. I'm sure I can buy out whatever's available in this store first."

And I found out that I could. The store didn't have a ton of food, but it wasn't too little either. The golem workers cooked fast. I stuffed everything they had into Vadeem's storage, and the total bill only came out to be 601 gold as well. I was starting to appreciate just how valuable this currency was. No wonder the regressor was surprised I had 500k on me.

We exited the restaurant, stomachs full and spirits high, and went to check out the various stores so we could properly supply our guild. Not to mention the fact that we would be staying in this particular town for the foreseeable future, some daily necessities, such as toiletries, clothes, and the like also needed to be purchased. I hadn't changed clothes in much too long.

"You sure you're okay with buying everything for us?" Yoona asked as we stepped into yet another store. The amount of stuff that we had purchased had necessitated hiring a team of delivery people to bring all the larger items back to our guild HQ, and it didn't look like we were close to finished getting everything we needed.

"I'm filthy rich right now." I shrugged. "And it's not like we won't generate more money later on, so you can think of it as me investing in the future of our guild."

The regressor and Noel had gone somewhere else a bit earlier, something about looking for a particular smith to reforge my weapon, and to get something better suited for the rest of us as well. The twins still needed proper gear of their own. I chose not to tag along; I'd found out quickly that trying to keep up with the guy who knew the future tended to be more effort than it was worth.

Yoona had wanted us to all stick together, but her brother stressed the importance of getting everything today while the streets were practically empty of aspirants. The stores around here would give you special discounts if you were among the first people to shop. That ignited everyone's drive to get as much out of this deal as they possibly could, and they went into overdrive trying to stuff the carts with as many items as physically possible. I was just dragged along like an oversized wallet.

I hadn't even bothered checking on prices given how much cash I was hoarding, but the others seemed enthused about the prospect of getting things for cheap. I just handed everyone some money and let them go wild.

"He's right, Yoona," Vadeem said happily. "We need the starting funds to get our little organization started, and Walter here is like the rich investor betting on our success. All we have to do is make sure that we live up to his expectations, and it's not a waste of money for him!"

"Well . . ." Yoona said, "I guess that makes sense."

"Which is why you should get as many things as you need now, while things are on sale! The more you buy now, the less you have to spend later!"

She couldn't argue with that logic, and reluctantly agreed, although I think Vadeem's encouragement was a little too effective. Once Yoona realized that she had to restock all the things that she used to take for granted when she lived back on Earth, the woman was like an unstoppable machine, going from store to store, buying practically everything in sight. She said that because we would be expanding our forces, we needed to make sure that we had enough supplies for our future guild members.

I didn't have to do anything other than hand out money after that. Was this how rich sugar daddies felt? It was just baffling seeing more and more hired help lug piles of stuff away. By the time we met back up with Noel and the regressor, the sun had already started to set for the first day. I felt more exhausted now than I had back in that damn trial, yet the others seemed more than happy to continue on. These people truly were freaks of nature.

In total, we spent close to a hundred thousand gold, most of that going to whatever it was the regressor needed. Yet even with all that spending, my available funds barely took a dent. Let's just say that I won't be running out of cash anytime soon.

"Did you get everything you needed on your end?" I asked Jae-Hyun as we met back up.

He nodded. "Yes, and management contacted me while I was away as well."

"Was there an issue?"

He smiled wryly. "None at all. For what it's worth, the people working for these trials have laws and regulations that they must abide by, and I was able to convince the nice employees of the legality of my purchase."

Damn, Jae-Hyun was able to out-legal literal demons and millennia-old monsters? Perhaps they were right to be afraid of him!

"Well, I sure as hell am starting to get tired, so let's head back and get some proper rest," Vadeem said as he looked at the twins by his side.

I think he was saying that mainly for the girls because although they looked the same as always, small hints of weariness were starting to show underneath their masks of indifference. It seemed that Vadeem was able to pick up on their micro expressions as well, which was honestly impressive considering he didn't have Noe with him.

Jae-Hyun nodded. "Were you guys able to get everything we needed for the future?"

"Most of it," Yoona said. "I think I might have to make another trip back here tomorrow, but we have everything the seven of us will need for the fore-seeable future."

"Perfect," he said. "Let's head back then, we still need to pick out places for all of us to stay."

We stopped by one or two more smaller stores before making our way back toward the building. Strangely enough, I could see the structure now on the horizon. I had asked him why and the regressor told us that it was only the case because we now officially controlled all of its various functions, although none of the other aspirants could find it without knowing the specific route to the building. It made for a neat secret base.

Additionally, our new guild HQ was way more high tech, or magical in this case, than I thought. There were a lot more functions that could be unlocked, and Jae-Hyun said he'd show us some of the more useful functions down the road. It seemed that there was a clear reason why he'd spent so much time planning to purchase this building.

The sun had fully set by the time we made it back to our new home, and the various hired helpers were still busy moving cart after cart of things into the building. The regressor and his sister had to step in to give them instructions on where to offload the stuff, but they were able to get everything settled in quickly enough.

Jae-Hyun looked at Yoona and pointed at the twins. "Hey, Yoona, do you mind finding a spot for the two girls to sleep? There should be spare bedrooms on the fifth and sixth floors. Make sure they have everything they need as well; they grew up in that weird darkness dimension, so they might need some help adjusting."

The twins looked at Vadeem, who nodded at them to go. "Don't worry, I'll get a room right next door, so you can holler—er, I mean knock if you ever need something!"

They nodded, a tiny hint of relief showing for just a microsecond, bowed to the rest of us, and walked beside Yoona. I think all the new things they'd seen and experienced that day were really starting to tire them out. The change from what they were used to and their new life would take a long time to digest fully.

"No problem, brother," Yoona said with a soft smile. "I'll get them settled in. And I'll let Vadeem know which room they chose. Just let me know if you need anything else!"

"Thanks, Yoona," Vadeem said, smiling. "And get some proper rest, you two. We have busy days ahead of us!"

Once the three girls were fully out of view, the regressor's entire demeanor turned dark. "We need to discuss the future of the guild, so if you three would please follow me."

I looked around and saw that even Noel's and Vadeem's usually light-hearted vibe was gone. They seemed to know exactly what Jae-Hyun wanted to do, while I could only guess that it was time to talk about the real side of the guild's management, the part that our leader didn't want the children to see.

No sense being the odd one out now, so I nodded and followed the others. Jae-Hyun quietly led us down a separate set of stairs into the building's basement, and into a darkly lit conference room. The room had bare concrete walls in a brutalist fashion, and only a small table with adjoining chairs furnished it. This was an intimidating space. It felt hostile just being in here.

The guild leader, now looking more like the head of a criminal syndicate, took a seat at the head of the conference table, and gestured for us to do the same around him.

We did. Jae-Hyun's mood was solemn, and I felt a chill when he looked me in the eye. I'd never seen the man like this before.

"Noel, Vadeem, Walter," he said as he turned to stare at each of us, his voice glacial, "to ensure the success of our future operations, I need the three of you to complete a couple of . . . minor tasks for me. There are some obstacles we need to remove."

CHAPTER SIX

Abyssal Operations

Noel and Vadeem grinned as if they had anticipated what the regressor wanted, the dim lighting in the room creating quite the fighting scene. I felt a little out of place, like I had just interrupted a secret meeting between mafia heads, but I didn't let it show. I'd see what the regressor had to say first.

"I'll reiterate, but the three of you know that running any new organization successfully needs some *unique* methods," the regressor started. "Especially if we are aiming for the top."

None of us disagreed. Even Noel was on her best behavior, although she had a knowing smile on her face.

"I will be frank with you," Jae-Hyun continued. "We must be prepared for what's to come, and the only way that we can ensure our own survival is if our guild is unequivocally secured as the number one power in Pandora."

Ah, so it seemed Jae-Hyun had bigger plans for his guild than I thought. He didn't just want the best guild, he wanted it to be the only true power here. Interesting.

He looked at us again. "Things will only progress in scale from here on out. We will be forced to take command of larger and larger forces in the future, and for us to maximize our chances of survival, we *need* to have full control over this city. We need to be the leading figures for Pandora. Without the people unified, we will only lose manpower as each subsequent trial whittles down our resources, and if we allow that to happen, then we will all lose once the . . . never mind. It's too early to worry about that."

He sighed. "To prevent the worst-case scenarios, we need to take some affirmative actions now."

Once again, no one said a word. We were all silently waiting for what he wanted us to do.

"And for that to happen," he said coldly, "certain sacrifices need to be made."

He took out four bundles of paper from his inventory, giving one each to me and Noel, while he handed Vadeem two. I saw that each page contained very detailed, not to mention professional, pencil sketches of individuals. On the bottom of each page was a list that included their names, height, ethnicity, and other identifying characteristics. Noel and Vadeem had a bunch of sheets in their piles, while mine only had one.

The regressor spoke before I could look at what my document contained in detail. "I've given you three portraits of key individuals to look out for."

I nodded and saw the other two do the same.

He turned to the redhead and gestured at her papers. "Noel, I need you to find those individuals in the coming days. They represent people who are most likely to oppose our plans in one way or another. It would be a terrible shame if an unfortunate 'accident' were to befall them. Most of the people on that list who need a . . . friendly visit are already in Pandora."

Noel smiled as she took another peek at her bundle of papers. "Accidents? That would be horrible! I'll make sure that I keep an eye out for these nice ladies and gentlemen, to make sure that nothing untoward happens to them, of course."

The regressor nodded in satisfaction and turned to Vadeem.

"As for you, Vadeem"—he pointed to one of the piles near the man— "the individuals on your left are people who have the most wealth among the aspirants, and it would be most welcome if you could convince them to, say, donate some of their wealth to a better cause."

Vadeem gave him a wicked smile. "I'm sure I could talk some sense into these lovely aspirants."

"The other pile is the important one," he continued. "It is a list of people who have classes and skills that are suited to the creation of goods and services. If you could also be so kind as to convince them that working for us is in their best interest, then it would greatly accelerate the growth of our guild."

"Using any means?" the big man asked.

"Within reason, Vadeem," he answered with a cold smile, "but remember that we need them to be productive, but only for us. Give them any incentives that you might think will help, feed whatever vice they might enjoy. Make them rely on our guild to function. No, make it so that they can *only* function if they are with us."

Damn, I did not think that Jae-Hyun could be so ruthless. I knew that he would stop at nothing to achieve his goals, but I didn't think he would show his true colors this early. But I guess there was a reason he recruited Noel and Vadeem first, which should say something about my own character since I was lumped with them and not Yoona.

Vadeem grinned again before stashing his set of papers away. "That I can do. I'll make sure you have the most productive employees possible, boss."

Jae-Hyun nodded again.

"Finally, Walter," he said as he turned his cold gaze my way, "you have one of the most important tasks needed for the future success of our guild."

I arched an eyebrow.

"Your particular set of skills is perfect for this role," he continued. "The man on your paper is someone that we must recruit at all costs. He will be a part of our . . . private meeting in the future, so do your utmost to ensure that he becomes a part of our organization."

I looked down at the sketch and saw a very plain-looking man. Jae-Hyun had drawn him with a modest smile, and aside from the clothes he wore, he didn't look all that special. He was wearing a black cassock and clerical collar, so he must be a priest by trade. The information below said that his name was Marcus Ashford, forty-nine years old, and that he should be arriving within the week if he wasn't already here.

"What's so special about this guy?" I asked.

"Many things that you will learn if he joins, but most importantly, we are missing a key figure in our party, and he's the perfect candidate to fill that void."

He paused but continued when he saw that I wasn't quite getting what he was saying. "We're missing a healer, Walter. You almost died in that last trial because none of us could prevent or treat ailments and diseases, and we can't rely solely on items to heal our physical wounds. You had to take on way more than was necessary, and I will not allow that to happen again. If we can get Marcus on our side, then he can fill that role."

I nodded. "And this priest will be okay with our, uh, interesting method of establishing control over Pandora?"

The regressor gave me an eerie smile. "He will be more than accepting of it, so do not worry."

"All right . . ." I answered as I put the drawing away, making a mental note of the guy in case he was here already.

Jae-Hyun continued. "And there's one more thing I need you to do, Walter."

"Sure," I answered with a relaxed smile. "What is it?"

"I need you to work on our guild's public image," he said, and I could already tell where he was going with this request. "I need you to ensure that the Abyss Guild's image is squeaky clean."

"So that no one would ever connect any missing people with our guild's operations?" I inquired with a raised eyebrow.

He nodded. "Not only that, but we have to be a power that the masses love and adore. We need to be a beacon of hope and authority so that no one would ever question why or how we got into power in the first place. This will be essential down the line. We need to be the rallying force behind all newcomers, so much so that the masses will quelch any discontent by themselves in the future. I need our guild to be the *only* authority that the people of Pandora will believe in."

Jae-Hyun looked at me hard in the eyes. "Can you do that, Walter?"

Several ideas were already forming in my head, and all I needed to do was to get a good sense of the people coming into Pandora to see which scheme of mine would be the most ideal. There were always ways to exploit people's desperation, and if there wasn't, then I just needed to create one myself.

I grinned. "Seems simple enough. I'll see what I can do."

"Good," the regressor said. "You have my full support if you need anything."

"Mine too, little bro!" Noel added in. "Just call me if you need someone to mysteriously disappear. I heard that's going to be a common thing in this town, a terrible thing, really."

"And you can count on me if you need a little show of force," Vadeem added with a smile.

Why did it feel like this was not the first time they'd done something like this? Man, what kind of strange people had I become associated with? Still, if they only needed a propagandist, they picked the right man for the job. Spreading misinformation and rumors I could do in my sleep, and that was before getting Noe's help and all those Charisma skills I had.

"Thanks, I'll keep that in mind," I answered.

"Perfect," the regressor concluded. "Please get those tasks done as quickly as possible, and I'm sure I don't need to tell you to keep things on the down low to the others?"

Noel gave him a thumbs-up. "Not a word out of me, boss man!"

And for once, I think I actually believed her.

Vadeem chuckled joyfully. "You know I wouldn't bring the children into these affairs."

"Got it, Jae-Hyun," I said last.

He gave us a silent look of gratitude before ending the meeting. "We'll have another meeting once this is done, at the same place, same time in a week."

I nodded. "What will you be doing in the meantime?"

He gave me another creepy smile. "I have some more things to plan out. We have a lot to do in the coming weeks."

With all of our tasks in hand, we left the dark conference room and headed back to the building lobby. The reception area was still empty, but I assumed that our promised workers would come sooner or later. As if the regressor had planned everything out, his sister came down only a few minutes after and greeted us.

"Sorry it took so long," the girl said. "I had to bathe the twins first. I don't think they had the chance to take a bath . . . well, ever, really."

"No worries, bestie!" Noel answered with a smile.

"Thank you, Yoona, I wanted to get them properly cleaned but . . ." Vadeem laughed awkwardly.

Yoona smiled in understanding. "It's not a problem. It's why my brother asked me to help. Are you guys going to settle in for the night as well? There are spare rooms on the sixth floor, where Ana and Eva are."

Noel shook her head. "I'm going to take a little nighttime stroll. Need to work off all that food I ate earlier, so head up without me for now. I'll find a room myself when I'm back!"

Yoona nodded. "Be careful out there. It could be dangerous at night!"

Yeah . . . I highly doubted it would be Noel in danger that night.

"I'll be careful!" she answered with a wry smile. "I wouldn't want to encounter any kind of *accidents* out there! Heard they can be deadly."

Yoona nodded innocently. "All right, just send us a message if you need help."

Noel waved goodbye and left the building, humming a happy tune all the way out.

"How about you, Vadeem?" I asked. "You also going on a stroll?"

He understood what I meant but shook his head. "Not this night. I'll go check up on the twins and hit the sack myself. I ate too much food today, even for me!"

"Fair enough. Suppose I'll wash up and head to bed as well," I added.

Jae-Hyun looked at us one last time before saying to his sister. "Yoona, do you mind if you help me out with something?"

"Sure thing, brother!" She turned back to me and Vadeem. "Good night, you two! I'll see you tomorrow!"

I took the elevator up to the sixth floor with Vadeem and left the man to find a room for myself. All the unoccupied rooms were open, so I just chose the one closest to the exit and made myself comfy. Right when I was about to take off my clothes and wash up, a new sound interrupted me, and a familiar figure stood by the room's entrance. I gazed back and nodded at the figure.

"Sorry for always catching you at inopportune times, Lord Arbiter," Q said with a low bow, "but I needed to contact you about the Tribunals. We can't push back the meeting any further."

CHAPTER SEVEN

The Tribunal Part 1

I sighed.

Well, there went any chance I had for rest. How was I supposed to ever get any when I had to do tasks for both Q and the regressor? One side believed that I could casually destroy planets just by breathing, while the other thought I had adequate downtime. It wasn't like I could just excuse myself to sleep for a while, saying that I was too tired. I was finally starting to see the downside of living this darn life of lies.

Well, sorry, Noe, but our conversation's going to have to take a rain check.

"It is okay, my host," she answered reassuringly. "I shall count the days until then. For now, please take care of yourself, dear Walter."

I refocused my attention back on Q. "What is it that you need to inform me?"

"Well, we have finalized the proper paperwork on my side," Q answered, "so I am here to formally invite you to the Tribunal as the representative of Site 1102."

I nodded. "How long will this take? You know that I can't leave the anomaly unattended for too long."

"Yes . . ." he answered hesitantly. "We have taken that into account. We will try to slow down this timeline as much as we can on our end, but given the temporal nature of our site's anomaly, that could prove to be an issue."

"I thought you had total control over the flow of time for your aspirants," I said matter-of-factly, using the information the regressor just gave me.

"We do, but something about Aspirant Kim Jae-Hyun is hindering our ability to tamper with any timeline that he is currently on, even on the Main Stage. This is not an issue since we can alter the timelines of the other aspirants to fit around this, but . . ."

"But he's here with everyone else now, so you can't do much for me," I answered for him.

Q laughed nervously. "Yes, but we can still slow down the passage of time on the Pandora Plane if I work with the other site admins, even if it's minor. We have dealt with other anomalies with chronological defects, but this particular case is extreme. I'm not sure what the Origin Matrix did to your charge, but it is unlike anything I've seen before."

Other site admins? Were the other nonhuman aspirants here with the rest of us? No, it didn't matter. That wasn't important for now. I could ask the regressor or Q later.

"Then that's all the more reason why I shouldn't be leaving this trial for any length of time," I continued. "You know how bad things can get if we leave even a regular anomaly unchecked."

Q was sweating now. "Yes, and I have informed Central as such. They have agreed to expedite certain procedures, and your stay should take no more than thirty-six to forty-eight Earth hours if all goes well."

Well, shit, there went all of the preview tickets I had, then. But I counted my blessings, because at least it didn't go over the time limit that I could afford. I just had to hope that everything went well for once.

"And how much time would pass here?"

Q looked even more nervous. "Well . . . given how difficult it would be to make any adjustments . . . it should be around eight or nine hours."

I gave him an annoyed glare. "Should be?"

"Not to worry, Lord Arbiter," he quickly added. "Even if something goes wrong on our end, we have your disguise covered."

Another flash of light, and a new figure popped into my room. It was . . . well, it was me. From head to toe, there was a perfect replica of myself. It looked like one of those golems I saw outside, but there was no way one of those things could fool the regressor. To make sure I didn't make a fool of myself and ruin my Grandmaster Alchemist disguise, I peeked into its info with my title skill.

QC1102.004: Level ??? Grand Doppelganger (Aspirant Walter)

"Hm, a grand doppelganger," I said, pretending to appraise the thing and not be completely freaked out. "Not bad. Did you design it yourself?"

He smiled with pride. "It is indeed one of my own, my fourth successful one, in fact. One of my pride and joys, if you don't mind me bragging a bit!"

I nodded approvingly. "And you are sure that your creation will not be noticed by our resident anomaly?"

He answered without hesitation. "At the current stage of the tests? It would not be possible, rest assured, Lord. And I will also limit what it does so as to not ruin your image or future plans."

The Walter lookalike nodded vigorously as if it was doing its best to assure me that it was going to do its assigned task perfectly. I wasn't sure what to expect from that thing, but I just had to take Q's word that it'd serve as an emergency replacement for me if needed. Just looking at a perfect, moving replica of myself was weird. I didn't like it.

"All right, then are we to head off now?" I asked.

"Yes, if that would not be a problem with you."

"Lead the way, then," I said with authority. I mean, it wasn't like I knew where we were going in the first place.

Noe, use one of my preview tickets once we're out of here.

"Acknowledged, my host," she answered warmly.

Q snapped his finger, and that familiar feeling of traveling through space instantaneously engulfed my being. I think I was starting to hate being teleported around.

I was instantly in my Xollon form when I rematerialized . . . or perhaps reatomized would be the better term? Restructured? Honestly, I have to figure out what happens when Q and his people teleport me around one of these days. There was still so much I couldn't understand about my situation that it was starting to frustrate me more than anything else.

Anyway, I was fully Xollon again, and the sweet release I felt was intoxicating. I stretched out my feelers in satisfaction. Q had taken me to a small reception room, and a familiar face greeted me there.

"Walter!" Xalla exclaimed. She looked like she wanted to come for a hug, but she saw Q beside me and stopped herself. "It's good to see that you're okay. I was worried about your experiments when you were forced into that abnormal trial."

I smiled and hugged her anyway. She blushed and quickly returned the gesture. Sure, she was working right now, but I was the lord arbiter, and I was pretty sure that I could ignore normal rules. What was the point of being in charge if I couldn't abuse my authority?

Q stood to the side and smiled. "My head of security almost lost her job trying to break into that trial, even when she was specifically told not to."

Xalla's gaze fell away from me, and she stroked her adorable frills in embarrassment.

I chuckled. "Well, thank you, Xalla, but you should know that I would have been fine either way."

"I know, Walter," she answered. "But I didn't want all of your hard work ruined because of a screw-up on our side. I know how important that human project of yours is, and if something is important to you, then it's also important to me."

I was about to say something else when the door swung open and two more familiar faces greeted us.

"Well," Rogue's jovial voice interrupted, "I am glad that my disciple didn't lose her job. It would have looked quite bad if I got to keep my position as a sponsor only to see my disciple lose her post as head of security!"

Big Bob, who still looked like a chubby human, joined in and dashed straight at me, giving me a huge bear hug. I was afraid that he'd impale himself with my spiky tentacles, but whatever his skin was made out of was damned hard. His hug felt strong even with my new body, so I can only imagine how much force this seemingly normal guy could exert.

"What are you guys doing here?" I asked as a smile started to creep on my face, or whatever the Xollon equivalent of that was.

Big Bob grinned. "We're going to the Tribunals as well, on super important, official business, of course!"

He looked at the older Xollon. "Uh, Rogue, what was the excuse we gave Central so we could tag along again?"

The big Xollon sighed. "Excuse? Nonsense! We are here because we officially represent the sponsorship program, just like how Walter is representing Q and his site. We're here to tell Central what we sponsors think of this situation . . . Or something along those lines in any case."

Bob smiled even wider and nodded. "Right, what he said. Not like they can say no when it's the two of us asking."

"And Xalla?" I asked, pulling the girl closer. She hesitated, but only barely.

"She will act as your bodyguard for the duration. Of course, normally such a position would be filled by someone lower down on the security team"—Q smiled and gave me a wink—"but seeing how Xalla almost disobeyed direct orders, she is on probation, and I have temporarily demoted her to serve as your aide for the duration of this trip. Terrible punishment, really."

Xalla cleared her throat. "I will do my best to ensure that no harm will fall upon you, Lord Arbiter."

"I'm sure my little disciple wants to do more than just protect yo—"

A swift jab quickly silenced the elderly Xollon.

"Wonderful strike, Xalla." Rogue groaned, rubbing his sides. "Whoever's teaching you is doing a great job."

Xalla rolled her eyes and ignored her master. "But I will officially be acting as your guide and aide during your time in Central HQ, so please tell me if you need anything."

"Thank you, Xalla," I said. "And will you be coming with us as well, Q?"

He gently shook his head. "I won't be attending, unfortunately. My role as the site admin keeps me busy, especially with the anomaly in play. It's endless nights of overtime for me."

Damn, I actually felt bad for the guy. I'm not sure how he's able to keep up with all the work Jae-Hyun's adding to his already full schedule.

"All right, take care, Q," I said.

"I always do, Lord Arbiter," he answered with a tired smile.

The others all bid the admin farewell, and he left the room by simply vanishing. I wished he would use the door more often.

"So, what's the plan?" I asked the other three. "Do we take the train over?"

"Oh, my friend, do I have a treat in store for you!" Big Bob said, his smile going even wider, "Central went all out on the VIP services this time."

Rogue added in, "I might have accidentally let word out that the legendary Arbiter W was back in town, and that he was going to be accompanied by myself, the venerated Xollon general, along with his mighty disciple and the illustrious Grand Alchemist Babylon. Well, let's just say that the people in charge took notice."

"This was all done accidentally, of course," Big Bob added in with a mischievous smile. "Otherwise that would be a gross breach of ethics."

"Of course, of course, totally unintentional," the Xollon said with his own smirk. "It would be unbefitting of our esteemed selves to abuse our powers and privileges like that."

Xalla only sighed. "I wish you two would act your age sometimes. I sometimes miss the war hero who made his recruits shiver in fear just by looking at them."

I looked over at Rogue, and I just couldn't imagine him as anything other than a really friendly old man. Perhaps in his younger days, he would have struck an intimidating figure, but now? Nope, a silly old grandpa was all I got from him.

"Oh, come now," Rogue exclaimed. "There's no wars for me to fight these cycles, so you can't expect me to be a military man all the time, Xalla!"

She sighed again. "Yes, but you should still be mindful of your image when we are out in public. You represent the best that Xolloid has to offer."

"Enough of that, Xalla," Big Bob said. "I bet you won't be saying that when you see what Central's got prepared. And let us old folks relax once in a while! Now let me show you just what's in store for us!"

He gestured for us to all get going, and with a grand flourish, he opened the door leading out of the tiny room. I peered out and saw that Central really had spared no expenses for this trip to the Tribunal.

I smiled. Maybe this trip wouldn't be so bad after all.

CHAPTER EIGHT

The Tribunal Part 2

When Big Bob said that Central went all out, he really meant it. Even Xalla, still trying her best to appear professional given her new assignment, couldn't help gawking every now and then.

For one, an entire ensemble of butlers took the four of us to a private loading platform and escorted us into the most luxurious passenger train I have ever seen. I'm not sure why all these multidimensional creatures traveled by train, but I wasn't complaining right now. The interior was much more spacious than it had any right to be and was decked out in exotic furnishings and artwork. The floors were covered with a soft white carpet that massaged my feelers as I walked, and a beautiful scent of iron-rich blood flowed through the interior.

On high golden display cases adorning each of the carved walls of the train hung living portraits made up of rare and wondrous species; some were opened up to show how their unique biology worked, and others were made into beautiful sculptures and chimeric creations. And the most wondrous thing was that none of their screams escaped the displays, instead, the soothing background music lulled me into a state of relaxation.

Huge windows made of the clearest glass I have ever seen showed off a view of the swirling galactic void as the train blitzed through the dimensions, the multicolored radiation warming up the interior nicely and providing a great ambient light source.

Big Bob showed me to the bar, where a team of homunculi bartenders awaited our orders. I sat down on the lavish stool, custom-made with living material so that my feelers were perfectly supported, and just took in the atmosphere.

"Like I said, Walter," Big Bob said with an even bigger smile, "they went all out for us."

"Damn, this place is impressive," I muttered as I glanced around my surroundings.

Rogue had ordered drinks for all of us, although Xalla refused hers since she was technically still working. It was nice to see that she was so dedicated to her job, especially when that job involved keeping me safe, but I did want to spend some more time with her outside of work hours. But surely there'd be time for that later.

I took a sip of whatever Rogue handed me. I didn't know what it was, but it was pretty damn nice, and asked absentmindedly, "Pretty impressive train, though I'd love to know the specs on this thing."

Rogue groaned. "Ah, Walter, why did you have to mention that?"

Before I could ask what he meant, Big Bob's face lit up immediately. "Oh you have no idea!"

Rogue sighed. "Here we go again . . . I'll have another, no, make that five more shots, bartender."

Big Bob turned toward me, and his eyes were glowing with excitement. "Walter, my friend, let me tell you all about this baby!"

Oh . . . Big Bob was one of *those* types of people. I gave him my polite smile and just hoped that he wouldn't talk about the train for too long.

I was wrong.

"This is the newest model made by the Karmen Corps, the LCVI 1200 Super, fully decked out with the latest and greatest," he continued without stopping. "And before you ask, yes, it is the same Karmen Corps that made most of the trials, but their interiors are all fully customizable. We have the Xolloid design today, but the best thing is that you can even combine different aesthetics. You couldn't do that in the 1100 model! Have you ever seen Xollon art mixed with Omni architecture? Well, you can here! And don't even get me started about the materials used on these trains . . ."

And on and on he went. My god, I have never seen anyone talk about one topic for so long. Rogue gave me the most scathing look I have ever seen him use, and I think Xalla dozed off for a bit halfway through his explanation.

"Yeah, that's great . . ." I mumbled as I nursed my sixth drink, or maybe it was my seventh? I had lost count after Big Bob went into excruciating detail about each of the train's ten carriages. I absentmindedly peered out the train, marveling at how beautiful the interdimensional chaos was. It was strangely welcoming.

"...and the new engines?" Big Bob continued, completely oblivious to his audience. "Unlike last year's make, these new ones can take you anywhere in the multiverse in one go, Walter. Anywhere! Do you know the kinds of engineering and alchemy needed to accomplish that? You're an alchemist yourself, so of course you'd know! But it took Karmen's R&D department over five cycles just to get the prototype working . . ."

"Yeah, anywhere, amazing. Prototype, yeah . . ." I knocked back another drink, hoping that Bob would finish his little speech shortly. Given Rogue's expression, however, I didn't think that would be the case.

". . . so all of that means that we can skip going through multiple parallel dimensions and go directly to our destination. Walter, just think of how much time and resources that saves! Gone are the days of tedious transfers and delays caused by scheduling errors! But you don't need to guess, because I have the data! According to last year's . . ."

I must have dozed off as well, but a slight shift in the compartment woke me up, and to my utter disappointment, Big Bob was still talking.

". . . this is one of only three in service right now, and we get to be a part of an exclusive group of people to travel on it! And the list of VIP passengers is quite astonishing. There's—"

"That's all wonderful and good, Babylon, but how about we talk about something else now?" Rogue finally said as he finished his latest drink. He'd had a lot so far, and his own tentacles seemed to flush a shade of pink now.

"But I was just getting to the good part!"

"But we need to get Walter caught up on, uh . . ." He looked at Xalla for help.

"What my mentor means," Xalla answered without missing a beat, "is that since Walter has been away from Central for over ten cycles, it would be best to update him on some of the changes that have occurred since he was last there. Unfortunately, that does mean that you'll have to explain the rest of this train's functions at a later date."

Big Bob looked slightly deflated, but nodded. "Yes, that is true. I'll make sure to tell you all about the rest when we get back!"

Rogue groaned. "Let's just save that wonderful conversation for another time . . ."

"Fine, fine," Big Bob conceded with a sigh. "I have no idea why you guys just can't see the beauty in a properly built train. Works of genius, really! Makes me regret choosing alchemy over engineering in my early days."

"So, what's changed in Central since I've been gone?" I asked before Bob could get distracted again.

Rogue was the one to sigh this time. "A lot, and none for the better. You would think that after ten cycles, Central would pull their heads out of their—"

Xalla gave her mentor another death glare.

"All right, all right, disciple of mine, I'll be professional." Rogue cleared his membrane and continued. "What I meant to say is that the core of Central has stayed practically the same."

"Yeah, still the same overseer as before, if you can believe it," Big Bob grumbled. "No shortage of coup attempts, but that old bastard is hanging on somehow. Now, I normally don't want to get too political—I enjoy being a neutral party for the most part—but even I can see that he'll drag the entire Central Collective down with him at this rate. I think things have just gotten worse since before you left!"

Hmm, more information I could use. "You have to be exaggerating. I mean, I heard about the budget cuts from Q, but that's been happening for cycles at this point. How can it possibly be worse than before?"

"Don't get me started!" Rogue added, looking more animated than ever. "That brain-dead overseer's been making one disastrous mistake after another ever since his best arbiter left. That's you, by the way. He's desperate, and he's doing anything and everything to get this to work his way, even if that means using force. He's still somehow incapable of understanding that he can't force anyone to work for him, and that pissed-off workers will make for damned useless ones! I'll bet you anything that he'll chew your frills off when he sees you again."

I shrugged. "Come on, he can't be that bad . . . and there's no way one arbiter would make that big of a difference."

"Now you're just being humble, my friend." Bob laughed. "You were practically holding the whole organization together near the end, and you know damn well that's the truth. You should have seen the Council's faces when they found out you disappeared. Ha, I think I have a recording of it somewhere. I have to show you!"

All right, so it turned out that this mysterious Arbiter W was more impressive than I had originally thought. He was a serious deal if everything went downhill the second he left. There was just the slight problem that I had to somehow live up to these ludicrous expectations again, and I didn't even have the damn Absolute Luck skill with me this time.

I took another look at my unused luck charges and despaired.

Luck Charge: 1057/1057
Transformation Time Left: 23 hours 44 minutes

All those tasty charges that I couldn't use, but at least I still had a lot of time left on my current transformation . . . Hold on, there was no way that only sixteen minutes had passed. I swear Bob's speech alone took hours, not to mention the time it took us to get to the private train platform.

Noe, what's going on?

"To clarify, my host," she answered cheerfully, "since Unit Noe's upgrade, I have been able to slightly alter the way your transformation works. I have taken it upon myself to sync all of your functions with the timeline of Pandora, whereas I could only use your local timeline prior to my shard's integration."

So that means that the twenty-four-hour time limit is going off the regressor's clock, and not whatever strange dimension I'm in now?

"That is correct, my host," she answered. "But do note that I cannot make further adjustments until more of my functions are unlocked. I apologize, dear Walter."

That's more than enough, Noe. You just got rid of the biggest headache for me! If I could kiss you, I would!

"Noted."

I smiled awkwardly. "Well, any specifics I should know? I have a feeling that the Overseer will try to rope me into more annoyances if my absence was that profound."

"Well . . ." Rogue said, "that depends on how strong your ties with Central still are."

Ah, he was afraid that I'd take offense, seeing as how I was a big shot at Central. Good thing I had literally no ties with them now!

"There was a reason I left for so long, Rogue," I said, reassuring him that he could speak the truth with me. "And I'm a Xollon first, so you know where my allegiances lie."

He gave me a huge grin before moving his gaze to Xalla. She had been quiet in this conversation so far, as she was here on official duty, but I could tell that she liked my answer. I felt like they'd just confirmed something about me during a secret discussion they'd had. A little concerning.

"That is certainly good to hear, and you should know that Xalla shares those sentiments," Rogue continued. "Why, she was thinking of saving up some cash and buying herself a nice little plot of land, maybe start her own brood with a handsome young m—"

Another quick stab of her feelers shut the man up again.

"Those aspirations of mine can be discussed later, Lord General," Xalla said, her tone icy, "without a third party giving their input on the matter. If you would please tell Arbiter Walter the rest of the information, the *relevant* information, that would be much appreciated. We are almost at our destination."

"She's got a fiery temper, that one," he whispered to me, ignoring another one of Xalla's death stares. "But anyway, to summarize fast, Central's war is still going strong, that idiot overseer burned more bridges than cycles I've lived, and Origin's getting overloaded trying to put all the fires out."

"A bit of an exaggeration," Big Bob added, "but not completely untrue. The Overseer is growing desperate, anyone can see that, and there are a lot of worrying rumors about some of the steps he's taken to solidify his quickly dwindling power. Some say he's even gone into the Origin Matrix's core and fiddled with its code, but I highly doubt he could manage that. I'm pretty sure he specifically summoned you here to rope you into his petty power struggles."

"An idiot decision," Rogue muttered. "We Xollon have long remained neutral. Does he honestly think Walter would change that?" He sighed and shook his head. "Never mind, it's an idiot decision made by an idiot. He'll try it."

"So what do you think will happen at the Tribunal?" I asked.

"It'll be a farce," Big Bob said with certainty. "They'll do everything to get you back into the fold, using whatever means they can. The Tribunal's a shell of what it used to be, and it's nothing more than a political tool now."

Big Bob smiled and gave me a friendly pat on the shoulders. "But knowing you, my friend? You'll be fine! Let them know what happens when they try to mess with the legendary Arbiter W!"

"Yeah . . ." I answered with a forced smile. "I'll make sure to do that."

I felt the slowing of the train we were on, and Xalla's warm voice welcomed our arrival.

"Lord Arbiter, Grand General, Master Alchemist," Xalla said in her most professional tone, "we have arrived at Central's base of operations. Please gather your things and follow me."

CHAPTER NINE

The Tribunal Part 3

We followed the Xollon out of the train and into a beautifully luxurious car, which took us the rest of the way to Central's headquarters. Like the others said, Central really had spared no expense when it came to our comfort.

"Xalla, oh disciple of mine," Rogue began as he gazed out the side window, "you know that it's just the four of us here. You don't have to be so formal. We're all friends."

"Unlike someone I know, *Lord General*," Xalla replied sternly, "I do not slack off when I am assigned official duties."

He grinned. "I'm pretty sure I saw you hugging the great lord arbiter back there."

Xalla gave him a deathly glare, and I quickly added before the old Xollon could lose a feeler or three, "That was completely my fault, Lord General. I overstepped, and Xalla was more than professional the whole time."

Rogue chuckled. "So you're abusing your power over a subordinate and engaging in sexual harassment at the same time, eh? Are you taking one out of the Overseer's playbooks now?"

Big Bob laughed at the exchange while Xalla rubbed her frills with a feeler. I think she had given up trying to get the old Xollon to behave in any capacity. And there was the mention of that damned Overseer again. I didn't know who or what this Overseer dude was, but the more I heard Rogue and Bob describe him, the less I wanted to actually meet the man.

"As I was saying," Xalla continued, "we have arrived at Central HQ. We are to head into the lounge and await our summons."

"You know how long that will take, Xalla?" I asked.

"I do not know, Lord Arbiter," she answered politely.

I shuddered a little every time she called me by my title. Xalla was so different when she had her professional maw on, which was completely unlike my first meeting with her. I guess she was stepping up her game now that she was representing Q and his site on a larger stage. And she had mentioned that she wanted to change the perception people had of the Xollons, but as much as I respected her dedication to her assigned role, I missed the more carefree and cheerful girl I saw on our date.

"But knowing the current political state Central is in," Xalla continued, "they will deliberately make us wait."

"For what?" I asked. "Just to spite me?"

Rogue grumbled, "That, and to show their dwindling supporters how much better they are than you. Useless gesture to make the fools think that you still worship the ground that the overgrown slimeball of an overseer walks on."

Big Bob chimed in as well with a chuckle. "Don't forget the part where they'll make a big fuss about making you wait, my friend! Then they'll apologize profusely and probably find a scapegoat to blame it on, another political rival most likely! You know the drill: They'll try to rope you in with promises, then when that inevitably fails, they'll go back to their threats. Rogue and I have watched this play out far too many times."

"Agreed, Bob," the old Xollon said. "But they are predictable, and a predictable enemy is an easy enemy. Especially for one so accomplished as the lord arbiter here."

I wished they'd stop hyping me up to be this unstoppable Xollon hero! I was going in practically blind here.

"Well, let's just go to the waiting room, then," I said, trying to change the subject. I still had some time to get as much information as I could out of them, so I'd count Central's display of power as a blessing in disguise. I only had my own skills to rely on to bullshit my way through whatever was coming my way, although if I could somehow rope in Rogue and Big Bob . . . Let's see what I could do.

Xalla led the three of us into a grand processional room. She called it the lounge, and yes there was no shortage of places to lounge around, but I'm pretty sure most lounges don't cover the area of several football fields, while also having an army of staff on hand to cater to your every need.

The staff were kind of strange looking, featureless gray humanoids with elongated limbs, and they moved rather jerkily. And when I say they were featureless, I meant it. They didn't wear clothes, but they had, well, nothing. No genitalia, no hair, no mouth or any other opening in their bodies. How they perceived the environment was beyond me. I wouldn't say they made for the best servants given their awkward movements, but there were so many of them that I don't think efficiency mattered.

The place was divided into many sections, all beautifully and tastefully decorated, which housed pretty much anything a guest would need to feel welcome.

There were private chefs waiting to take our orders while servants scrambled to get anything and everything we might need for a meal, no matter how outlandish the request. Professional massage artists (these ones seem to be hired help) were at our beck and call, every single one of them proficient in relieving stress, regardless of what kind of anatomy their guests had. Next to the manicure and massage parlors were several heated pools, although I couldn't tell what liquids made up their contents.

All the while, the halls were filled with a nice ambient music that seemed to permeate from every corner of the room. And of course, it wouldn't be a lounge without places to sit. There were sofas, chairs, and even living slime-like organisms that contoured their shape to maximize comfort.

I grabbed one of those and settled my feelers into its cool folds. One of those featureless manservants was already by my side, as if it already knew that I was about to order another glass of Xollon wine. Honestly, if making us wait here of all places was a vain display of power, then they could take as long as they possibly need to show off. Shit, I could get used to this type of lifestyle.

Rogue sat beside me, nursing his own glass of wine, while a few serfs were massaging his bottom feelers.

He sighed in pleasure. "Well, they've really outdone themselves this time. This whole place must have put a dent in Central's operating costs. I'm guessing the Overseer's really desperate to have you back on the team."

Big Bob was relaxing face down on a nearby tanning bed, enjoying the artificial sun one of the servants had brought over for him to use. "Yup, I've been affiliated with Central for close to 200 cycles, been a sponsor for damn near 150 of those, and they've never once rolled out the VIP treatment for me."

Bob flopped onto his back now and allowed his pale stomach to roast in the sun. I'm pretty sure that the temperatures that he was experiencing could melt steel, but the chubby human-looking man didn't seem to mind.

"But damn, can I get used to this," he mumbled. "Walter, my friend, please get into more trouble so we can tag along to your Tribunal summons in the future."

I laughed and agreed, although I wish I felt as relaxed and in control as Bob was or had even a fraction of the confidence he had in my success. The original W, wherever he was, was lucky to have a friend like him.

Seeing the two sponsors so relaxed, I turned my attention back on to Xalla. The Xollon girl was standing at attention by the other Central attendants, her gaze constantly searching for threats, although I think she knew that we were safe until at least the start of the Tribunals. I doubt the Overseer would try to harm me before attempting to rope me into his crew.

"Xalla," I said, waving a feeler over at her and beckoning her to join me on the squishy slime sofa thing. "Why don't you come over and relax for a bit. There's a lot of other guards stationed around."

I could tell that she desperately wanted to do just that, her cute little frills fluttering against the urge to join me. I liked seeing the slightly flustered girl, even if I probably shouldn't.

"I must decline, Lord Arbiter," she said after a few moments of hesitation. "I was tasked to serve as your bodyguard and aide, so I cannot afford to relax."

I smiled mischievously, although I'm not sure how that gesture translated in a Xollon body, but whatever gesture I did make was noticed by Xalla.

"Well, as my bodyguard," I started, "I think it would be more efficient if you were closer to me."

Xalla frowned.

I looked at Rogue for support.

He smiled and obliged. "He's right, you know. There are deadly assassins that could strike at our poor arbiter friend, and that could have all been prevented if someone were to be guarding him closer. Say, by sitting right next to the vulnerable man."

I scootched over and patted the empty spot beside me. Reluctantly (or maybe not), Xalla came over and sat down. She still seemed on edge, but I used a feeler to bring her a little closer, enjoying her warmth against the cool sofa creature. Once she was firmly by my side, I felt one of her tentacles wrap around me, holding me tight.

"And," Big Bob added when he saw the situation, "I think we also need this bodyguard to test Walter's drinks and food for any poisons."

The big man then gestured to one of the many attending servants to fetch Xalla some wine as well.

"Indeed, Big Bob," I answered, knowing full well that nothing short of the heat death of the universe could harm a Xollon, let alone some mundane chemical or virus. "I could fall dead at any moment from deadly poisons."

Xalla sighed and went along with it, accepting the offered drink and taking careful sips with her proboscis. Even the way she drinks was cute!

"Fine," she mumbled, "you guys win. But if anyone asks, I was doing my job."

"What do you mean?" I said in mock confusion. "You're still doing your job right now. No would-be assassins could strike me with you by my side, and I can rest assured that my drinks are free of toxins."

"Yeah, yeah," she said as she placed her head on my side and relaxed for the first time. "And you don't get to make fun of me for this after, Rogue."

"Wouldn't dream of it, little disciple," he answered with a chuckle.

"Before we all fall asleep," I said with a smile, "there's something I'd like to discuss with you three. Any way to keep would-be eavesdroppers at bay?"

Big Bob snapped his finger, and the air around us visibly tightened. If it hadn't been for my enhanced Xollon perception, I wouldn't have thought that anything had happened, but something was different for sure.

"Done," he said, voice still relaxed. "Unless there's another Xollon here, no one should be able to hear us now."

"Thank you, Bob," I said with a nod. "Just wanted to clarify some things before the meeting starts."

Bob and Rogue nodded.

"First of all, I can assume that you have no love for the Overseer, correct?"

"Like that wasn't obvious before, Walter." Rogue snorted. "I was never a fan of that bastard."

Big Bob shrugged. "He was fine before all the power got to him, a bit stuck up now, and I certainly wouldn't help him if he were in trouble, but I remain a neutral party for the most part. Central makes up a large portion of my customer base, after all, even with its recent decline."

"You know my stance, Walter," Xalla answered. "I'll stick with any decision you make. I've always been a Xolloid first kind of gal."

"Good," I said with a smile, "then you should be fine with helping me out for a bit."

They nodded.

"I'm sure you know that the Overseer will try his best to rope me back into Central's side, but we can all see that it's a sinking ship."

"No kidding," Rogue said. "I'll give it thirty, maybe forty more cycles before something gives in. Hopefully the thing that gives first is that idiot of an overseer."

I continued, "And you also know that there's no way I would abandon my role in Q's site for whatever offer he gives."

"That's a given, Walter!" Big Bob answered. "I wouldn't either if I was testing out the biggest breakthrough in alchemical research. You made a damn soul! Making one for a new life-form is easy enough, but one that you can use yourself? You still need to tell me how you did that, by the way, but I'll let you do the fine-tuning first."

I ignored Bob's last remark and continued, "So there's a couple of things that I might need your help on when we meet the Overseer and his tribunal."

"Sure. I'm game if you're not asking for much," Rogue agreed. "And Xalla here would probably do anything you ask of her. *Anything*, Walter, if you catch my drift."

Another death glare from the girl by my side, but she was too close to me this time to attack her mentor, much to his relief. She also didn't correct him, which I wasn't sure was a good thing.

"And you know that you can always count on me for another one of your crazed schemes, Walter." Bob laughed. "Reminds me of the old days!"

Huh, was the original Arbiter W more like me than I thought? The fact that Big Bob hadn't pointed out any dissimilarities should mean that we were. Strange.

I spoke again. "Then I need you three to back me up if things go like I think they will . . ."

I went over my plans, wrinkling out some details here and there, and before long, an attendant came to take us to the Tribunal. Big Bob undid whatever he'd done and allowed the guide to take us away.

Well, I had to hope that all my crazy plans worked out this time because I'd need all the luck I could get to make it out in one piece.

CHAPTER TEN

The Tribunal Part 4

Xalla

Xalla didn't want to leave Walter's presence as the attendants came to finally take them to the Tribunal. She was always calm whenever he was by her side, and just feeling his skin on hers made her feel safe and comfortable. If only she wasn't here on official business! Maybe she could use her status to book one of those nice spas in Xolloid for the next time they were free.

Still, now that she had finished hearing about the arbiter's plans, she realized just how amazing Walter was. Sure she had heard about the legendary Arbiter W's exploits in the past—you couldn't find anyone working in Central who hadn't—but the information she'd heard second hand were just lists of accomplishments. It was all one emotionless accolade after another, about how many rebellions he had quelled, how he saved this site from collapse or made these deals with this race. He seemed too perfect in those reports, and Xalla always suspected that a lot of the rumors and reports were exaggerations of the truth, although she had to admit that if even a fraction of his exploits were true, then he had been an impressive figure for Central, even by Xollon standards.

One thing she wasn't sure about before was why Arbiter W had stayed as an arbiter. He was offered various positions of power over the cycles but had turned each one down. But Xalla thought that she could understand why Walter had made that decision now that she knew him better, and more importantly, found out that he was a fellow Xollon.

Like her, he must have wanted the freedom to explore the universe and meet other higher species. Sure, the offered promotions came with power, but what was power to a Xollon? Instead, he chose the one position that gave him the option to move around freely, and it was such a position that Xalla had wanted to attain for herself as well. So now that she had seen him in person and had gotten to know him, if only just a little, she understood how he could have risen to such an exalted status.

There was this intangible charisma that Walter exuded in everything he did. He seemed like he had plans upon plans, that he had a solution for every situation, and she just knew that nothing could go wrong if Walter was tasked to fix it. Even when Central lost control in that last trial, and Walter was cut off from all support, he never panicked. He was able to contain some artifact that was able to influence even the Origin Matrix, and he did so while still maintaining his human disguise to boot! The man just seemed to shrug off seemingly impossible tasks on a regular basis, the events were so mundane in his life that he probably didn't understand how amazing even one of his achievements would be for the average person.

Impossible was definitely the right word for it. Xalla couldn't even imagine how he could have done such a thing in such a feeble body. The whole situation was so secretive that most of the information about the incident had been redacted by the Overseer, and even she, the head of security for the site affected, had only limited knowledge of what happened. Yet before she could even try to intervene and help Walter out, he had already somehow solved the issue! Of course, her outburst also landed her in hot water, but Q was kind enough to "punish" her by allowing Xalla to act as his bodyguard and aide.

Some irrational part of her just couldn't help but want to help this man, and she still sometimes questioned why he had decided to date someone like her. But it was just more motivation for her to be the best Xollon that she could so that she could one day stand proudly by his side. She was just glad that he liked the little gift she and Raffiel had prepared for him. That insignificant aspirant David was spreading the lord arbiter's influence rather effectively after she had tweaked his physiology a little bit. She did get a harsh lecture about interfering with the trials after that, though.

Now, Xollon didn't necessarily need worshipers, unlike some of the lesser gods of the minor planes, so Xalla wasn't sure if Walter would appreciate the extra attention. Sure, having some extra peons to help with mundane tasks was useful, but they could get tiresome with their constant needs and prayers. It was the main reason why Xalla had destroyed all of hers. Thankfully, he must have seen her hesitation and silently approved of her actions by establishing a cult in that second trial.

Plus, she also learned of his designation! Xalla allowed her imagination to run wild, against her best judgment. The *Devourer of Truth* . . . it just rolled off the maw. She subvocalized the title again, this time adding her own along with it. The *Devourer of Truth* and the *Anguish of Eternity*. She thought that they sounded perfect together! And perhaps if they ever had a hatchling of their own, they could take after them both and be the *Devourer of Eternity*, or perhaps the *Anguish of Truth*. Or maybe they could have twins, and that way, both options could be used!

Xalla sighed and cleared her mind. Well, that was a bit too optimistic, even for the cheesy romance shows she watched. They'd gone on one date; they weren't even an official couple yet. She had the terrible habit of getting ahead of herself and had ruined many potential dates in the past. Well, that and a lot of the men she used to see were only there for her status. She resolved to fix all those issues with Walter.

Xalla's daydreams were only broken when the attendant led them into the council chamber, and she forced her professional maw back on. Although Walter did not give her any specific duties in his plan, she was still tasked with providing backup and ensuring that nothing would harm him.

The four of them walked into the grand hall, up the wide staircase, and approached the podium that faced where the Overseer and his two most trusted advisers oversaw everything. There had been many more advisers in the past, their ghosts still echoed by the empty seats beside the three, but that had been many cycles ago. Unlike the empty tribunal stands, however, the spectator seats on the sides were packed to the brim with every important figure in Central, and their hushed whispers echoed across the hall. This was the first time so many people had gathered all at once. News of Arbiter W's return was overwhelmingly effective at gaining attention.

The noise only stopped once Walter took his spot in the center of the room.

"Welcome, or should I say welcome back, Lord Arbiter W!" the Overseer said, his voice booming, "And I welcome the Grand General Rogue and Master Babylon, who represent the sponsors for Site 1102. I apologize for making you wait, but getting everyone here screened and seated took longer than anticipated. A cause of celebration, of course, for your arrival has only reinvigorated the souls of all the important figures of the Central Collective!"

Xalla gazed at the thing called the Overseer. He was a strange creature, all things considered. Even her Xollon senses couldn't see past the veil that shrouded the man. It made his features blur and shift like billowing smoke, and even his size couldn't be properly measured. It extended to the clothes that he wore as well—they were ever changing. Sometimes it was a royal robe, other times it turned into a beggar's cloak, never staying in one shape or color for long.

What was annoying for Xalla was that she couldn't properly assess the Overseer no matter how hard she tried. There weren't a whole lot of ways to deceive a Xollon's senses, especially for someone of Xalla's caliber, but the figure had somehow managed. That made him dangerous.

"Thank you, Overseer," Walter replied, his beautiful voice calm and assertive, "but I am not here for pleasantries, nor do I care for them. Why am I called here?"

The Overseer laughed. "Always the pragmatist, Arbiter W. I see that hasn't changed since your disappearance."

"Get to the point," Walter stated.

"And as rude as ever." The other man chuckled. "But you are right. Let's get to the main point. That is why so many of our esteemed guests have taken time out of their busy schedules to be here. You, Arbiter W, are here to represent Site 1102 on the matter of the abnormality of the Second Earth Trial. And as much as I would love to hear an explanation on why you were gone for ten cycles, this is not the time or place for that discussion."

Walter nodded, still looking impatient. "What do you want to know?"

"You were present in that trial and saw firsthand what happened there. You know that our monitoring process was hindered by the abnormalities, so why don't you give the people here a summary of what happened."

And Walter did as he was told. Xalla was also interested to know exactly what events transpired, as she had only been able to take disjointed glances into the trial. She already knew that he was able to convert a huge portion of the population into his worshipers—that kind of event was hard to miss as a Xollon—but she didn't know how he had done so without revealing any of his Xollon abilities.

He had managed to use the outdated title system to gain the trust of the locals and launch an offensive against the source of the corruption: the shard. Xalla wanted to know more about this object, but it seemed that Walter's knowledge of it was also incomplete. He only knew as much as the rest of them here, that it was somehow able to affect the planet it was on, as well as the Origin Matrix.

The Overseer interrupted Walter's explanation. "So you're saying that you have never seen this shard before, or know anything else about it?"

"Nothing that Q wouldn't have already told you," he answered calmly.

"Yet you were able to somehow contain this object?"

Walter shook his head. "Not contain, I destroyed it."

For the first time, the mask of cool the Overseer had on started to slip, and he almost shouted. "You did *what?*"

Walter remained nonchalant. "I destroyed the source of corruption. It was a hazard to Central's operations and had the ability to influence Origin."

He stared directly at the Overseer then, his tone challenging, "Why, did you want to have it for yourself?"

The Overseer gritted his teeth. "No, you did . . . exactly what you were supposed to do, given the situation. I applaud your dedication to your work. However, if you encounter these shards in the future, you are to contain and bring them back to Central. They are valuable research material."

Xalla scoffed at that. As if this man wouldn't use the shards for his own gain, especially if it had the ability to change Central's greatest asset. There was no one in the audience who didn't understand his true intentions, but without proof, they also couldn't voice those thoughts.

"So, there are other shards out there?" Walter asked with a raised frill. "And why are you not tasking other arbiters and staff to get rid of them, or in your case, securing these shards for 'research'?"

"Because, Lord Arbiter W," the Overseer said again, trying in vain to hide his growing frustrations, "none of the other arbiters or administration staff were able to even approach these shards, let alone destroy one."

Once again, Xalla was amazed that Walter was able to casually do something that no one else could. It was almost as if the shard had just invited him over, given how easy it was for him to solve this problem, as ludicrous as that sounded!

"So let me ask you once again, Arbiter W," he continued. "How was it that you were the only one who was able to do what all my other staff could not?"

This time it was Xalla's mentor who spoke up. "Oh, come now, Overseer, this wouldn't be the first time that Arbiter W has done the impossible. You can't expect him to just give up the secrets to his success."

The Overseer thought for a moment but nodded in the end. "That is true. We will speak more on this matter at a different time, away from so many guests."

Walter shrugged. He seemed like he didn't have a care in the world, as if all of this current situation was completely beneath his notice. And in some ways, that was true. Xalla knew that he held no love for Central, and it was only a matter of time before he integrated back into Xollon society. Central was dying, it was plain to see, and a small part of Xalla was a little sad that she might lose her little security gig in the foreseeable future.

Perhaps it was finally time to search for a home of her own, preferably somewhere close to her parents in the countryside. While she liked the bustle of the city and her current hectic work environment, there was just nothing like the nice and quiet of the great outdoors. Hopefully, a small part of her thought, Walter would like it there too.

The Overseer's voice brought Xalla out of her delusions. "Which brings us to the next point that I want to discuss."

Here it was, Xalla thought, the part where Central would try to derail Walter's experiments and rope him into more politics. No matter what happens, there was no way that Xalla would stand to lose Walter and see him transferred to some backwater dimension or war front, but she trusted in his ability to solve this issue himself.

But if worse came to worst . . . she and her mentor had plans of their own.

"For your continued service, and for brilliantly solving this crisis in Site 1102," the Overseer said with a smile, "I am using my authority as the head of the Central Collective to reassign you from your duties at the Training Center and into a more valuable position by my side at our main headquarters."

He stared directly at Walter. *"This is not a request."*

CHAPTER ELEVEN

Drastic Decrees

would have to kindly decline," I answered calmly, keeping my voice and tone neutral.

"Did you not hear me, Arbiter W?" the Overseer asked in puzzlement. "I said that this was not a request. You do not have the option to decline my *command*."

"I heard you," I answered. "And I will repeat myself: I will have to kindly decline your *request*."

Now the Overseer was getting annoyed. "You still work for me, Arbiter W, and as long as I am still running the Central Collective, you will obey me. You will find that things have changed in the ten cycles that you were gone."

I continued, my voice calm and even. "And I will remind you that my duties as an arbiter, as Rogue so kindly affirmed, is to first and foremost settle disputes between anomalies and the Origin Matrix. Why don't I ask one of the other Tribunal members to clarify this point? I haven't heard them talk at all yet."

I looked at the Overseer, his once-calm façade now completely broken, even under that weird shroud he had going on. Oh yeah, this was a person who was not used to having his commands disregarded, but thankfully I found out very early on that Central worked and thrived on rules and regulations. I was betting that not even the Overseer could arbitrarily break those.

The figures beside the Overseer didn't have the same disguise going on and were instead dressed in simple robes. They were freakishly tall, maybe twelve to fifteen feet from head to foot, but the black dress obscured all visible features. The other two silent men finally woke up from whatever trance they were in and looked at the fuming Overseer before speaking for the first time.

"The rules for an arbiter are clear," the one on the left of the Overseer said. "They serve the training sites directly, and to deviate from those duties would constitute a break in the contract."

The robed figure on the right of the Overseer also chimed in. "In order for the Overseer's decree to pass, it would require the lord arbiter to accept a change in designation."

The Overseer gritted his teeth. "And I can assume that you will not choose to accept a promotion, Arbiter W?"

I smirked. "Have I ever?"

"You have not," he answered. "But this time is different. If you will not accept a promotion, then I can demote you."

I raised a frill. "On what basis?"

The man smiled this time. "For the neglect of your duty in the past ten cycles, for one."

"Oh, come now, Overseer," Big Bob said. "We can hardly blame him for that disaster ten cycles ago. If anything, the fact that Arbiter W survived at all should be celebrated, not punished."

Now I was really curious about this mysterious Arbiter W I was impersonating. I'd have to somehow gather more information about him later, although I couldn't exactly ask others to tell me about my own biography. That would have to be yet another task to do in the future.

"Perhaps, Master Babylon," the Overseer said, "there might have been extenuating circumstances for his initial disappearance, but there certainly wasn't any for his return. He did not follow through with proper procedures and infiltrated Site 1102 without contacting Central first. Not to mention that working as an aspirant is highly unusual. For all of these infractions, I am well within my right to reprimand the arbiter. Does the Tribunal agree with these facts?"

The two cloaked figures thought for a moment before speaking as one. "The Overseer is correct, although no fault can be attributed to W for the incident ten cycles ago. Nevertheless, Arbiter W's actions at Site 1102 were highly unprofessional and irresponsible, and a demotion is well within the boundaries of appropriate punishments."

"Do you have anything to say, W?" the Overseer said with a smirk. "Or will you accept your promotion and work with me?"

"There will be a bit of a problem with that, Overseer," Rogue spoke up this time, exactly as I had instructed him to.

I knew this slimeball of an overseer would bring up my mysterious reappearance sooner or later, since I doubt I did anything the standard Central way given my unique situation. I got this fake position through literal luck, so although I didn't know what rules I had broken, I was certain that I had broken a whole bunch of them.

"And what would that be?" he said impatiently.

"The lord arbiter, or should I say Aspirant Walter, has already fully integrated himself into the trials with Origin's approval."

"Then he will simply fail them." The Overseer shrugged. "Say that he died in his sleep from a heart attack, humans tend to do that a lot if I recall."

Rogue smiled as he continued. "Normally it would be fine to have one or two new aspirants disappear like that, but Walter is in a special spot within the trials."

The Overseer frowned, not liking where this was going.

"You see," the Xollon continued, "the arbiter has already integrated himself into the anomaly's team and is a founding member of his guild."

"Fine," the Overseer said. "Then we can simply wait until the start of the third trial and have him die there. I am willing to make such a concession."

"But," Rogue continued, "that would be a gross breach of the terms of my contract with him if he were to deliberately lose."

"Explain," the Overseer muttered.

"I have offered him an official sponsorship, as is my right, and we have already signed the contract sealing this." Rogue then pulled out a piece of paper and threw it at the Overseer. I wasn't sure when a physical contract was signed, but I wasn't going to complain now.

The other man read through the contract quickly before tossing it back. "And it says that you have given up all rights to anything W does in the trial. This hardly counts as a contract of sponsorship!"

"But it is one." The Xollon smiled. "Tribunal, do you agree?"

Once again, the two figures beside the Overseer woke up from the weird trace they went into when they weren't addressed, and they spoke as one. "That is correct. General Rogue can freely give up the rewards if he wishes. The contract is valid."

Rogue continued, "So it would be against regulations for him to give up his position as an aspirant, or to willingly die or give up in the trials. After all, I have a vested interest in the success of my recipient, reward or no reward."

Now the Overseer was angry. "And if an accident were to happen that caused W to somehow leave the trials early?"

"Are you threatening to interfere with the trials?" I asked.

"No, of course not," he answered, lying through his teeth. "I am just giving a potential hypothetical."

This time Bob chimed in with a smile. "Well, since I designed the monitoring systems in the trials, and I am also actively monitoring Aspirant W's activities, this hypothetical accident would be really, *really* unlikely to happen if it escapes my notice."

"It would be," the Overseer answered, "but it can still happen. As skilled as you are, Master Babylon, your creations are not infallible."

I shrugged. "If that were to happen, then I would simply quit my job as an arbiter and live on Xolloid."

Now the Overseer's disguise was starting to falter, and I could briefly see his true face for a fraction of a second. It was a hideous thing made of patchwork skin and other organs, as if he was doing everything in his power to keep his physical form from deteriorating.

"You would leave everything that you built up over the years to live in a backwards place like Xolloid!? After everything that I have done for you?"

"Careful what you say," Rogue said, his voice chilly. "Remember that we Xollon do not like to be insulted. We remain neutral in the current war solely because my disciple works for your site."

"And I will also be inclined to leave this position if Walter is impacted in any way," Xalla added. I gave her a quick flick of the frill in thanks. She didn't have to do that for me. "And the lord arbiter has done more for Central than you have ever done for him."

"Fine!" the Overseer screamed, all pretense of calm completely gone. "But the gross negligence of the arbiter must be addressed. If he refuses to take responsibility, then that responsibility rests on the site administrator!"

A flash of light appeared, and Q was standing a distance away from the four of us. He was still in his human disguise, although he quickly shed it when he saw the situation he was in. His new form, or his real body in this case, was marvelous. He was still vaguely humanoid in shape, but his physical body was made out of a clear, glass-like substance. Inside that glass structure was a swirling mass of nebulae and galaxies, almost as if he housed an entire universe inside himself. It was beautiful.

"You, Site Administrator Quasar of the Omnipotent Race," the Overseer said with rage, "will be relieved of your duties due to your failure to properly inform Central of the arbiter's return, and for allowing multiple anomalous phenomena to occur unheeded in your site."

I was about to protest, but Q, still as calm as I've ever seen him, raised a hand and gestured for me to remain quiet. I didn't mean to cause him to lose his job! He was being blamed for something that I had done, and there was no way I would allow that to happen.

The Overseer continued. "A new site admin will be chosen to take over, on my recommendation, and you will have until the last aspirant arrives on the Main Stage to transfer all necessary power and privileges over to the new staff."

"I understand," Q answered emotionlessly. "Will that be all?"

"Yes, you are dismissed," the Overseer spat. "Leave at once."

Q nodded, gave me a reassuring wave, and disappeared just as quickly as he came. Fuck! I hadn't meant for that to happen. I'd make sure I set things right with him if it was the last damn thing I did. I still have a bit of time to think up a way to fix things.

"You four are dismissed as well," he grunted. "I will also designate someone to *help* the lord arbiter in his tasks when the new staff arrive."

Great, looked like his man would hold a grudge for a long time.

We were about to leave when the Overseer stopped us one last time. "Oh, and W?"

I looked back but didn't say anything.

He grinned. "I will summon you again privately once the change in staff is completed, to discuss all of the changes in Central over the last ten cycles. I'm sure we will see eye to eye then, this time without the Lord General and his people to distract you from our conversation, of course."

Shit, did this mean that I had to use the last of my preview tickets just to deal with this petty overseer? I looked at the remaining time on my transformation and saw that I still had over fourteen hours left on it. It seemed like a waste to have to go back to human form so early.

"Do not worry, my host," Noe chimed in. "With the Gamma upgrade, I can store the unused transformation time for future use."

I almost danced in joy at hearing this first little bit of good news to come but just twitched weirdly instead. Xalla and Rogue gave me a weird look but didn't comment on my sudden movement.

Thank you, Noe, you are the freaking best!

Refocusing on the present, I forced myself to smile. "I look forward to that, Overseer."

"You should," he answered with a mocking smirk. "Now please leave. I have work to do. Termination papers to sign. It's a lot of work, finding a new site admin."

No wonder Rogue hated this guy's guts! This piece of shit was the most petty person I had ever met. But he would curse the day he pissed me off, that I promise.

CHAPTER TWELVE

Brewing Issues

The trip back to Site 1102 was a solemn affair, even if we technically achieved every goal that I had. The issue with Q didn't sit well with any of us, and Xalla looked especially concerned about Q's future. I couldn't blame her, as she had known the man personally for a lot longer than all of us, and she thought of him as a genuine friend.

"Well," Big Bob said as we neared our destination, "it's not all bad for Q. I've been trying to poach him to join my company for the longest time, so he will be financially stable at the very least."

Xalla sighed. "I know that, and I'm sure Q does as well. But . . . you've seen how much he's given up over the cycles for his site. He practically built it from the ground up, despite all the budget cuts. I'm pretty sure he's paying some of us out of pocket."

Xalla squeezed my feeler tight. "He loves the place."

Big Bob grimaced. "I know. He's had every opportunity to leave a dead-end job like that, but he didn't. It's not the pay that's keeping him, anyone can see that. Damned shame to see someone like him go."

"I just never expected the Overseer to be so petty," I muttered as I pulled Xalla closer. I needed some warmth right now. "He's willing to lay off one of his best employees, all for what? Revenge because he didn't get his way?"

Rogue shook his head. "He's changed, my friend. The Overseer was ruthless in the past, everyone knows that, but never so vindictive. He's afraid, but he wants everyone to know that he's still in charge. I don't know what's gotten into him these past few cycles."

"Look, let's all go speak with Q first," Big Bob said. "I'm sure a man like that has something up his sleeves. He must have known that Central's been going downhill, and I do not believe that he wouldn't be ready for a situation like this."

I nodded. "And I need to apologize for getting him in this mess."

Xalla shook her head. "It's not your fault, Walter, you know that."

I sighed in response. That might be technically true, but there was no way that I had no part in him losing his job. I lied for a living, I knew that, but seeing someone I actually cared about get hurt from my own actions sat wrong with me.

"Unfortunately, I won't be able to join you," Rogue said. "I've been away from my official duties for too long, so I'll be getting off after you three. But say hello to Q for me and let him know that I've got his back if he ever needs help."

I nodded.

"Come on, we're almost there," Bob said with a forced smile. "Let's not meet the man looking like this."

"You three take care," Rogue added. "I'll see if I can do anything for our situation on my end. I'm sure I can pull in some favors. At the very least, I'll try to make sure that the Overseer's not bothering you in the immediate future. Like I'll allow him to just make arbitrary calls like this one going forward."

I nodded and thanked the old Xollon before following the others out of the train. Xalla had distanced herself from me and put on her professional demeanor once more, although none of her normal cheer and energy could be seen now.

If there was one thing I'd learned from interacting with her and the other Xollon, it was how rare they were seen working for any other race in the multiverse. For her to stick with Q for so long meant that the man had earned her trust and support, a rare thing indeed.

Q was standing by his desk when the three of us arrived to meet him. He had a bittersweet smile on as he was shuffling around various files and reports. I was back to my human form at this point, having decided to conserve as much of that cooldown as I could now that I was back in the same timestream as the regressor.

"Hey, Q," I said tentatively, not sure how to talk to the man now that I was responsible for him losing his job, "I um, I just wanted to apologize for what happened."

He turned to me and smiled, but it didn't reach his eyes. "It's all good,

Walter. I knew this day would be coming sooner or later. I can't say that I'm surprised, to be honest."

"I'm sure we can appeal your dismissal," Bob added. "There's proper procedures that need to be done, and I'm sure that we can at least delay his decision. I can get you my best lawyers on the job right now."

Q shook his head. "It's all right, Lord Babylon. I've . . . I've grown tired of my role here. Perhaps it's about time for me to move on to something else. I can't say that I won't miss it, but there's no point making all of you work harder when we all know that the Overseer will just find another reason to fire me even if this decision is overturned. Let's not delay the inevitable."

Xalla looked like she wanted to say something, but she ultimately held herself back, not wanting to make the situation any more awkward.

I noticed that he had a little framed photo made of some kind of metallic material in his hands, and I had to move a little to see what it was. On it was a picture of Q, not with his human suit on, but I somehow knew he was a lot younger in that photo, holding a little placard. I couldn't make out what was written on it, but from the bright smile that plastered his face was a memory that he cherished.

He noticed my gaze and smiled more warmly this time. "That was taken during my promotion to site admin, almost 138 cycles ago to this day."

He held it up and chuckled a little. "You wouldn't believe how much time I put in to get that position, and it was the first time that my hard work paid off. I thought the world worked on hard work and effort back then. Maybe it did, when Central and its training facilities were still respected." He sighed. "But that's not the case anymore, is it?"

I frowned. The man had been nothing but kind to me during my stay so far, and to see him so down was starting to get to me as well. I swore that I'd think of some way to make it up to Q.

"Well, it was a great 138 cycles in any case." He chuckled quietly, putting away the little picture frame. "But my time here is about over. It was a good run, if I do say so myself."

"Look, it's not over yet," I said. "We still got something like a few months before the last aspirants make it to the Main Stage, right?"

Q nodded. "It will be thirty-eight days until the start of the third trial, then about two more months before the last batch of aspirants arrive, so yes, around three months total. Time sure goes by."

"That's a lot of time," I continued. "I'll think of something to fix this mess. Just . . . don't give up yet."

Q laughed. "I appreciate the sentiment, Walter, but don't beat yourself up trying to reason with the Overseer. Central's been a sinking ship for a while now, and I think it's about time I take Lord Babylon up on his various offers."

Big Bob smiled. "I guarantee the pay's better than what they're giving you here!"

"But if you could have your old job back, if something could be done, " I said again, "would you take it?"

The other man shrugged. "We'll see. Sometimes I feel like being a site admin's not as great as it used to be. The budget cuts and new rules were bad enough already, but now even Origin's on the fritz. I don't think I'd come back if the Overseer was still around."

Then I'd just have to make sure he wasn't, but I didn't voice that out loud. Not here. Instead, I just gave Q a quick nod.

"Still, I was the cause of this, so if you need anything, Q, anything at all, just let me know. Rogue said the same thing before he left, so you have most of Xolloid backing you."

He smiled, this time regaining some of his old mirth. "Well, I don't think I'll need the Lord General's help for now, but you still owe me a trip to the alchemy labs. I guess that can wait a little longer, though."

Right, I had forgotten all about that promise I made when I first met the man. With so many things going on, I could hardly keep track of everything.

"Well, if you do decide to show him some tricks," Big Bob added, "you'll find that my labs are better than anything Central's got. I'd love to see what kind of research you've been hiding during those ten cycles."

"I'll show both of you a new thing or two," I said confidently. "Although I can't give up the secrets to making a soul that easily!"

Q chuckled. "I wouldn't dream of it."

He then turned his attention to Xalla. "And Xalla, well, it was a pleasure working with you. I hope you remain at this site to make sure everything's all right when I'm gone."

Xalla nodded but didn't say anything. Her frills were trembling.

"Don't be like that," he said. "It's not like you can't visit with Walter. The new site administrator might have their biases, but even they can't overrule regulations, and the regulations state that you are entitled to do whatever you want during your breaks."

"Of course, Q," she finally said. "It just won't be the same without you here."

He shrugged again. "Well, at least I'll be seeing you next time as a friend instead of your boss."

Xalla smiled back. "Yes, that would be a nice change."

"All right," Q said, a little of his old cheer back, "I've taken up more than enough of everyone's time here. I still have a lot to do, and I'm sure the three of you do as well. Almost ten hours have passed in Pandora since Walter was gone, and I'm sure his charges are looking for him by now."

Shit, had that much time passed, even with the slowed time flow? I had better go back before Noel did something stupid.

"And I'm sure Master Babylon and Xalla have other matters to attend to as well."

"Unfortunately, we do," Big Bob answered dejectedly. "Well, I'll get the paperwork started on your transfer. I'll be in touch."

Q nodded.

"I'll see the lord arbiter out," Xalla said, and she walked me out of the office and opened a portal back to my dorm.

"Look after him for me, Xalla," I said, turning back toward the direction of Q one last time. "I'll see what I can do on my side."

"I will, Walter," she whispered. "And take care of yourself as well."

I nodded and stepped into the portal . . .

Only to be greeted by the sight of my clone wrapped up in layers of blankets with a wet towel over his head. There was a basin of water by the side, and he looked to be squirming under the heat.

"What on earth are you doing?" I asked my doppelganger, still unsure what caused this situation.

"Ah, it be Master Walter the first," he said, his voice creepily similar to my own. "I has been told to lie down on thine bedding by friend Vadeem and Yoona."

I frowned. Why was he talking so strange?

"But worry not thine head, Origin Walter, for I hath been acting in your absence, as was originally mine directive."

"Wait a second," I muttered. "Why are you speaking like that?"

"Like how so, Walter of the First?" he replied innocently.

"Like that . . ." I continued, then a thought hit me. "Wait, is the Origin Matrix translating what you're saying into English?"

"It not be," my clone answered. "Origin Matrix only transmogrifies the languages of the aspirants, and I not be an aspirant."

"Right," I said slowly. "So how did you learn English?"

"I consummate the knowledge through what the humans dub the internet," he answered with pride. "It be most productive and useful. Many billion of pages of information freely use for learning. Marvelous invention for less good species to creation!"

Yeah . . . that explained a lot.

"You can speak in whatever native language you want now," I said. "And uh, please learn English from a native speaker when you have a chance."

The fake Walter's speech instantly improved as he changed back to his native tongue. "Was my Earth English not adequate, my lord?"

"No it's just—"

A knock on the door stopped my explanation short. The other Walter noticed the situation and immediately turned himself into a sludge-like form, spraying me with some sort of liquid in the process, before squirming away to hide under the bed. The damn stuff I was coated with smelled like old socks and gym sweat. I tried not to puke.

Not sure what had just happened and still recovering from the smell, I just stood there confused before the door opened and some concerned individuals came in.

"Walter, what are you doing up?" Yoona said with a concerned look on her face. "We told you to stay in bed! And why are you changed?"

"What? No, I—"

Vadeem frowned. "I told you that damn darkness did a number on his mind! Don't worry, we bought a doctor over. He'll make sure you're fine."

Jae-Hyun and Noel came in next, followed by another man holding a doctor's satchel. Each of them looked at me with pity and worry.

"Is this my patient?" the older man said as he looked me up and down, before frowning as he saw the state I was in.

"Yes." Vadeem nodded. "We told you about what happened in our last trial, but there must have been a delayed reaction, because Walter damn near lost his mind this morning!"

Jae-Hyun came over and forced me to sit down. What the hell did that stupid clone of mine do in the short amount of time he took over for me?

"It'll be fine, Walter," Jae-Hyun said calmly as he gave me a reassuring pat on the shoulders. "Mental pollution isn't that rare, and we caught it fast. Just relax. We'll have you back to normal in no time."

"No, really, I—"

"He don't look too good, boss," Noel said, interrupting me. "Little bro, you're sweating buckets." She sniffed a little. "Smells a bit off too."

The regressor frowned. "That's not good. If it's gotten to the point where the contamination is leaking out of his body, then it could be very serious."

The doctor shoved his way forward. "Please get out of the way. Make some room for me to work."

"Look, doc," I managed to say, "I'm fine, really."

Yoona gave me a pitying look.

"And you will be, Walter," the doctor said with a kind smile. "You will be."

Before I could react, he plunged something into my side, and I fell into a deep sleep.

CHAPTER THIRTEEN

A Normal Day in the Abyss

My mind was in a haze when I woke up, and my eyelids felt like lead. I felt oddly fatigued, so I stayed in my bed, eyes closed, trying to recall what had happened. There was a strange, dull ache in my left side. Why was that there? I was still too drowsy to remember what I was doing in this bed, but slow memories were resurfacing.

I frowned as I felt something tickle my nose. It was like a warm breeze hitting my face rhythmically. I twitched a little and used what remaining strength I had to force my heavy eyes open.

And I saw a face not two inches from mine.

It was my face, looking down with unblinking eyes, staring straight into my soul.

"Ah, good morning, Lord Arbiter—"

I screamed. The sudden shock made me forget everything for a moment.

My doppelganger, which I just had the clarity of mind to remember was who that being was, once again turned himself into goo to hide. He sprayed me with whatever the fuck that horrible liquid was again in the process.

I heard fast footsteps before the door to my room was slammed open.

"Walter, are you okay?" Vadeem asked in panic before more people entered the room again. A strange sense of déjà vu hit me, and then I remembered everything that happened last night.

"Yeah," I muttered. "I was, uh . . ."

Well, I couldn't say I panicked because I woke up seeing my own face hovering two inches in front of me.

"It was just a nightmare," I said again. "It's nothing."

The regressor nodded and gave me a look of understanding. "Nightmares . . ."

He sighed and shook his head in sympathy. "It's not nothing, Walter. I . . . I know what you're going through, and I won't say the nightmares will go away, or that they'll be easy to deal with, but if it's any consolation, you will get used to them. I'll get you something to help you sleep at night."

Vadeem also gave me a pitying look. "Look, let's give Walter some room, let him get changed. Um, I'll go get you a nice hot cup of coffee, and we can just pretend nothing happened, yeah? Just take it easy, my friend, and if you need someone to talk to, you always have Vadeem on your side."

Noel nodded, and even she was uncharacteristically sympathetic for once. "Take care of yourself, little bro. Some hot breakfast will help."

What on earth did these people think happened to me? I wanted to tell them that I did not suffer some kind of strange trauma due to that last trial, but I saw the futility in that endeavor. I was too tired to even try to correct whatever misconceptions they had right now.

"And there's some medication on your nightstand, Walter," Vadeem added. "Take it twice a day. It should help with your condition."

I nodded and saw a little bottle of pills on the counter. I might as well use it since I did have some mental contamination from earlier, although that was completely separate from what happened in the second trial.

"Um, thanks. I'll take a shower and get changed," I answered. "Is there a cafeteria or something in this building to get food?"

"Yeah, just go to the lounge and we'll meet you there," Vadeem replied. "We'll all have breakfast together, maybe make it a guild tradition to share at least one meal a day with the whole group. It's a great way to stay connected when things inevitably get busier as our organization grows."

I smiled and agreed. That sounded pretty nice, honestly. I didn't exactly grow up with a lot of friends or family around, so being in this kind of atmosphere was a nice change. If only Noe could join in as well.

"I wish for the same, my host," she answered.

Well, I'm sure you can figure something out when we get all those shards of yours.

"I look forward to that day, dear Walter."

Once the last of my friends left my dorm, I walked up to the entrance and pressed my ears against the door. Satisfied that no one was out there eavesdropping on me, I told my stupid doppelganger to come out of hiding. I had some choice words for it.

"Yes, my lord Walter?" he said with an innocent smile as he reformed his body from that sludge-like substance to be like mine again. I could never get used to seeing the damn thing. It wasn't conventionally creepy like 90% of Q's staff was, but there was just something so unnerving seeing a perfect copy of yourself move. No wonder people feared body doubles and skinwalkers in myths.

I sat down and tried my best to look my clone in the eyes. "Okay, tell me, from the beginning, what happened when you took over for me."

"Of course, Master Walter!" my clone replied. "But let me begin by saying that I am a huge fan of yours! I have done my utmost to ensure that your exalted self was not diminished in any way while I was taking over! I've studied every file there was on you, and I'm sure that I have done an adequate job to ensure your pristine and exalted reputation!"

I nodded. It seemed like he was another idiot fan of Arbiter W. That man must be something else to have all these die-hard fans even after being MIA for however long ten cycles was.

He continued. "One of your charges, the big one called Vadeem, came to your dorm in the middle of the night. He said he wanted to discuss your tentacles."

I nodded. I was expecting him to come talk to me about what had happened in that trial; I was dodging a lot of his questions back then, and I owed him some kind of explanation. I just hoped my stupid clone didn't reveal too much, but given my friends' earlier reactions, the fake Walter probably said something so ridiculous that no one would believe what he said to be the truth in the first place, even if what he said was technically correct.

The doppelganger continued. "I believe that these nighttime rendezvous are a part of the human mating ritual, according to my internet research, but I also knew that you had the lovely Miss Xalla, so I kindly rejected Vadeem's advances for coitus."

I blinked. "You . . . what?"

He smiled again. "Not to worry, I simply stated that I did not wish to mate with him, using the most polite language that I could, and stated that your tentacles were taken. I also managed to explain that it was only natural that another fellow human would be attracted to your esteemed self."

My mouth hung open. I didn't know what to say.

"That was when he looked at me with his lustful eyes," my clone continued with grim determination, "before running to get the other members of your party. I believe this is the standard human reaction when faced with rejection. Humans behave in the strangest ways.

"After that, they made me lie on the bed and wrapped me with that fabric." He shuddered. "I feared the worst. I knew that no human would be able to keep their appendages off your body, hence the restraints. Thankfully the lord arbiter came back before the worst could happen."

I felt my eyes twitch.

"I . . . see," I forced myself to say. "Was there anything else?"

He shook his head, his smile never faltering. "That is all, my lord."

I took a deep breath, calming my nerves. I was thankful that I had all those opportunities to control my emotions because if I hadn't, I would be strangling Q's fucking clone to death right this instant!

But instead, I said, "Thank you. Please go back to Q, and while you're there, take some of those Intro to Earth classes with the rest of the staff."

He nodded enthusiastically. "I shall do as you say, Lord Arbiter! I shall endeavor to learn all that I can about Earth and its humans!"

I smiled. "Good, you may go now."

I took a step backward this time and avoided his splash of liquid when he turned into sludge and disappeared. I was going to just pretend that I never heard the thing's explanation, and hope to God that Vadeem never, ever brought up what happened last night with the others. I shuddered in primal fear thinking about what would happen if Noel ever caught wind of that.

Another deep breath, and I was relaxed enough to just let the whole situation pass through me. I was zen. No need to be upset. Q's got enough on his plate right now, so let's not add any more stress by complaining about his worthless, garbage, mentally deficient doppelganger. I thought these things were supposed to be good at mimicking others, so what the fuck went wrong with this one? And it was a so-called grand doppelganger as well?

No, let's not get angry. Zen, Walter, zen.

Forcing myself to calm down like I had in the last trial, I took a nice cold shower and thoroughly cleaned myself, my mind utterly empty of thought.

I got dressed quickly and headed down to the lounge to meet up with the rest of my friends. I almost jittered a little when I saw Vadeem, but the big man didn't seem to mind what happened last night or had the decency to chalk it up to my mental corruption. Yeah, if anyone asked, it was all mental corruption.

"I can see you're feeling better now, Walter," Vadeem said with a smile. "And sounding better as well. Sorry, we should have had you checked out immediately. I had forgotten how bad things were for you."

"It's fine," I said quickly. "I'm better now. I'll take the medication, so let's just move on to brighter topics, please?"

He nodded, and the others agreed as well.

Now that I had the chance to see everyone all rested up and properly bathed, I almost didn't recognize some of them. The twins had changed into more modern clothing, now sporting matching black long-sleeve shirts and comfortable-looking shorts. They were looking a whole lot better after a proper bath, although nothing could hide the scars that covered their skin. Still, no one else here seemed to care, and their complexions had turned a lot pinker. Even their hair was starting to really grow out. A few more days and they'd be sporting pixie cuts.

The girls were still huddling mostly beside Vadeem, although they would venture out of his immediate vicinity every now and then. I guess they were still reliant on the big man, but they were warming up to the rest of us.

Vadeem was still wearing a checkered shirt and some cargo pants, while the regressor was wearing a black T-shirt and loose sweatpants. Noel was wearing a new red hoodie and tight-fitting pants, while Yoona had a simple white dress on. We almost looked like a normal set of friends.

"Come on, let's get some food," Yoona said. "We still have a lot of things to set up after. This will be the first day of operations for the Abyss Guild! I'm a little excited about getting everything set up for the future."

I smiled as we headed to the building's eatery. It turned out to be a fully decked-out restaurant, the really fancy kind as well, but it was a bit weird seeing as we were the only ones there. There was no one around, not even the servers and staff.

"Sorry," Jae-Hyun said as we grabbed a seat at the nearest table, "but the guild staff won't be here for a little while. We'll have to tough it out with whatever's in Vadeem's storage for the time being."

"The food that we got yesterday was amazing," Yoona said, "so it's not like we're toughing it out in any sense of the word, brother."

Noel chuckled and grabbed Vadeem's suitcase out of his hands. She opened it and grabbed herself more steak and ribs.

"Still nice and warm!" Noel exclaimed. "I knew I should have gotten one of these myself!"

"How are you able to eat something like that in the morning?" Yoona asked.

"You want some too?" the other girl answered between mouthfuls, then handed the high schooler the briefcase so that she could choose what she wanted herself.

"Um, no thanks, I'll get something light," Yoona replied politely. She looked around in the case for a bit before pulling out a bowl of soup, careful not to spill any, and some fried eggs.

We passed around the storage and each got what we wanted. I had to admit that Vadeem's purchase was quite handy, even if it nearly bankrupted him like he said. I'll make sure to properly stockpile the thing with all the goodies Pandora has to offer soon.

By the time we were done with the food, all of us excused ourselves one after the other. We all had our assigned tasks, after all, and it was about time for me to do mine. Let's take a look around Pandora and see what kinds of interesting schemes I can come up with to better my new home.

I chuckled. After all the craziness with Q and the trials, I was happy to finally be back in my own element. Pandora's people won't know what was coming.

CHAPTER FOURTEEN

Pandora and Propaganda

I stepped out of our new base of operations and took a breath of fresh air. Something I hadn't noticed about Pandora was just how crisp and clean the air was. Growing up in the city, there was the ever-present air pollution and stench of unwashed bodies and garbage permeating the more unsavory corners and alleyways, and it was strange not having to deal with any of that here. It was why I had moved to the countryside later on, just before I got kidnapped here.

Even the strange modern part of Pandora, a sight that I was so familiar with, had a different feel to it, and that's not mentioning the gorgeous outskirts of the town. I only had a quick glance at the plains outside the city walls, but I can imagine that they'd be just as nice, although whatever monsters roaming the fields might ruin that atmosphere. I guess that's what happens when humans haven't had the chance to ruin everything with their presence yet. I hoped this peace would last for a good while.

I took another deep breath and felt refreshed for once. A small, mounting feeling of anticipation grew in me as I walked around the streets of Pandora. Yes, I was back in my element wandering the streets, out of sight and out of mind. Sure, after two days Pandora was still mostly empty, with just a few thousand people scattered around a huge area, but I could find where most of these new aspirants were.

If there was one thing I'd learned over the years, it was that people liked to settle where other people were. We were social creatures, and except for the strange hermits and extreme introverts, we needed social interactions to thrive. That was why I headed straight to the shopping and eating district, the same one my new friends and I visited yesterday.

Unsurprisingly, the place was packed—well, perhaps not packed, but busy given how few of us there were. I moved to a quiet little corner away from the busiest footpaths and observed the gathered people for the next while.

The first thing that I noticed was just how strangely everyone was dressed. I knew that the various groups all went through different trials, so not everyone would be as haggard as my party was, but it was clear that the aspirants who made it into the first or second group in the world had gotten some sweet rewards for their hard work.

Some individuals were sporting futuristic suits made out of strange metallic materials, others had gaudy trinkets and jewelry whose functions must be pretty good if they chose to wear those ugly things in public. Weapons of all shapes and sizes were on full display as men and women chatted happily and frequented the various stores, and everyone in this group looked content and deadly.

These types of people made up about 30% of the individuals there. This was a bigger percentage of the elite than I had expected, but I guess it made sense if you considered that only the best parties were able to make it to Pandora this early. They were the ones who obtained the best results in whatever trial they experienced and were set to do well in the future.

The regressor was right, Central really did want the strong to get stronger while everyone else was trampled underneath. These people looked like they didn't have a care in the world despite the crazy situation.

There was another, less noticeable crowd gathered here, and although they outnumbered the first group, it certainly didn't feel that way to anyone watching the scene. These people didn't walk in the middle of the streets with their heads held high and items on full display. They were not quite hiding, but were moving by the side of the streets, gazes kept low. I could already see this group of people increasing in number as more and more parties joined the Main Stage.

Good, these were the people I was looking for. These were the aspirants who didn't quite do as well as their peers. This group was dragged along to victory by stronger members or had suffered significant injuries that left them less capable than the others. Some of them were still gathered with their original party members, even though they were being ignored or ostracized.

Thankfully they were also easy to spot if you knew what you were looking for. Even without the clear difference in the quality of these lesser aspirants' equipment, they looked defeated and worn down. The ones who still remained with their original party were a step or two behind the main group and not joining in any of the laughter and small talk.

These were the kind of people that might need a little pick-me-up, a bit of extra hope. But not now. They needed to suffer a bit more indignity first. They needed to properly resent the difference in treatment between the two groups.

It was a good thing that I could speed up this little conflict on my side.

A newly formulated plan was swimming in my mind, but first, I needed to gather a few props and helpers. A quick visit to the nearby shops quickly solved the first need, while some private messages to Noel and Vadeem provided me with the second. I was a little hesitant to include Noel in my plans, but I needed more than just Vadeem for what I had to do. Thankfully, Vadeem vouched for the crazy girl's ability to follow orders when she had to.

We met up at a quiet spot away from the crowds a little while later, and I told them what I needed from them.

"Walter," Vadeem muttered as he took the strange costume from me, "you make the strangest damn schemes."

Noel had already come out of the restroom and changed into the clothes that I had given her. "Ignore Vadeem, he's too dumb to think of ideas of his own or use his brain at all, really. I think your plan is awesome, and you can count on me, little bro!"

I looked at her dubiously.

"Boo!" She pouted. "I know that face. You don't think I can be serious."

I nodded slowly.

"Well, ask Vadeem!" she continued, pointing at the big man. "My old job had me doing a lot of acting!"

I raised an eyebrow and glanced at Vadeem. "Seriously?"

Vadeem shrugged. "Yeah, I didn't believe it at first either. Noel can be a bit . . ."

"Awesome?" she filled in.

"Stupid," he said, "but she can act surprisingly well."

She poked Vadeem with a finger. "Well, I had to get into some tricky spots in the past, and being super sneaky-like doesn't always work. You need to be sexy and charismatic as well!"

"I don't think you're either of those things . . ." Vadeem muttered under his breath.

"Huh," I said, ignoring the exaggerated frown Noel was giving me. "Then this will be easier. I need to get changed as well, so just give us a sec, and we'll be ready to move out."

Noel had the biggest smile on her face. "I always wanted to be a pampered lady! Go fast!"

And we did, since I didn't have to coat Vadeem in buckets of paint and mud this time. I'd learned to keep my designs simple, well, simpler in any case, to the benefit of everyone involved. Once I came out, Vadeem and I were wearing the gaudiest, most expensive clothing that I could find in my limited run at the stores. I was freakishly rich, and I needed to use that to my advantage. I wanted to get something that screamed how stupidly wealthy we were.

Vadeem was wearing a crystal-and-jewel-encrusted suit that was a bit too small for him, and I also had him wear ten rings, one for each finger. I even got him some leather boots made from some exotic animal that glittered in the light. As for accessories, he was wearing three huge gold necklaces and some idiotic designer shades. I even gave him a gold fedora to accentuate his look and gelled back his hair so that he wouldn't be instantly recognizable in the future.

My goal was to disguise Vadeem, which was a bit harder given his enormous size. However, there were, surprisingly, quite a few others who were in his weight and height range here, and I doubted anyone could recognize the man in his current outfit. Vadeem was normally a very laid-back individual, which was the opposite of what he looked like now. Just the light bouncing off all the jewels covering him would blind anyone who tried to get a good look in.

As for me? I had on the shiniest and most intricate armor that I could find in short order, and wearing it made me look like some kind of lordling trying their best to show off their wealth to the masses. The metal visor was shaped like a dragon, the plate mail had so many engravings in it that it just looked like a mass of lines at a distance, and it was all polished to a mirror shine. Everything just had the smell of obscene money to it.

The only one who wore something even slightly tasteful was Noel. It had taken a lot longer than finding random crap to throw onto Vadeem and me, but the results were amazing. It had better be, considering how much I paid to hire a professional to give her a complete makeover.

Noel had a beautiful, yet simple silk dress on. The material glistened in the light and perfectly accented her slender figure. Some fine jewelry adorned her neck and wrists, and she had a huge ruby earring that tied into her natural hair color. The makeup artist did a fantastic job making slight adjustments to Noel's features, and she looked like a completely different person once everything was in place. She looked like a high-class lady instead of an ordinary person that you wouldn't look at twice passing on the street.

Even Noel's normal aura of indifference and playfulness was gone, and she had fully immersed herself into her new role. I wish I could say the same thing about Vadeem . . . but after watching his performance back in the second trial, I had given him an easier role to play now. He didn't need to speak much for what was to come.

All in all, I think I outdid myself this time. There was no way that anyone would be able to connect who we were with the Abyss Guild now, even if we needed to use these disguises for an extended period of time. This was exactly what I needed for my harebrained scheme to work.

Now, was what I was about to do all that practical? Almost certainly not. It had way too many moving parts and was too reliant on the acting abilities of my friends. But I didn't care. I needed a way to relieve my stress after all this time, and I couldn't think of a better way to do that than this. I think I deserved some fun every now and then, and I was going to treat myself to just that.

"Okay," I said, my voice horribly muffled through the stupid helmet I was wearing. "We all know the plan, roughly speaking?"

"Seems easy enough to follow," Vadeem said as he (tried) to give me a thumbs-up. The various rings on his fingers made the gesture awkward. "Although I have some qualms about the role you gave me."

I shrugged. "We all ready to go?"

Noel answered smoothly, her usual flippant tone gone. "Of course, bodyguard Winslow, love. Let my husband, Veda, take my esteemed self to the marketplace."

Huh, Noel didn't even make fun of Vadeem when she said that. I guess she really could be counted on for stuff like this in the future.

"As you will, Lady Nora," I replied.

She took Vadeem's arm and gracefully walked out into the streets. Vadeem had an easy smile on his face and followed her lead.

Hm, should I have picked pseudonyms that were a bit different than our actual names? Ah well, too late now. And it was easier to remember if I kept them simple since I might need to use these disguises again in the future.

And so, Lady Nora and her husband, Veda, accompanied by Knight Winslow, strode into the heart of Pandora's marketplace with their heads held high, ready to create some sweet, sweet mayhem.

CHAPTER FIFTEEN

The Play

Just as I had predicted, we were immediately the center of attention when the three of us arrived at the market. Although you would have to be practically blind to somehow miss us considering how much light was being reflected off Vadeem and me. My big friend was practically a walking disco ball with the amount of gems sewn into his suit, while I was a walking mirror. Damned suit of armor was also acting as an oven. I needed to keep things short before I boiled alive under the metal.

But complaints aside, the real star of the show was unmistakably Noel. The way she strode into the road left no one second-guessing who was in charge. She walked with a grace that spoke of class and sophistication, which made me question why she never chose to show any of us this side of her before. Where Vadeem and I were gaudy to the extreme, she was all grace and sex appeal (words I never thought I would say about Noel), the perfect contrast.

Once I was sure that enough eyes were on us, both from the well-to-do gang and the stragglers, I signaled my little hired help to initiate the next step of the plan. It's surprising what people will do when they're desperate and you offer them enough money. It seemed that the warmth of friendships meant nothing next to the cold, hard comfort of coin.

One of the aspirants that I had a chat with earlier saw my signal, along with the promise of more gold to come, and shoved one of his friends right into the path of Noel. His friend looked at the other man in confusion while some of his other buddies tried to help him up. However, this group quickly stopped what they were doing when Vadeem glared at them with unrestrained rage.

Good. Now the stage was set. If I wanted the regressor's guild to be the beacon of justice, then there must be a contrasting foil to his ideals. I didn't have time to wait for one to appear naturally, so what else could I do but create my own conflict and sell the resolution? It's a time-tested method proven to work.

I smiled underneath the helmet. Let the play begin in earnest now.

On cue, Noel exaggerated shock that someone would dare get in her way and made a faint cry of alarm. I went straight to her side, almost trampling over the people in my way, and offered an arm to support her. Vadeem was on my tail and rushed toward the side of the fallen man.

"How dare you try to rob my wife!" Vadeem screamed as he glared at the poor man on the ground. "It wasn't enough that you useless peasants were able to ride off our coattails to the Main Stage, but you choose to bite the hand that feeds you?"

The guy sprawling on the ground looked confused. Everyone close by could see that he'd been pushed to the ground, but unfortunately for him, the only people who saw what had happened were the other unfortunate, not-so-well-off aspirants. Let's call these people the B Group. They knew that everything Vadeem was saying was clearly slander, but that was the point.

The well-to-do aspirants, or the A Group as I'll call them, were sufficiently far away that they didn't quite see what had transpired, but a small crowd of them were already coming to see what the commotion was about. And who would they believe in a situation like this? The party with the gorgeous lady and her entourage or the beggars on the street?

"We—" the man on the ground started. But I wasn't going to let him speak, not quite yet. I needed the proper amount of resentment to brew in these people.

"Don't just lie there on the streets! Have some self-respect as a human being!" I approached him angrily and forced the man to his feet. While he was distracted, I secretly slipped a little present into his pockets.

"Now what is it you wanted to say?"

"I—I," he stammered, "was pushed, my friend—"

He turned around to point at where his friend was, but the man had already long fled. Now he just looked like an idiot trying to blame someone else for his error, and the A Group wasn't buying it.

"What friend?" Vadeem asked angrily.

"He was—"

"We caught you red-handed!" I screamed, then politely gestured to the well-to-do aspirants gathered. "Unless you think one of these nice gentlemen did it?"

Giggles and whispers of mockery were already filling the crowd, and I added some fuel to that fire. "Not only were you the only one around us, but does anyone here honestly think that one of those lovely people would lower themselves to stealing? These aspirants have class, unlike the scum here!"

I pointed to the B Group with undisguised disgust. Louder shouts of agreement started to fill the air; the A Group was enjoying the schadenfreude at seeing the scene before them. Good, let them get riled up. Make them lose themselves to the moment so that all thoughts of morality would be lost to the joy of seeing the suffering of others. I gave a silent signal to Noel.

"And we are not blind, peasant," Noel said with a haughty attitude and pointed at the bulge in the man's pocket. "You stole one of my husband's jewels right there."

The man looked surprised, then reached into his pocket to pull out a huge ruby. He stared at it in confusion before realizing what must have happened. He gave me the dirtiest look, but I lifted my helmet just a smidge to give him a shit-eating grin.

"You fucking bastards!" he screamed, finally losing to his rage. "You think you can just frame me? Don't you have anything better to do with your damn time?"

I scoffed while Vadeem took a few steps forward threateningly.

"For what reason would we have to frame you?" Noel asked. "Do you think we have nothing better to do than stir up trouble with the rabble?"

More mocking laughter filled the air.

"But we are merciful," Noel said with a graceful smile. "Hand the jewel back, get on your filthy knees, and apologize, and we can pretend that this never happened."

"Or don't," Vadeem added with a deadly smile. He flexed his muscles, which told the other man exactly what would happen if he refused Noel's suggestion.

The poor man gritted his teeth in frustration before one of his friends quickly whispered something in his ear. I would see his pride trying to surface, but it was quickly crushed when he saw the sneers of hatred from the onlookers. This man was smart enough to realize that pride would do no good against a mob of angry superhumans. Reluctantly, the man handed the gem back to Vadeem and got on his knees to apologize.

I laughed, which prompted the others to do the same. "Look at him, and the people around him! They have no dignity! Oh, how embarrassing to be seen in the same location as these miserable cretins. I say we outlaw them from this glorious marketplace. Let them squabble and pollute somewhere else."

More cheers of agreement filled the air, and the people around me started to chase out the people who didn't belong out of the market. Now the seeds of resentment and class inequality were firmly planted, all I had to do was wait a little to see the results. For now, Winslow, Veda, and Nora had to firmly establish themselves as important figures to the A Group.

"Come," Noel said with a charming smile. "Now that the filth has left the streets, I wish to celebrate this success with a meal. On me, of course."

No one here refused the offer, and the three of us spent the next few hours entertaining the various aspirants. I noticed a few people in the crowd who were a part of Noel's list and saw that she was secretly eyeing them up as well. Guess the amount of people we had to impress would be a tad shorter the next time we came disguised.

After the meal, we all excused ourselves as politely as possible. Once we were out of the bog of people, we found a safe spot to change back to our normal clothes and finally took a breather.

"Ugh, Walter." Noel pouted, her earlier elegance nowhere to be found. "I feel all icky pretending to be married to Vadeem. It makes my skin crawl."

Vadeem just sighed but didn't make a retort.

"Well," I said, "thank you both for playing along. I still have a little bit more work to do on my end before I'm done."

Vadeem nodded. "Not a problem, was barely any work on my part!"

"And I like the attention!" Noel added with a smile. "It's a nice change of pace from my usual work. Although speaking of my usual work . . ."

Right . . . guess some more people would be meeting with unfortunate accidents tonight.

"I got my assignments to complete as well," Vadeem said. "Let's all meet up for breakfast again tomorrow if I don't see you."

"You bet!"

I nodded. "Sure thing."

We each went our separate ways for the night after that, each of us having distinctly different but equally important jobs to do. I made one more costume change before heading out to start the second part of my plan: injecting some hope into the hearts of those poor, poor mistreated aspirants.

Since I was the one responsible for kicking the people out of the markets, I also knew where the B Group congregated afterward. I had seen them gathered away from the main streets and in the shadier back alleys, and they should have had enough time to congregate by now. These people still had some money to spend and had decided to drown their woes in cheap beer and ale, which made my job a lot easier. Drunk aspirants were a lot more gullible than sober aspirants.

Well, it was time for my entrance.

I lowered my posture and slouched, my eyes were downcast, and I looked as miserable as I could as I entered the bar. I just had to remember the disaster that was Q's stupid doppelganger to achieve the correct level of misery and resentment to complete my look. I fit right in.

The bar patrons noticed my entrance and welcomed me with open arms. They saw someone else in the same shitty situation as them, and as they say, misery loves company. The interior of the place was already starting to look a little disheveled, which was impressive given how this place was only used for a handful of hours. Beer and men were sprawled on the ground in equal measure, while chairs and bar stools were strewn all over the place. The atmosphere of discontent was almost permeable.

"You too, bud?" one of the disgruntled aspirants asked and gestured for me to grab a seat alongside his party. The group of four, two men and two women, looked like they'd had a few too many to drink already, and showed no signs of stopping. Their shirts were stained with spilled drink and food particles but were not otherwise dirty.

"Yup," I muttered soullessly as I sat down beside the others. "I was just told to fuck off after surviving three weeks in that last bloody trial helping out my good-for-nothing teammates. All because I don't have a fucking combat class. And what do I get after repairing all of their items and keeping them alive?" I laughed bitterly. "One hundred goddamn gold! Well, I'm bloody well using that here! Bartender, give me and my new friends a fresh round of beer. I don't care what it is, just keep the tab flowing!"

"Cheers to that, friend!" one of the men said to me, and he took another huge swig of his drink. "Here's to those damned bastards who think they're so high and mighty!"

I cheered to that as more beer flowed between my new friends. "So what happened with you four?"

They told me about all the unfair and biased treatments that befell them, how they'd tried their best to remain useful in their parties, or how an injury caused them to fall behind, but one fact remained the same: It was always someone else's fault for their failures, never their own. They made all the classic excuses and shifted responsibility to things outside their control, and after listening to them talk for a few minutes, I finally understood why they were not a part of Group A.

I sighed to myself.

Of course, I didn't show my discontent with their attitudes, and I nodded along to their grievances, gave some words of encouragement here, some well-timed curses toward their aggressors there, all expertly placed. Well, of course it wasn't your fault that you couldn't keep up with the rest of your team, it was your unlucky class that was at fault. And how could he choose someone else over you, even though you're so much better than her? You would have certainly come out on top if only this had happened instead.

It's never your fault. You were just unlucky. The world is just out to get you.

By the end of the night, they were practically addicted to the praise and reassurance I was giving, undoubtedly due in no small part to all those Charisma passives I had. I wasn't just William, another poor sob who couldn't make it to the top of the food chain, I was their friend now. They could trust what I was saying because I always had their best interests in mind.

I ordered another round of beers for my new best friends, and once they had their fill, I started to talk.

I gave them my best smile. "Hey, did you hear this rumor . . . ?"

CHAPTER SIXTEEN

Rumors and Role Models

"What rumor?" one of my new friends asked. I couldn't for the life of me remember or care what they were called or even looked like, to be honest. They were just a faceless mass of bodies in my memories.

"Apparently we're in the same city as Kim Jae-Hyun and Kim Yoona," I whispered conspiratorially, my eyes darting around as if I was afraid someone would overhear what I was about to say.

"You mean those freaks that got first and second place in the world during that zombie disaster?" the nameless female questioned. "Didn't they kill something like 10,000 zombies each?"

"You can't kill a zombie, Sarah!" the first one slurred, clearly more drunk than the rest. "They're, like, already dead. God, you're stupid! No wonder Mason chose that other bitch over you!"

The girl, apparently called Sarah, snarled back, "Fuck you! And you know what I mean!"

"Yeah, yeah, so, uh . . . we're in the same place as another bigshot," the first man continued. "So what? Just another stuck-up snob to spit on our faces. Big fucking deal."

"Fuck them!" agreed the other man in the group, I think his name was Nick or Nolan or something. "Just you wait, we'll show them all how wrong they are once we get to the third trial."

I nodded and smiled at N-something or other. "You're right, they'll be sorry once they see your true abilities. You just got a clearly unfair second trial that didn't allow you to show off what you can really do."

He nodded enthusiastically at that, almost drooling at the praise. Was my ability to influence people getting stronger or were the people I was using my charms on earlier just abnormally resistant? Thinking back on all the "people" that I had been interacting with, it was most likely the latter. I honestly hadn't given my Charisma stats or the various passives much thought so far, but the way these fools were eating up everything I said was crazy.

"No," I said, and the attention of the others instantly turned to me. "I heard those two are different than the others."

They were about to dismiss my idea, but I held my hands up and spoke before they could formulate too many ideas that I didn't approve of. "Hear me out first. I know, it sounds ridiculous, given the shit we just went through."

They agreed reluctantly but still listened to what I had to say.

I continued. "But I heard the two actually care about folk like us."

They looked at me dubiously.

"Sarah, you have a production class, right?"

She nodded. "Yeah, I got the Rookie Potion Maker job."

"Right," I said, "and it'll be absolutely vital once those idiots realize that someone needs to supply them with healing on the fly. They're just too stupid to understand that brute strength can only go so far in these trials!"

She laughed and instantly held her head up high in pride.

"Well, I have a production class as well, and I've been in talks with others like us."

"And?" she asked.

"And I heard that those Kim freaks started a guild and were actively recruiting people like us. I even heard that they offered really good terms if you work with them, protection, stable wages, all that jazz."

Sarah looked enthusiastic and wanted to hear more.

I turned to her. "My buddy just got scouted, and he said that they live in this huge tower in the center of this place, but they use that huge space not to show off, but to support artisans like you. They have the best facilities, and they treat you like human beings for once. None of that better-than-thou garbage like the others."

"That does sound nice . . ." the girl muttered. "Do you think they'd take me in?"

I gave her my most charming grin. "I don't see why they wouldn't."

However, the other three without a purely supportive class were not quite as enthralled with the prospect. They were frowning, but that was fine for now. No rumors could spread in a day, and I'd already successfully planted the idea that the regressor's guild treated noncombat jobs with sincerity and respect.

Mike, or Nick, or whatever his name was, spoke up next. "So what? Maybe that's great for you two since you can make a quick buck off your class, but the rest of us are still fucked."

All right, it was time to start altering the others' way of thinking as well. This would be slow work, but the results should speak for themselves down the line.

"Hey, I know what you mean," I answered as smoothly as I could. "But think about it. Those two are starting a guild, and they got an entire building to themselves, yet they're only hiring trades folk like us right now."

"So?" the last girl in the group, who didn't talk much, said finally. "They probably just want to use you guys to make them even more rich."

"And what's wrong with that if they're paying us proper?" the Sarah girl spat back. "It's how companies worked before all of it went to shit, so why would it change here?"

"Wait, wait, I'm not trying to say that," I interrupted, trying to defuse the situation. "What I mean is that they're not hiring those assholes out there with their shiny new weapons and armor. Instead, they're looking after guys like us."

The four intoxicated aspirants thought about that for a while, although I could tell that they were still not completely buying what I was saying. Or perhaps they were just too drunk to reason properly.

I sighed. "Don't you think it's weird that they've just started a guild but didn't expand their numbers? I'm sure there's loads of successful aspirants hoping to ride their glory, but none's joined so far, or more like, none of them *could* join so far."

They all nodded finally, starting to see my flawed logic. Now, were there a lot of holes to my story? Of course there were! First of all, how the hell would I even know the inner workings of this hypothetical guild in the first place? Not only that, but they had no reason to even believe that the regressor and his sister were in this town let alone the fact that they had started a guild. Even the tiniest amount of critical thinking would rip my wild rumors to shreds.

Yet they still chose to believe every word I said, because between their beer-soaked brains and my charming voice, there just weren't enough brain cells left for logical thinking. What I said was taken as fact, as far as those four were concerned. And the fact that Vadeem actually was tasked with finding talented people would only reinforce what I said as the absolute truth when they went out to confirm my words later . . . If they bothered to do that at all.

But for now, I needed them to spread what I'd said to the masses. I needed the idea that the regressor had started a guild to become common knowledge, and most importantly, that they had the common folk's best interests in mind.

He needed an air of awe and reverence to gather before Jae-Hyun made his appearance properly next time.

"Look, I know it's hard to believe," I said again, making sure that my Idol Voice was turned to the max, "but there's no way that everyone out there is a selfish degenerate, right? Our society would have gone to hell if that were the case."

"That is true . . ."

"So why would it be so hard to believe that there's someone out there that genuinely cares about us?"

"I mean . . . it's not impossible, sure."

"And I'm telling you, my sources say that these Kim people are legit. Just ask others, tell them what I told you and you can see for yourself."

"Well, yeah, we can do that."

"Good," I said with my most flattering voice. "It'd be really helpful for me if you could tell others about what you've learned. You know, get the word around so that people like us have something to look up to."

I turned to each of them, looking right into their eyes. *Can you do that for me? It'd mean a lot.*

"Yeah . . ." they said as one. "We can do that for you, William."

I smiled. "Good. Remember to put the word out. Now, if you'll excuse me."

"Are you leaving already?" the quiet girl asked. I could hear a strange desperation in her voice. "But you just got here. You should stay, chat some more."

The others agreed. It seemed that my charms were working a little too well.

"I'd love to," I answered, "but I have to head off for the night. If you guys do what I said, then I'm sure I'll be able to come back and have another round of drinks with my new best pals."

"Really?" Sarah said with wide eyes. "You will?"

"Of course," I replied with a confident smile. "But only if you do your part!"

They all replied with affirmations. Damn, they kind of looked like how Patar and his group were acting. I needed to get myself out of this little situation before things escalated. I hoped the minor amount of makeup I applied to myself would prevent them from recognizing me later on.

I bought the group one final round of beer and quietly made my escape while they were guzzling down more alcohol. I drank a whole lot that night as well but felt nothing aside from a very full bladder. I remembered that my Soul Title had upgraded to the point where I had immunity to most poisons, so that would explain things. Pity I couldn't enjoy a nice buzz every now and then, even if I was never the biggest enjoyer of beer and booze.

After emptying my really full bladder, I wiped away the cheap makeup and grime off my face and changed back into my regular clothing. The filthy stuff I had worn during the first trial was a great way to blend into the crowd here, but it was starting to become a little too filthy even for me.

But after getting refreshed, I was satisfied with what I had accomplished for the day. If human nature hadn't changed completely overnight, then word of the regressor and his fancy new guild would be all over the place soon. And as all rumors go, the things that I said today will be greatly exaggerated down the line. This would normally be a problem, but if I could subtly adjust what the rumors morphed into by frequenting a few more locations? Well, let's just say that Jae-Hyun would get his shiny guild image.

Yet my work wasn't quite done yet. Rumors alone wouldn't be able to completely consolidate Jae-Hyun's reputation. To do that, the man needed to defeat adversity and crush some kind of injustice. For now, I needed to create that problem on my end for it to be fully destroyed at an opportune time, and what better injustice was there than a classical class divide?

For the next few days, I spent my time going with Vadeem and Noel and hanging out with the rich kids while introducing the daily intake of newcomers to our ever-growing exclusive club. Our activities mostly involved tormenting the weak and spending money like no tomorrow, all while flaunting our wealth and power to those who didn't have either. Trampling on people's pride and segregating the poor was also a favored pastime of ours.

Then at night, I'd frequent the dirty alleyways and hidden bars, engaging the people I was literally just crushing underfoot, and selling them a tailored lie of hope. I stroked the egos of the battered men and women, while simultaneously lamenting on our growing struggles. But each time I would leave by singing the praise of the regressor and his group. And best of all, other yes-men confirmed my increasingly insane statements about the guild.

I could feel the tensions growing with each passing hour, and I knew that things would erupt in one way or another soon. All it would take was a spark and a guiding hand, and things in Pandora would change for the rest of its history.

I smiled in anticipation.

It wouldn't be too long before the fruit of all my actions would fully mature, and I could move on to the climax of my little orchestrated charade. I had told the regressor of what was to come, and after getting the thumbs-up from the man in charge to proceed, I gathered the last of the equipment and personnel that I would need, and the curtains rose for the grand finale of this little show.

CHAPTER SEVENTEEN

Closing Act

I was about to start the final stage of my little plan when I heard a nostalgic beep. It had been so long since I got a notification from Noe that I had almost forgotten about it.

"Congratulations, my host," Noe's soothing voice said, "you have earned your third legitimate secondary title."

That was a pleasant surprise, but not wholly unexpected, given the amount of work I'd been putting in for the last five or so days. I wanted to end this a little faster now that my mandatory rest period was also coming to a close. I was itching for a little bit of combat after all this time. Between frequenting the undercity bars and my excursions with Noel and Vadeem, I had done practically nothing else but sleep. It was good to see that my hard work was paying off, even if it didn't immediately increase my attributes or combat abilities.

"Displaying information now," she continued. "I hope you continue to grow in the future, my host."

Secondary Title: The Devil's Advocate (B Rank)
Title Description: Your silver tongue sows discord and chaos wherever you go, and you can bring societies to its knees with a whisper. You aim to fool those closest to you and bring ruin to your enemies from within. Beware the Devil's Advocate.
Title Passives:
Charisma +25

Charisma +10% when user is speaking with another.
Title Actives:
The Devil's Temptation: You can make a person with significantly less Charisma than you believe any one piece of information you say as fact.
Cooldown: One use per day.

Now that was what I was talking about. Not the most useful thing to have in combat, but with the insane growth that my soul title had gotten, I was okay with fighting for the time being. The passives were a nice boon for my already impressive Charisma score, bringing it all the way up from 78 to 103, and that was without counting that 10% bonus when I was speaking. If I were to add in the bonuses from my Light Bringer title when it was dark out, then I was going to be a propaganda machine!

Of course, the active was also useful, although I was limited in what I could do with it. It was only usable once a day, and one drawback was it only affected one person, but the payoff could be huge. But once again, I was seeing the issues with these skill descriptions. A lot of the time the information given was a little vague. What did it mean by significantly less Charisma, or how did a will save even work?

I frowned. Just like Noe's Gamma class that she gave me earlier, I would need to test out these things on my own. Perhaps that was the purpose of giving the users incomplete information, as it incentivized the aspirants to test out and more naturally get used to the tools at their disposal. Having complete knowledge could lead to complacency and stagnation. If everything was spelled out for you, then fewer people would bother with experimentation or try to use their skills in creative manners.

I dismissed the stat page and focused on my task at hand. The boost in Charisma would have been nice if I had gotten it a bit earlier, but I couldn't complain. At least I had the title to use now instead of having it after all of my plans were complete. Any extra boost in Charisma would be helpful now, and having the active as a backup was a nice touch of reassurance in case anything went wrong on my end.

But first, I had to do the part I was dreading. I went into my room and called forth my stupid doppelganger. Thankfully his ability to communicate in English had improved drastically since his first appearance, although that unpleasant memory would resurface every time I saw the man.

I needed him to do one simple job since I couldn't be seen in two places at once. All those social gatherings I had with Noel's group meant that some people had seen my face under the helmet even though I tried to keep it on for as long as possible. I doubted people could remember what I looked like in great detail, but I could not afford to take any chances. No one could be allowed to link my two identities together. There were already rumors that I had to quash going around that William and Winslow were the same person, or at least related, and I couldn't have that continue.

Having someone look remarkably like me would be a hard sell, but if they saw the two of us at the same time? Well, there'd be no doubt that we weren't the same person, and I could even spin it as slander if I wanted.

As for how I explained his existence to the rest of my party? That was honestly quite easy given the new world that we lived in, where skills and abilities that regularly spat in the face of physics existed. The Walter lookalike was simply hired help that had the ability to change his form to match mine, and that explanation wasn't even a lie.

The doppelganger appeared in my room as expected, now looking like the beggar version of myself. There were just enough differences between his features and mine that it would be hard for someone to notice the similarities if they were only seeing us from afar, which was hopefully where most of the snobby crowd would be. I planned on ditching one of these disguises in any case, and I planned to take full advantage of the creature's abilities to transform.

"You read over everything I need you to do?" I asked it.

It looked at me, wide-eyed with glee, and I almost puked seeing myself make a face like that. "Of course I have, Lord Walter! I have memorized my part in full!"

I nodded. "Good, and you're sure you can mimic a human death convincingly?"

He gave me a confident smile and handed me a piece of paper. Confused, I took it and saw that it was a report detailing my clone's grades in his Intro to Earth class. He scored remarkably well, all things considered, but more specifically, he got a 98% on the Human Anatomy and Physiology subsection.

"I have studied the subject extensively!" he answered with pride. "I shall do you proud, Lord Arbiter!"

"And you know how to behave around the anomaly and his friends, right?" I asked dubiously. The last incident was still fresh in my mind, even after all this time.

"Yes." He smiled. "I have studied your instructions thoroughly, and I will not let you down."

"So what would you say when you first see them?" I tested.

"Nothing!" he said with a smile.

I nodded. "And what do you say if they ask you any questions?"

He smiled again. "Nothing!"

"And what will you say if you ever see them again after?"

"Nothing!"

Perfect, he couldn't fuck this up.

"All right, let's go introduce you to the rest of them, and then you can go prep for your part."

"I will do my best to fulfill your expectations!"

Well, here goes nothing. I walked him out of my room and into the basement where I told the other three to meet me. For obvious reasons, Yoona and the twins were not included in my plans. The regressor told me that they would be out of the picture until the time was ready, and I trusted his judgment.

"Damn, little bro!" Noel said the second we entered. "He really does look just like you!"

She all but ran up to the doppelganger and started looking him up and down, which made Vadeem do the same.

I greeted my friends and explained to the new member, "This is the guy with the skill I told you about."

"You sure you can trust someone else with such an important task?" Jae-Hyun frowned. Was he suspicious about the origins of the doppelganger, or just the trustworthiness of the man? I mean, I knew that he had insider information given his unique nature, but surely not even he could know the abilities of every aspirant in the world, especially after things had deviated so much from his first iteration. Hopefully, he was just cautious about letting a stranger know a little about his guild's operations.

"I paid him more than enough for that, and if things don't go as planned . . ." I glanced at Noel. She gave me a polite nod back.

That seemed to satisfy the regressor, and he welcomed my clone as well. I think he agreed more readily after seeing firsthand my ability to manipulate the populace and had started to trust in my planning skills. That was one of the nice things about Jae-Hyun—the man knew when to trust the opinions of others when he knew that they were an expert in that field.

Vadeem also shook fake Walter's hands and gave him a quick inspection. His face was scrunched up in concentration.

"Impressive skill . . ." the big man said. "I can't see any difference between you two, other than the makeup."

"That is a very useful skill," Jae-Hyun agreed. "Can you freely change what you look like whenever you want?"

My clone didn't respond.

"Uh, his ability to speak is limited when he's using his skill," I said quickly before they could question the stupid thing further. "His skill's not perfect, but he can do what I assigned him when the time comes."

The regressor seemed to buy what I said and nodded slowly. He turned his attention back to me. "You're sure that your plan will succeed?"

"Yeah, I've been putting in the work these last few days, and all that's left is the appropriate spark to set things off." I smiled. "All you have to do is fix the mess that I make, and I can guarantee that you'll win over the hearts of all the less-well-to-do aspirants."

He raised an eyebrow. "And the others?"

Vadeem grinned menacingly. "Leave the disgruntled elites to me and Noel."

"We need them alive and on our side for the future," Jae-Hyun clarified.

"Don't worry," I said. "We're not approaching this group with the usual pitch. I have plans for those people after."

He gave me a long stare before finally nodding. Good, it seemed like he was trusting me more and more now.

"All right," I said finally, "Fake Walter, you go ahead and get in position."

My clone nodded and left the room, giving everyone a thumbs-up before going out of view. The others waved back, and I forced myself to do the same. I really didn't want to deal with him any more than necessary.

I turned to the regressor. "You too, Jae-Hyun. You know the signal for when you should make your entrance?"

"Yes," he answered simply.

"All right," I said. "Then let's put our costumes on and head out. Hopefully, we can wrap this up and get some dinner after."

"I like the sound of that!" Vadeem answered with a mighty grin.

Vadeem, Noel, and I were the last to leave our guild headquarters, now fully dressed up as Veda, Nora, and Winslow. After spending five days and about a thousand times that number in gold, we were the center of attention for the A Group aspirants and were greeted warmly when we arrived at our usual hangout in the market.

We welcomed the gathered people and waited for more of the aspirants to show up. I had told them that we were going to have some extra-special fun today, so I was expecting quite the crowd. The A Group was so used to bullying the weak at this point that they were drooling at the mouth waiting to see what I had in store for them. Well, it would certainly be a day that they never forgot.

Once everyone was there, I led them out of the market and into the slums—the fact that a proper slum could be developed in just five days should speak volumes to how much harassment the B Group was taking every day. Just as I predicted, or more accurately, planned, there was already a horde of people waiting for us there. And they were pissed and weren't afraid to show it.

At the center of the irate B Group, riling up the crowd, was my doppelganger. Now was the perfect time to finally let all this brewing tension ignite, and what better way to do that than with the death of one of the leaders? Things would quickly devolve into beautiful chaos soon, but more importantly, I was just itching to accidentally "kill" Q's clone.

CHAPTER EIGHTEEN

Curtain Call

What are you rabble doing all huddled together?" Noel said mockingly when she saw the gathered aspirants.

"We're tired of being treated like second-class citizens!" one of the B Group members shouted.

"You can't do this to us!" another yelled.

I laughed. "Look, the idiots think they're second-class citizens!"

Mocking laughter erupted behind me as I continued. "No, you're less than that! If it weren't for the entertainment value that you provide, we would have long since left you to die outside these walls. You all should be glad we're allowing you to live here at all!"

"Fuck you!" one of them screamed. "Just because you guys were able to get ahead doesn't mean that we can't fight back!"

I snickered. "Yes, yes, keep telling us those jokes. It's quite entertaining."

I could see the rage in the eyes of the B Group. It was just about time for them to explode. We just needed one last push.

"And I heard you have a leader amongst you?" I said as I scanned the crowd. I saw the doppelganger and pointed at him. "That one, right?"

My clone stepped up as planned and glared at me.

"And I've heard some interesting rumors about you as well," I continued. "It's quite impressive that you were able to become the king of the trash heap."

More sneers and whispered mockery accompanied my speech from the onlookers on my side. They were loving the display so far, but I had to get them riled up as well.

I looked my clone hard in the eye and spoke with as much visceral hatred as I could—it wasn't hard. "But what I want to know is why you thought you would be able to get away with killing one of ours!"

Now that got everyone's attention.

"You thought we wouldn't notice the constant disappearances around us?" I shouted again. Of course, those disappearances were due to Noel, but as far as I knew, no one was able to find out who was responsible for all those assassinations over the last few days. I'll admit, the redhead was good at what she did.

"Now you slander us further?" the other crowd shouted, but they were ignored.

"That fucker is responsible?" one of the A Group aspirants spoke up. I believe this was someone close to one of the people who had an unfortunate Noel-related accident.

"Yeah," I said with confidence. "I saw him give Thomas something to drink right before he went missing. I'll bet you anything that these pathetic degenerates realized that they couldn't beat us in a fair fight and resorted to poison. We all know that most of them have worthless production classes."

My logic was sound enough to have the A Group believing everything that I said, and thankfully laws and courts didn't exist in Pandora, so it wasn't like the other party could even defend themselves. Oh, how I loved this place.

As I had said before, I knew of two surefire ways of making people believe in a cause, or a person in this case. I already used religion in the second trial, and it was time for me to make a living legend out of Jae-Hyun. If the people needed a hero, then I would provide the villain for the hero to stomp all over, and the stage was set for a hero to be born.

I was about to proceed with the next stage of my plan, but something unexpected happened. What I didn't account for was the reaction from the guy who asked me the earlier question. Once he heard my explanation, all reason seemed to have left his head, and he summoned a staff out of his inventory. I wanted to stop him from ruining my carefully planned play, but he moved fast. With a flick of his wrist, he threw a fireball right at my doppelganger, and true to my clone's word, he was ready for whatever violence was headed his way and embraced the attack a little too melodramatically.

Then he exploded.

Like, into a shower of flying bits. I was pretty sure he was fine since the little pieces of exploded Walter jiggled ever so slightly as they expanded outward, but why had he chosen such a weird way to die?

Shit! That was not what I needed to happen! My original plan was for me to assault the Walter clone, beat him up a little, and hold him hostage so that

I had more leverage with the B Group. I was only going to get rid of him once Jae-Hyun was safely in the picture. I wanted the people to hate me so that the regressor could absorb all the adoration once he solved the situation and fought off the villain.

But that plan was out the goddamn window now.

Vadeem and Noel looked on in shock and gave me a questioning gaze. Even the man who cast the fireball was stunned.

I sent a private message to Vadeem and Noel.

> **Walter's Fine:** Uh, that wasn't part of the plan.
> **Vadeem the Dream:** That much is obvious. Well, at least we don't have to worry about any information leaks in the future.
> **Lady Awesome:** I was gonna visit him after this anyway, so you just saved me a trip, little bro!

Right . . . thankfully my new friends had different moral standards than the average person. If their only concern about having hired help die was that it saved them future trouble, then I was just glad that I was on their side and that they weren't paying me anything to be on that side.

Once the shock of seeing someone literally explode wore off, everything devolved into complete anarchy quickly. It was too late to fix this, so I'd just have to improvise. Seeing their leader, the guy who helped buy everyone round after round of beers, explode right before their eyes was the last straw, and the B Group was taking up arms against their oppressors. This was also the situation I really hoped to avoid, because I could already see what was about to happen.

Now, on paper, the oppressed group had the advantage in numbers, and if this kind of event happened in the normal world, some of the aspirants in the A Group might have been killed or at least injured when the mob attacked. But this wasn't the normal world anymore, and it was an absolute one-sided slaughter.

The B Group was, quite honestly, pathetic. They were woefully slow, and I saw maybe a dozen class skills being used in total. The difference in skill was absurd. They could barely use the weapons they were holding, and even if they had managed to get in a solid blow, the armor of their foes made their opposition all but invulnerable.

The same could not be said about the other side. Waves of magic took out dozens of aspirants at once while martial artists destroyed their opponents up close. Healers were in the back making sure that anyone who was wounded quickly recovered, and I was starting to fear that the B Group would just be wiped off the face of Pandora.

Some of them even tried to get to me, but a casual swipe of my hand sent them flying back. I hadn't realized just how weak the normal aspirants were. I was worried that the B Group might be a little too weak.

> **Walter's Fine:** Jae-Hyun, there's a change of plans, I think you should go in now. They're getting slaughtered.
> **Jae-Hyun:** In a moment.
> **Walter's Fine:** Uh, I think we're losing dozens of them every second. You sure it's wise to wait?
> **Jae-Hyun:** Your plan might have changed, but the goal is the same. They need to suffer some casualties first, otherwise what you've been doing will not be memorable enough.

Well, shit. The regressor was absolutely ruthless. He didn't see the other aspirants as people, but just as sacrificial pawns that he could use to advance his plans. I don't even think I was that bad. Between Noel, Vadeem, and the regressor, I think I can safely say that our guild was, indeed, evil.

I sighed. Time to just make the best out of a bad situation.

> **Walter's Fine:** If you say so. Just go in when you can. I'll make do with the new situation.

I watched the scene before me with growing anticipation, wondering when Jae-Hyun would make his move. I winced as the number of aspirants decreased steadily. It wasn't until maybe a minute after the slaughter began that the regressor finally made his move, and although I questioned why he decided to wait so long, I couldn't say anything about the way he made his entrance.

He leaped off a nearby building and slammed down in the middle of the conflict. The force that he landed with caused every set of eyes to land on him, and he pointed a spear at the A Group.

I sent some rapid instructions updating my party on what to do, and on cue, Noel and Vadeem quietly left the venue while everyone was distracted. Noel slipped off easily enough, but Vadeem . . . Well, he wasn't the sneakiest individual around, and with his outfit on, he needed a little bit of extra help to go unnoticed. Jae-Hyun had to slam his spear into the ground to create a huge dust cloud to conceal his movement. I regretted making his costume so ridiculously shiny.

Once the two were safely out of the picture, they'd also need to make an appearance once changed. I screamed at the regressor at the top of my lungs.

"Who do you think you are?" I said with a scowl. "You're clearly someone capable, so why are you standing in our way?"

However, Jae-Hyun didn't even need to introduce himself. My rumors about his guild had spread like wildfire, and a few aspirants in the crowd already worked for him. Soon, whispers of Jae-Hyun and the Abyss Guild filled the air, growing louder and louder by the second. This was eerily similar to the reactions those crazy cultists had when they saw me. Oh well. I was sure the regressor could handle insane fans better than me.

"Shut your filthy mouths!" I screamed at the people, and took out my old spear from my inventory. "Do you think one man can protect you from all of us?"

Their fervent cheers died down a little when they saw that Jae-Hyun was alone. They were starting to doubt his ability to protect all of them. That was good, because what better way was there to build a legend than for one man to go against seemingly impossible odds?

The regressor ignored my provocation and drew a simple line on the ground with his spear. "Just try to get past me. I will not allow anyone on Pandora to be taken advantage of."

Hmm, his acting could use a little work, but the sheer coolness that he exuded made up for any shortcomings his poor line delivery might have. I still envied how effortlessly he made everything look. The man oozed main-character energy.

"Fine!" I continued. "If you want this place to be your funeral, then so be it!"

I threw the spear right at his face. It was a pretty horrible throw, all things considered, but my insane stats made the weapon travel faster than the speed of sound. A little sonic boom accentuated the attack, but what really sold the performance was when the regressor simply caught the spear with his hands. He didn't even flinch.

"How . . . ?" I muttered in actual disbelief. "It doesn't matter. I'll admit you're better than me in combat, but are you better than all of us?"

I gave the people behind me the signal, and we all launched various attacks on the man. It was, of course, absolutely useless. Now I knew how much of a monster the regressor was, having seen him fight firsthand, but it was quite the treat for those who had never seen Jae-Hyun in action. He was deflecting everything that was heading his way, not allowing even the smallest of wounds to appear.

And worst of all, he made it look effortless. Magic attacks just seemed to pitter into nothing as they approached him, and anyone stupid enough to get into melee range was quickly sent back. Yet most impressive was how he fought without killing a single person. He was basically doing everything that a Goody Two-shoes hero would do. Once I was sure that everyone was sufficiently impressed with the regressor's abilities, I gave out the next set of commands.

"Attacking him is useless!" I screamed in false rage. "But he can't protect the trash behind him!"

The others realized the logic in what I was saying and started to launch attacks aimed at the people he was trying to protect. In response, Jae-Hyun started to move at insane speeds, deflecting and parrying every single attack and projectile that tried to go over the little line he drew in the dirt. Yet the sheer number of people launching various assaults on the group behind him was starting to overwhelm even his speed.

That was when Jae-Hyun's reinforcements arrived. Just as the first stray fireball was about to pierce the gap in the regressor's defenses, Noel appeared seemingly out of nowhere and parried the attack. Vadeem was right on her heels, having copied Jae-Hyun by jumping off a roof to make his entrance. Of course, he landed more like a meteor, as he was already transformed into his titan form on arrival.

With the new members here, the initiative swung in the favor of the three members of the Abyss Guild. This was met with overwhelming cheers from the B Group behind them. Now instead of purely defending the position, Jae-Hyun would take steps closer to our position, while Noel and Vadeem held their ground behind him. With every step forward he took, more and more of my forces would be pushed back, and it was only a matter of time before the morale of our loose group of aspirants collapsed.

"Shit!" I muttered. "We run for now!"

Well, most of my group had already done so I was mainly speaking for the sake of the victors. Still, seeing one of the A Group's leaders all but give up provided a huge boost in confidence to the B Group, and they cheered even louder for the regressor's party.

"Abyss Guild!" one of the aspirants chanted in victory. "I knew they would save us!"

"Thank you!" another added. "Give it up for Kim Jae-Hyun and the Abyss Guild!"

More and more shouts of elation joined the first couple of voices, which signaled the end of my little performance. Although my work wasn't quite finished, as I still needed to assuage the growing unrest in the A Group, the status of the Abyss Guild should be through the roof for the common man.

That day, a hero was born, but everyone knows that for a hero to truly shine, a villain needs to be in there to contrast his deeds. But the birth of that villain could wait for a little while. Let the people of Pandora rest, let them sing the praises of Kim Jae-Hyun and the rest of the guild before I brought the next stage of my plans to life.

CHAPTER NINETEEN

The Priest

I made my way out of the ensuing fight as quickly as I could. Between the panicked aspirants and the general chaos of the situation, it wasn't hard to lose myself between the various winding streets and low walls despite my gaudy outfit. Yet even in the crowd, I noticed someone staring at me as I was running away.

Off in the side, up a small hill, a group of a few hundred new arrivals gathered. These aspirants weren't integrated into either the B or the A group yet, having just arrived on Pandora less than twelve hours ago, and were acting as interested spectators to my orchestrated play. They, like the people who had yet to arrive, would be brought into the fold soon enough in the coming days, but that wasn't what caught my interest.

Among the spectators was a man I recognized, not because I knew him from my past, but because he was the priest that Jae-Hyun wanted me to recruit at all costs. I had made it a priority to find him before, but he must have only arrived with this new batch. The timing was a little off from what the regressor predicted, but given how many changes had been made in this timeline, discrepancies would naturally appear as more time passed.

I wondered what Jae-Hyun would do when he couldn't rely on his past knowledge anymore, but knowing him, he probably had fifteen different plans in place for such an inevitability. Thankfully we were still early in the trials and we could rely on his foresight for a bit longer.

I refocused my attention on the priest, and I swore I saw him smile at me when our eyes met. But there was no way that he would have any insight about what had happened. I was almost completely sure that he hadn't even been here for longer than a day . . . right? Then again, what use was there for common sense when it came to people who had interested the regressor?

Either way, at least I knew that he was in the town, so I'd have to make some time to make proper introductions, but not now. After organizing everything that had happened in the last few days, I was thoroughly tired and needed a little break. I quickly changed back into my normal clothing and finally slumped down in exhaustion.

Vadeem, Noel, and Jae-Hyun would be busy for a while longer sorting out the mess that I had created, and Yoona and the twins should be well on their way to helping out now. That left me with some time all to myself.

Now, I could have sworn I had to do something when I had the chance to relax for once, but I couldn't remember what it was for the life of me. I was pretty sure that it was important as well.

Hey, Noe, you remember what it was I was supposed to do?

"Negative, my host," she answered.

I felt my muscles ease and relax just hearing her voice.

Noe continued in that lulling tone. "But I am sure that it is not important if you cannot recall. I would suggest that my host take this time to relax and enjoy the atmosphere. There is a lovely bench around the corner for you to soak up the sunshine."

Yeah . . . that's not a bad idea.

I followed Noe's advice and found the bench in question. It overlooked a gentle stream that curved its way out into the horizon, and I just bathed in the sunlight for a little while. All the tension and stress just seemed to melt away. I was sure that I'd remember what I had to do later on.

I must have dozed off at some point because the sun was setting when I looked up again. I was just about to get up to move my aching body when I saw that someone had taken the seat beside me. It was that creepy priest.

"Can I help you?" I asked.

"I believe so," he answered simply as he stared off into the horizon. "But let's enjoy the sunset for now."

"Yes, we should," I answered calmly. "It is a lovely time of day."

I was so used to dealing with insane people that I'd kind of expected something like this to happen. If the man just wanted to watch the sunset while being super creepy, then we'd just watch the sunset and be creepy together.

And so the two of us just stared off into the distance and watched as the sun dipped below the horizon and dusk's cool air washed over us. It was a pretty sight; I've always liked the twilight haze.

"Thank you for allowing me this moment of calm," he finally said. "It is rare to see a kindred soul so far from home."

Okay, so I had no idea what he was speaking about, but my weeks of dealing with Noel had taught me a thing or two about these types of people. Time to put that valuable practice to use. I was a different man now that I'd been dealing with constant random bullshit!

"It is indeed. I was hoping to see someone with the same mentality here," I answered with the creepiest smile I could muster. "What brings you to my neck of the woods?"

He returned the smile, and I swear he was trying his hardest to out-creep me at this point, no one could force their lips to move in such an unnerving manner. I saw a strange light pass through his eyes as he smiled even harder.

"I wanted to introduce myself after seeing your beautiful performance tonight," he answered with a whisper. "It was masterfully done."

So, he somehow knew I was responsible for everything that happened, even though he wasn't even here when I first set up most of my plan. That was fine, not the strangest thing I'd seen so far.

"Ah, you liked that little play of mine?" I said casually. "Not many would understand the artistry behind my actions."

He nodded. "But I can understand your actions, Walter."

Yup, and he even knew my name. Fine, if he wanted to be so damn eerie, I could be as well.

"Thank you, Father Marcus," I answered. "It saddens me to see so many who do not understand what I do."

"Yes, the masses need a symbol of hope and clear leadership to grow in these trying times. The Lord's trials will push everyone to their limits, and I fear that many would not make it if not for your actions."

I nodded. "But I fear my actions will not be enough."

"No," he agreed, "but that is why you were seeking me out, was it not?"

I turned toward the priest and looked at him fully for the first time. Time to see what I could see with my Rookie Arbiter skill first.

Class: Priest of Profane Promises (S Class Support)
Description: ???

Strange . . . I couldn't see his full information.

"Ah, my apologies," he said. "Here."

> **Class: Priest of Profane Promises (S Class Support)**
> **Description**: Lead the masses into the Promised Land, let them hear what they want to hear, and see what they desire to see. You will rescue the common folk from their feeble lives with the Promises of the Profane.

Goddamn it, why was everything he did so uncanny? Not even the regressor could tell that I was looking at his information, but not only did this man know about it, but he could somehow stop my title's skill from working. Yet he just allowed me to view it anyway?

"Thank you," I answered. "And yes, this is why I sought you out, although you beat me to it, it seems."

He laughed. "I do like to take the initiative at times, but I feel like the Lord has chosen to guide me to you for this particular meeting."

"Then it is good to finally meet you, Father," I said and extended my hand in greeting.

He took the offered hand and shook it. However, I could swear that I felt a slight movement under his skin. It was so weird that I inadvertently twitched the feelers that were hidden in my palms.

A look of shock filled his face as he felt the strange sensation, and he burst into laughter. His face and body started to move as if thousands of insects were crawling just under his skin, and I was honestly afraid that he would burst into something horrible if he didn't stop laughing.

"I apologize, Walter," he said at last, and I saw that the last of the weird movements stopped as he composed himself, "But I never thought that we would be so similar. Yes, I believe that we will get along splendidly!"

I matched his madness and laughed as well. "Yes, indeed!"

His laughter stopped abruptly. "But you are not the sole leader of this operation."

I nodded. "I am not. Our guild is run by another. I merely help out in the shadows."

"A noble cause," Marcus replied. "One that I will surely help with, but let us go meet your leader first. I wish to see the organization that I will be a part of in the future, and if it will meet my needs."

"I'm sure they will," I assured.

Yeah, let the regressor deal with this new lunatic since he seemed so keen on collecting them. But I will admit that as creepy as this priest was, he possessed abilities that not even Jae-Hyun had. I can't even imagine what else he could do, especially considering what I'd just witnessed earlier. I didn't think I wanted to know the full extent of that particular ability of his, however.

I quickly sent a message to the regressor, letting him know that I had Marcus coming over to meet the rest of the gang. I wasn't sure if Jae-Hyun wanted him to meet his sister so soon, so I didn't message the rest of the guild members. He could bring whoever he thought appropriate.

He immediately agreed to meet us back at the guild headquarters, instructing me to lead him to that underground meeting room. I guess he wanted Yoona introduced to him after, maybe to force him to keep his horrible uncanniness in check before he scared the crap out of the teens. Normally, I would be against keeping Yoona and the twins in the dark for this long, but I'd make an exception for this dude.

"My leader has agreed to see you," I said to him. "If you would please follow me, I'll take you to our headquarters."

Marcus nodded gently and walked with me to the guildhall. We took our time, and while I wanted to say that we enjoyed the beautiful dusk atmosphere, I would be lying. He hovered just about a step or two back, never walking with me or in front of me, and he stayed completely silent. All I could feel was a pair of eyes staring into my back, right through me. Holy shit, I couldn't wait to get away from this man.

Where the fuck had the regressor found these goddamn weirdos? I tried to outweird him, but it was clearly futile.

Marcus never said a word, even when he saw the strange building appear out of nowhere, and never asked me how we were able to afford to purchase this plot of land in the first place. It was like he either knew the answers to all of these questions or simply didn't see the point in asking. I suppose it was nice that I didn't have to talk to him any more than I needed, but surely he would be curious about *something*.

But no, he continued in utter silence even when we arrived at the underground meeting room. He naturally took one of the seats by the table and patiently waited for the regressor to come. Jae-Hyun didn't make us wait too long, and he brought the usual gang with him as well.

Marcus greeted Vadeem, Noel, and the leader kindly in turn before putting his creepy smile back on as he waited to see what Jae-Hyun had to say.

CHAPTER TWENTY

Final Party Member

Thank you for taking the time to see me," Marcus said with his usual smile. "I know how busy you all must be."

The regressor nodded. "Thank you for being here. I assume you already know why we wanted to meet you?"

"Only the surface-level things," he answered. "I can normally perceive much more, but your group is special, always hidden, but I can feel great potential in the four of you."

"Then I'll make our plans clear to you," Jae-Hyun continued. "We wish to establish an organization that will control every facet of Pandora and become a force that will guide the aspirants in the future."

Marcus stared straight into the regressor, as if he could see something that I couldn't. He thought for a second before slowly nodding. "I see."

"The upcoming trials will be trying, and I need everyone on the same page to succeed. We cannot allow others to do as they please when our very survival is at stake, and for that, we need someone to lead them."

"And you wish for my help in leading those lesser aspirants, correct?"

"Yes," he replied, "I need you to guide them onto the right path."

Which I'm sure meant his path, regardless of what the people wanted themselves. Now, was the priest going to be okay with such a radical approach?

Jae-Hyun looked the priest hard in the eyes. "So you approve of our little guild?"

He thought for a moment longer before finally agreeing. "If Walter hadn't already convinced me, then seeing you most certainly did. It is a noble cause that you are pursuing, one that will be difficult without my aid. Many will push back if they ever realize what you are doing, so I will help you in this endeavor and ensure that no one will find out."

The regressor smiled. "Good, then you're a part of the guild now."

"Thank you, guild leader."

"You know what you need to do right now?"

"The flock is in turmoil, and they need a guiding voice to bring them to heel," Marcus said calmly. "I shall be that voice. I shall guide them so that they will behave when you call for them."

"Go," Jae-Hyun said. "You know what to do."

Marcus got up and quickly left the building.

Wait . . . was that it? The exchange between him and Jae-Hyun hadn't lasted longer than maybe sixty seconds. Where was the exchange of information or negotiating of terms? Jae-Hyun made it seem like I had to get this guy on our side at all costs, yet when he finally met him the whole exchange was over in less than a minute? Noel and Vadeem looked equally confused. They didn't get more than a word or two off in that entire exchange.

Jae-Hyun noticed our confusion and clarified, "The priest sees the world . . . differently than we do. Please excuse his odd behavior."

"Uh, I know how sensitive you are toward Yoona," I said. "Are you sure you're okay with her interacting with Marcus?"

Vadeem looked at me with confusion. "What do you mean?"

"I mean how goddamn creepy the guy is!" I answered. "Did you not see that?"

"Yeah," Noel agreed. "He was kind of sus. Never seen anyone like him before, but my little bro's right, he's definitely creepy."

Now Vadeem's confusion increased as he furrowed his brows. "He seemed nice enough to me. A little taciturn, sure, but looked like a nice enough fellow."

Was Vadeem seeing the same thing as I was? In no universe was Marcus anything other than creepy and weird.

"Jae-Hyun," I asked, "he was super creepy for you as well, right?"

"That's one way of putting it," he answered slowly. "But the fact that you could see through his skill means that you have more Charisma than I thought, Walter."

"Wait," Vadeem added, "so he's using some kind of skill on us? But how come Noel noticed it too? I'm pretty sure that her Charisma's in the single digits!"

Noel poked a finger into the big man's ribs. "Hey! I totally do not! I got, like, a trillion points of Charisma! It's why everyone loves me."

The regressor ignored her. "No, Noel and I have abilities that mitigate outside forces from influencing our minds. It's why we were fine for the most part in the second trial."

"But you're saying that a high Charisma also counters whatever Marcus has going on?"

"Yes, but it's got to be really high to do that," he replied. "What's your attribute at now, Walter?"

"Uh, with all the bonuses I got, it averages around 120," I answered truthfully, "but that doesn't seem all that high. Vadeem's got, what, 300 Strength now?"

He smirked. "434 now! I'm starting to fear my own abilities!"

"And I'm starting to fear that you're getting stupider. You probably have negative intelligence, Vadumb," Noel added. "All that muscle's taking away any nutrients that would normally go to your brain."

"Then I just have to eat enough for both!" Vadeem grinned.

"Yup . . ." Noel sighed. "You're a lost cause."

I ignored the two bickering friends and asked, "So he's got like four times my attributes in Strength, how is my puny 120 points high at all?"

Jae-Hyun shook his head. "Physical stats are a lot easier to accumulate than the more nebulous ones like Intelligence and Charisma. There's no job that I know of that increases that attribute like Vadeem's class does for Strength or Dexterity. Even titles that give out those bonuses are rare. I think Walter has some of the highest Charisma stats among all the aspirants right now."

Well, that made me feel a little better. I was also willing to bet that Marcus also had some insane Charisma scores of his own. Now that I thought about it, my abilities and Marcus's seemed to overlap a lot. Was the regressor's original plan to have the creepy priest guy do what I'd been doing before he met me? It would make sense since I was never even originally supposed to exist in Jae-Hyun's mind.

"So, what does his skill do?" I asked.

I knew that at this point Noel and Vadeem trusted anything that Jae-Hyun said without question. All of us no longer cared about how he was getting the information that he had. Jae-Hyun's ability to earn the respect and admiration of the people he interacted with was quite laudable, especially given how serious he generally was.

"It's hard to explain," he muttered in thought. "Think of it like a barrier that distorts how people view him. If you don't have a skill to counter his, or enough Charisma to counteract it altogether, then you'll see him as any normal priest."

"Wait, so I'm seeing a fake version of the guy? Does he have tentacles growing out of him like Walter?" Vadeem asked. "Should I keep my guard up?"

"No," the regressor answered firmly. "He's officially a part of our guild now, and he will never betray us as long as he is with us."

"Never?" I asked, uncertain how that could be possible. "That's hard to believe."

"Believe it or not, it's the truth," he answered simply. "You'll quickly see that Marcus doesn't operate like the norm."

"So he's like Noel, then," Vadeem mumbled. "Wonderful."

"Hey!" the girl added. "I'm totally less crazy than that dude! Even I can see that!"

"All right," Vadeem said slowly. "If you say so, boss. Our guild's not exactly normal in the first place, so I'm sure having an extra weirdo won't make too much of a difference."

"Speaking of which," I added, "shouldn't we let Marcus know about sleeping arrangements and all that? In fact, he hasn't even met the other three members."

The regressor shook his head. "I'll call for a guild meeting in a few hours. Yoona and the twins are still busy helping out with the aftermath right now, and I believe Marcus will be busy on the sidelines as well. I'll send everyone a message over the system and we can have our introductions then. There's something I want to show you now that we've settled in properly."

"Oo," Noel said. "What is it? Is it a super-awesome surprise?"

"Something like that," he replied with a small smile. "It'll be useful for our growth in the future in any case."

"Cool!"

Even I was wondering what he wanted to show us at that point. Jae-Hyun must have prepared something special if it was important enough for the whole guild to be notified, but it didn't seem like he'd tell us right now. He never did.

After being dismissed, the three of us decided to spend some time exploring the new building. Now that most of the staff had arrived, a lot of the stores and amenities that were empty could be used, so Noel, Vadeem, and I decided to see just what we had available for us in this huge building we practically stole.

To the surprise of no one, Vadeem wanted to check out the gym first, and it was as impressive as any facility that I'd seen back on Earth. It also passed the Vadeem test, and we had to practically drag him away from all the fancy new equipment. It wasn't an easy task. We also passed by various stores, spas, medical offices, and more office space than I knew what to do with, although we only took cursory glances in those places.

What we did decide to end our little tour of the building on was the pool and hot tub. These were a little too inviting not to try out for ourselves. It was a nice way for the three of us to unwind after a long day.

True to his word, the regressor sent us a message a few hours later. However, instead of meeting at the lounge like normal, he told us to meet him all the way up at the fourteenth floor. I don't believe any of us had been up there yet, seeing as there really wasn't a point. The three of us changed and headed to see what this so-called surprise would be.

The elevator took us to the designated floor, and the same series of corporate hallways greeted us. Yoona was already with the regressor, and the twins popped out from around the corner when they heard the noise. They immediately went to Vadeem's side, much to the big man's amusement. He ruffled their hair and flexed his muscles in greeting.

Marcus was the last to arrive. He still looked horribly off to me, but whatever skill he had seemed to be working on the three girls, because they just greeted the man like they normally would. I think even Noel shuddered when she saw him.

"First of all," the regressor began, "thank you for taking the time to see me in the middle of the night."

Noel gave him a thumbs-up, but the rest of us didn't speak.

"Noel and Vadeem have already met the priest," Jae-Hyun continued as he faced the three girls, "but he will be the newest and final member of our core group. I'm sure we will all have time later to get better acquainted."

"Hello, Father," Yoona said with a smile. "I'm Yoona. It's nice to meet you, and welcome to the Abyss Guild. Sorry about the ominous name; it wasn't my idea. The two beside me are mute, but they're Ana and Eva."

Marcus gave his signature smile and shook Yoona's hand. "Pleasure is all mine. I hope to work with all of you thoroughly in the future."

"So what's the surprise, boss?" Noel said impatiently. "I wanna see it!"

"I was getting to that," he said. "Follow me, please."

We did, and Jae-Hyun led us to a discreet door at the end of one of the hallways. He unlocked it and we entered a huge room. The gym-sized place must take up at least three or four floors in height, and in the middle of the otherwise empty space was a huge metallic sphere.

Various cables ran across and into the structure, and a small control panel was hooked up to it. Next to the control panel was a small slot. It was empty at the moment, and I was pretty sure that something was supposed to be housed there.

I spotted a small door leading to the interior, while a larger screen was hooked up to its side. Perhaps this was to show what was going on inside the thing when it was turned on? Still, it looked fancy, and I was sure that it did something amazing. Jae-Hyun went to the controls and gestured to the machine.

"This," he said with an uncharacteristic smile, "is why I wanted the building."

CHAPTER TWENTY-ONE

The Omen Machine

We all stared at the thing in awe, although no one besides Jae-Hyun knew what it did. I couldn't wait for him to explain it, so I took the time to see if I could glean some information with my Arbiter skill.

Omen Machine: A machine used for training purposes. It can recreate any foe that the user has encountered before, allowing up to 10 party members to practice their skills against these recreations without the fear of death.

"This is the Omen Machine," he explained. "It allows us to fight against preprogrammed enemies if we enter that sphere. There's pretty much every kind of creature available in there. It's the perfect training tool."

Hm, so he wasn't telling the whole truth there. Although it was basically the same thing if we're using the regressor's memories to power the thing. I was pretty sure he'd faced every foe imaginable in his past life. I thought about it more—this would be the perfect tool given Jae-Hyun's unique situation; he should have a pretty good idea of what kinds of creatures we'd encounter in the future, and if we could practice fighting them before the actual trial, then we'd have an overwhelming advantage. We could even test our tactics against future bosses with this thing.

"I'm assuming that we can't die in there?" I asked tentatively. It wouldn't be a very good training tool if we all got killed while in it.

"No," he answered, "but you will still feel the injuries, so we can't use it constantly. It is otherwise safe if we limit how often we go in."

"How about using it to gain experience and levels?" I added.

"Unfortunately, it is a training tool only, so we can't use it to cheat the system."

Damn, there went my hopes of using that thing to cheat, killing the same bosses over and over again to level up like crazy.

"However," he continued, "leveling up is not the only way to improve, nor is it the most effective. Increased stats are worthless if you do not have the skill to back them up, and we can hone our abilities to the extreme using this."

I nodded, agreeing with the reasoning behind what he said.

"Which brings me to my last point," the regressor added. "I'm sure everyone here, except our newest member, saw the problems that we faced in the last trial."

Vadeem frowned. "The darkness did a number on all of us?"

"That was one of the problems," he answered calmly, "but not the main one. Father Marcus should alleviate those types of issues in the future, even with Walter's unique constitution."

Oh, he was able to help me out? I wondered how that worked . . . although my gut was telling me that it would be anything but pleasant. The creepy priest gave a small nod of acknowledgment, which only reaffirmed my fears.

"Our real problem is that we have no experience fighting as a team," Jae-Hyun continued. "We are not using our strengths to the fullest when we fight a singular foe, and we will be facing increasingly more challenging enemies in the future that require proper coordination and teamwork."

Well, that was some ominous news. I certainly didn't want to face any more kaiju-sized stone golems or six-armed giants in the future, but what choice did I have in the matter? The damn Origin Matrix had its metaphorical eyes set on destroying me and Noe, and I was willing to bet my left feeler that it would send us on more bullshit trials in the future.

"All right, let's try it out, then!" Noel said with glee. "I wanna try out this sweet new tactic I've been cooking up!"

"Huh," Vadeem added with a smile. "And I got a few moves I want to practice as well. A little bit of the Vadeem team special!"

The regressor calmly shook his head. "Unfortunately, we can't use it at the moment."

I frowned. "Why not? Do we not have access to it fully?"

"No, we just don't have the fuel necessary to start it up."

I nodded. Made sense. There was no way something like that would be available for us to use for free, even if they never initially intended for any aspirant to own the thing.

"So how do we power it up?" Vadeem asked as he studied the structure closer. "I assume we can't just plug it into the mains."

"No shit, Vadum— Um, pardon my language," Noel answered before pointing to the small opening on the side. "I'm assuming we put something in this little slot thing?"

Jae-Hyun smiled. "Exactly, which brings me to tonight's meeting."

We all turned to face him.

Jae-Hyun had this uncanny ability to capture your attention when he wanted to discuss something important.

"We need the cores of monsters for this machine to function, or more specifically, processed cores," he continued.

Wait, I thought I remembered hearing about them before, when Raffiel said I caused some core resonance when I used Noe on that first zombie. I was pretty sure that the regressor also used some to make those defective flares of his, but I never gave the subject much thought before.

"I don't think we saw any in the second trial," Vadeem thought aloud for a moment. "You have any of those, Marcus?"

The priest shook his head gently. "No, I don't believe I saw any either, although I'm to assume that there is a special method to their extraction."

"Exactly," the regressor affirmed, "but we can talk about how to extract them later. It's not difficult once you know what to look out for. Just know that we need to make it a priority to acquire as many cores as we can."

"So we hunt critters and get their cores?" Noel asked.

"Partly, but the eight of us will never get enough to power the machine," he continued. "Which is why I wanted us to have a firm foothold on Pandora."

"Ah, so we're to buy them off the others," I said. "Are the cores useful for anything else?"

"Minimally for now," Jae-Hyun answered. "But they will explode in value soon. We can keep prices low while they're still relatively useless, and I've already made plans to have the aspirants here collect and process them. I've already distributed the method to harvest cores, and the next step is to teach the noncombatants how to process them for use."

Thank goodness our leader had all of that stuff figured out, but that was the power of knowing the future for you. I wasn't sure how valuable these core things would be, but if we controlled all of the people who could process them, and had a huge hoard of them stored up, then I could only imagine how rich we'd all be in the not-too-distant future. Perhaps my 100 million would be but a drop in the bucket for the Abyss Guild's coffers.

"But," the regressor continued, "we cannot slack off either. The other aspirants might be able to get us a lot of cores, but the quality of the ones that the masses can get will be low. In order to do what I want with the machine, we'll need to hunt down foes that they cannot."

"Right," grumbled Vadeem. "You did say that there are enemies that we can destroy outside these walls. We've been cooped up here for so long that I almost forgot. Man, do I need some proper exercise."

"All right," I added, seeing where this conversation was going, "so what's the first mission for the Abyss Guild?"

Jae-Hyun flashed me one of his rare genuine smiles. "We go on an expedition, of course. However, I will have to ask you to stay back, Father."

The priest nodded. "I understand. There is still much chaos that needs to be quelled with the aspirants, and they will need a guiding hand in the coming days."

The regressor smiled. "Thank you. I apologize for having you work just after joining."

"It is not a problem," he answered with his own, distinctly creepier smile. "I am just glad to be the guiding hand that leads the masses. It is my calling in this life, and I am helping a noble cause."

The meeting concluded quite quickly after that. The regressor had to make plans for an extended absence, but since our guild was so new, it wasn't that big of a deal if most of its core members left for a while. The few production workers we had hired were already busy with their various assignments, and they could be trusted to work independently for a week or two; the uncanny father could take care of the rest.

Jae-Hyun told us that this would be the only time that we could afford such luxuries, unfortunately, and I could only imagine how much his little organization would grow in the future. Either way, it did take another two days to get everything set up for our voyage, and as always, our quiet leader chose not to enlighten us on where exactly we were going. Apparently, Yoona didn't know either, although we did our best to bribe some information out of her.

"You sure you can't get doe-eyed for your brother and get him to tell us where we're going, bestie?" Noel pleaded. "You know he's got a soft spot for you!"

"I can't, Noel," Yoona said with a sigh. "And he has enough things to worry about. He doesn't need me to get in his way."

Vadeem had gone out with the twins to get some last-minute stuff for the trip, while Marcus was gone doing whatever creepy thing he normally did with the aspirants, so it was just the three of us hanging out in the lounge. Without the internet and modern technology, there just wasn't a lot to do for fun other than chat and relax.

"And plus," Yoona continued, "we'll all be leaving in a few hours. I'm sure my brother will tell us his plans then."

"Yeah, yeah," Noel grumbled. "Just wish I knew what we were getting into so I could prep better. All we know is that it'll be a long trip."

Yoona looked confused. "But Jae-Hyun told you what to bring."

"I know that," Noel answered with a pout. "But I want to bring stuff myself this time. Our leader's like, omniscient, but that doesn't mean that he should have all the fun when it comes to choosing what to bring!"

Yoona sighed again.

"And I say we take some board games with us!" Noel continued. "And maybe some snacks for when we get hungry. I don't want to rely on Vadeem's stupid suitcase for everything."

And on and on the two went, although it was mostly Noel talking, with Yoona doing her best to keep up with the other girl's ramblings. I tuned out of their conversation quickly and just wished there was something else for me to do other than wait. There weren't even any books around here to read; you'd think that you could buy a nice novel with everything else available here. I swore I'd use my wealth to commission proper literature later on.

However, before too long, the regressor completed whatever last-minute planning he had, and called for everyone to meet up in front of the building. Noel all but jumped out of the place, while Yoona and I followed. I knew that it would take us a few days to get to whatever destination Jae-Hyun had in mind, so I expected transportation of some sort, maybe some sort of carriage or the like, but I wasn't expecting what I saw.

Outside of the guild building was a square, bus-shaped object that looked like it had enough room to more than comfortably house the seven of us. It wouldn't have been strange if it was pulled by horses or some other four-legged creature, but instead, it was tied to the underside of a goddamn dragon. A big red one at that. Where the hell had the regressor found that thing?

The massive creature was at least the size of any modern commercial aircraft and maybe twice as wide. The thing seemed docile enough, although every twitch and breath it took would shake the air around it. A person was riding the impressive creature's head, nestled away on a comfortable-looking seat, but he was so far away that I couldn't make out any features.

Wrapped around the dragon's stomach with various ropes and chains was the traveling compartment, and I was a little dubious about the safety of such a setup. We all looked at our transportation in awe. Well, Marcus didn't seem to have any reaction to it, but that was mainly because nothing seemed to faze the guy. And it wasn't like he needed to get on it either, so that helped.

"Uh . . ." I said, still not believing what I was seeing. I couldn't find the right words to say, so I just remained slack-jawed.

"Wow . . ." Noel added with as much awe as me. "I've always wanted to ride a dragon . . ."

Vadeem looked a little dubious. "Is that, uh, safe? Look, riding a dragon's cool and all, but I, uh, I don't do heights or flying really well."

The twins looked on with mouths hanging open, and they didn't need to speak for me to understand how much they wanted to ride the thing. However, when they noticed Vadeem's hesitation, they gave him gentle pats on the back, letting him know that everything would be fine. It honestly looked pretty funny seeing them comfort someone so much bigger than they were.

"It's completely safe," Jae-Hyun answered. "And it's the only way to get where we need to go. Hop in. We'll talk more on the way."

"Right . . ." I muttered as I stepped into the housing area. "And how did you manage to rent a dragon of all things?"

He shrugged as he forced Vadeem on. "You can do a lot if you have the necessary funds, and thanks to you, we have a lot of money to go around."

The rest of the party stepped on calmly, and that was the start of our first expedition via dragon. If only I had known that our method of transportation would be the least outlandish part of the trip.

CHAPTER TWENTY-TWO

Skyward

Things calmed down, relatively speaking, once we were in the air and the horrible shaking of the dragon minimized. Things got bumpy when the massive creature took to the skies; liftoff was not a smooth affair when our ride had to use wings to do so. Vadeem seemed like he would have a heart attack every time the cabin shook, and it took the concentrated effort of the twins to ease the man's suffering before he destroyed the whole cabin with his jitters.

Honestly, I'm pretty sure that Vadeem would do more damage to the earth than it would to him if he ever fell from the sky. I could see him cosplaying as the meteor that ended the dinosaurs if he turned titan-sized in his descent, although I didn't share this little nugget of information with the big man himself. We all allowed him to suffer in peace. Even Noel was uncharacteristically quiet when she saw him like that.

At least Vadeem managed to regain some of his composure once we reached cruising altitude. I wasn't sure exactly how far up that was, but it must have been a lot lower than the standard 30,000 feet for modern airplanes; after all, we weren't freezing to death so far. The added benefit was that we were still below most of the clouds, so the view from the windows was gorgeous.

Once we all felt safe, our group of seven naturally splintered off into two sections. Noel, Vadeem, and the twins sat in a back corner, away from windows, and were playing a board game that the redhead had purchased. It seemed to help with the big man's nerves, having something to focus his mind on.

That left me with Yoona and her taciturn brother for company. Kind of reminded me of when we first met, way back in that zombie hellscape. It hadn't been that long since then, relatively speaking, but after everything that we'd been through, it felt like I'd known them for a lot longer.

The cabin area was spacious enough to house all of us comfortably, and even had various comfortable seats and tables around for us to use. I had underestimated the size of the place when I first saw it, thinking it was only the size of a bus, but it was a lot larger. Nestled in the back were some small bunking areas where we could rest, also a singular toilet, while the rest of the area provided plenty of space to walk around in.

Naturally, the first thing that I did was to go to the front where I could take a proper view of the land around us. There was even a little patio-like area where you could enjoy the fresh air. The observation deck was small, maybe just a few feet in all directions, but there was more than enough room for a small group of people to enjoy the wind and fresh air. I was joined by Yoona and her brother.

"Quite the view, isn't it, Walter?" Yoona whispered as she gazed into the distance. "I never thought I'd see something like this in my lifetime."

I glanced down at the beautiful landscape before me and agreed. It was probably impossible to see such clean ecosystems devoid of the corrupting influence of humanity anywhere else, and just seeing nature run its course was beautiful.

"Yeah . . ." I muttered. "It really hits you that you're not on Earth anymore."

Yoona chuckled. "And the zombies didn't tell you that before?"

I laughed back. "Well, not in the good way, at least. It's been one horror after another since we all got sent here. Guess we never saw the beauty before."

"Those last few trials feel like a lifetime ago." She smiled. "I like it here, with everyone helping out. It's nice to feel like I belong to something larger than myself."

I nodded. I was starting to see why the regressor wanted to keep the shady sides of his operations a secret now. With how absolutely messed up our guild was becoming, I think we all needed someone like Yoona to keep things in balance. We all needed a little light in this new world.

I gazed down below for a bit longer, enjoying the breeze in my hair. "So where are we going that we need to get there by dragon? I know that I said I had a lot of money, but this must be pretty expensive to rent."

Jae-Hyun moved over and leaned on the railing by his sister. I think he was also enjoying the rare moment of calm.

"You'll see," he said simply. "And we need to get there by air because we can't reach it by land."

I sighed. I hated how the man would never just tell us things straight up. Would it kill him to just let us know ahead of time, or was looking at us squirm in anticipation the only form of entertainment left to him?

"Fine," I grumbled, "but at least tell us how long it'll be. I think Vadeem will have an aneurysm if we don't get down to the ground soon."

"Vadeem will be fine," Jae-Hyun answered. "The priest gave us some of his own medication we can use on him."

"Oh," Yoona answered innocently. "That's very kind of him!"

Oh, indeed . . . How I wished I had less Charisma at times like these and saw the creepy man in the same way that Yoona did. I wasn't going to trust anything that came from Father Marcus's own stash of goodies, but at least Vadeem was in the same boat as her, so whatever undoubtedly horrible cure the priest gave wouldn't look so bad on his end.

The regressor continued. "It will take us maybe a full day's trip, depending on the weather. No more than a day and a half."

Well, that wasn't too long in any case, although wherever he was taking us sure was far given how fast we were going. Of course, Noe was still upgrading, and that wouldn't end for another week at least, so I'd have to get through whatever the regressor had in store for us by myself.

But that was a worry for Future Walter. Now Walter would relax and just look at the pretty scenery and not dread what was to come. The various hills and rivers were passing by our dragon quite quickly, and I even saw a few small village settlements down below.

"Say," I said, now that a new thought hit me, "I never had the chance to ask, but just how big is this place they've thrown us into? Actually, just where are we, anyway?"

Jae-Hyun smiled. "I was wondering when you would ask that."

Noel and Vadeem heard the conversation and stopped their board game to hear his explanation as well. Although Vadeem stayed as far back as he possibly could.

"Yeah," Noel added, "never thought about it, but we've been flying for a while, so this place must be pretty expansive. This whole world can't all be run by those creeps, right?"

The regressor shook his head. "No, the people in charge of the trials did not make this place they call the Main Stage from scratch, nor do they control every facet of its operations. But they are the ones with the most power here."

"Makes sense," I said, then remembered all the budget cuts that Q was complaining about. "I'm pretty sure not even these mysterious kidnappers could fully control a whole world. Still, what is this place we're in? I'm seeing medieval villages below, but we also have the strange urban stuff near our base. That can't be natural."

"And you'll see even stranger things as we go farther from Pandora," Jae-Hyun continued. "You can think of the world that we're in now as a patch-work planet of sorts."

"So like, what, a bunch of smaller worlds all smushed together and made into one big world?"

"Something like that. It's why Pandora's the way it is," he answered. "I don't know the exact details myself, but I know that the Main Stage is huge and you can find practically anything here. It's also more or less completely governed by the System."

"Then is this whole place made for the exclusive use for the aspirants?" Noel asked. "Cause that'd be a little lonely if this place is so big. Reminds me of that stupid zombie city."

"No." Jae-Hyun shook his head. "Locals here as well, but they tend to stay away from where the aspirants are. Remember that other towns out there where others are going through similar experiences, and not all of them are human. We aren't the only people they took."

Noel's eyes went wide. "So you mean Raffiel and his crew kidnapped aliens as well? Oh my god, I've always wanted to meet an alien!"

Yoona sighed. "It's not all good news, Noel. My brother said that it's pretty hostile out there, but the, um, aliens are far away enough that we won't see them for a while longer."

"Aw." Noel pouted. "I wanted to see an alien, or at least fight one! But aren't you curious about what an actual alien would look like?"

Yoona hesitated a little, but Noel's enthusiasm was infectious, and soon the two girls were discussing all the possibilities about what an alien would look like. Even Vadeem joined in a few times, while the twins were listening in with fervor. I drowned out the noise as best I could. I had other things to contemplate.

I was having a hard time trying to picture how everything slotted into place. There were still so many questions left unanswered. Was this Main Stage the location where all the aspirants gathered, regardless of which site they belonged to? It wouldn't be impossible if Central had control over the timelines of various other sites, but I doubt that aspirants from other dimen-sions would also gather here. If that were the case, then this place would have to go on near forever, and I couldn't imagine how Central could keep that much chaos contained.

So that probably meant that the Main Stage, or at least our Main Stage, was local to this dimension or maybe some adjacent ones. But if that was the case, then was it the Overseer who was responsible for all the aspirants? No, that couldn't be the case either, as he barely seemed to care about how we were doing when I met the man, and was probably too busy with whatever war was going on.

Which that meant that someone else was in charge of the Main Stage's operations. I'd have to confirm all of this when I saw Q again. Maybe this was the angle that I could use to get the man's job back and get rid of that piece-of-shit overseer. I'd need powerful allies for that, and perhaps I could leverage my status as the legendary Arbiter W to see if I couldn't worm my way into the good graces of whoever was in charge.

I smiled. This was the start that I needed.

"All of that will only matter in the far future," Jae-Hyun said. "For now, get some rest. We'll be busy once we land."

The others agreed, Vadeem especially so, as he quickly went back to his little corner away from the exposed elements. The other three followed him, and they continued with their board game while the regressor went back inside the cabin to do whatever it was he did in his spare time. It seemed like a lot of planning and brooding, but what did I know?

Yoona stayed for a little longer before heading inside. I remained for a long time, just gazing at the distant horizon, before hunger finally got the better of me and I went inside to join the others.

CHAPTER TWENTY-THREE

The Island in the Sky

The journey to our destination went by faster than I thought, although that was mainly due to the great company that kept us entertained. Between a few naps and some rounds of board games and trivia, it felt more like a cozy get-together than anything else. Even Vadeem seemed to grow accustomed to flying after a few hours in the sky, although he would still stay far away from any windows.

But the cabin started to shake as the dragon slowed its speed, signaling the end of our journey. Vadeem almost had a heart attack and immediately grabbed onto the closest object. He all but flattened the table, which was something that would probably come out of my pockets to fix. Much to his relief, we stopped shortly after, having arrived at wherever it was that the regressor dragged us to.

We followed Jae-Hyun off the platform once we came to a complete stop and set foot on a goddamn floating island in the sky.

"Wow . . ." Noel whispered, and even she was at a loss for words gazing at the new locale.

The dragon blimp thing flew a little off into the distance, finding a more spacious space to wait for our return, which left me with a jaw-dropping view of the place. We were just barely above the lowest cloud cover, which made the landscape before me look like it was floating in a sea of white. The place was large as well. I couldn't make out the full scale of the island even when I was on the dragon, as a lot of our view was obstructed by the ancient buildings that dotted the landscape.

Now, the buildings themselves were awe-inspiring. They were massive monuments that seemed to have been built in a bygone era, and they seemed to stretch impossibly high into the sky. Moss and vegetation covered the huge stone pillars and large archways, and everything seemed to be too large for normal-sized humans to use comfortably, which suggested that this place had been made for beings that were perhaps much larger than its current guests. The marble pathways and steps were still visible under the grass and flora, and a gentle breeze blew steadily.

It looked like we'd just stepped into a set piece right out of a fantasy movie.

The regressor stepped in front of us and smiled. "Welcome to Mount Olympus, or at least an old version of it."

"Olympus, as in the place where all the Greek gods used to live?" I asked in disbelief.

"Yes," he answered, "but it's the outdated version, like I said. There are many variations of Mount Olympus, Asgard, or Heaven scattered between the dimensions when the gods are involved."

"Wait," Vadeem added, "those old gods are real? Zeus and Poseidon and all that?"

"And many more besides," Jae-Hyun answered. "We stepped onto a larger stage the second we were taken to the trials. Expect things to be very different from here on out."

"Well, shit . . ." the big man muttered. "Won't they mind if we're trespassing in their old home, then?"

Jae-Hyun laughed bitterly, and I could tell there were some hidden grievances behind that bitterness. "They will not, nor will they care. They barely notice us now, but they will once we are further into the trials. You know that sponsorship Walter gained?"

The rest of the group nodded.

"The people doing the sponsoring are what we generally know as gods."

"Damn," Vadeem said as he looked at me in earnest. "You got the attention of some kind of tentacle god? Well, that explains a lot."

"Maybe it's the Flying Spaghetti Monster that sponsored him!" Noel added with glee. "I knew he was real!"

The regressor shook his head and his tone became serious. "I'll say this now, and I'll remind us again when the sponsors come in full force, but *never* accept help from them. They are not your friends, although some of them will do their best to convince you otherwise. Their terms are never fair, and they all want you to suffer in the long run."

We all saw how serious Jae-Hyun was and quickly agreed. I was willing to bet anything that he'd had a lot of run-ins with various sponsors in his previous life, and none of those meetings were positive. There was still so much I didn't know about the man.

"But what about Walter?" Yoona asked. "He's already accepted one."

Her brother frowned for a second before quickly composing himself. "There are ways to undo that in the future. It won't be easy, but it's not impossible. If it's only Walter that has a sponsor, then we can still do something about it."

I thanked him, although I most certainly didn't need whatever help he was offering. Not that I'd tell him that, of course. Still, it was nice to see that I was important enough for Jae-Hyun to go out of his way to help. Hopefully, this also meant that he'd try his best to save me from whatever horrible future disaster did him in the first time.

"But enough about the sponsorships. We can worry about that when it's relevant," he continued. "For now, I want to talk about why I brought everyone here."

"Finally!" Noel added. "You have a horrible habit of keeping all these juicy things under wraps!"

The regressor shrugged. "It's faster to just show you, and I hate repeating myself."

"All right, all right, you are the boss after all, boss," pouted Noel. "So what's so special about some abandoned buildings?"

"Other than the fact that they were used by the literal gods?" Vadeem added incredulously. "That's not special enough for you?"

The other girl shrugged. "It's all abandoned now, so what?"

"So what?" Vadeem muttered. "How can—"

"It's important," the regressor interrupted before Vadeem and Noel could get into another one of their dialogues, "because while the gods have abandoned this place for greener pastures, these ruins are not completely empty. Other, lesser beings have inhabited the mount while it was vacant, and this is the perfect opportunity for us to gather cores and other material that we can't find elsewhere. There is also one particular place I want to visit as well."

Noel sighed. "So we're just collecting the unwanted stuff the gods left behind? We're like, glorified garbage collectors, ew."

"But it's godly garbage, Noel!" Vadeem smiled with excitement. "Imagine what they've left behind!"

"Well, you can go pick up godly toenail clippings or something," the redhead mumbled. "And I got excited for nothing."

"It's not that bad, Noel," Yoona added softly. "There's bound to be hidden treasures and artifacts as well, plus there's a lot of aliens you can fight as well."

"My sister's right," Jae-Hyun said. "The gods are never exactly thorough when they move homes, so there are things in there that will be worth our time."

That perked up the redhead a little. "Well . . . I guess it's not too bad, and I always wanted to go search for ancient ruins one of these days."

"That's the spirit!" Yoona exclaimed with a cheerful smile. "So what's the plan, brother?"

"Yeah," Vadeem added. "Got traps and stuff we have to watch out for? Magic barriers we need to avoid like last time?"

The regressor shook his head. "No, it's more standard here, like I said, that last trial was abnormal. We'll set up camp close to the dragon—it's part of the reason we rode here on one in the first place. I'll tell the driver to detach the cabin for us to use."

"Good idea," I muttered. "I doubt anything will want to get too close to that thing."

Jae-Hyun nodded. "Yeah, she'll stay put for a week before we have to go back, so we'll use that time to thoroughly explore this place. Our goal is to gather as many cores as possible. Treasures are a secondary concern, but most importantly, we need to practice our formations and synergies in a fight."

Yoona nodded. "I'm still a little hesitant to shoot when you or Vadeem are too close to an enemy."

"And you have two other archers to account for as well," Vadeem added. "The twins are good, but they're more used to scout work than fighting in a team."

Ana and Eva started to flex their arms to affirm what Vadeem said, but Yoona quickly corrected them, and they nodded instead. I guess they still defaulted to the Vadeem method of communication even after all this time. However, I knew that the big man was still teaching them ridiculous things when he thought the others were not looking. I didn't think he'd ever stop, regardless of how many times he got scolded by the others. I think Ana and Eva secretly liked the ridiculous gestures as much as Vadeem did.

"Right," I said, "we've never really had a proper chance to fight together, what with us being split up before even starting the trial. I still don't know what Yoona's class does, come to think of it. Or that weird thing Jae-Hyun did in that last fight."

Jae-Hyun spoke before his sister could answer. "It's easier to get the proper feel of things in combat than just explaining."

"We're not all like you, brother. It'll be easier if I actually told them," Yoona said with a sigh. "But generally speaking, I can imbue my arrows with mana and give them different properties. I think you saw me control their flight well. There's a bit more nuance, but you'll see when we fight."

"All right, enough talking!" Noel joined in. "Let's go stab some baddies already! I've been cooped up in that box all day. I need to stretch my legs a bit."

I actually agreed with Noel for once. As fun as that trip was, it had been over a day since we were able to stretch ourselves properly, and I wanted to test out my new class passives as well. I'd yet to see just how much more damage I could do with my luck charges completely full. Then another thought hit me: Just how much damage could I do in my Xollon form combined with Noe's new class?

"I'll speak with our driver and we'll head out after," the regressor said. "We might need to camp out for a night or two inside the ruins, so keep some supplies ready."

"Got it, boss!"

"Oh right. Walter?" he asked as he turned to look at me.

"Yeah?"

He took out something from his inventory and tossed it over. I barely managed to grab onto it without cutting myself. That would have been embarrassing if it had.

"Your weapon's fixed. It's not the sturdiest thing, but we can find something better here."

Ah, the damn whip-blade. I'd almost forgotten about it, but it wasn't like I could actually use the stupid thing when Noe's Absolute Luck was out of the equation. I still planned to use it in the future. I had the idea that I could swing the thing in my left hand randomly and let Noe do most of the work on that front while I concentrated all my attention on using my right feeler to attack. That way, it was like having two people fight at once, although I'd still have to see how feasible this plan of mine was. Honestly, with the use of my tentacles, the necessity of an actual weapon was becoming less relevant.

But all of that would wait for later, once Noe's upgrades were complete. Instead of swinging it around like an idiot and letting people know that I had no actual ability to use it, I stashed it in my inventory and pointed to my open palms.

"Thanks," I said, "but I want to try out my new abilities this time since we're here to practice. I know you don't like the fact that I got a sponsorship, but I might as well use the tools I'm stuck with, right?"

The regressor slowly nodded. "Fair. It's best to make use of any advantages you have, and as I said, I'll make sure that we fix your particular problem later on."

I watched the regressor head toward the dragon and felt a mounting anticipation of what was to come. The feelers in my hands were wiggling happily as well, just waiting for a chance to be free. I was never one who welcomed violence, yet I was strangely amicable to the idea right now. In fact, I was practically scrambling at the chance to fight. Was that the Xollon in me speaking?

Thankfully we didn't have to wait for too long, as our leader came back within a few minutes. He did, however, make us do one last check to make sure that all of our gear was ready. If there was one thing I'd learned from my interactions with the regressor, it was that he never wanted to go into any situation unprepared.

Once things were all accounted for, the seven of us walked with glee into the ruins, all of us glad to be on our feet once more, anticipating what was going to be in store for us.

CHAPTER TWENTY-FOUR

A Delve into the Depths

Jae-Hyun led us into the ruins casually while the rest of us followed with anticipation, weapons out. Walking through the windswept alleys and disused buildings was a surreal experience, especially coupled with the fact that we were all in the air. Our footsteps echoed between the huge monoliths and crumbled archways, giving the whole journey an eerie feel.

"You don't have to be so on guard," the regressor assured us. "There's rarely any enemies above ground."

We relaxed a bit but still had our weapons at the ready. Rarely didn't mean never, after all. Nobody but the regressor felt comfortable being so out in the open on unfamiliar ground.

"So that means we're, what, going belowground?" I reasoned.

"Yes, we're headed to the middle of this island," he continued. "There's an entrance where we can enter."

"Wait." Vadeem furrowed his brows and interrupted. "How's there a belowground when we're not even on land? Won't we just fall through the sky?"

Jae-Hyun gave a small laugh. "It's called Mount Olympus for a reason, we are technically on a mountain."

I gave him a confused look. How was that possible? When we were landing here, I could have sworn that I didn't see any mountains around us, although the low clouds did obscure some of my view. Still, when we were near the edge of the island structure, it was just a vertical drop down, with no mountain ranges or the like in view.

"I know what you're thinking," he said again. "It doesn't look like any mountain you've ever seen, but it is one. Think of it like taking a huge chunk of land and placing it on top of a very tall, narrow rock."

"Well," Yoona added, "I think the Greek gods didn't really have to bother with common sense when they built the place."

Vadeem chuckled. "No kidding. Who needs structural engineering when you have magic?"

Noel smiled. "Like I said, everything here's just magic! The faster you peeps accept that, the fewer times you'll all be surprised when stuff like this pops up."

That was true. I'd seen some of the insane stuff that Central's people created, and having an island balanced on top of a tall rocky skyscraper was the least outlandish piece of architecture I'd encountered. Pity, though, because I really wanted to explore an actual sky island for once, but maybe I'd have a chance to do that one of these days.

"So where are we going, boss?" Noel added.

"To the middle of the island where we can head down."

"Wait," I asked, "why are we going belowground in the first place? Shouldn't we explore these ruins for stuff first?"

Jae-Hyun shook his head. "Everything aboveground has long been scoured clean at this point. We're not the first people to have explored these ruins, but very few have traveled Mount Olympus's underbelly. We'll take a look aboveground once we're done searching below first."

"So all the good stuff's underneath because no one could find it?" I asked hopefully.

"That," he answered, "and because that's where the gods left their unwanted kin behind. You heard of Tartarus?"

I recalled my knowledge of Greek mythos and remembered it faintly. "Something like a big hole where they stuck the Titans?"

Vadeem frowned. "Hm . . . you think there are any Titans left down there?"

"It's not just the Titans that were housed there, it was everything that displeased one of the gods, and a lot of beings displeased them," Jae-Hyun explained. "But no, Vadeem, they took the Titans with them when they left."

The big man nodded slowly, seemingly lost in thought. I guess he had a deeper connection with them than I thought. The twins noticed his unease and moved closer to him, almost as if they were doing their best to guard the man while he was feeling down. It was kind of cute seeing them so attuned to Vadeem's emotions, although I still wished they would interact with the rest of the group more. I was sure that would come with time, though.

"So it's just the minor stragglers that were left behind?" I inquired.

"Something like that, at least close to the surface. I'm not sure what's housed deeper down."

"Huh," Vadeem said. "Didn't think there was anything that you didn't know about."

"Yes," Jae-Hyun answered with a sigh. "There are things that elude me. But enough chat, let's move on. We're close to the entrance now."

We traveled for another ten minutes or so before the regressor stopped us and led us into a seemingly ordinary pile of rubble. How he was able to remember all of these things was still a mystery to me. The man must have had thousands of points in Intelligence if he was able to recall information this well.

"Vadeem," Jae-Hyun said as he pointed to the fallen debris, "can you clear that for us?"

The other man grinned back fiercely. "You don't even have to ask."

Almost casually, Vadeem chucked the huge stone fragments off to the side, with some pieces larger than SUVs, and he didn't even need to transform to do so. In less than thirty seconds, the pile of broken buildings and other stone-work was clear, and I could make out an opening.

We walked closer, and after clearing away the last of the loose rubble, we peered down to see an ancient set of stairs that spiraled ever deeper into the earth. I couldn't see how far down it went, even with my enhanced vision.

The regressor then turned his attention to me, "Walter, can you still use that halo of yours?"

I nodded and turned the thing on. I peeked my head into the opening and saw, much to my surprise, that the halo's light reached much farther than what I had experienced in the last trial. Made sense, now that I thought about it, since I was fighting supernatural darkness then, and I was just dealing with normal darkness now.

What was even more surprising was that although my light was bright, brighter than it had any right to be, honestly, it was not blinding. None of my friends had to squint their eyes when they saw me, which would have been annoying if that hadn't been the case.

My friends joined me at the entrance to the hole in the ground, all trying to see just how far down it went. We couldn't tell. It must extend pretty far down if even I couldn't see the end, what with my title giving me perfect night vision and all.

"Looks ominous," Vadeem muttered. "But I guess it has to be if it leads to Tartarus."

Noel sighed. "Don't tell me you're afraid of tight spaces as well as heights."

"No," he answered, "I'm not, but I am worried about how well I can fight if I can't move without collapsing the damn roof."

Okay, that was a pretty logical concern. Vadeem wasn't known for his grace and subtlety, and I'd seen what he could do to buildings and infrastructure.

"You don't have to worry," Jae-Hyun explained. "It'll open up once we go down. There's some narrow passages we have to pass, but we won't be fighting there."

"It's still ominous . . ." Yoona whispered as she squinted to see if she could see a little better. "But I guess we have to get used to situations like this. Just going in the dark reminds me of that last trial . . . I'm sorry I wasn't of much help then."

"It's fine, Yoona," I assured her. "We all got out of it fine in the end, and you did save Vadeem's big butt at the end."

"That she did!" Vadeem grinned. "The damn rock monster almost had me if she didn't kill that barrier thing."

Noel sighed again. "Sometimes I wish she hadn't . . ."

The twins glared at her again. Pretty sure they had some choice words for her if they could talk. Noel chose to ignore them.

We gathered our courage and stepped into the void. The stairs were steep, and the shorter members of our party had to practically climb down each step given how high they were. Once again, I was reminded that his place wasn't designed with humans in mind. Still, Yoona and the twins were nimble enough that it didn't pose any problem for them.

Step after step we went down, farther and farther, until even my superhuman stamina was starting to feel its limits. These damn stairs seemed to go on forever, spiraling ever downward, and I almost slumped to the ground when they came to a stop eventually. The expertly carved stairs leveled off and opened up into a massive chamber.

This new place was so huge that my halo's light couldn't illuminate the other side of the cave clearly, but what we could see was a huge chasm that seemed to descend into the very depths of the earth.

There wasn't a lot of room to maneuver, as we found out rather quickly. Our exit ended on a very narrow ledge, maybe only a few feet wide, facing the sheer drop. Vadeem looked like he would drop to the ground at any moment before he quickly made his way back into the safety of the stairway.

"It's like dragging along a big baby." Noel chuckled as she sneered at the cowering man. "So do we head down there, boss?"

"That's the plan," he affirmed.

Noel shrugged before hopping down into the abyss. I thought she'd fall to her death as I peered down after her, but she had transformed halfway down and floated to the bottom, and, as if to spite Vadeem further, she flew back up and gave him a huge smirk of triumph.

"It's not that deep," she said with a shrug. "I say we throw Vadeem down. I think he'll survive."

I actually agreed with her assessment but didn't voice it out loud. My big friend was giving the redhead the most scathing look I'd ever seen.

"We climb down," Jae-Hyun said firmly. "Take out your flashlights. Walter's halo might not be able to illuminate everything."

Yoona and the twins did just that, although Noel didn't seem like she needed to. I heard Vadeem mumble something not quite appropriate under his breath, but he did what was asked of him, despite his fears.

"All right," Noel said once everyone had their lights pinned, "I'll head down first. Meet you there!"

And just like that, she jumped off the ledge and disappeared into the depths below once again. I followed, using my feelers to impale the rocky surface of the cliff to rappel down safely. It was kind of fun.

Yoona and the regressor came down next. Yoona's feet seemed to glow ever so slightly, which I assumed was from the use of mana, and she gracefully hopped down, her feet sticking supernaturally to tiny imperfections on the rock. However, while Yoona was all grace, her brother chose the direct approach and just jumped down. He took out his spear and dug it deep into the wall to slow down his descent when he neared the bottom.

Which left only Vadeem and the twins. The two girls had coaxed the big man to the edge of the cliff, urging him with their gestures to climb down. Eventually, Vadeem was able to overcome his fear, if only so that he wouldn't look so lame in front of the kids, and slowly, ever so slowly, he planted his feet on the rock face and started to climb down. The twins were cheering him on silently in the background. Soon Vadeem was able to get all four limbs on the wall, and all seemed well.

"Oh my god, Vadeem!" Noel yelled from below. "Hurry up! We'll be here all week if you don't move your big butt! The damn dragon will leave without us at this rate!"

That slight distraction was all it took for things to go downhill. Vadeem must have gripped a little too strongly because he pulverized his only handhold. He lost balance quickly after, and he fell. He also shouted some not-very-nice things on his way down, which got more chuckles out of the redhead.

Vadeem came crashing down like a meteor of muscle, the impact of his fall sending tremors through the ground. The twins saw what happened and quickly climbed down themselves to make sure that he was okay. They were fast and moved like a couple of spiders. It was honestly a little creepy.

They ran up to him and started to slap his face. I wasn't sure how that was supposed to help an injured person, but Vadeem did seem to be receptive to whatever they were doing and quickly composed himself.

"I'm fine, I'm fine," he grumbled and dusted the dirt off his clothes. "Honestly thought that fall would hurt way more than it did."

"Told you it would have been faster if we just chucked him down here in the first place," Noel added with a smile. "Let's go with my plan the next time we need to go down a cliff."

"Quiet!" the regressor said. "Get ready. Something's coming this way."

I nodded and refocused. I'd have been surprised if nothing was coming our way after Vadeem's fall. It probably alerted everything within the cave system with the noise and shock wave.

"Good," Vadeem grumbled, "I need to work off some of these nerves. I'll just pretend each foe has Noel's stupid face. That'll help with motivation."

The twins nodded their agreement as they stared daggers at the offending woman.

"All right, I'm sorry," Noel said. "Sheesh, it's not fair having kids defend you, Vadeem."

"Enough talk," Jae-Hyun said again. "Here they come."

CHAPTER TWENTY-FIVE

A Delve into the Depths Part 2

Remember," the regressor said calmly, "our ultimate goal is to improve our teamwork, but I want to see how we react naturally as a group first. The enemy's weak, so limit your skill use. No transformations."

"Aw, that's no fun!"

Yoona nodded. "Understood, brother!"

Vadeem grunted an affirmation before taking out his massive maul, eager to meet the foe head-on. I just noticed that he was able to hold and use that thing even without transforming, although I had no idea how he did so without sending himself flying with the momentum. Seeing everyone else ready for a scrap, I set my feelers free and waited for the enemy to approach.

Soon the first signs of what was coming flew into view. They were humanoid birdlike creatures, all female, apparently, with wings and wicked talons in place of arms and legs. Its feathered body was impressive, although it was still smaller than the average person. If this was the Olympus of old, then I was pretty sure that this is a harpy, or more accurately, an entire horde of them. The creatures flew through the air, shrieking and fluttering just above our heads.

The twins were the first to act, having already taken out their bows. Yoona joined a second after, and they unleashed a torrent of arrows into the oncoming mass. The regressor's sister had previously said that she could add properties to her shots, and it was clear to see how effective those additions were.

Some of the arrows she shot burned a trail through the mass of enemies, while others froze them in place. More importantly, each arrow did not stop after hitting one or two birds but tore through them like a high-powered rifle shot.

Whereas Yoona took her time to aim and shoot, the twins focused solely on speed. They stood next to each other and made pertinent use of their infinite supply of ammunition. Unlike Yoona, their arrows didn't have special effects, but the sheer speed at which they were able to draw was impressive. I could hardly see the movement of their hands once they were fully in the zone.

Now that I thought about it, I hadn't bothered checking their information with my Arbiter skill. Between my hectic schedule orchestrating the little play from earlier and my meeting with the Overseer, I barely saw the twins at all outside of breakfast.

I took a peek at their most relevant info.

Ana – Level 39 CORRUPTED CLASS

Description: User is not registered with Origin Matrix, please contact the Administration for further support . . . Unknown Aspirant . . . *you cannot take from us!*

Eva – Level 39 CORRUPTED CLASS

Description: User is not registered with Origin Matrix, please contact the Administration for further support . . . Unknown Aspirant . . . *you cannot stop us!*

Noe . . . did you bring the twins over?

"Affirmative, my host," she answered. "I saw the opportunity to interfere with its operations when the Trash Matrix was at its weakest. I hope you do not mind."

Noe had been taking a lot of initiative lately, which I suppose was a good thing, but I just wished that she would let me know about these types of things first. But still, it wasn't like I was the boss of her, and I never did like to micromanage everything. I'd be content as long as Noe was on my side, even if she was becoming more and more independent.

Well, it's good to have them around. Thanks, Noe. Just a little bit of a heads-up would be nice in the future if it's not too big a bother.

"I will do my best to ensure that you are properly informed, my host," Noe answered calmly. "But please note that it might not be possible, as I can only exploit the Trash Matrix when it is vulnerable. I apologize, dear Walter."

I focused my attention back on the flying birds above. They seemed to be gathering in number, but none of them were attacking us quite yet. Were they waiting for a critical mass to gather before swooping in?

Their numbers were increasing faster than the three archers could cope with, but they were still too high up for me to hit. I could occasionally stab one that got knocked down by its fellows, but those were rare and far between.

Noel was in the same boat as me. Without her skill, she was pretty much worthless in the fight since she couldn't fly in to just drown her foes in her creepy black fire. She realized this as well, and simply gave up trying to fight and just found a spot to sit down. She even got some popcorn out at one point.

Vadeem had it even worse; he had remained normal sized, as per the regressor's instructions, but the harpies instinctively fled away from him. In fact, there was a radius around him where no fliers would dare approach, and he was left flailing his hammer uselessly. Were they mistaking him for an actual Titan, even in his normal form?

If they were, then the class system was a little more complex than I had initially thought. It would mean that Vadeem did have Titan blood flowing through him, which begged the question: Had he always had that in him, or was it given to him when he got his class? Yet another question that I didn't have the answers to.

Lastly, Jae-Hyun was just off the side, not engaging the birds at all. Unlike Noel, he looked like he was analyzing the battle instead of just slacking off. No doubt he was trying to gauge our response to a flying enemy, and I'm guessing he did not like what he saw.

Once the last of the harpies had exited their caves and gathered above us, an unseen signal was sent, and they all started to dive at us. Noel quickly stashed away her food and grabbed her swords again, rushing to meet them head-on. Vadeem tried to do the same but the harpies would swerve wildly whenever he approached them, and he was way too slow to outmaneuver his airborne foes.

I did the same, using my tentacles to intercept anything that got close. I had a lot of experience doing so fighting those human-grasshopper things, and the harpies behaved in a pretty similar manner. They couldn't change their flight path when they decided to swoop, so all I had to do was make sure that a feeler was placed between me and its path of attack. Momentum did the rest.

Eventually, Vadeem just screamed in frustration, as nothing he was doing was working. He decided to ditch his weapon and just chuck rocks at the things. Honestly, it was pretty effective, all things considered. The rocks that he threw were the size of basketballs, and they were launched at cannonball velocity. The only downside was that it would cause horrible debris to litter the battlefield when the rocks inevitably hit the cave behind the foe.

"Stop throwing them!" Yoona shouted. "I can't see anything with the dust in the air!"

After analyzing the situation more, I think that Yoona was right. Vadeem's random throws were helping the enemies more than it hurt them, even if they killed a few unlucky harpies here and there, not to mention he risked collapsing the whole cave system if he threw them any harder. I certainly didn't want to be buried alive in literal Tartarus.

"But I can't fight 'em any other way!" Vadeem replied with a shout. "The damn flying turkeys keep avoiding me!"

"It's cause you're so ugly!" Noel shouted back as she eviscerated anything that even approached her. Seeing her work was still impressive.

"Don't push it, Noel!" Vadeem said, his tone angry. "I've just about had it with these damned winged fu—I mean, things!"

Well, that was cute, he chose not to swear after seeing the twins off to the side.

"All right, all right," the girl returned. "Just don't lose it. Your wife will kill me if anything happens to you. God forbid you burst a blood vessel in your head and get even stupider."

He grunted and turned his attention to Jae-Hyun. "You sure I can't just go titan-sized and squish these stupid birds?"

"No," Jae-Hyun answered calmly, "take it as a learning experience. You can't always rely on your skills to overcome every situation. You've learned that airborne foes are a problem, so we can prepare properly next time."

Vadeem took a deep breath and sighed. "Fine, do you have any suggestions on how I can fight them now, though?"

"I do," he replied. "But just watch for now."

"Fine," he grumbled and took a seat beside our leader, arms folded in frustration.

Well, I was starting to hope that he would give his advice soon because I was starting to get overwhelmed by the sheer volume of the flying turkeys myself. And the worst part about it was that I couldn't even properly test how much more power Noe's class gave each of my strikes. The birds all died in one strike if they hadn't impaled themselves onto my feelers.

Now, I could test my defenses, but that was something that I did not look forward to, although it appeared that it would be an eventuality soon.

Right at the tipping point, when it seemed like our forces would be overrun and we'd have to rely on class skills, the regressor joined the fight. He launched himself off ledges and walls, darting between areas and killing all but the farthest harpies. He made use of tiny footholds on the cliff to propel himself up higher and higher before allowing gravity to accelerate his downward assault.

He made it all look so easy.

"Vadeem!" he called. "Let me show you what you can do in a situation like this."

The big man obliged and ran toward where the regressor landed.

"If there is ever a foe that we cannot reach, say, because there weren't any walls that I could use to launch myself, then I want you to throw me as hard as you can into the enemy."

"As hard as I can?" Vadeem asked dubiously. "You'll splatter into paste if I do that."

"I will not," he answered confidently. "Trust me."

"Are you sure?"

Jae-Hyun gave him a hard stare. "Just do it."

Vadeem slowly nodded. "Okay . . . so how do you want to do this?"

"I'll launch myself off you. Just give me a proper boost when I make contact."

"All right, and full force?"

"Full force."

Without another word, Jae-Hyun dashed toward the other man. Vadeem barely had time to get into position before the regressor's feet landed squarely on the big man's interlocked hands. With an audible grunt, Vadeem used that momentum to push Jae-Hyun off him as hard as he could, sending the regressor flying straight into the densely packed harpies.

All of us stopped what we were doing to see just how this would play out. Jae-Hyun was swinging with alacrity as he traveled through the air, basically vaporizing anything that was caught in his spear's radius along the way. However, the regressor was going at such insane speeds that I was pretty sure that he'd be at least injured if he crashed into the walls, if not outright killed.

Yet right when he was about to splatter into the wall, he abruptly stopped, his momentum seemingly disappearing completely, and he gently landed on his feet. It was like watching a poorly edited film, seeing him completely stop like that.

"What the hell did you do?" I asked. "How'd you stop like that?"

"A skill," he answered. "My class allows me to control time very briefly, so I slowed it down right when I was about to hit the wall."

That hardly seemed like a time ability, but who was I to argue with the guy? That was when another thought hit me. "Wait, what about all that energy from you speeding off like a bullet? Where'd it all go?"

He smiled. "You noticed, that's good. You might want to cover your ears, but watch."

Not sure what he meant, we did as instructed. Jae-Hyun saw a low-hanging harpy. It was disoriented and still trying to recover from the regressor's earlier assault. Our leader slowly stabbed his spear toward it, his movement slow, almost lackadaisical. The spear tip made contact with a soft touch.

Then the harpy vaporized.

It, along with everything in a cone-shaped area behind it. A huge shock wave of force rocked the six of us, and we all stared wide-eyed at the scene before us.

Jae-Hyun grinned. "That's where the energy went."

We all stared at the scene in disbelief. None of us had anything witty to say. Even his sister was surprised at the destruction her brother could unleash.

His one strike practically killed off the entire horde of harpies, and the cleanup was easily done by our three archers. I was still in shock at the true capabilities that the regressor possessed as the last of the flying monsters died.

"What are you all waiting for?" Jae-Hyun said as he walked forward. "Let's get going."

"Yeah . . ." I muttered as I took one last look at the sheer, casual destruction that he just caused. I made a note never to antagonize that goddamn freak of nature.

CHAPTER TWENTY-SIX

A Delve into the Depths Part 3

The six of us followed Jae-Hyun closely behind, still a little shocked at his earlier display of power. Only his sister's expression was different; she showed off a proud look, clearly happy with her brother's abilities.

"What the hell did you do, boss?" Vadeem finally asked. "It looked like you nuked the damn birds from orbit."

He smirked. "I stored all that potential energy from your throw and unleashed it all at once in a concentrated cone. You have yourself to thank for the power behind that strike."

"Damn . . ." Vadeem muttered before flexing an arm and smiling to himself. "I'm good!"

Noel rolled her eyes. "It was the boss who did all the hard work."

"But I provided the muscles!" He smiled back. "I'd like to see you do that, Noel!"

The twins nodded approvingly as they flexed to show their solidarity for Team Muscle. I hoped it was just a phase they were going through and they didn't actually end up Vadeem-sized in the future . . .

"How come you didn't use that trick when we fought the six-armed guy or the golem back then?" Yoona asked. "It would have saved us a lot of time at the second trial."

"I couldn't use it then," he answered simply. "I just unlocked the skill after clearing that stage, and it has its limitations as well. Can't use it that often."

We waited a second for him to elaborate on what those limitations were, but of course, he didn't choose to do so. Well, not that I blamed him completely; the less we knew about his weakness, the less likely that kind of information could be spread to people he didn't trust. The fact that we knew that it couldn't be used continuously was good enough, I suppose. But the fact that there were limitations at all was good to know. It meant that not even the regressor's absurd class was without its downsides.

"What about the cores from those harpies?" I asked as I finally remembered why we were here in the first place. "Shouldn't we get some from the bodies you didn't vaporize?"

"No point," he answered calmly. "They're not worth the effort; we'll get more cores of that quality from the other aspirants than we can ever harvest for ourselves. For now, we need to head in deeper. I'll let everyone know when we need to be careful about how we dispatch our enemies."

"Aye-aye, boss!"

We followed the regressor down seemingly random passageways and tunnels, occasionally having to bend down and even crawl when the passages became too narrow. Thankfully we seemed to have eliminated the entire harpy community around here and were not harassed further. Still, the dank network of cave passages made for dismal travel, which was made worse by how large Vadeem was.

I wasn't sure how the regressor knew where he was going, but his strides never faltered for even a second, and we eventually made it out of the increasingly narrow cave tunnels and into something that resembled a man-made passage. The rock walls and ceilings were still untreated and bare, but at least clear signs of excavation could be made out, and it only improved as we went farther and farther down the downward-sloping walkway.

Our group eventually reached the end of the passage. The tunnel had long since morphed into an industrial hallway, although not a very well-maintained one. Our journey down the creepy hallway ended in a large metal door, where a complicated-looking lock had sealed the entrance shut.

"Wait," the regressor said as we stepped in front of the firm barrier, "there's something else that we need to be mindful of when we're working as a group."

"Man, it's like you're teaching a bunch of kids," Noel mumbled. "Can't we just go in real quick-like and explain this stuff after?"

The regressor shook his head. "No, this is probably our only opportunity to learn firsthand the skills we'll need for the upcoming trials. Our main goal is to learn, so we do this the slow way."

It seemed like Jae-Hyun was really reflecting off that disaster that hit us in the last trial and was pushing for us to learn the necessary information and ways of thinking that he undoubtedly had to learn the hard way in his past life. It wasn't that bad, as the regressor made for a pretty good teacher, all things considered, and these were important skills that were necessary for our survival. I couldn't say no to not dying!

Noel sighed but ultimately saw the wisdom in Jae-Hyun's words as well. "Fine, we do it the boring way. What's the thing we have to be mindful of, boss?"

"It's how we deal with unknowns," he continued as he gestured at the door. "For instance, how would you open this door?"

"Break through it, of course!"

"Find an alternative passage?"

"I'd try picking the lock."

Vadeem, Yoona, and I all spoke up at the same time, and I frowned when I realized that all of our answers were different. I was pretty sure I was right, though. Vadeem's strategy left no room for subtlety, and Noel? Like, how would we even look for another passage right now? Waste all of our time going back and testing out random tunnels until we found the right one?

The regressor chuckled. "All three answers are fine on their own, but we won't know which course of action is correct without more information. We will not act rashly without more information, especially in the future when we cannot afford to make mistakes."

"So we need scout work! You should have just said that first!" Noel answered brightly. "Oh, oh, let me do it this time, like we did in that creepy dark place!"

I raised an eyebrow. I hadn't been with the regressor's group when they were separated back in the second trial, and I'd only been told the general information about what had happened on their end. Getting more concrete information out of Noel was a lesson in futility, and it wasn't like the regressor was the most social person in the world. This meant that the only person I could ask was Yoona, but she had been unconscious for most of the trial, and I didn't want to stir up any uncomfortable memories for the girl.

Jae-Hyun nodded and gestured for his sister to do something.

The other girl took out an arrow and looked at the rest of us. "Um, you guys should stand back for a bit."

We did so, unsure what she was about to do.

"Thank you."

She held the arrow's shaft and furrowed her brows in concentration. Soon, the tip of her arrow started to glow a bright red before turning white hot. The temperature around her grew steadily until it reached an uncomfortable degree. This process continued for about a minute before the girl was content with the progress, and she shoved the white-hot arrowhead right into the door.

The metal door sizzled as the area contacting the arrow melted rapidly. The door was thick, maybe several inches, clearly designed to keep things contained, yet it was no match for whatever Yoona did with her arrow. It took the high schooler almost no time at all for her to form a hole the size of a baseball into the side of the door. She smiled in satisfaction.

"Do we . . . peer into the hole?" Vadeem asked as he inspected the new opening. "I guess it's one way of scouting."

"No, Vadeem," Noel answered with exaggerated annoyance. "Watch how Noel does things!"

Noel transformed into her strange flame form and squeezed her incorporeal body into the hole. It was a little strange seeing something human-shaped just flow through an opening that small, but then again, so was seeing someone melt solid steel with an arrow or explode a group of supernatural monsters with a spear. You would think I would be used to such sights by now.

Noel emerged a few minutes later and gave us a thumbs-up before turning back into flesh.

"Situation looks clear on the other side," the girl said. "But the other side's just more hallways and stuff. There's some abandoned jail cells and other locked doors everywhere on the sides, but no people or baddies."

"Thank you, Noel," the regressor said. "No immediate danger on the other side, but we should still be cautious. Vadeem, would you do the honors?"

"With pleasure!"

We all moved back as Vadeem's massive paws sank into the door, the force of his hold so strong that his fingers made dents in the metal. With a grunt, the door, and more concerningly, the entire foundation, shook before the hinges gave out and the huge metal object was lifted free. He gave us a smile of triumph and placed the door gently to the side.

"And that, Noel," Vadeem said with a condescending grin, "is how Vadeem does things. It's better than her way, right, girls?"

The twins bobbed their heads up and down before flexing their own muscles.

"You're going to rot their brains." Noel sighed.

"Um, usually I don't always agree with Noel, but you should correct their strange behaviors, Vadeem," Yoona added.

"I will," he answered, which I was almost certain was a lie, "but let's go in first, yeah?"

"Once again, wait," Jae-Hyun said as he blocked Vadeem's path with an arm. "Remember that this place was meant to keep things contained; it's one of the exits to Tartarus. Do you think that the only safeguard in place was one door?"

"So what," he answered, "expect traps?"

"Yes, although most of them should have been deactivated by now, but we must still be careful."

Vadeem sighed. "So more scout work. I wasn't built for this slow-going cautious approach."

Yoona poked her head through the newly created opening. "Should Noel go again?"

"Let the twins have a try," he answered. "It's what they grew up doing, and it's their primary role in our party. Let them practice in an unfamiliar environment."

"Won't that be dangerous, though?" Vadeem added. "You said these traps were built to contain enemies of the literal gods. Those must be lethal, even with our abilities."

"As I said, most of the dangerous stuff's been deactivated already, and these levels only house very minor entities. This isn't even technically a part of Tartarus proper. Do you honestly think a metal door would contain Titans and the Kraken?"

Vadeem grumbled but ultimately relented to the regressor's words. He was still protective of the two girls, having all but adopted them, but he also understood just what situation we were all in. He couldn't shelter them, not completely at least, without stunting their growth, although I don't think he liked that fact.

The twins looked at Vadeem and gave him a thumbs-up.

"All right," the man sighed. "Just be careful."

They skirted off into the entranceway, wearing expressions of intense concentration, and entered the empty hallway on the other side. I sat close by so that my halo could illuminate as much of the interior as possible, which also gave me the best view of what they were doing. This was my first time seeing the twins work up close. They had always been with Vadeem or off on their own.

Now, I wasn't exactly sure what to expect when it came to scouting. Maybe they would inspect each floor tile for traps or dodge laser beams like in the movies, but the actual thing was different. It was a lot more dull.

The twins just moved slowly. They would glance down every now and then, sometimes one of the twins would point at something before communicating in their unique, silent way, but there was literally nothing of interest to see as an observer. They just moved about. So I just sat there and provided light as the twins meticulously swept the area for traps. Occasionally they would note something and avoid an area, but that was it.

They came back maybe half an hour later and did their best to report what they found. I could understand that they were trying to say thanks to Noe, but the others, even Vadeem in this case, seemed utterly lost.

"Uh, I can translate," I offered. "I've been with them for long enough, and that skill that allows me to understand what those villagers said works a little with body language as well."

"That's useful," Yoona said with a smile. "Wish I had a cool innate ability like that."

I nodded. "Speaking of which, what innate talent do you have?"

"Um, just a better grasp on mana," she answered. "I guess it's nice to have, but I wouldn't know what it's like if it wasn't there, so I can't really say how useful it is."

Yoona looked at me before quickly adding, "Not that it's important to have mana, of course. Um, it's not all that great, honestly, so don't feel too bad."

I smiled at her consideration for my unique situation before turning to Vadeem and Noel. "And what about you two? Don't think you ever told us."

Vadeem shrugged. "Yeah, 'cause it's not that impressive, honestly. All it does is give me more strength, not that I mind, though."

"I got one that focuses on endurance," Noel answered next. "I guess all of these innate abilities are passives, huh?"

Come to think of it, she was right. My actual innate ability was that Calm Mind/Awakening Mind skill, which just sat there in the background doing its thing. I wouldn't have even noticed it if it weren't for how strange our last trial was. The more I learned about how Central and its stupid Trash Matrix worked, the more I realized just how structured things were. This was good, because structure meant predictability, and predictability meant that I could anticipate what the Trash Matrix could do. But more importantly, I could find ways to exploit those limitations.

The twins were annoyed at the interruption of their report and nudged Vadeem to do something about it. I guess they were still a little too shy to bother me about most things. Vadeem gave me an apologetic nod, telling me to focus on the two instead.

"Oh, sorry," I said quickly. "I got off topic. Uh, tell us what you two found, please."

They made strange gestures, sometimes pointing at a wall, followed by some hand signals. I had no idea how they came up with such a complicated communication method all by themselves.

"All right," I translated, "so here's the areas that we should avoid . . ."

CHAPTER TWENTY-SEVEN

A Delve into the Depths Part 4

Yoona imbued her arrows with more mana and sent them flying toward the locations that the twins marked. Most of the hits didn't seem to have any visible effect, but a few that landed on odd spots made an audible pop followed by some static discharge. Whatever Yoona's arrows were doing was activating the traps but didn't cause them to set off.

"Okay, that's all of them," Yoona said. "Are there any more spots we have to watch out for?"

The twins made more complicated gestures as I translated. "Uh, they're saying that the doors look, sorry, I mean they feel strange, so you should be careful if we want to open them. Other than that, there's . . . Uh, sorry, some of these gestures don't translate well into words."

The twins sighed and slowed down their hand signals. "Okay, so there's also another set of stairs going down farther along the path, and they say that they don't like the feeling of what's down there. Not because of traps, but it's the feeling they got when they used to scout for danger. That about accurate?"

The twins nodded.

"Then we're good for now unless we want to open those side doors, and there's more danger if we go down the stairs," Vadeem summarized and ruffled the twins' hair. "Sounds simple enough. Good job, you two."

The two smiled more expressively than I'd ever seen them show previously, before that fleeting smile disappeared just as quickly, and they focused their attention back on the present.

Jae-Hyun gave us the all-clear, and we entered the new room. Like what I had seen in the hallway, the room was just one wide corridor with small jail cells locked with sturdy-looking metal. None of the cells were occupied, or even showed signs that they once were. They were entirely empty, without even a raised platform to use as a bed and looked more like unused storage areas than anything that used to hold people.

In fact, the interior was too barren of anything. Other than the minor security measures that the twins delt with, there was nothing in this huge chamber. Even with ruins or abandoned buildings, it wouldn't be uncommon to see decayed furnishings, rust stains, and broken materials strewn about. After all, the distinct signs of use would be otherwise impossible to hide even if someone tried their best to thoroughly clean the place out.

But this place looked like it was abandoned before it ever got to be used. Yet it clearly was used, or at least partly, if someone went through the trouble of rigging those traps. Even the bars and cell doors looked to be in relatively pristine condition, aside from the fine layer of dust that settled on everything here. This strange disconnect made the entire place feel suffocating.

"It's getting creepier and creepier the farther down we get," Vadeem grumbled. "Feels like something'll just pop out of a corner and ambush us at any moment."

Noel nodded. "Kind of like one of those sci-fi horror movies. Always loved those films! You think there's something stalking us in these hallways? I bet it's got big teeth and acid spit!"

Yoona shuddered. "Please stop. I don't like the thought of being followed like that . . ."

"If it's any consolation," I added, "we have faced worse in the trials so far."

That didn't help the girl's unease, and she shuddered a little harder. Jae-Hyun noticed and moved a little closer to his sister.

"There's nothing stalking us," he said sternly. "There won't even be any living creatures until we move farther down, but it's nothing we cannot handle, and it won't sneak up on us if we scout properly."

"What about the ominous feeling the twins got earlier?" I asked. "There's something down those stairs."

"That's where Tartarus starts officially," the regressor explained. "We're in the holding cells right now; it was barely used even back when the Olympians used to live here."

That would explain why this place was so empty, and I doubt they'd keep the really nasty stuff just locked up in simple cages. Not like that would do anything to stop those monsters from escaping.

"Is it a good idea to head down there, then? You even said you don't know what's down there . . ." Yoona asked uncertainly. "I'm not too well versed in the myths, but even I know that Tartarus isn't a place you'd want to visit."

"While I don't know what's at the bottom," he said, "I do know what's near the surface. Tartarus is divided into different sections, with the worst inmates housed at the bottom. The situation is still the same now—the weakest creatures will be found near the top, away from the resources. We won't go past a certain layer, at least not now, and even then, most of the really nasty things have already been moved out of here."

I just hoped Jae-Hyun wasn't simply overestimating our abilities. Even if the gods took the really problematic creatures out, I didn't think even minor creatures of myth would be an easy foe for newly awakened aspirants, no matter how abnormal our situations were. Then again, Jae-Hyun did bring his sister with us, and I doubt he'd allow much harm to befall her.

"What can we expect down there?" I asked. "In the first layer, I mean."

"Hopefully not more of those damned winged freaks," Vadeem grumbled. "I don't do well with anything flying in the air."

"You'll get your wish, Vadeem," Jae-Hyun answered. "The harpies only have a nest deeper in the cave system. They're not actual residents of Tartarus."

"Good."

"What's at the end of that staircase," the regressor continued, "will be the weakest of the leftovers. We can't be sure until we arrive, but whatever's down there will be half starved and half dead. However, a word of advice: *Never* underestimate anything that appears in Tartarus, no matter how pathetic they look."

We all gave Jae-Hyun various forms of affirmation before heading down the stairs. These ones were narrow, much more so than any of the passages we came from, and Vadeem had to move sideways just to fit.

"These stairs better end soon," Vadeem muttered as he forced his way through a particularly tight area, "or this passage will become Vadeem-shaped very soon because I'll have to force my way through!"

"There'll be another locked door down below, then it'll open up from then on out," the regressor's muffled reply came somewhere behind the big man. I couldn't see him since I was in front of Vadeem. "We don't have to worry about traps there, just burst through the door when you see it."

"Understood!" I said at the front. "I'll do the honors this time. I don't think I want to see Vadeem try to get past me."

"I heard squid could fit in really small holes, though!" Noel said beside me. "Maybe you can do the same!"

That was a disconcerting thing to imagine. I highly doubted I wanted to test out Noel's hypothesis to see just how squid-like the Xollons were.

"I think I'll just open the door myself," I answered instead.

To everyone's joy, we reached the door soon after, and I was able to yank it free of its hinges easily enough. My feelers provided an easy grip for me to hoist the door right off, and I was quite amazed by how strong I was. I mean, I knew that my stats had grown astronomically—I had a pathetic 4 Strength when I first started out—but I never really internalized how much growth I'd undergone.

All the fights that I'd gone through felt too surreal. My brain wasn't really processing what it meant to kill strange harpies or mutated horrors since there was no normal analog for that action. That was why it wasn't until I effortlessly dismantled this door that I finally realized how far along I'd gone, and I felt a little giddy seeing all this. I felt like a superhero, and maybe even understood Vadeem's need to lift really heavy stuff for fun, just to see my limits.

Once the door was clear of the passage, the seven of us entered one by one, with Vadeem having to all but destroy the doorframe to get in. True to the regressor's words, the interior expanded, but what he didn't choose to mention was that the interior of Tartarus proper looked like another dimension entirely.

I was pretty sure that the space we were in couldn't physically exist, unless my spatial reasoning completely lost it, because the "room" we were in extended as far as the eye could see. The only wall visible before us was the tiny doorway that brought us here, and the ceiling loomed hundreds of feet above us, glowing faintly with some kind of iridescent blue light. Maybe it was some kind of bioluminescence, but the twinkling lights looked remarkably similar to the night sky.

Stranger still, Noe notified me that my nighttime passive was activated the second I stepped foot into this place, which further confirmed the fact that we must have been taken to some kind of alternative plane of being. The faint illumination provided us with enough light to operate even without my halo on, and I chose to deactivate the thing so that I wasn't a beacon informing everything in Tartarus of our presence.

"Where the hell are we?" Vadeem muttered as he bent down and touched the ground. The big man picked up a handful of dirt and sniffed it.

"Why are you smelling the ground?" Yoona asked. "Is there something special about it?"

He shook his head. "No, but I felt weird the second I stepped in here, and I think I know why. The dirt doesn't . . . I don't know, it doesn't feel right. Like it's not the stuff we see out in Pandora or even in that strange corrupted Earth. Feels wrong."

Noel looked at the big man with confusion. "Dunno about you, Vadeem, but I kind of like it here. Feels homey."

"Wait, you can . . . feel the earth?" Yoona interrupted. "Is that a skill?"

Vadeem shrugged. "Something like that, I guess, but I've always felt closer to the earth even before all this nonsense hit us. Felt it stronger when I got through that zombie level. Think it's from my class."

Vadeem's behavior was most likely caused by his Titan-related job, but if he'd always had an affinity with the earth, then it pointed to my second theory that the classes given by the Trash Matrix used information already present in the aspirants. Most likely the same thing was going on with Noel and her underworldesque class. That was good to know, although I wasn't sure when this information would prove useful.

"Still, this place is so . . . strange. I don't get any of the comforting vibes you have, Noel," Yoona remarked as she gazed into the distance. "It's like we're in another reality altogether."

"It's because we are," Jae-Hyun answered. "Or, more accurately, it's a pocket dimension."

"Uh, and we can leave this place anytime we want, right?" I asked, looking at the stairs, fearing they would just vanish at any moment.

"We can," he assured. "It wasn't always the case, but even Nyx's enchantments are corroded with the passage of time."

"That's the, uh, night goddess, right?" I asked. It had been a long time since I'd read up on the gods after all.

"One of the primordial gods, in fact, and consort to Erebus." The regressor nodded. "Avoid her and her husband at all costs if you ever meet them."

"You say that like we'd actually meet gods." Vadeem laughed. He quickly stopped when he saw that the regressor wasn't joking. "Uh, we're not going to actually meet gods, right?"

"I'd want to meet one!" Noel chimed in with a smile. "I mean, they must be awesome to be called gods, although I'm not a mythology nerd like you guys are. I bet it'd be cool to pick their brains!"

The regressor gave her a hard glare, his voice icy. "Never do that."

Even Noel shuddered at his unconcealed fury. She quickly put her hands up and muttered, "Okay, okay, I'm just joking! I'll, um, I'll make sure I don't talk to godly strangers."

"We get it. We do not speak with the gods," I said. "So what's the plan from here on out? Just find random stuff to kill? There doesn't seem like there's a lot here."

Which was true. Aside from the noise from our chatter, nothing else could be heard. If anything was around us, they most certainly would have noticed our arrival.

"We're heading farther in," he explained. "We'll mark this location so we can get out, but there is a specific spot that I want to reach before we head back."

"And that is?" I asked.

"One of the hidden forges of Hephaestus."

CHAPTER TWENTY-EIGHT

The Search Part 1

Wait, why would Hephaestus have a forge all the way in Tartarus?" I asked. "I thought this place was a prison for the Olympians' enemies, not for one of their gods."

The regressor laughed. "You should have paid more attention to your classes if you think the smith god was treated the same way as the others. He was despised by most of his peers because of his deformities, especially by his mother. They thought that the gods should all be perfect, as if any of them were."

Jae-Hyun gave a mocking, bitter chuckle. "Hephaestus has probably spent more time in Tartarus than on the outside because of one perceived infraction or another. His hatred for the gods most likely eclipses my own. It's why he's the one god that has most likely left something for us to steal."

"Why do you hate them so much, boss?" Noel asked, uncharacteristically curious for once. "You must have met them already, right?"

"I have my reasons," he said in that same voice that left no doubt that he wouldn't explain further.

Yoona quickly noticed his unease about the topic—she was most likely the real reason he was so bitter—and decided to speak up. "And they threw him in the worst place on earth because of that? That seems unnecessarily harsh, brother."

"You will find that the gods are always harsh," he replied. "Their way of thinking isn't the same as ours, and things like familial ties do not exist between them."

Vadeem looked at the twins with a hint of worry before replying with a sigh. "That's rough . . . family's important."

He walked over to the twins and gave the two a friendly pat on the shoulders. "I'm not sure how you two lived before, but we're family now, all of us here, okay?"

Ana looked over at her sister and nodded slowly. Eva gave the big man a thumbs-up before both of them were engulfed in a massive bear hug.

"I've always wanted a sister, or two in this case," Yoona said with a smile. "It's always been my brother taking care of me all this time."

Even the regressor looked at the two girls with a silent smile. I think he was too embarrassed to say anything else. Noel just shrugged as if what Vadeem said was already an established fact.

"Well," I said finally, "welcome to the Abyss family, then, Ana and Eva."

The two were still hesitant to interact with me too much, maybe because they still thought that I was some kind of deity, but I'd noticed that their behaviors had started to shift in the last few days. I think they realized that I wasn't a literal god, or at least not the holier-than-thou kind that the regressor seemed to hate, but they still needed some more time before they could feel completely comfortable around me. I wasn't going to rush them.

"So do you know where the forge is located, boss?" Noel asked. "Let's get there fast so we can focus on getting cores! I'm itching to fight something that doesn't fly!"

"I do not," the regressor admitted. It seemed like this is a rare case where the man didn't have all the answers. I guess he never had the chance to fully explore Tartarus in his past life.

"Um, so we just search the whole place?" Yoona asked. "Won't that take too long?"

"There are hints," her brother answered. "The layout of Tartarus used to change daily to prevent escape attempts, but that function has long since ceased to work. But that wasn't the case before, so Hephaestus had to have created something to guide him back to his forges each time he got sent back here. We look for those."

"Do you know what exactly we're searching for?" Yoona inquired again. She seemed pumped to help out after her extended absence in that last trial.

"No," Jae-Hyun said. "But check for inconsistencies around, maybe a small mark on the floor, places with condensed mana, anything that looks like it doesn't belong. It shouldn't be too well hidden. Nothing else in Tartarus back in the day, at least on this layer, would have tried to look for these clues."

"Understood, boss!"

"We split up to search," he continued. "There doesn't appear to be any-thing near us, but if you find trouble, we regroup and fight together. Use the system message to communicate, and if there's danger, Walter will use his halo and we use him as a beacon to meet up. Don't leave the immediate surroundings of the staircase."

I was a little peeved that I was being used as a portable light source again, but I guess that's life. We agreed with the leader's suggestions, not that we ever had anything to critique his strategies.

"Wait a second," I said before we could all scatter, "why can't the twins use the system chat to talk?"

Everyone stopped what they were doing and frowned.

"I tried that before," Vadeem said, "but I didn't know how to have them use the system chat. I always thought they couldn't use the same tools we did." Vadeem turned to the regressor. "I mean, they didn't come into the trials the normal way."

The two girls looked at the rest of the party in confusion. They weren't sure what we were talking about.

"Um, let me ask," I said. "Ana, Eva, do you see any see-through screens sometimes?"

The two nodded, then made a series of gestures.

"Oh," I continued as Noe did its thing. "They say that saw it, but they couldn't read any of the information. I guess the system doesn't translate writ-ten text."

"Will the things they say be translated into English if they use the chat, though?" Yoona asked. "It won't be much help if they send us text we can't read."

"That shouldn't be a problem . . ." Jae-Hyun said after thinking for a while. "At least that's the case with the chat system when it's used between two normal aspirants. You can think in Korean and it'll still look like English on their end, Yoona."

Yoona: Does it really do that?

"Yeah, it does," I answered, "unless you thought that part in English as well."

"But . . . can they even read at all, though?" Yoona added. "They've been in that weird Earth all this time, so what if they're illiterate?"

"That shouldn't matter, either," her brother answered. "It should translate directly into a language they can understand. At least with the system chat. There are a lot of others here who can't read or write."

The regressor then knelt down and spoke to the twins. "All right, I sent you two a party invite, so a screen should have popped up. Can you just say yes in your head?"

They nodded and did so.

"Okay, good, I'll need you two to do this . . ."

The regressor then took the next ten minutes trying to find a way for them to access the party message system, having the girls draw out what they saw on their end on the floor so he could properly navigate them through the series of screens. I didn't know that the Trash Matrix mainly communicated its features through text, which was so unlike Noe.

"It is because I am better, my host," she chimed in.

Yup, you certainly are!

Muscle A: Are we doing this right?
Muscle E: Is this ok?

"It works!" Vadeem shouted as he rushed up to hug the two. "You can talk! Well, sort of!"

Muscle A: You are squeezing us.
Muscle E: But we do not mind.

"Okay," Noel added, raising an eyebrow. "I know that I'm not one to talk, but those nicknames . . ."

Vadeem put down the squashed children and glared at Noel. "And what's wrong with the nicknames they gave themselves? This is probably the first time they've chosen anything on their own. Are you saying their naming choice is bad?"

The redhead shivered. "Um, no, it's nothing! I, uh, I just wanted to say that you two did good!"

"That's right," Vadeem grumbled, still giving the woman a warning look. I guess Vadeem could fight back when he really wanted to, and Noel knew what buttons to not push on her friend.

"It's good to see that you can communicate with us now!" Yoona added to defuse the situation. "Um, it's good to properly greet you!"

Muscle A: Thank you, Sister Yoona.
Muscle E: Thanks.

The high schooler almost melted when she read that, although they dodged her attempts to hug them. Guess she really did want a little sister of her own. It would be good for them to properly tell us what they thought. I'd mostly forgotten that they were there most of the time given how eerily quiet they were most of the time. It would be interesting to see how the two differed since they'd pretty much always remained together. I kind of just lumped them in as one entity most of the time.

The regressor nodded at the progress made but quickly refocused us on the task at hand. We weren't in a safe location, so the proper introductions could wait. Once the novelty of the situation wore off, we all went our separate ways to see if we could find Hephaestus's elusive clues.

I looked around the barren ground, not entirely sure what I was doing. Occasionally I'd use a feeler to turn around some big rocks, but I was more or less wandering around. With my Bringer of Dawn's Light passive, I could see perfectly well in the darkness, and I was pretty sure that there was nothing of note in my patch of Tartarus. The place was just an eerily flat expanse of dirt, rocks, and that ever-present glowing moss.

I was certain that there was nothing here, unless Hephaestus decided to bury whatever he decided to use to guide him to his forge. I noticed the others in the distance looking a lot more productive than I was. Noel was even flying through the sky, checking out the various areas that we couldn't get to on foot. All I did was poke my feelers into the ground every now and then, hoping to find something. It was awfully boring.

"Brother!" Yoona shouted, just as I was contemplating what kind of shadow puppets I could feasibly create with my new limbs. "There's something strange here!"

Yoona: Sorry, I forgot you said to communicate using this. Um, there's something strange over where I am.

Lady Awesome: I see you. My little bro's close by as well. We can use his lightbulb head and meet up.

Walter's Fine: Hey, I resent that. It's a halo!

Vadeem the Dream: I'm afraid it does look like a lightbulb from farther away, my friend.

Jae-Hyun: Meet up with him there.

Muscle A: Got it, boss!

Muscle E: Ok.

We used my halo to meet up shortly after, and Yoona pointed at a spot on the ground. It looked like all the other spots on the ground to me.

"There's an unusual flow of mana there. Can you guys feel it?" the girl asked. "Maybe I'm looking too hard."

Vadeem stepped closer and brought some of the dirt closer. "Yeah, it's a little different, you're right. This patch feels more like the earth we have upstairs."

Jae-Hyun joined him and dug his spear into the spot. He did something with his weapon, the same black electricity crackling from the tip before a faint glow erupted from the ground and formed a line. No, it formed a path.

"Right," I muttered, "of course it's got to do with mana."

Yoona winced; she must have felt bad about my condition since she was the most mana-sensitive out of the whole group.

"It's fine," I reassured her. "At least I got cool tentacles."

Vadeem gave me a cautious glance and whispered, "Walter, uh, you might not want to say that in front of the ladies."

I sighed. Yeah, that was probably true. It seemed that even my most powerful tools were creepy.

"Let's follow the trail before it fades," Jae-Hyun added quickly, his voice cutting in and stopping our banter.

His job had been increasingly more about keeping our party on task and focused lately, as we tended to go off-topic whenever there was even a slight lull in the atmosphere. Probably something else to work on in the future if I knew the regressor's standards for discipline.

"All right, let's go deeper, then."

CHAPTER TWENTY-NINE

The Search Part 2

We went off, following the trails left behind from an ancient god who used to dwell here eons ago. These sorts of insane situations had become so mundane that I didn't even question things any longer. I started to wonder when my mindset had become so warped. Well, I guess too much of anything and you start becoming desensitized.

The guiding light of mana crossed over barren, dead land for a significant amount of time. So long, in fact, that we had to set up camp for a while just to take a breather and get refreshed. I suppose between the harpies, the climbing, and everything in between, a lot of time had passed, and I hadn't noticed the accumulating fatigue until I sat down for the first time.

But our rests were never more than a few minutes long, just enough time to eat some solid food and get a drink of water. The regressor was quite the stickler for proper nutrition and hydration, and he seemed to have some kind of supernatural talent for finding the perfect time to order one of these rest periods. These breaks were timed perfectly right before any one of us would become too tired that our thinking and performance were negatively impacted.

Honestly, Jae-Hyun made for the perfect leader for any excursion. He was knowledgeable, deadly, and most importantly, he knew the limits of every single one of his charges. I felt pretty happy to just let him take control and follow blindly, even with my unique situation within Central.

I could only imagine this man growing further and further. Maybe I could help accelerate that growth and point him the Overseer's way . . . but I'd also have to somehow prevent him from damaging the people I cared for. I still had to properly think about how to approach this particular problem, but that was something for later.

Eventually, the regressor saw that we had rested enough and made us leave again. The glowing mana trail had started to dim a little, so we had to pick up our pace. It wasn't until late in the evening—according to Noe, in any case, as it was hard to tell the time of day when the Tartarus was completely underground—that we reached the end of the trail. By that point, the only one who could still sense Hephaestus's signal was Yoona, and we had to trust her instincts to guide us the rest of the way.

After a certain point, we didn't need Yoona to show us the way anymore, since we were going toward the only structure that we'd seen so far. Well, perhaps *structure* wasn't the right word for it. There was a single entrance, and all around it was a solid wall that stretched all the way up to the ceiling.

"Think there's a minotaur in there?" I joked, pointing to the labyrinth's entrance.

"There is one," the regressor said softly. "It'll be easier to explore the place once we've gotten rid of it."

"You're joking, right?" I asked. "We're not fighting that thing that almost did in Theseus, right?"

"We are," Jae-Hyun answered. "Although it's probably not the same creature. That one's been dead for a long time."

"Lovely . . ." I muttered. "And I suppose you have a ball of string we could use to find our way out again?"

The regressor shrugged. "Why would we need that? Once we find and kill the beast, we'll have Vadeem open us a shortcut. Why did you think I asked him to buy that maul in the first place?"

Wouldn't that be cheating, though? But then again, when did the regressor ever operate on normal-people logic? I almost felt bad for the guy responsible for building this elaborate structure, probably dreaming up the best ways to trap unsuspecting trespassers, only for a big dude with an even bigger hammer to smash all of his hard work into nothing. But I suppose we couldn't just spend the time navigating the maze the old-fashioned way. It was a pity, though, because I learned some labyrinth-solving techniques back in the rest area after seeing how complex Q's workplace was.

"I like the sound of that!" Vadeem added. "Do we smash first and find the minotaur to kill, or kill first and then smash our way through?"

"We go in first," Jae-Hyun answered. "We need the minotaur's core, and I can't risk scaring it if we go in like that."

Oh . . . so it wasn't us who should be afraid of the minotaur like I had thought—it was the other way around. Now I was starting to feel a little bad for the creature like I did the maze's architect. I wouldn't want to be anything that got in the way of the regressor's plans.

"How do we attract the big cow?" Noel asked. "I say we roast Vadeem a little over a fire and use him as bait. I'll bet the minotaur'll come rushing out to eat him."

I looked at the big man. "He's too gamey, too lean, probably won't taste too good."

Vadeem looked at me and grumbled, "Not you too, Walter! Noel's infecting you with her stupidity."

"I'm joking," I said seriously. "I'm sure you'd be delicious, Vadeem."

He just sighed and walked toward the others, shaking his head. Noel gave me a thumbs-up.

"You're all being distracted again. If this happens when we're in the trials, then it could prove deadly," the regressor grumbled. "We'll have to address this problem once we're out of here."

"Sorry, boss!" Noel apologized. "Can't help myself."

"I was getting carried away as well, sorry," I admitted. "Just wanted to lighten the mood was all. So what is the actual plan?"

"Noel's idea isn't technically incorrect," Jae-Hyun said. I saw Noel about to say something witty, but a quick disapproving glare from the regressor shut her up again. "The minotaur is sensitive to smell. It was a part of the reason these labyrinths were built in the first place."

"Ah, the food suitcase then?" I asked.

He nodded. "Yes, the food suitcase."

Vadeem took the thing out from his storage and opened it up.

"What do minotaurs like to eat?" he asked, peering into its bottomless contents. "Walter's been busy stocking it up with practically everything in Pandora, so we're spoiled for choice."

"Meat," Jae-Hyun said, "raw meat, preferably. You should have some cooking ingredients in there as well, right?"

Vadeem took out an entire boar carcass from his case. It still had most of the fur on it. How it even fit in there was beyond me, and I was definitely not the one who bought that thing.

"Way ahead of you, boss." He smirked, putting the huge slab of meat on his shoulder. "I think this will do nicely."

"The boss said we shouldn't be distracted," Noel muttered, "so I won't question why you thought it would be a good idea to bring that with you, but . . ."

The regressor gave her another one of those chilly stares.

"But I won't say anything this time," the redhead continued. "See? I can follow instructions, too! Unlike Vadeem, I can actually learn!"

"You didn't have to add that last part in, though." I sighed.

The regressor nodded. "Good, now there's something else I want us to work on, and it's how we lead a group."

"But you're the leader, leader," Noel said quizzically. "You're going to do all the leading."

"We can't count on that all the time," Jae-Hyun explained. "Who's to say something like the last trial won't happen again? Walter did a great job guiding Vadeem, but what happens if he's with me and the rest of you are together instead? Would you know who will be in charge then?"

"Oh," Noel replied. "Good point. I'm more used to working alone, and Vadeem . . ." She gave the man a disapproving glance.

Vadeem sighed. "I will readily admit that I am a poor leader. I've already told Walter as much. If we only followed the stuff I think of, we'd probably still be in that damn creepy darkness. I'm sure I can work something out if it's just me and Noel together. We've worked fine as a duo before, but with the others to consider . . ."

"It'll be a mess," Noel finished. "So we follow . . . Yoona, then?"

The high school turned wide-eyed. "I—I can't do that! You two are a lot older than me, so surely it'll be better to follow Noel, at least?"

The other girl laughed. "Yeah, as awesome as I am, that's not really an option, bestie. I'm not the best at telling peeps what to do."

Yeah, that was for sure. If even I had a hard time trying to guess her nebulous methods of thinking and communication, then I could only imagine how impossible a task that would be for anyone else. If Vadeem made for a poor leader, then Noel made for an absolutely terrible one.

"You're used to giving orders already," the regressor added. "You were the captain of your archery team back home."

Yoona blushed. "But those were other kids my age. I mean, I can't tell people like Vadeem or Noel what to do. They probably know a lot more than me."

"We don't," the both of them said as one, finally agreeing on something.

Jae-Hyun continued. "We're in a whole new world, Yoona, the things that we know back on Earth have very little bearing on the current situation. And you should get used to such a role soon. You are second-in-command, after all."

"But . . ."

"Hey," I added, "no one's expecting you to be perfect the first time around, and we're all friends here, so it's not like we're going to judge you. Hell, I messed up the most around here, what with my sponsorship nonsense, and you guys were supportive of me. We'll be the same."

The girl slowly nodded. "All right . . . I'll give it a go. But I apologize in advance if I make mistakes. I'm not like my brother."

Vadeem chuckled. "I don't think anyone is like him."

Noel nodded. "All right, so what's the plan, new boss?"

"Before that," the regressor interrupted, "let's ease Yoona into the role first. The minotaur will be an easy foe compared to the golem or that hybrid we faced earlier, so we won't all need to act. Let Walter and I take a more passive role this time, so you can focus on leading a team of four. That's the standard size of most parties in the trials."

The regressor's sister took a deep breath and gave a firm nod. "I'll do my best."

I stood near the back with Jae-Hyun while the other five entered the labyrinth first. Yoona, despite showing hesitation earlier, was honestly pretty good at taking charge of the situation. She was giving short and concise instructions for each of the members, even putting in the stuff her brother taught us earlier.

She sent the twins ahead to scout for any movement, telling them to be extra mindful of any noise that might be coming from each corridor. The labyrinth was pure stone walls and nothing else, which made for an effective echo chamber. Additionally, she put Vadeem near the front with the carcass out, and whenever we reached a fork in the road, she would wait for the twins to guide them down the path with the most sound or vibrations.

It didn't take us long before we didn't need the twins to locate the minotaur in question. Vadeem put away his boar carcass when the echoes of the bull's rapidly advancing footsteps became too loud to ignore, and everyone got ready to meet the enemy head on. The labyrinth corridors were wide enough that we didn't have to worry about the use of space, much to the joy of Vadeem, and I was about to join in before the regressor put a hand on my shoulder and pulled me back.

"Not this time, Walter," he said. "Let's watch them on their own, and we'll help if needed. I want to hear your thoughts on the fight."

CHAPTER THIRTY

The Search Part 3

You want to hear my opinion?" I asked. I honestly didn't think he would bother asking for anyone else's input given his knowledge and experience. This was definitely a first.

Jae-Hyun sighed. "As much as everyone thinks that I know everything, I am still just one person. I can make mistakes, as you saw in the last trial. I trust your opinion on these things, Walter, so yes, I want to hear your opinion."

"All right," I said, "I guess I can provide some play-by-play commentary. Uh, analytical play-by-play commentary, of course."

He nodded. "It's coming. Let's move back and give them room to work."

The regressor and I moved back a little more. I couldn't see things too well from where I stood, so I used my feelers to latch myself onto the side of the wall to get a better vantage point. Plus, I could launch myself off the way real quick in case I needed to get involved in the fight. Jae-Hyun saw what I was doing, and he joined me by stabbing the wall with his spear, using that as a ledge to sit on. He looked relaxed as he silently peered down at the huge approaching monster.

The minotaur was . . . Well, it wasn't as impressive as I thought it would be. All those movies and game depictions of the mythological monster made it out to be a massive creature of unstoppable destruction, but the specimen charging in front of Yoona and her party was shoddy at best. It was like the runt of all minotaurs.

First of all, while it was certainly tall, it wasn't nearly as large girth wise.

In fact, it was downright lanky, with its muscles wasted away from malnutrition and an obviously poor diet. Some of its fur was patchy and disheveled, its horns looked a little flaky, honestly, and it was foaming at the mouth. Even its teeth and eyes were a horrible jaundiced yellow.

"That's . . . that thing is a minotaur?" I asked skeptically. "I thought it would be a lot more imposing. Doesn't it look kind of, I don't know, sickly?"

The regressor chuckled. "I know what you mean. That particular specimen doesn't exactly strike a threatening pose. We wouldn't stand a chance against a healthy one as we are, but against that?"

I looked at the monster's quite underwhelming charge. It was easily stopped by Vadeem matching its strength, and my friend didn't even need to transform to do so. Even Vadeem himself was a little surprised by how easy it was to stop his foe.

"Why's it so weak?" I asked. "It looks like it'd fall down even if we didn't fight it."

"What did you expect? There's nothing around here for it to eat, so it's been starving ever since the gods left. Worse still, it can't even leave the labyrinth with the enchantments in place. But weak or not, its core is still that of a real minotaur, so just consider yourselves lucky for being able to get a high-quality object with minimal effort."

"I kind of feel bad for it, then," I replied with a wince as I saw it being bombarded with a torrent of arrows. It was howling in rage and pain as the three girls riddled him with their shots, and the minotaur soon looked like it ran through a field of cacti with how many arrows were sticking out of it. It was howling in pain, but even its cries were hoarse and raspy.

"It's just going to be a one-sided slaughter," I said. "Noel doesn't even have to do anything."

In fact, she hadn't been doing much of anything so far. She slashed at the minotaur's heels every now and then, when she saw an opportunity, but she was a passive observer for the most part. It wasn't so much that she didn't want to help out, but she seemed like she couldn't be bothered when the end result was already clear to see.

"That's the problem with Noel," Jae-Hyun said, "she gets distracted and bored when she's not challenged. She thinks the fight is already over, so she won't give it her all."

"The fight's not practically over?" I asked.

He chuckled again. "Diminished and half starved as it is, that thing is still a minotaur. Just wait and see."

I looked dubiously at the fight to see what Jae-Hyun was talking about. It still seemed like a one-sided affair to me. Vadeem was smashing its shins with his hammer, and I wouldn't be surprised if its legs gave out completely soon, while the three archers prevented it from dislodging the man from his assault. Noel had managed to slip through to the back of the creature and was chopping away at its calves.

"Just wait for it," the regressor stated calmly. "Things will get interesting once it's wounded past a certain point. Should be any second now. Noel's in the worst position. She's strong enough to take the impact; it'll be a learning moment for her."

Impact? Before I could ask, I saw what Jae-Hyun meant. Once it was hurt to a certain point, something seemed to trigger the wounded beast, and it exploded in a rage. Its entire form seemed to shift; the creature's once-matted fur instantly turned full, and the minotaur's withered frame filled in substantially. Just the air around it shifted, and I automatically knew that this was a creature to be feared.

"Don't warn them; let them figure it out themselves," he added as he looked at the unfolding scene. "It's a good opportunity to see how they handle unknown situations, or when their initial plans don't work."

The minotaur howled in rage and instinctively kicked a leg backward, hitting Noel right in the abdomen. The woman managed to move back a bit so that some of the force was lessened, but she still took tremendous damage from the hit.

"Noel!" Yoona shouted as she shot another mana-infused arrow at the minotaur. "Are you okay?"

Noel winced and tried to say something but only a wheeze came out. She concentrated and spoke again. "Yup, think I broke something, though. I can still fight; just give me room to drink a potion."

"You got careless!" Vadeem grunted as he turned Titan-sized and tackled the monster. "Use your skills. It's gotten a lot stronger."

Yoona composed herself before giving out more instructions. "Vadeem, hold it off until Noel recovers! Ana, Eva, aim for its eyes, make sure that it can't shake off Vadeem!"

Muscle A: Got it.
Muscle E: Ok.

The regressor sighed. "Told you, Walter. Now let's see how they fare against an enemy that's more on their level while on the back foot."

I nodded. "Well, it's their first time fighting something that gets a lot stronger when it's injured. Even I would have been complacent in that situation, so you can't fault them too much."

Noel tried to retreat as far as she was able to, but she didn't make it far. Once she was out of immediate danger, she pulled out a vial of green liquid from her inventory and drank it. She struggled to move, so it was evident that the blow did more damage than she cared to admit. However, the spot she chose to retreat to was the worst one possible, and she backed herself into one of the labyrinth's many dead ends.

"And she didn't bother to check where she was retreating to before," I said as I saw her face as she realized that she couldn't move back farther. "You're right. Noel doesn't plan ahead in situations like this."

Meanwhile, the other four were trying their hardest to keep the minotaur distracted, but it could smell the blood in the air and was trying its best to ignore the other combatants and focus on the wounded member of the party. And it was strong.

"Shit!" Vadeem swore. "It's too damn strong. I can't keep it from moving!"

The thing was dragging Vadeem with it as it moved closer and closer to the injured woman. The big man was doing his best to try to prevent the minotaur from advancing, even trying to pick the massive creature up, but its hooves were dug deep into the ground and nothing he was doing seemed to work. The creature just took step after slow step, dragging the Titan with it. It would only be a matter of time before it reached the injured girl.

"Why doesn't Noel just go into flame form?" I asked as I saw the girl in question just sitting there waiting. "A lot of this could be avoided if she did that. I'm not sure if the minotaur could keep up with her if she just flies away, assuming it can even harm her in the first place."

The regressor slowly shook his head. "She can't. Like I said, all skills have their limits and weaknesses, and this is hers. Noel can't transform unless she's completely unharmed."

Now that I thought about it, I had always seen her use it before the start of a battle, and never during one. That was a pretty steep downside if our enemies could plan for it.

Jae-Hyun spoke again. "She's way too careless in these situations; she knows full well what would happen if she gets hurt, and now she's paying for it. She just assumes that she can quickly heal up with a potion, but even the best ones take time to work, especially if her injury is severe."

"Damn," I muttered as I analyzed the scene. "And they're not using the environment correctly either."

Jae-Hyun raised an eyebrow. "Explain."

"If Vadeem wants to keep the minotaur away from Noel, then he needs to secure himself to the floor. The big cow's strong enough to move his weight, but if he can tie himself to something larger, then it can't do that. If I were him, I'd hook that huge hammer into the floor and use that as an anchor to prevent the monster from moving. He's not using that huge thing of his for anything other than fighting."

The regressor nodded slowly. "True. Anything else of note?"

"Yeah . . . The three girls are starting to panic as well," I said as I continued to watch them let loose endless volleys. "It's clear that their arrows are doing minimal damage, so they should use their time better. The minotaur's still bogged down by Vadeem, so one of the twins can easily slip past it and help Noel on the other side."

"But like you said," Jae-Hyun continued, "they're overloaded with information and aren't calm enough to think of that. They default to shooting even when it's obvious that it won't work."

"That's going to be a hard skill to master," I replied. "But I guess it's something else to note down to improve on. Should we help them out?"

"Not yet," he said. "I think Yoona can still salvage this situation."

I continued to watch, now ready to intervene if necessary. Vadeem was still trying in vain to stop the minotaur, while the twins were still letting loose an endless stream of arrows. Eventually, the first person to snap out of the shock was Yoona.

"I'll freeze the ground around the minotaur!" she shouted. "Jump when I tell you to, Vadeem."

"Got it!" he shouted back. "Don't miss!"

Well, Yoona's strategy would probably work if she made it so that the ground around the creature was slippery, but it was a lot less efficient than my suggestions. But still, a strategy was a strategy, and I saw the girl grimace in concentration as she imbued her arrow with ice. I just wished I could see what was going on, but my damn lack of any mana affinity made that impossible.

"Jump!" Yoona shouted as she unleashed her charged shot.

Vadeem did as he was told, and the high schooler's arrow narrowly avoided hitting the big man. The shot struck the ground right beneath the struggling minotaur, freezing the surface almost immediately. The monster began to lose its footing, and Vadeem took advantage of that moment to yank the creature away from Noel.

Without a solid footing, the minotaur was powerless to stop Vadeem, and the Titan launched it against the wall, briefly disorienting it.

"Hold it down for a bit," Yoona said again. "I'll try to freeze its feet to the ground. It should give Noel enough time to recover. She can finish it off!"

"Understood," Vadeem grunted and threw himself at the monster, doing his best to pin it against the wall. "Hurry up, though, the thing might be stronger than I am!"

"Got it! Ana, Eva, go help out Noel!"

The twins nodded and ran toward the injured girl. Vadeem and Yoona were able to keep the minotaur occupied long enough for Noel to recover, and soon the redhead flew back, body covered in those familiar dark flames, and the tables quickly turned in their favor.

"Good," the regressor said. "Not perfect, but they were able to get the situation under control better than anticipated. Let's end this little test and get that core."

CHAPTER THIRTY-ONE

A Panicked Beginning

We joined the others once it was clear that the minotaur was fully and completely dead. Noel had melted its head off, so I really couldn't see how it would be getting up after that particular wound. The other five all slumped down in exhaustion once it was clear that the threat was over, and sighed in relief

"Good job, everyone," the regressor said. "That went better than I thought."

"Then you really don't have much faith in us if that was better than what you thought," Vadeem mumbled. "We almost lost to a crippled old cow."

"You got careless. Especially you, Noel," Jae-Hyun said. "I did warn you never to underestimate anything from Tartarus, and you saw the reason first-hand. But you recovered well enough." He turned to nod at his sister. "Good job, Yoona, for taking control of the situation once your initial plans failed."

"I still panicked at the start, though," she said, looking down. "Noel could have been in serious trouble if this wasn't a practice run. She could have died."

"But it *was* a practice run," I added quickly before Yoona's self-confidence could be destroyed. "And it was your first time leading a squad. You'll get better with more time and practice. Plus, I'm pretty sure it was Noel's own fault for half-assing things at the start there."

"That was dumb of me," the redhead answered with a pout. "I'll admit it, lesson learned."

"I hope so," the regressor said sternly. "Your life's on the line, along with everyone else's. Never forget that, Noel."

She nodded grimly, looking properly chastised, but only time would tell if Noel would learn from this particular lesson.

> **Muscle A:** Sorry we were not more helpful.
> **Muscle E:** We are not used to fighting, that must change.

I grimaced. I didn't expect everyone to take this scuffle that poorly. Even the kids felt responsible. Looking at how depressed everyone seemed at their performance, I didn't think it was a good idea to point out all of their faults, at least not at the moment. I gave a questioning glance over at the regressor, and I think he understood what I meant. We'd hold off on critiques until later.

"Look," I said again, "you made it through the fight mostly unscathed, and you know what to do in the future, so I'd chalk that up as a win. Think of it as motivation to improve!"

Vadeem sighed again. "Yeah, I think we all know that. Failure's the best way to learn. It doesn't make it any less awful, though."

"Agreed," Noel added in. "Especially if you mess up the most. Sorry, gang, I goofed."

"It's fine, Noel," Yoona replied. "I was the one in charge. I should have given everyone clearer instructions."

"No, it was—"

I needed to stop them before they could continue their game of who was more to blame. That was never a good route to go down.

I coughed to get everyone's attention and said, "Look, we can all review what went wrong later. For now, let's just collect the minotaur core and go from there."

"All right, that's fair," Vadeem said after taking a deep breath. "So how do we find the core thing?"

"It's in the area with the densest mana," the regressor explained. "Hard to spot when a creature's alive, but it should be the only thing emitting mana now that it's deceased."

Ah, of course. It had to do with mana again. I honestly hadn't thought much about it when Q first told me about my strange disconnect with mana, but it was becoming more and more clear that everything seemed to use it in one way or another. This damn condition was more debilitating than I thought. I'd have to find a way to compensate for it later if I wanted to somehow keep up with the regressor and his growing cohort of freaks.

The others didn't have any trouble locating the core while I just sat around, unable to help at all. This time I wasn't really complaining, though, because getting the thing out of the dead minotaur was a . . . messy affair, to say the least. I'll save everyone the grisly details, but suffice it to say that you would need a strong stomach to extract cores in the future. Perhaps not having mana was not that bad of a thing if I never had to deal with *that.*

"Sorry, brother," Yoona said as she tried her best to not gag. "Is . . . is this really the only way to get cores?"

Jae-Hyun was waist deep in dead minotaur as he spoke. "Yes, unfortunately, unless one of us can use telekinesis."

His sister sighed. "I don't think I can ever get used to this."

Noel shrugged as she shifted around the carcass. "It's not so bad once you get used to it. Just think of it as pork intestines. I heard some cultures eat it raw!"

And that was when Yoona lost her cool and quickly ran to a corner to empty the contents of her stomach. Which was understandable; I wasn't anywhere near the thing and I was already nauseous, the core was located near the stomach of the minotaur, so the smell was just too much.

Yoona came back a few minutes later, and just as we were about to regroup and head farther into the maze, an unexpected message showed up.

> **Notice: Due to a change in scheduling, the third trial will begin in exactly one hour. All aspirants, please gather within Pandora's walls with your party members. Failure to do so before the time limit will result in abnormal conditions within the next trial.**
> **Once again, the third trial will begin in exactly one hour. All aspirants, please gather . . .**

Hadn't the regressor said that the third trial wouldn't start until the last batch of aspirants arrived? I was pretty sure that even Q said that it should take a little over a month for that to happen. That was when the realization hit me, and I swore—it was that piece-of-shit overseer again!

I had thought that he would wait until Q was out of office before acting. He practically said as much when he talked about replacing Q with one of his goons, but why had I trusted him to stick to his words and do that? He had every incentive to lie, and here I was, gullible enough to believe otherwise.

"What's going on?" Yoona asked as she quickly finished cleaning up. "What's the schedule change about?"

The regressor was silent for a moment, lost in thought, before finally answering. "Something's wrong. I . . . I'm not sure what's going on, but panicking helps no one in this situation. We're leaving Tartarus if we can."

I'd be surprised if Jae-Hyun was somehow expecting this situation. It was that goddamn Overseer doing his absolute best to make sure that I failed one of these trials so I'd be dragged back to his side. Too bad he didn't know that if I failed, I'd also be dead! I cursed myself again for allowing that piece of shit to fool me into believing that he'd just stay on the sidelines until our next meeting.

"What, why?" Noel asked. "We're so close to the forge thing, though! Plus we'll never make it back to Pandora in an hour anyway, so I say we book it to the treasure!"

"No, we leave now," he said again, and this time his tone left no room for argument. "We can't afford to be transported in such a dangerous environment, much less a place enchanted by Nyx. I am not chancing something going wrong if I can help it."

He pointed toward the general direction of where we came from. "Vadeem, make us an exit!"

The big man stuffed the core into his inventory and nodded.

"Got it, boss," he said as he transformed, hammer ready for action. "Make way!"

We steamrolled through the labyrinth, although the structure could hardly be considered a proper maze when Vadeem just bulldozed through the walls instead of around them. Yoona could still follow the faint traces of mana we used to get to the maze, and we made a beeline toward the staircase that we came from, all the while a little countdown timer was ticking down in my retina.

But after running for a while, it was clear that we weren't going to make it, even if the speedier amongst us ran ahead. The regressor realized the same thing when the timer hit ten minutes and he instructed us to stop.

"There's not enough time," he grunted. "We'll have to make do with going into the trial here."

"Do you know how that will affect us?" Yoona asked. "The notification said we could experience abnormalities if we're outside Pandora."

"Expect the worst."

No kidding. I bet the Overseer would do everything in his power to make sure that we were as screwed as possible. I was just hoping that there were only so many legal loopholes he could exploit before being stopped from straight-up killing all of us the second we set foot in that trial. Bureaucracy and rules seemed like a big part of Central, so I was fairly certain that there was only so much he could do . . . hopefully.

"Man," Noel grumbled as she came to a stop. "How come we always get the crummy luck?"

I saw the briefest hint of guilt flash across the regressor's face before he composed himself again. It was clear that he thought that he was the cause of all our misfortunes. If only he knew the truth.

Yoona noticed as well and quickly covered for her brother. "We're probably the best aspirants around, so maybe the System just wants to challenge us further."

Noel sighed. "Yeah, I guess so. We're just too awesome to leave alone."

The timer hit eight minutes.

"Just listen for now, save the banter for when there isn't a countdown looming over us."

We nodded and allowed Jae-Hyun to continue. "I don't know what's going to happen, but assume that we will all be split up. Unless things are really wrong, all guild members should be grouped together, but we might not all be in the same trial. If that is the case, try to reestablish communications with the party chat, and if that fails, focus on your own situation, and do not trust anyone you do not know."

"Even if we're partied with other aspirants?" Yoona asked.

"Especially other aspirants, Yoona," he said coldly. "Other people are often more dangerous than the trials themselves."

Noel gave him a knowing smirk. "Understood, boss!"

"This is still the third trial, so even if our own goes wrong, it should still follow the general rules set for it. It is designed as a bonus round to reward the aspirants with the most potential. If there's one thing I know about this place, it's that they have set regulations that must be followed. There's only so much leeway for change."

"Which means what?" Vadeem asked.

"Which means that we shouldn't expect battle like the other trials," Jae-Hyun answered. "It shouldn't be dangerous, but . . ."

"But our situation isn't normal," I said for him, "so expect a place that's not dangerous in the conventional sense."

"Exactly," he said. "And for the twins . . ."

Everyone looked at the two girls. We all had the same thoughts. Were they going to join us in the trial? They came in via a really unconventional way, and even their classes were corrupted. It was anyone's guess what would happen to the two if we left, and as far as I could tell, they didn't even have access to the inventory system.

Vadeem frowned and held out his food suitcase. "Take that in case you two get stuck here. I don't know how long we'll be gone for, but just wait for us to return if you can."

The two didn't look like they wanted to take the offered item from Vadeem, but he shoved it in their hands and didn't give them a chance to argue. I could tell that the big man didn't want to be separated from them any more than they did.

The regressor nodded and scribbled something on a small piece of paper. "If we're gone for longer than three days, head back out and give that to the driver. He'll take you back to Pandora."

Muscle A: We want to stay with Big Muscle.
Muscle E: Don't leave us.

Vadeem's face was hard to read when he saw their message. He walked up to them, bent down, and gave the twins the most reassuring smile I'd ever seen him use.

"Look, you two will be fine no matter what happens. You've survived far worse," he said. "Maybe you'll be paired up with one of us, but even if you're not, always remember that we will be back. There's no trial that's tough enough to stop these muscles!"

The twins gave him a weak smile. I didn't need Noe's translating abilities to know that it was forced.

"And take the flask with you," I added, tossing over the little container I got from my first trial. "It'll provide you two with all the water you need."

Ana caught it and stuffed it into one of her pouches.

Muscle A: Thank you.
Muscle E: Please be safe. Please come back.

The timer hit three minutes.

"We will," I reassured them.

"One more thing," the regressor interrupted. "If, on the rare occasion, our trials have special rules in them, ensure that you *never* break them."

I quickly went over the contents of my own inventory to take stock of what I had access to. There weren't many healing potions left, but it would have to do.

Two minutes now.

"Anything else to add?" I asked, feeling nervous as the timer went ever downward.

"Stay safe," he said simply. "Make sure to send a message once you're out."

"You too, brother," Yoona replied. "And everyone else, too."

One minute.

Vadeem was by the twins, hugging them tightly as if being in physical contact could ensure that they were sent to the same place. Noel took out her swords, looking as if she anticipated what was to come, while the two Kim siblings were seated together, simply waiting for the clock to run its course. I took a deep breath and waited for the inevitable feeling of disorientation. It came not long after.

It was basically a habit at this point to survey my surroundings whenever I get teleported like this, but I checked to see if anyone from my guild had joined me this time. Thankfully I wasn't alone here, although I was conflicted. The regressor was here with me in the trial this time, so it would be my first time properly working with him, but right beside him was the newest member of the guild . . . Marcus.

Unlike the regressor or myself, the priest looked comfortable in the new environment, which is saying something because the place we were all sent to was just as uncanny as he was. The three of us were standing in the lobby area of what seemed like an old hospital, not the modern ones that are all white walls and sterilized surfaces, but the eerie ones seen in horror movies.

Facing our backs was the only exit, and there was an awful storm raging outside. The howling of the wind was barely contained by the thin glass, and it made the entire place permeate with a layer of gloom. Strangely enough, I couldn't see past a certain distance outside even with my title's passive ability, which meant that the only thing I could take stock of was the interior.

This was a hospital sporting aesthetics from before the turn of the century, when modern technology was still being developed and ethics were a lot looser. There was just something about the drab, yellowing wallpaper and overused rugs that seemed to soak in decades of abuse and suffering. Even the faux leather chairs by the waiting area were flaking and wrinkled with age.

"The Trash Matrix is sending new information about the trial. Displaying information now, my host," Noe's clear voice cut through the gloom, and I almost shuddered at the sudden interruption.

> **Welcome, Aspirants, to the third trial! Due to an error in your party's registration, the contents of this trial have deviated from the standards. We apologize for the inconvenience.**

Apologize, my ass! I bet the Overseer was laughing his blurred ass off right now.

> **Clear Conditions: Survive and [CONTENTS CORRUPTED DUE TO ERROR 2353].**

Yeah, it was undoubtably the Overseer's work. Of course my trial's clear conditions just so happened to be corrupted because my party was conveniently away from Pandora when the trials started. All of it could be argued as pure coincidence if it was ever brought up to the Tribunal in the future. Too bad he didn't seem to understand the exact nature of Q's anomaly if he thought that's going to hinder me at all.

And also, why did we always get these damn horror-set knockoffs for trial locations? At least Father Marcus looked like he fit right in. There was one last point of interest that I wanted to observe closer, that being the weird nurse stationed at the reception desk, but the regressor quickly pulled the priest and me back toward the exit.

> **The trial will begin in five minutes. Please gather with your teammates in that time. We wish you the best of luck.**

"We don't have time, so listen to me carefully," Jae-Hyun said quickly, the look on his face furrowed with concern. I'd never seen the man like this before. Just how bad was our current situation for him to act like this?

"Please explain," Marcus said evenly. "Walter and I trust your judgment."

He looked at me. "Remember when I said there might be the rare case that we enter a trial with rules?"

I sighed. "Let me guess, we're in one of them right now?"

"Yes," he muttered, "and it's one of the worst ones."

CHAPTER THIRTY-TWO

Start of the Third Trial

O f course we're in one of the worst ones," I muttered mainly to myself. "So what do we need to know?"

Our five minutes were counting down fast. I hoped Jae-Hyun was concise with his explanations.

"We're in a unique trial," he explained as he took out some pads of paper and began to scribble something on them. "I don't have enough time to explain how to clear the stage, but I need you two to do some tasks I'm writing down. I'll give you further instructions later on, but for now, read these over when you have time. We won't have access to most system functions here, so don't bother trying to communicate with the chat. If it's you two, then I know you'll be able to get them done somehow."

Marcus and I nodded and allowed the regressor to speak.

"The important part is the special rules you'll have to follow here," he said quickly. "The nurse will give you a handbook once you've established your roles here. Make sure that you never, *ever* break those rules. You are safe if you do things according to the regulations."

"Roles?" I asked quickly. "What do you mean?"

"I was getting there," Jae-Hyun said as he checked how much time was left. "Once we talk with the nurse to start the trial, we will be assigned roles in this hospital. Normally we would all be patients undergoing treatment, but that can be changed."

"I see," Marcus said calmly, his smile never leaving him even in this situation.

The regressor continued. "If you two introduce yourselves to the nurse at the reception with a strong role in mind, then we can manipulate the trial and have you become that person. The nurse is the key, she is the one who determines what or who you will be here, but you need to make a very strong impression to solidify that persona."

"Make a strong impression of a particular role, got it," I repeated. "So what roles do you want us to take?"

"One of us will have to work as a patient for this trial—I'll do that. If we're in the corrupted version, then we're here later than the others. I'll take care of the things needed on the patient side of things," Jae-Hyun answered with a grimace. "I need you two to work in areas that I won't have easy access to. Marcus's role is easy; he can be a priest here to give the dying their last rites. He'll have access to all the patient wings that way."

"Easily done," he replied. "I have done so many times already."

"And Walter," the regressor said as he turned to me, "I need you to present yourself as a doctor."

Now, I knew nothing about doctoring, but I didn't think this particular hospital worked the normal way. I was sure I could figure something out.

"Any particular doctor?" I asked.

"Anything that you think will work best, but make sure it's a *doctor*," he answered. "I trust your judgment, but make sure you strike the strongest first impression on that nurse. Your disguise will be stronger if she firmly believes that you are who you say you are. Just know that your tasks will require you to move a lot and skirt around the rules and access the various staff areas, so it'll be ideal if you can think of something to help with that."

"I can think of something," I said quietly.

The little countdown timer showed that we had a little over two minutes left.

"One last thing," he said, this time slower. "Once you are assigned your roles, make sure that you stick to that disguise until this trial ends, even if you meet with me or the others. Marcus won't have any issues here, but Walter, you will not survive if you're seen through, do you understand?"

I almost smiled. My disguise failing? I had a lot of experience making sure something like that never happened.

"I'll manage," I answered simply.

"I trust you," he said. "And remember when I said that things will go very badly if you break those rules or if people doubt who you say you are?"

Marcus and I nodded.

"It works both ways," he continued. "Everyone in this hospital has to live by the rules, and you can make them break those rules or have enough people doubt their identity. Use that to your advantage if you face difficulties with other aspirants."

"Other aspirants?" I asked. "We're not the only ones? I thought we're only in this mess because of the error."

"Yes and no. This is one of the trials used to punish aspirants who break the rules, but we're in the worst version because we came from Tartarus," he replied cryptically. "Just . . . just know there will be other parties who have already started this trial, maybe for a few days already, but they will be in slightly different situations. Being late won't matter if we follow my plans. I'll explain when we have more time; all you have to know right now is that this place is dangerous even without it being corrupt."

"All right . . . so we're late and we get the special treatment here," I answered. "I think I get the gist of it."

"I as well," Marcus added. "Is that all we need to know?"

"For now, we don't have time left, so let's go," the regressor started to walk back. "And I'm sure that I don't have to say this, but this is not a normal hospital, so don't react to anything that seems strange here."

"Naturally," Marcus stated. "Shall we introduce ourselves?"

The regressor passed us the notes he wrote and nodded. I could see a tiny hint of nervousness on his face, which was an expression I had never seen from him before. Just how bad was this trial for it to make even this man on edge? Thankfully this was a trial that played to my strengths, which was a godsend because I still didn't have access to the Absolute Luck skill. It wasn't like I could do anything about it since we were all stuck here. I just hoped the other members of the Abyss Guild had easier trials.

"Marcus, you go first," Jae-Hyun said. "I don't think you'll have any issues here since you're not really pretending to be someone you're not, but be careful in any case."

The priest nodded and walked up to the reception desk with a calm purpose. The regressor and I stayed just a few steps behind, observing how this would play out. I was also a little curious about the exact rules that this trial played by. We still had a minute to go so I could hopefully squeeze in a few final questions as I watched.

The regressor said that we had to make a strong impression on the nurse so that she believed that you were some kind of personnel working in this creepy hospital, but that would require her to have prior knowledge of me at the very least, or at least some kind of established connection with the hospital. This is especially the case if you were trying to convince her that you worked here as a doctor. I doubted even a new intern or med student would just show up one day without any warning.

If that were the case, how would that work? If I said that I was Dr. Smith, who'd worked here for fifteen years, then would she just fill in the inconsistencies herself? Would she "acquire" memories of this random doctor? I was sure that wasn't the case, because the regressor wouldn't have stressed the importance of the first meeting if I could just say a role that wanted. Most likely only small pieces of inconsistencies would be filled in.

"Hey," I whispered to Jae-Hyun while the priest was approaching, "how does choosing the roles work? Will the nurse make up memories of my persona if I hint that we've met before?"

"To a limited degree, yes," he whispered back. "If what you're saying is plausible enough, she will make up the background information for your role to work, and once your role is fully realized, the others here will also inherit those memories. She's the key to this trial. But if you say something unreasonable, then you'll default to a patient again, so be careful."

I acknowledged that and quieted down once the priest reached the receptionist nurse. I had no worries at all that Marcus would fit in. If I didn't know better, I could have sworn he was another Central worker assigned for this gig.

"Greetings," Father Marcus said warmly, "I am here to cleanse the souls of the dying and ease their journey into the embrace of the Lord. I heard that my services are needed here."

The nurse stared at Marcus for a long while, her stare unblinking, before something clicked in her mind, and she returned the welcome with a warm smile.

"Thank you, Father," she said with a small bow. "Our facility is in desperate need of your services. Do you know which ward you are headed to?"

Oh, it seemed like she'd ask questions as well. Was that to make sure that our identities were solid?

Marcus replied with a soft ease that showed no hint of worry. "All souls are under my care, Sarah."

And he obviously knew the name of the creepy nurse as well, just like how he knew mine. God, I could never get used to the man.

"Of course," she answered back with a bigger smile, like she was visibly easing up to the man. Marcus was giving her the right answers it seemed.

"I feel much suffering here," the priest continued, "and I feel that I will be busy, but I am a man of devotion, and I will help any who needs my services. I am sure that I can guide the unwilling into the afterlife."

The nurse's smile grew wider. "Yes, you will find that many here do not understand that they are already bound for death. I hope you can do as you say and help them transition. One more question, Father, but you will find that our hospital houses unique patients."

"All souls are unique, Sarah," he added.

"Of course, Father! But many under our care will resist your help. They will deny our treatment and insist that they are not fated for the grave. What would you do in that case?"

"Many poor souls are unable to understand the end of their own mortal coil, and it is my job to make them understand even if they are in denial. It is not my place to neglect my duties because of the delusions of the sick," he replied. "Now I must attend to the dying and dead, if you will please send someone to assist me, that would be most helpful."

"I understand, Father," she answered. "And please take your guidebook with you."

He did so and thanked the woman. I felt an intangible wave of energy. Now the smile on the nurse's face was genuine. Marcus must have passed whatever test was in place and was accepted as a proper priest for this weird hospital.

The nurse said something incomprehensible into an old intercom system, and within moments another priest—equally creepy as Marcus—came to get the man. I couldn't see his full features since he was wearing one of those old-fashioned, raven-shaped plague masks. Marcus didn't seem to even notice that.

They communicated something so quietly that I couldn't make out what they were saying, even with Noe's help, but the two seemed to be chatting hap-pily after a while as they left down the unusually dark corridor. Marcus gave us one small nod before disappearing into the depths of the hospital for good.

"Good," Jae-Hyun said in relief. "He's through, so it's our turn now. My part is easy. I don't have to say anything special to get the default role, so I'll take your lead. Do what you think is necessary."

"Got it. I'll introduce you as a new patient and go from there," I said as I immersed myself into the role I would have to soon play. "Let's get this over with."

CHAPTER THIRTY-THREE

The Newest Arrival

The regressor and I approached the reception. He was all grim determination while I took a final breath and got into character. If I needed to skirt around the rules, then I knew what role I had to play. If this dull-looking nurse was the key, then I was going to make one hell of a first impression.

"Hey!" I greeted with my brightest tone. "Sarah, babe! How've you been? Never did hear back from you after that steamy night out!"

Jae-Hyun looked at me as if I had just lost my mind, but I needed to do this. How she reacted to this prompt would determine how much leeway I had with this role. The best-case scenario was if she filled in what I said with matching information on her end, sort of like an improv performance, but I could play it off as an inappropriate joke if that fell short.

She stared at me vacantly for a while, her hazel eyes glazed over. This was the same thing she did when the priest first introduced himself, and she only became animated a short time later.

"That's not an appropriate conversation to have here!" she answered with a crimson blush on her otherwise pale face. "That's not something—"

"Not something the illustrious Dr. William Walter would say? I guess I am the best physician in the building! You saw my knowledge of anatomy first-hand, after all," I added with a light-hearted laugh and a wink. It seemed that the best-case scenario was most likely, which meant that I needed to cement my identity as quickly as possible.

Without missing a beat, the nurse replied sarcastically, "I would hardly say that you're the best doctor, or the most knowledgeable."

Good, so the nurse would, for the most part, follow the prompts the aspirants gave her. If that was the case, then there was something else that I could use to my advantage: that sweet, sweet active ability from my new title. I had the perfect idea of what to say, but first I had to speak with the nurse a little more.

"All right, all right," I answered and entered the woman's personal space; she didn't immediately flinch back, which I took as a good sign.

I gave her my most charming smile. "I got a new patient here. You know the drill, love."

Sarah sighed again. "Don't call me that, please."

"That's not what you were saying the other night."

Now she was a little flustered with a hint of anger showing. "Dr. Walter, please! We have a new patient here. I know how hard it is for you to act professionally, but this is too much, even for you!"

Good, now she was getting angry. Time to use that little active title.

Noe, do your thing!

"Acknowledged, my host."

I stared at the nurse, maintaining eye contact, and I felt the new power in my voice. "You know that I don't need to do that. *The normal rules don't apply to me. The hospital's director loves me too much to get rid of me.*"

The nurse froze again as if some kind of conflicting force was raging inside her. Even Jae-Hyun looked at me in question, but he was smart enough not to speak out of turn at such a crucial moment. A visible shudder was felt in the building, as if the very foundations of the place were changing and an invisible force seemed to sweep through everything around us, but the tremors quickly subsided. Eventually, the woman unfroze, although that slight daze in her eyes never left.

"Yes . . . right . . ." she muttered before the cheer in her voice returned. "I know the director has a soft spot for you, which is why you shouldn't advertise our little meeting so vocally! You know how she gets!"

Now it was my turn to pause. What?

Whatever. I didn't have time to contemplate what random background information the nurse gave to my made-up doctor identity. I'd just go with the flow for now and deal with the consequences later. Sorry, Future Walter!

"True, even I know my limits," I said with an exaggerated sigh. "I know all too well how she can get. But can you please have someone take the patient to the wards? You know I'm far too busy to do such drudge work. I have people to fix, work to do, bodies to get rid of."

Sarah sighed again. "As if you do much work around here, but I'll have another nurse have him processed."

She turned to Jae-Hyun, and her friendly tone turned ice cold instantly. "Here is the patient handbook. Make sure you follow the rules to the letter. Failure to do so will result in the appropriate punishment. We hope you will get the proper treatment here."

He took the little booklet silently, and the nurse whispered something else into the intercom. Strangely, I couldn't tell what she said even though I was right next to her.

Soon, another masked man—this time there was no mistaking the inhuman nature of the being—came in to take Jae-Hyun away. The new nurse looked like he came right out of a slasher flick. He was abnormally huge, maybe over seven feet in height, and wider than Vadeem. His skin was a patchwork of sewn bits and decaying flesh, and a grotesque surgical mask obscured his face. Were the other workers here equally horrible?

The creature nodded at me, and the receptionist took out an awful-looking needle and jabbed the regressor right in the neck. Jae-Hyun passed out immediately and was dragged away into the depths of the hospital. The strangest thing happened once he entered the hallway: his normal clothes were replaced with an inpatient gown, and even his appearance was slightly altered to look more sickly.

I guess that signaled his integration into this weird hospital's structure. Father Marcus hadn't seemed to change earlier when he passed through, but then again, he was already dressed up as a creepy priest.

Once the two were fully out of view, I turned my attention back to the only normal-looking person in the hospital. "So, Sarah, about that night . . ."

She rolled her eyes. "You have work to do, Doctor."

"You know you can call me Will," I said with a wink. "You were practically screaming it before."

She blushed. "Don't talk about that! And go, before both of us get in trouble. Take your handbook, although I'm sure you'll never read it anyway."

I grabbed it off the desk and gave her a friendly wave before turning to the dark hallway. "You know where to find me in case you get lonely again! Take care!"

"I swear you'll be the death of both of us!"

I laughed and gave her a little wave of goodbye before heading into the hospital proper. Much like Jae-Hyun, my clothes had changed as well, and my comfortable sweater and trousers morphed into a decrepit surgeon's uniform. This thing looked more like a Halloween costume than the real deal, what with the random brown and red stains on it, but it fit this hospital's setting well enough. I could only imagine that the rest of me transformed to match the outfit.

I sighed and got ready to see what kinds of horrors I'd face here. But first thing's first, time to see what the rules were and what the regressor needed me to do. I found a quiet corner and pulled out the rulebook first to make sure I didn't accidentally die because I broke some random law.

Physician's Handbook:

NOTE: ON THE ORDER OF THE DIRECTOR, ANY PHYSICIAN CAUGHT NEGLECTING THEIR DUTIES WILL BE SEVERELY PUNISHED.

FAILURE TO FOLLOW THE INSTRUCTIONS OUTLINED BELOW WILL RESULT IN PUNISHMENT.

FAILURE TO ADHERE TO HOSPITAL PROTOCOLS WILL RESULT IN PUNISHMENT.

THE DIRECTOR RESERVES THE RIGHT TO ADD ADDITIONAL REQUESTS AT HER LEISURE.

FAILURE TO MEET THE DEMANDS OF THE DIRECTOR WILL RESULT IN PUNISHMENT.

Well, that was an ominous start. I was pretty sure I never wanted to find out what this punishment was.

INSTRUCTIONS FOR CARE:

ALL PATIENTS IN THIS HOSPITAL ARE SICK. THERE ARE NO EXCEPTIONS.

DO NOT ENGAGE IN CONVERSATION WITH A PATIENT OUTSIDE OF TREATMENT SESSIONS OR DESIGNATED LUNCH HOURS.

IF A PATIENT SPEAKS ABOUT IMPOSSIBLE EVENTS OR A TRIAL, THEN THEY ARE SICK BEYOND HELP. THEY ARE TO BE REPORTED TO THE DISCIPLINARY DEPARTMENT OR THE DIRECTOR IMMEDIATELY.

IF YOU SEE A PATIENT BREAKING THE RULES, THEY ARE SICK AND NEED IMMEDIATE TREATMENT. THEY ARE TO BE REPORTED TO THE DISCIPLINARY DEPARTMENT OR THE DIRECTOR IMMEDIATELY.

Well, there was a problem here: I didn't know what the rules were for the patients. I couldn't exactly report patients for breaking the rules if I didn't know them! That was going to be something that I had to find out immediately before I headed to where they were housed. I read on.

PHYSICIANS MUST SUPERVISE AT LEAST THREE PROCEDURES PER DAY TO ENSURE THAT DOCTORS ARE PERFORMING THEIR DUTIES ADEQUATELY. THE PHYSICIAN MUST REPORT ANY DOCTOR FOUND NEGLECTING THEIR DUTY TO THE DIRECTOR.

Damn it, I had no idea what the duties of a doctor were, something else I had to find out ASAP. Hopefully, my status as the director's pet would give me a little leeway on the rules here, although I don't want to see how far that grace would go.

> THE PHYSICIAN MUST MAKE AN IN-PERSON REPORT TO THE DIRECTOR AT THE END OF THE WORK SHIFT.

Fuck, even more unknowns. At least that was all the rules I had to follow, but this situation was looking worse and worse. First of all, what was I even reporting about? I didn't know where the director was, or even when work hours ended. I was starting to curse my idea of being someone so important to this stupid hospital. The regressor's trust in me was too high if he thought I could get through this crap with ease.

Speaking of the regressor, I still had his little note to read. I hoped he remembered to provide me with some basic information in addition to telling me what I needed to do for him. I pulled out the crumpled note and quickly read. As always, the regressor was all work and efficiency, even in his writing.

> *Work hours: 8 a.m.–8 p.m. The trial starts at 8 a.m.*
> *Lunch at 12, never miss it. Dinner and breakfast are safe.*
> *Your dorm number will be in the registry in the Admin building.*
> *Be careful when you operate after work hours, it is exceedingly dangerous. Beware of dogs then.*
> *Director's office is on 2nd floor, Room 201. Don't go there unless you are thoroughly prepared. I'll give instructions on what to expect later.*

Ah . . . well shit, I had to go to the director's office tonight, and I highly doubted Jae-Hyun was in any condition to give me the instructions today. Guess I'd have to wing it . . .

> *Be wary of the physicians here, and especially the director.*
> *Avoid her at all costs.*

Well, double shit. Looking back, I guess the regressor's exact words were for me to go in as a doctor and not a physician, but who the hell knew those were different roles in this damned hospital? I thought the words were syn-onyms. In fact, I was fairly confident that they were!

Map of the hospital is found at the reception hall, ask for one.
Say it's for an intern.
Other rulebooks for various staff can be found in the relevant
wards. Ask the workers to give you one.

I need you to do the following:
—Get me a key to unlock the patient wards
—The password to the director's computer
—Uniforms from one of the other roles, preferably a doctor or
nurse
—Keycard to access the basement
More instructions to come once those are done.

Good luck, Walter.

And that was all the instructions that I got. I read it over one last time to make sure I committed it all to memory before stashing it into my inventory. I took a few more moments to compose myself, working out the order that I should do things in. I needed to ensure that I lived first, so finding out the basic information about the patients and doctors was number one, followed by figuring out what on earth I was supposed to report about at the end of the day. The regressor's tasks could wait until after.

Thankfully I had a full twelve hours to work with, but there was a lot on my plate already. I couldn't be complacent. For now, I'd get that map so I knew where I was even going. Guess it was time for Dr. William Walter to start his first day on the job.

CHAPTER THIRTY-FOUR

William Walter, MD

With my list of priorities set, I had clear goals in mind that I had to finish. Normally I enjoyed this systematic approach, as it made things so much easier when you just had one task to focus all your attention on, but the consequences of failure, or worse yet, not finishing on time, were a little steeper than what I was used to. But there was no sense in worrying; that just wasted more time I didn't have.

After making sure that my rulebook and the regressor's notes were safely stashed away in my inventory, I turned around and returned to the reception area to find that map. I couldn't make much progress if I didn't know where anything was located after all, and judging from the hints left by Jae-Hyun, I was going to assume that this place was enormous.

Now, I thought I was prepared to face anything this haunted horror hospital had to offer, but apparently, I was woefully wrong. I also almost had a heart attack when I reached the entrance and saw my own reflection in the rain-soaked windows. Holy shit, was that what a normal physician here looked like? That nurse who took Jae-Hyun away looked bad enough, but a physician was downright disgusting.

First of all, although the shape of my body remained more or less Walter-like, albeit a lot bigger, I could not say the same about the rest of me. My face was hideously wounded and deformed. It looked like someone was in the process of skinning me alive and just left me to die halfway through. The wounds looked fresh and were leaking an awful mixture of pus and blood. I didn't even have lips, so my decayed and yellowing teeth were exposed. Some sort of rusty metal apparatus was stretching my features to inhuman degrees, and my eyes were permanently open, with some metal wire pulling my eyelids apart.

Worse yet, my entire body looked like it was pox-ridden with disease! Pieces of my skin were actively falling off in maggoty clumps and parts of my body looked like they had been replaced with random bionics and even the grafted pieces of unidentifiable creatures. Coupled with the creepy doctor get-up, I was straight up an abomination!

Yet strangely, what I was seeing couldn't have been what I actually looked like. I didn't feel any different, and the fact that I could still blink meant that whatever was happening was either an illusion or something more complex at work. Even weirder, now that I was properly studying myself, I did feel stronger and more in charge than I normally would be. I instinctively felt for my face and was glad to feel normal Walter skin instead of whatever horrible thing I saw earlier.

Um, Noe, you have any insight on what's going on here?

"Affirmative, my host," she answered. "I do not have the full picture, as I only have partial access to the Trash Matrix's databases, but from what I do know, you have been fully integrated as a physician in this trial. The use of your skill during the initiation process also activated some unknown effects to your surroundings and most notably the native inhabitants of this trial, but I will keep an eye on that. Your form has changed to reflect this integration, but Unit Noe has insulated your mind from the changes so as to minimize further mental corruption."

Great, things only get worse . . . Wait, only my mind is insulated? So I do look like that right now?

"It is not permanent, and any changes experienced in this hospital will cease after trial completion, even with the skill's interference," Noe assured. "Please be at ease, dear Walter. Unit Noe will be with you even if your form changes once more."

That's . . . I mean, okay, if it's not permanent then . . . let's just not think about it. Thanks Noe.

"You are most welcome as always, my host."

Well, guess I'm a freak of nature that came right out of a horror movie for the remainder of this trial . . . Hopefully Jae-Hyun and Marcus recognized me when I saw them again. Somehow, I didn't think they'd have trouble if it was those two, although Yoona would probably have a stroke if she were here. I'm glad the kids were somewhere else at least. I doubted any other trial would be as bad as this one.

"Are you looking for something, Dr. Walter?" the nurse asked when she saw me stop for a while. Right, I had almost forgotten why I was here in the first place.

I put on my best smile once again. "Hey, Sarah, you know, I just had to come back to see you again."

Sarah rolled her eyes. How come she was the only normal-looking person here? Was Father Marcus also changed when he went out of view? Just thinking about the priest normally made me shudder in disgust, but what if he somehow got creepier? Great, more goodies to look forward to.

I continued my performance with a mock sigh. "But I'm also here to get a map of the hospital. I got stuck with a new intern, if you can believe that."

"You should have said that at the start, Will," Sarah replied, shaking her head. "I don't know what the director sees in you."

"Oh, come now! It's because of my charming smile, of course." I had to suppress a wince when I remembered what my face looked like right now. Could you even make a smile without lips and with only a fraction of your actual face remaining?

Sarah pulled a piece of paper from her drawers and gave it to me. "Just go before the interns make a mess of things again. I don't know where we got so many of them at once, but we've already had a handful of them sent down for punishment . . . again, and the workday hardly started. There's only so much biomass that could be processed at once; it's going to be a busy week."

Wait, already? Were these intern roles played by other aspirants? I couldn't think of another case where they would mess up that badly in under 10 minutes. The regressor said that the default role was a patient, but that doesn't necessarily mean that other special roles didn't exist here. The intern role seemed harder than the patient one just based on what Sarah said, and I could see this role being other people who couldn't make it back to Pandora in time for the trial's start.

"I know!" I answered with a frown. "And I heard we got a whole lot of new patients as well recently. There's no way that we can work with those numbers, and we've got how many doctors again?"

Sarah sighed. "It's why we have all those useless interns. We're still only at sixty-eight doctors and the five physicians. Good luck, William, you'll be working hard for once."

"Don't remind me, love," I muttered. "I'll get back to the grind, got to fill my daily quota otherwise the director'll chew me a new one!"

"She'll do more than that if you slack off this week! She's been livid ever since we got the new staff two days ago."

Two days ago? Well, that was a nice bit of information to have. I guess Jae-Hyun, Marcus, and I are only late by a few days. Not too bad, all things considered. I said my goodbyes and started to head out again when a new idea formed. I might as well take advantage of the current situation and my buddy-buddy relationship with the nurse. I could get a little more information out of the woman before I left.

"Oh, right," I said, turning my attention to the nurse one last time. "I think the director will be in a foul mood with all the chaos going on, any recommendations on how to ease her stress with my reports tonight? It'll be better for all of us if she's feeling better."

Sarah stopped and thought for a moment. Was she assessing if the question I asked was congruent with my persona? The nurse seemed to have these weird pauses every now and then, and I was almost certain that it had to do with all these roles and disguises everyone here was forced to use. I took a mental note to be more cautious of what I said or did in the future, as whatever system was judging my performance was thorough.

The nurse snapped out of her trance and nodded slowly before replying. "Well . . . I think it'll help if you inform her of how well all the new people are integrating into the hospital and assure her that everything is still operating optimally."

Good, I was getting some pieces of information about these reports I had to make. I couldn't push how much I asked for fear of breaking character and going for a round of "punishment" myself.

"Good idea," I said. "Anything else? I feel like a lot of rules will be broken soon, and when that happens . . ."

I deliberately left off the last part of my speech to see how the nurse filled in the information.

Sarah didn't pause this time but just shuddered. "We all know how the director gets when people blatantly ignore her rules . . . Um, Will, can you do us all a favor and maybe let her know if there are any especially incompetent patients or staff here? Just let the disciplinary staff know that you're sending them to her directly. They'll understand if it's you asking. I find she gets a lot more manageable when she punishes rulebreakers personally, especially if it's a gift from her favorite physician."

"I'll do you one better and find as many as I can," I answered. "Hopefully that'll make her a little calmer."

"Thank you, Doctor," the nurse said with genuine appreciation. "I guess you can be more than just a pretty face at times."

The nurse thought my current face was . . . pretty? Then what the hell would the unattractive or downright ugly people look like? You know what, I didn't want to know. God, I hoped I wasn't going to be spending too much time here, even with Noe insulating how much crap I saw and experienced.

I walked back to my quiet corner near the reception and took a peek at the map. This hospital was, as I'd expected, huge. No wonder they were short-staffed if only eighty-odd healthcare professionals worked here. It took me a while to find where I was since this place spanned multiple buildings as well as an exterior courtyard. Various wings and smaller structures were labeled with their respective uses, and it didn't seem like it would be too difficult to make my way around, although walking around would take some time.

For now, I made a mental note of the key locations: the cafeteria, the surgical wing, the new patient wing, and the administration building, which I could only assume was where the director was situated. The hallway where I was now led directly to the main medical center, so I'd head there first and survey my situation. It was close to the cafeteria, which I needed to go to in a few hours anyway, so it was my safest option while I was still unsure of the current situation.

Noe, can you remind me when it's 11:30 so I don't miss lunch?

"Acknowledged. I shall do so."

Thanks.

I gathered my wits about me and made my final preparations for what was to come. If the regressor was right, then I was Dr. William Walter right now, the director's favorite physician, so I had to act the part. The second I stepped into that medical wing, I couldn't afford to let this disguise slip, especially without Noe's help to get out of any sticky situations.

I closed my eyes and mentally went over the character I needed to play, over and over again, immersing myself deeper and deeper into the character that I needed to be. No, he wasn't a character, he *was* me. I opened my eyes again, and the illustrious Dr. William Walter walked down the hallway with gusto, without a care in the world. After all, he was the most important person in the building aside from the director; why would he have any worries at all? It was time for the good doctor to do his part for the well-being of this hospital.

CHAPTER THIRTY-FIVE

The Dreaded Doctor

Hospital

D r. William Walter walked into the medical wing with a relaxed smile on his superbly augmented face, and his casual strides down the hallway made all around him unconsciously glance to peek at his impressively modified physique. This was a man who had reached the pinnacle of their craft, but the other doctors and nurses still gave Walter a wide berth. It was not because they were afraid of the doctor himself, but because of his association with the director.

Everyone in the building knew of his personal relationship with the ominous woman in charge of Hope's Memorial, and aside from Nurse Sarah, who worked mainly in Reception, no one else dared to get too friendly with him for fear of retribution. Sarah's spot in the hospital's hierarchy was unique, so it was understandable why even the director would give her some leeway, but the same couldn't be said for the others.

In fact, if it weren't for his well-known affiliation with the director, the other hospital workers would have adored someone so dedicated to his art. He was the most complete among the doctors and surgeons working here, and his impressive body was a testimony to his mastery of the human form. Many nurses and doctors alike had lost their lives trying to court the good doctor, enamored by his abilities and magnetic personality, and it was only stopped once the director made a rule specifically to stop such an event from happening in the future.

That wasn't the only change the director made after the doctor caught her interest. More than a dozen unwritten rules were put in place to ensure that Dr. Walter's position as the unofficial second-in-command of the hospital was unquestionable. It did alienate him from the others, and although Dr. Walter was generally a cheerful man to be around, he was equally unpredictable. It was impossible to know just how he would react in any situation, or worse yet, who he would include in his infamous end-of-day reports to the director.

Very few people wanted to risk getting on his bad side for fear of getting on his dreaded list. Any poor soul who was named on it would have an inevitable visit to the director's office, and no one had ever come back from one of those meetings the same. That was why the doctors and nurses were glad that his attention would be focused on the massive intake of new patients and interns. Anything that would distract him was a boon for the others.

William walked into the busy wing and surveyed the area before him. The place was busier than it had been for years, with every able-bodied nurse, doctor, physician, and other support staff working hard to process the sheer number of new patients that arrived recently. These new patients were incurably sick, with many who would unfortunately never get better.

The janitorial staff were working overtime just trying to get the various blood, body fluids, and other viscera off the floors. The yellowing floor tiles were slick with liquids as the rusted drains quickly started to overflow, and the decrepit gurneys were constantly wheeled from place to place. Other menials were carting off discarded body parts and the dying into the morgue, and they moved hurriedly out of the physician's path, doing their best to make sure that their eyes never met the good doctor's. Failure to do so would be a gross breach of the rules.

Dr. Walter navigated his way nonchalantly through the chaos of hospital staff to the front of the intake center and grabbed a spare rulebook. No one dared question why he had chosen to do so, although it could be surmised that he wanted to review the intern's guidelines since so many were present now. He flipped through the pages casually, whistling a happy tune, before putting the little pamphlet back and picking another one up. William read through several more before heading into a busy surgical theater.

He slammed the door open and greeted the nervous doctors and nurses. The three interns almost fainted when they saw who had entered.

"Greetings!" he said with his iconic smile. The way that his mouth widened all the way to where his ears used to be was an impressive sight. "I'm here to supervise things, but no need to be nervous, I'm mainly here to make sure that the new interns don't make any mistakes."

The chief doctor in charge of today's cure turned off the electric bone saw and quickly bowed to the new visitor. He was heavily modified in his own right, with the entire left side of his body replaced with various body parts harvested from the best specimens that could be found, but he was a far cry from the perfection that was William Walter.

His face still had most of its flesh intact, and his head had pockets of blond hair that clung to the man's rotting scalp. His left hand had been surgically removed, and a massive set of needle-sharp blades were attached to his stumps, yet his right hand was woefully unchanged. Alas, the chief doctor still retained much of his original body, a far cry from completion.

"Physician Walter," the doctor said nervously, "it is an honor to have you supervise my craft."

The various other hospital staff also bowed and greeted the chief physician. Aside from the clueless interns, everyone else knew just how important it was that today's procedures go flawlessly. One could not afford mistakes when the chief physician came to personally oversee an operation. The new staff would have to learn the hard way what it meant to displease Dr. William Walter.

Dr. Walter nodded, his exposed windpipe wheezing pleasantly as he did so, and glanced at the subject of today's operations. Lying on a cold, corroded metal table was a man of indeterminable age, his features covered with grime and the corroding oils dripping from the various machines that hung around him. He was strapped onto the structure securely, but his struggles caused the leather restraints to tense and shake. His left hand was a work in progress, but the rest of him was still pink. For a person to have no augments at such an age showed just how neglectful he was.

"What does the file say on this one?" William asked as he surveyed the room. One of the nurses almost winced when he realized that he had forgotten to place the severed fingers into their proper storage containers. The nurse only hoped that the physician didn't notice.

"One of the new patients," the doctor answered quickly as he gestured to the squirming man. "He was caught neglecting his breakfast. He did not finish all of his allotted meal, but he was still deemed salvageable once today's treatment finishes."

"I see," William replied. "And what would the procedure be for such an infraction?"

"Of course, it would be—"

"Not you," Dr. Walter interrupted before gesturing to one of the cowering new staff. "I want to hear it from the intern. I believe the rules state that each of them should know the proper cure for such cases."

The new staff member quivered in fear as the full force of the physician's attention was upon him. "Yes! I, uh . . . the file says that a full modification of his arms is enough."

"Is that all?" Dr. Walter asked.

"Yes?"

The physician sighed. "Failure to address me by title . . . that's quite unfortunate because your answer was correct, Intern Adrien Smith."

The intern's eyes went wide in shock. Adrien had been so intimidated by the doctor's presence that he had forgotten that little rule. There were just too many for a new intern to follow, after all. He felt the slow tendrils of dread creep up; he had been in the hospital for long enough to understand what it meant to break the rules.

"S-shall I call for security?" one of the nurses asked, his hands already reaching for the intercom for the Discipline Department.

"Normally, yes," Dr. Walter answered before pulling out a little pad of paper from his coat. The others all felt nervous seeing the dreaded List. "But I will make a note of this personally and let the director deal with this issue."

"Yes, of course, sir," the nurse answered quickly.

Now Adrien was sweating profusely. He didn't know what a visit to the director entailed, since he had only arrived here recently, but he knew instinctively that it was something to be avoided.

"But I—I didn't mean to forget your title, sir! I don't even know your name! I was going to add it after, I swear!" the intern said. "I'm sure you've made a mistake!"

The other veteran staff all flinched.

The idiot had to break one of the biggest rules in the entire hospital: Never question the words of a physician, especially if that physician was William Walter. The temperature in the theater immediately dropped, and an intense sense of dread and suffocating nausea infected every corner of the room. It seemed that the director herself had taken notice of this blatant disregard for her rules. No one other than William could even move at that moment as they felt the full force of the director's displeasure.

Walter shook his head in disappointment, his demeanor still appearing calm, but the veterans knew that this façade would quickly break. "And you just had to say that . . . I will make this part abundantly clear for everyone present."

The physician's face distorted in rage, his once-calm visage turning monstrous in moments, and his voice rose to deafening levels. "I, Dr. William Walter, *never* make mistakes! Do you understand me?"

Everyone in the room aside from the target of his rage nodded quickly.

William turned to the first doctor, his pus-filled eyes red with anger. "Get me security, right now! I want him contained until my talk with the director!"

The other man practically leapt to the intercom. Within moments, a set of disciplinary staff rushed through the door, but even their massive gene-enhanced bodies hesitated when they felt the sheer displeasure of the director's aura coupled with the seething figure of the physician. The security quickly recovered when they saw the familiar scene and dragged the paralyzed intern away.

"D-do we take him for holding like usual, Dr. Walter?" one of the two guards asked.

"Do I have to spell everything out for you?" the furious doctor shouted. "Use your brain! This isn't the first time that someone broke the rules in front of me, and I have his name written down already! What do you think you're supposed to do?!"

"Of course, sir," the other guard answered. "We'll keep him for the director, sir. Sorry, Dr. Walter. I'll make a note of what happened!"

One of the nurses stepped up to give her report to the disciplinary staff. "I'll tell him what happened! To give a full report later!"

"Go, both of you!" he screamed again. "Get out of my sight!"

The two disciplinary staff and the nurse quickly left after, and the director's gaze slowly lifted from the surgical theater once she saw that the situation had been resolved. The other staff finally let out a small breath of relief.

Dr. Walter's mood instantly recovered as his bright smile returned. "Now, what was I talking about again?"

"The procedure, sir," the chief surgeon answered. "You were questioning the new staff about the procedure."

"Oh, right!" he said happily and turned his attention to the next intern. "All right, can you please tell me what the cure is for this particular patient?"

"Of course, Physician, sir!" the woman said quickly. "The procedure for his infraction is the complete modification of his arms, Dr. Walter, sir! We are to use standard replacement procedures outlined in Guidebook 103, sir!"

"Excellent! That's the correct answer! How long have you been here for?"

"This is my second day, Dr. Walter, sir!"

Walter thought for a moment. "Hm, so you're still too early to help out with the actual surgery."

"Yes, sir!" she agreed quickly. "That will not happen until the fifth day, sir!"

"All right, then observe quietly." Dr. Walter nodded and dismissed the interns. "And for the rest of the lovely doctors and nurses here, please continue with your operation; I am here to simply observe. I'm sure that you will finish such an easy cure without issue."

The others quickly went back to work, not wanting to risk the physician's wrath once more. They were quick and efficient, having done similar procedures a thousand times already, but they could only afford to relax once Dr. Walter was satisfied with their work and left their room.

Similar events played out two more times as the chief physician made his rounds in the surgical wing, and many a poor intern and unwilling patient were doomed to have a private meeting with the director in the not-so-distant future. The other hospital staff were only too happy to have all the attention turned to the new members, and they all relaxed once the physician's daily quota of observations was met.

CHAPTER THIRTY-SIX

The Doctor's First Day

Notification, my host," Noe said as I finished up with the last of my observations for the day. "It is fast approaching noon, and Unit Noe suggests that Host Walter head to the cafeteria for lunch. It is imperative that you do not miss the meal, both for the trial and for your health."

Right, I had been so busy trying to memorize all the rules for the interns, doctors, and nurses that I had completely forgotten about lunch. I probably would have messed up somewhere down the line had it not been for Noe. I had been treating the little system like I had been before her upgrade and thought of her more as a tool than an actual companion, but I had to change that way of thinking now that she had most of her emotion shard integrated.

Noe was a lot more autonomous and even suggested helping me out with the trial when she saw me struggling with all the new information and rules I had to be mindful of. I also noticed that she was a bit more . . . mischievous? Well, Noe had changed, but she still seemed to have my best interests in mind, and I should accept that.

Strange quirks aside, having Noe help out was a welcome relief. Trying to make sure I didn't break any of my own rules was hard enough, let alone trying to be mindful of everyone else's. But nothing could compare to the unfortunate interns; they had it especially bad.

They had over thirty-five different stipulations that had to be adhered to, and that was just for surgeries. I didn't even look at the multiple pages that outlined their conduct outside of those times. I'm honestly amazed that so many interns even made it past day two, but then again, I didn't know how many there were starting out.

Either way, I didn't have to worry too much about keeping track of all that, since I could let Noe do a lot of the analysis on whether someone was breaking a rule or not. That way I could focus all my attention on the acting department.

This would have been so much harder if you weren't helping me.

"It is a pleasure to be of assistance, my host," she answered back. "I have also taken the liberty of further insulating your mind from the corrupting nature of this trial. I hope that my host does not mind."

I honestly didn't even know what she was doing in the background, but I guess Noe must have been doing something important since I had so little trouble with the trial so far. In fact, aside from the creepy appearances of the doctors and nurses, everything else looked mundane. The hospital looked old and worn down, sure, but it was clearly a building made with medicine in mind. Even the procedures were tame, much to my surprise. That last patient I supervised was only getting some minor dental work done, even if she was squirming an awful lot.

Can you explain a bit more, Noe?

"I can, my host. Unit Noe has detected elevated levels of mental pollution that may negatively impact my host's performance in this trial," she replied. "I have taken it upon myself to negate as much of this pollution as possible by slightly altering your perception. This is all to safeguard your mind, dear Walter."

I remembered how I didn't feel my changed appearance and thought that was most likely for the better. I didn't want to find out what it felt like to have half my skin flayed off.

That's all that you're doing, right?

"Of course, my host," she answered with a light chuckle. I hadn't heard her do that before. "I always have the host's best interests in mind, even if you do not know what they are, dear Walter."

Um, I trust you, Noe. Keep it up if you think it's for the best. I don't want to go insane if I can help it.

"I will as I always do, my host."

With my head held high, I walked out of the medical hall and toward the cafeteria. The other staff quickly shifted out of my way. It was still a little strange seeing all of these deformed creatures being terrified of me, as if I were the monster here. I couldn't get used to it.

Even my time pretending to be an arbiter wasn't like this. Central's staff were more in awe of me there than scared. I was still trying to wrap my head around exactly who this Dr. William Walter was for everyone to be so on edge whenever I even looked in their direction. Whatever background the nurse gave me must have been impressive, but I was worried about my alleged ties with the director. In hindsight, I probably should have worded things better when I used that skill . . .

The hallway ended in a large glass door that led into the cafeteria. Prominently displayed on the wall was a huge sign that outlined how everyone should conduct themselves during lunch hours. No surprise as to what would happen if someone chose to ignore those rules: more punishment.

LUNCH HOURS: 12 P.M.–1:30 P.M.
Failure to follow the code of conduct will result in punishment!

RULES OF CONDUCT FOR ALL STAFF SAVE DR. WILLIAM WALTER:
All staff and patients must eat the cafeteria's daily menu.
Absolutely no talking or loud noises in the cafeteria.
All food must be eaten at your assigned seating.
All visitors to the cafeteria must remain in their seats from 12:20 p.m. until
1:25 p.m. without exception.
No food is to be left uneaten.

Wait a second, I was exempt from the rules here? Well, I did stipulate that the normal rules didn't apply to me when I had that initial chat with Sarah, but damn, was the outcome nice. That meant I have a lot more wiggle room to work with. I mean, I doubt I could get much information in my lunch hour if no one else was allowed to talk, but that didn't mean that I couldn't use my time well. I still had that meeting with the dreaded director tonight, and I needed to make sure that I was thoroughly prepared.

Without any information about what the woman was like, other than the horrifying rumors surrounding her, I was going in blind. All I knew was what Sarah told me about her need for law and order and punishment. That generally meant making a nuisance out of myself so I could get some more scapegoats to absorb her displeasure. Better they suffer her wrath than me!

I peered through the glass before making my entrance, trying to see what to expect. Although I couldn't see the whole room, I could make out most of the front. As cafeterias went, this one was pretty standard, albeit strangely laid out and rather large. The room was divided into two main sections, one large one that seemed to seat mainly patients, while a smaller clump of metal desks seated the rest of the hospital staff.

In the back corner, just barely in my line of sight, was a long lineup of mainly patients nervously accepting the food being handed out by the workers. The sound of food being dropped on the metal trays was the only noise I could hear through the doors as each person hurriedly grabbed their lunches and went to sit down as quickly as they could. Everyone looked nervous.

The tiled floors were neatly swept and clean, and a whole army of disciplinary staff that acted as guards were lined up along the walls, hawkeyed and ready to detain anyone who so much as broke a single rule. Seeing that I couldn't get any more information, I shoved the doors open and sauntered in.

The security detail stationed at all sides of the cafeteria almost leapt to their feet when they heard the commotion, ready to take away the idiot who dared to ignore the first rule of the cafeteria so blatantly, then immediately retreated when they saw who it was. It was eerie seeing just how silent the room was; even the sound of mastication was muted.

Now that I was inside, I could fully appreciate the oppressive atmosphere in the cafeteria. This was normally a place where people relaxed and chatted, but it was the total opposite in this hospital. There was a dark air of paranoia present that infested everything here. I tried my best to ignore it.

I was about to walk up to the serving area for my meal when I noticed something strange. In the very back of the cafeteria, in a strangely dark corner, was a small girl who couldn't have been older than seven or eight. She was deathly pale with almost translucent white-blonde hair, and her dirty white dress almost camouflaged her with her surroundings. I almost thought she was a ghost that only I could see until I saw that everyone near the child was taking nervous peeks in her direction. Well, maybe she was still a ghost, it's not like they'd be invisible in a setting like this after all.

Either way, it was clear that everyone was very, very afraid of her.

Even the disciplinary members were giving her a wide berth, and stranger still was the fact that she was obviously ignoring the rules put in place here. If she had the ability to circumvent the rules, then she must be someone or something important, yet the regressor's notes made no mention of the girl. That was probably what put me on edge more than anything else. Could it be something that he hadn't accounted for, or had he simply assumed that I would never encounter her?

Squinting my eyes, I could see that she was playing with a doll, one of those horrible cursed Japanese ones by the look of it, and she was muttering to herself every now and then. I glanced around to see if anyone could give me some insight on who that was, but no one was willing to even acknowledge her existence, or more accurately, no one dared to. What was it about her that caused everyone to be so afraid?

She didn't seem to have noticed my arrival yet. Now I was faced with a question. Would it be wise of me to try approaching her? I debated this question for a long time but ultimately decided that avoiding the creepy ghost child in the room wouldn't do me any good. For now, I'd eat my food and observe her before making my move.

I'd already accepted the fact that there would always be a degree of risk with everything that I did regarding the trials. I couldn't simply avoid my problems any more than I could just blindly follow Jae-Hyun's instructions. I'd realized for a long time that I had to be proactive, and I trusted my bullshitting abilities to get me out of any tough situation. This weird girl was an opportunity to find out more about this hospital.

My turn for food arrived, and I absentmindedly grabbed my lunch. I looked around for a spot to sit, preferably one close to the strange little girl, and saw that Marcus was among the people present. He saw me and gave me a small nod of acknowledgment before turning back to his meal. Jae-Hyun was missing today, although that could be because he was still unconscious from whatever the nurses drugged him with.

Marcus took a bite of food, and I shuddered when I saw that the inside of his mouth was a void of crawling insect limbs and wings. A huge bloat fly even managed to escape his mouth, fluttering around the priest briefly, before it crawled back into the man's goddamn eyeball. He didn't even blink. How was it that the priest was still the creepiest person around? Even the other priests around him, all horribly deformed with various burn marks and scars, looked practically nondescript compared to him.

I gave him a little wave back and then promptly ignored his existence. It was better for my sanity that way. I could always work with him later, much, much later. For now, I slowly ate my meal and quietly observed the girl. My Rookie Arbiter skill only displayed her name with nothing else being relevant: Alice. Even after finishing everything on my plate, the girl didn't really do much other than sit around and play with her doll. I half expected her to do something creepy.

I was about to get up from my seat and speak with the only unknown entity here when I noticed that a patient was standing right behind me looking more and more nervous by the second. It was clear that he wanted to say something to me, but I remembered that he couldn't due to the rules. I just looked at the patient, unsure of what he wanted as he frantically flailed around trying to communicate something to me.

I wasn't sure why Noe's gesture translation wasn't working here, but it wasn't until the clock hit 12:20 p.m. did I understand what had happened: I had accidentally sat on someone else's seat. He was practically begging me to leave, but it was already too late, the guards standing by saw that one of the patients was out of their seat and promptly took him away.

I frowned. I had to remember to be a little more mindful of what I did since I was a lot freer to act than anyone else here, and although I wasn't too concerned about the other patients here, I didn't want to be the cause of too many patients failing this trial. Everyone here represented someone who could help the Abyss Guild after all. It was just so easy to overlook everyone else when I was in such a unique position.

I pushed away these distracting thoughts and approached the weird ghost girl.

CHAPTER THIRTY-SEVEN

Exceptions to the Rule

After seeing the poor patient being dragged away, I gathered my focus and approached the only strange figure in the room. All right, time to see who this strange girl is and more importantly, why no one around here seemed to care or mind her doing whatever she wanted.

"Hello!" I said to the girl with that same practiced happy tone. "What are you doing here playing all by yourself?"

I was a little hesitant to ask that. Was Dr. Walter already supposed to know about this weird girl and what she was doing here? However, I couldn't think of any other way to break the ice. I was getting more and more worried by the second as the strange kid looked up from her doll and stared unblinking into my eyes. Every nerve in my body screamed that she was extremely dangerous!

I felt a strange sensation in my brain then, as if something horrible was invading my mind and thoughts. It was distinctly different from what I experienced when Rogue gave me that sponsorship, but paradoxically similar.

"Warning, my host," Noe said. "Unit Noe detects extreme levels of mental corruption. Unit Noe is allocating maximum resources to impede this progress and requires the use of the host's soul title. May I continue?"

Yes.

"Acknowledged," she answered. "Host's Xollon Anatomy Stage 1 passive is sufficient for this task."

The feeling immediately disappeared, and my mind was clear again. God, I thought I was starting to get used to dealing with things that could casually destroy the normal mind at a glance. I wasn't sure that was a good thing and wondered how the other aspirants could possibly survive without an awesome system helping them out. The answer was easy: They probably didn't.

The girl broke off her stare and smiled at me. "You're not like the others."

Ah yes, the classic creepy-ghost-girl dialogue. I could work with that.

I sat down beside her and returned her smile. "Well, that's for certain. I'm Dr. Walter, after all! And you're not like the others, either."

"No," she said simply.

I turned my attention to her doll. "And who's that?"

By this point, our conversation was starting to attract the attention of everyone else in the cafeteria. We were the only people making any sort of noise, but strangely, everyone was also trying their best to avoid making it obvious that they were listening in. They would occasionally make a quick half-second glance over before quickly shifting their attention back onto something else.

"That's Molly," the creepy girl answered. "Say hi to Dr. Walter, Molly."

The doll moved on its own—because of course it could do that—and turned my way. It gave me a little bow and a little twitch of the head. That meant . . . she was asking me how I was doing. Wait, Noe could translate doll gestures now?

"Correction, my host," she replied. "Unit Noe has always had the ability to translate the gestures of sentient beings."

Oh, so I guess the doll was just sentient. Nothing special there. I'd just treat the thing with respect so it or the creepy ghost kid didn't murder me in my sleep. If there's anything that I'd learned from watching horror flicks, it was that freaking out or treating these things with fear and discomfort usually led to very horrible ends.

"Well, hello, Molly," I said back and presented the thing with a finger to shake. "I'm doing well, thank you for asking. And how are you doing this fine day?"

The doll shook the offered finger and then bobbed its head slightly, translating to something like happiness and curiosity. There was also a clear sign of hunger mixed in, but I didn't want to know what it ate.

"Great to hear!" I exclaimed, choosing to ignore that last part of Noe's translations. "We need more joy in this hospital!"

"You can understand Molly?" The girl's eyes went wide. "No one else but Mom can."

"But of course I can understand her," I answered with confidence. "I'm Dr. Walter. I can do anything! And what's your name?"

"I'm Alice," she said and gave me a clumsy curtsy. "It's nice to meet you, Dr. Walter."

By now more and more patients were listening in on the conversation.

I could feel eyes darting back and forth, taking cursory glances our way. I couldn't blame them. Here were two people blatantly ignoring every rule in the cafeteria, and nothing was happening. The glares got to the point where I couldn't ignore them anymore.

That was when Alice's entire demeanor changed. She froze up, and the air around me started to drop. The air condensed around me and frost was starting to appear on the sleek floors. I didn't feel cold, but I chalked that up to whatever Noe was doing to keep me from going cuckoo.

"Someone's staring at me," the girl said. "I don't like being stared at. My mom always said that it's rude to stare."

She turned to face one of the aspirants. This man tried to turn his head away, but it was like he simply couldn't. His muscles were straining, trying uselessly to move away, but nothing he tried worked. Alice just watched him before gesturing for her doll to do something.

The patient's eyes went wide as he saw the Molly doll inch ever so slowly toward him. Its tiny porcelain legs moved excruciatingly slow. I saw the man's eyes watch the whole scene in dread as it crawled up his legs, then onto his chest, before finally stopping just inches from his face.

It then . . . well, let's just say that the doll's hunger was satiated after that.

Molly finished her meal and quickly ran back to Alice's side, every gesture radiating contentment . . . and something else. Then the doll looked into my eyes. Something made my mind collapse upon itself. It was like a distant memory was just out of reach . . . What was it that I was forgetting?

"Warning," Noe said. "Unit Noe is initiating emergency protocols. Extreme countermeasures are activated to ensure the host's continued mental well-being. I am using my authority to further integrate into Host Walter to do so. Please be advised that prolonged exposure to mental contamination will lead to unknown consequences."

Uh, got it, Noe, I answered absentmindedly.

Primary Soul Title: It That Sleeps at the Edge of Dusk (??? Rank)
Progress to Awakening: 11.58%

My mind cleared again as I saw the small doll sit down beside us.

"Thank you, Molly," Alice said, her old cheer returning. "I hate it when people stare at me."

"But I'm staring at you?" I asked quizzically. "You don't seem to mind."

"That's because you're nice," she answered. "And Molly likes you. You must be the doctor Mom always talks about."

Speaking of Molly, I noticed that the doll had a bit of some kind of sauce on her smooth cheeks, so I took out one of my napkins and helped wipe it off. Guess she was a messy eater . . . although for the life of me, I couldn't remember what it was that she ate. The doll allowed me to get the last of the mess off her before I put her back on the ground next to Alice.

"I apologize, Dr. Walter," Molly said. "I was too hungry and made a mess."

"Just take it slow next time," I answered with a smile. "A lady should eat with grace; it's not good if you rush like that."

"Exactly!" Alice added. "I always tell her to eat slower, but she never listens to me. But you should listen to Dr. Walter. He's an adult, he knows best."

Molly looked at me for a second, then back at Alice, before saying, "All right, I'll do as he says, but it's because he is a doctor. The other adults don't like us, Alice, but Dr. Walter is fine."

Alice lit up with excitement and hugged her doll. "Yay, thank you, Uncle Walter! See, Molly? You'll be a proper lady in no time."

The small kid turned to me again. "Sorry, I meant to say Dr. Walter. The grown-ups told me to call people proper-like."

I chuckled. "Well, I'm also a grown-up, and I say that calling me Uncle Walter is fine."

Her smile returned. "You're different than the others. Most of them are no fun."

"That's because I'm Walter, I'm special like you."

The girl nodded happily. "Would you like to play with us? We can make Molly new clothes since she got her old ones dirty!"

She pointed at a pile of strangely wet pink cloths near one of the tables the patients used. I didn't remember seeing that there before, but then again, I was in a strange hospital. Who was to say that random stuff couldn't just appear out of nowhere?

"I am not dressing up again," Molly mumbled. "And it's still wet."

Alice glanced at the fabric and frowned. The stuff seemed to levitate before all of the moisture around it exploded outward, covering some of the unlucky patients around in the disgusting floor liquid. One of the poor sods let out a half-muffled scream as tears ran down her face. It seemed like an overreaction on my end, as it was just a little bit of mop water, but either way, she was taken away promptly by security.

I shrugged.

She was never going to last for long if all it took for her to disobey a rule was getting wet. The trials weren't meant for the weak. Speaking of trials, I had almost forgotten why I had decided to talk with Alice in the first place. I still needed to gather as much information about my situation as possible, and maybe this weird girl could be the key. She was also obviously unique to this trial, so maybe she also represented the chance to get some of those hidden rewards that I never managed to acquire prior.

The cloth pieces floated toward the three of us and fell on the floor.

"There," Alice said with a little smirk. "Now it's not wet!"

"It's still in pieces," Molly answered with a sigh. "But I know you'll fix that as well."

Alice nodded and did something to make the broken fabric reassemble. Whatever use the strange material had before it was broken didn't quite make sense to me. It wasn't a solid geometric shape like you'd think a blanket or mat would be, but it kind of resembled a starfish, with one of its five limbs looking like a stub. There were some holes in the fabric, which looked like someone chewed on it, but I didn't expect random pieces of cloth to be complete in any case. Well, it was certainly large enough to use if it was just to make some doll clothes.

Another aspirant puked then and was promptly taken away like the last one.

I was starting to get annoyed at the constant interruptions and was wondering why these idiots couldn't follow such simple instructions. It was like they just all wanted to go to punishment. I could understand how seeing a creepy ghost girl using telekinesis could be terrifying, but for them to throw up from seeing that? There were way worse sights in this hospital. You'd think the least surprising thing here would be the ghost kid having psychic powers. I'd be more surprised if she didn't have them!

Alice produced scissors from somewhere and handed me one. She was using safety scissors herself, while Molly got a tiny toy pair. I hadn't agreed to play, but I guess that was a forethought now. I just went with the flow and tried my best. It was also a good opportunity to ask Alice some questions while her mood was good and she was distracted. I wouldn't want to know what telekinesis could do against someone she didn't like.

"Say, Alice," I said as I tried to make a little dress for Molly. "How come you're all alone in the cafeteria?"

"It's because Mom gets mad at me if I get in the way of the workers," she answered. "She said to play in the cafeteria because no one's moving here. It's nice and quiet as well, and me and Molly get snacks sometimes."

I guess that made sense, since there wasn't a lot of free space for a kid to sit down and relax without getting in the way of others.

"So, you're here all day?" I asked. "That can't be very fun."

She shook her head. "No, I go on walks with Molly. Molly protects me, so it's safe. It's fun playing hide-and-seek with some of the sick people, but they're not very good at hiding."

Molly sighed. "They're really not, Dr. Walter, they don't even last two minutes when we're trying to find them. And no one's having a good day if Alice gets upset."

"I'll bet!" I answered. "But I'm sure it's because Alice is so good at finding people."

I mean, how could they hide when they were trapped by so many rules and regulations? One of Jae-Hyun's tasks was to find a key to get out of the patient ward, so they probably couldn't even move freely.

"The other doctors are no fun either," she muttered. "They don't like playing with me. Mom said she's making me a new friend, but all the ones she made before were no good. I'm still glad you're nice, Uncle Walter, and Mom likes you, too."

I was getting a sneaking suspicion about who her mom was . . . but there was another piece of information that was more useful to me right now. If she was free to walk around unimpeded, then this might be a good opportunity for me to go places that I normally wouldn't be able to without a good excuse.

I didn't want to take any risks of my disguise failing, and I couldn't think of any reason why a famous physician would be going around the hospital poking his nose into departments that didn't concern him. I originally planned to get some of Jae-Hyun's requests done sneakily at night, but why risk the danger when I had this opportunity? If I just told everyone that I was supervising Alice on her walks . . .

"Say," I said casually, "do you normally walk around the whole hospital?"

"Yeah, and sometimes outside as well," Alice replied. She had gotten some glue sticks a while ago and was sticking little cut-out flowers on the dress she was making. "Mom said it's important that I exercise, so I walk lots. But it's lonely with just me and Molly."

Good, this was the chance I was hoping for.

"Well," I said with a smile, "I'll be glad to go on walks with you. I'm special as well, so I don't have a lot of work like the other doctors."

She looked up at me. "Really?"

I nodded. "Yup! You and Molly can show me all the cool spots you've found!"

She looked at her doll expectantly, as if she was checking in with Molly for permission to go with me.

"The madam trusts Dr. Walter," Molly said after a while. "So he's safe. You can trust him too, Alice."

"Awesome!" the girl exclaimed. "Let's go after we finish making Molly's dress!"

Jae-Hyun's Struggles

Jae-Hyun's time in the third trial would be considered a living hell for anyone but the man who witnessed the end of everything, yet even he was filled with worry and stress. Not because of his own experiences in the hospital, they were horrific, but Jae-Hyun could deal with pain, and he could endure the loneliness and the despair. Those were only temporary. No, what he was worried about was the welfare of the others he decided to trust in this new life of his.

The regressor wasn't worried about Father Marcus. That man survived almost as long as he did in the first round, and Jae-Hyun was certain that this particular trial wouldn't pose any problems for him, even if he joined as a patient. Now that he'd infiltrated the hospital as a priest, Jae-Hyun was even less worried that he might make a mistake. It was the other man that worried the regressor.

Walter had astonished him with his accomplishments in the short time that they had met, and he was beginning to doubt how someone so obviously talented had died so early on in the first timeline. Perhaps helping him survive was the greatest accomplishment of his regression, because Walter had single-handedly accelerated most of his plans for the future. Jae-Hyun had never seen someone so capable of manipulating the masses while being simultaneously skilled in battle. Yet Jae-Hyun feared that he was putting too much responsibility on Walter.

That was especially the case for this trial. Jae-Hyun cursed himself for not giving his party members clearer instructions. He wanted Walter to go in as a doctor and just assumed that Walter would use that term, yet he forgot to account for the difference in language. Of course Walter wouldn't know that a physician was not the same thing as a doctor here, how could he? Yet the man was paying the price for Jae-Hyun's error.

The changes to Walter's body after integrating into the hospital as a physician would have given even Jae-Hyun trouble, and he'd endured agony that would have crippled most veteran aspirants. However, not only did Walter have to endure the torment of a physician's body and form, but he couldn't show any of it for fear of breaking his persona. The human mind can only take so much before breaking.

Yet if that wasn't bad enough, he was also tasked with the responsibilities of a physician, and any mistake would result in his death. No matter how indomitable Walter's will was, there was only so much one individual could endure before his body or spirit gave in. Jae-Hyun expected the worst, and he hated himself all the more for forcing his friend into this situation.

"Patient 004!" one of the attending doctors voiced, breaking Jae-Hyun's thoughts. "It is time for your treatment!"

Jae-Hyun sighed and quietly made his way to the doctor. His new modifications made each step he took excruciating, the metal implants and surgical wounds scraping along each nerve of his body, but he hardly paid attention to them. What was pain to a man who had already embraced death?

"Good!" the doctor said, his grotesque, tumor-riddled face contorting into what could barely be called a smile. "You have adjusted to the procedures excellently! The director has high hopes for you, Patient 004. I have high hopes for you, too."

Jae-Hyun didn't respond. It wasn't like he could in any case. One of the core rules here was that patients couldn't speak outside of very specific times. He couldn't even answer direct questions outside of procedures, which was a lesson that many of his peers learned the hard way. Instead, Jae-Hyun just stared at the doctor with a blank face, not making a sound or moving.

"Excellent!" The doctor's hideous smile widened. "Come with me, patient, just a few more key procedures and you will be fit to meet the young miss. Come with me to the operating room."

Jae-Hyun suppressed a wince and followed the doctor. That was one of the two individuals in the whole hospital that he dreaded meeting, yet it was a necessity if he needed to clear the corrupted stage. Alice, the sole daughter of the director, was as unpredictable as she was deadly, and Jae-Hyun had only heard second-hand accounts of the strategies for interacting with her. He was thankful that one of his guildmates in his past life survived a run-in with Alice and told him all about it after one drunken night out, but he also wished that he had probed his old friend for more information.

All he knew was to treat the doll that was always with the girl with extreme care and attention, and to never accept an invitation to play with her under any circumstance. Yet Jae-Hyun was also instructed to always try to agree to her other requests and to keep her mood up. It was a hard balancing act, and Jae-Hyun knew that fighting against the child was out of the question. His old friend had faced this particular trial much later on in the Ascension process, and even then, he was overwhelmed by the girl's sheer presence. As they were now, in the third trial, he stood absolutely no chance against Alice.

So much had changed since his regression that Jae-Hyun was almost fearful that his increasingly inaccurate knowledge was fast approaching its uselessness. He had to make sure that the Abyss Guild's foundation was as solid as possible so that he didn't have to rely on his past knowledge. Trials that were corrupt or should only appear much later were popping up with increasing regularity, and he was sure that it was because of his unique situation.

Jae-Hyun went into the operating theater and sat down on the cold metal table as instructed. He separated the portion of his mind that would experience the awaiting agony and used the rest of the time to formulate new plans and ideas. It was one of the only benefits of these "enhancement" sessions—there was nothing that could distract his thoughts aside from the pain.

"Today," the doctor explained, "we will restructure your musculature and skeletal system so that you are sturdy enough for what's ahead. Rejoice, for you shall be stronger than all the other patients! Do you have anything to say before we begin, Patient 004?"

"Just get on with it," Jae-Hyun muttered as he emptied his mind of useless feelings and distractions.

The operation started, and the cold surgical tools started to do their work on Jae-Hyun's body, yet all he could think of was what he could do to help Walter out. The regressor only hoped that he would be fast enough to do so before his friend's sanity gave out. He knew just how corrupting this particular hospital could be.

CHAPTER THIRTY-EIGHT

An Escaped Patient

Making clothing for a doll was harder than I had initially thought, and it kind of gave me a new appreciation for actual tailors who used to do all this by hand. Molly's clothing that Alice and I made was . . . Well, let's just say that she put them on for a while before we all agreed that it was probably best that the doll wore what she had originally.

"I told you it was a waste of time to dress me up," the doll complained. "It's pointless if I'm just wearing what I had before."

"It's not a waste of time!" Alice exclaimed. "It was fun! And I know you liked the hat Uncle Walter made for you!"

Molly sighed as she clutched a tiny hat. "Fine, I'll admit I have a soft spot for the beret."

"And the flowers I put on it?"

"Yes, Alice, I like the flowers you put on it as well."

"See? It's not a waste of time," Alice said with triumph. "You're just grumpy."

"Well," I added, "I think it's about time we take the grumpy Molly on a walk. Maybe that'll cheer all of us up!"

Alice cheered up immediately and practically rushed to get going. However, she was stopped by her doll right away.

"What did the madam tell you to do after playing?" Molly added, pointing to the mess that we made.

Alice pouted. "To make sure I tidy up . . . but I want to show Uncle Walter all the cool spots we found!"

"But it is important to clean up after yourself, Alice. Look," I said, "I'll help out, too, that way we can finish faster. We'll get you a snack after as well. How's that?"

"All right . . ." the girl finally agreed. "And can I get any snack I want? I'm normally not allowed to eat too many snacks . . ."

"I don't see why not," I answered. "And I'll keep it a secret if anyone asks."

The girl brightened up immediately and started to clean the area. I didn't have to do much, honestly, since she just moved all the trash and loose fabric with her mind. The only thing I did was mop up a little. We were done cleaning in almost no time at all.

"Let's go, Molly!" Alice shouted. "Let's go get a cookie from the back!"

Her doll sighed again. "You'll spoil her like this, Dr. Walter."

I shrugged. "It's one cookie, I think she deserves a treat."

"I guess so," the doll agreed. "It has been a long time since I've seen her so happy, so one cookie can't hurt. Thank you, Doctor. I'll let the madam know that you cheered up her daughter."

Well, that confirmed things. Before I could talk any more, Alice picked up her doll and dragged me toward the back of the cafeteria. No one tried to stop us when we entered the staff-only area and reached the kitchens, although the various chefs were clearly unnerved when they saw the two of us stroll in. They stopped butchering their cuts of meat and looked like they weren't sure what they were supposed to do.

"Carry on," I said quickly. "Don't mind us, we're just getting a cookie."

One of the chefs glanced over at a guard, who just nodded in turn. Once everyone knew to just leave the two of us alone, they returned to their work and all but ignored our existence.

"The cookies are kept here," Alice said, pointing to a non-discreet jar tucked away in the back of the storage area. Two members of the disciplinary staff seemed to be guarding the container for whatever reason. In fact, the whole area was pretty well defended. Guess they really didn't want Alice sneaking away a few snacks, although it seemed a little excessive in my eyes.

The three of us approached, and the guards looked at me in puzzlement.

"Just here to give the young lady a cookie," I said casually. "Please step aside."

They didn't, although I could see a bit of hesitation in their actions. The two huge men quickly glanced at Molly, who only gave them a little nod, before silently shifting positions. Why were they so on guard about a harmless snack?

"All right, just one cookie, Alice," I said as I unscrewed the glass jar, the lid stuck on tight. "Any more's not good for you."

"I know, Uncle Walter," she answered and took a snack from the offered container. "Mom and Molly always tell me to eat healthy so I can grow up to be big and strong."

"You should have one as well, Dr. Walter," Molly said. "It's not every day that we get to have one of those."

I frowned and looked at a new cookie that I had taken out. It looked like any other chocolate chip cookie that I'd ever seen, but then again, why would the director assign staff just to guard them?

Noe, you notice anything weird about the food?

"Negative, my host," she replied. "The cookie is perfectly edible and will even improve your form after consumption, but please do not eat more than one per day."

Okay . . . I mean, it wasn't like I was addicted to snacking, so I never planned to eat that many in the first place.

Either way, if Noe said it was safe to eat, then I didn't see why I should decline. I stuffed the baked snack into my mouth and chewed. It was pretty good, all things considered, but it wasn't so good that they were addicting. Either way, I finished the cookie and felt a pleasant warmth flow through my body. I dusted off my fingers. They were probably handmade as well. Kind of tasted like the shoggoths I ate as a Xollon, now that I thought about it. I could have sworn that I heard a barely audible wail when I ate it, although I was pretty sure that was just my imagination.

Primary Soul Title: It That Sleeps at the Edge of Dusk (??? Rank)
Progress to Awakening: 12.61%

"And what do we say to Dr. Walter?" Molly reminded the girl after Alice had eaten her fill.

"Thank you, Uncle Walter," the girl said with a little bow.

"For what?" Molly added sternly.

"For the cookie," Alice replied quickly. "And for being my friend!"

I chuckled. "Well, you are most welcome, Alice. You think it's time for us to exercise a little after all that food?"

"Yes!"

I nodded. "All right, since I'm going to tag along with you, why don't you decide where you want to go first?"

My main goal today was to get a better idea of the hospital layout and just see how the staff and patients behaved. I wanted to ultimately see what was in the basement, but something told me that causally mentioning it was a bad idea, even to a child. The hospital's basement was on none of the maps, and the regressor's insistence in getting the key to unlock it suggested it was a place that was restricted. I'd play it safe and focus on the other tasks before delving into the literal underbelly of this horror hospital.

"Oh, oh, Molly." She smiled, swinging her doll around, much to Molly's displeasure. "Why don't we show Dr. Walter all the sick people? There's a whole bunch of them now, so we can play with the new ones!"

Not a bad idea. One of the regressor's instructions was to get him a key to get out of the patient ward, so checking out the layout and general security of the place was useful. Plus, I needed to read up on the patient's rulebook as well, or more accurately, have Noe memorize it. If we were going to see the new patients, then I could also potentially pass on a note to Jae-Hyun as well, if only to let him know that I was doing fine.

"Well, if Dr. Walter's with us, then it should be fine," the doll answered. "But be mindful of the other doctors and nurses. Remember the trouble you got into when you played with too many of the patients last time?"

Alice's expression turned sour as she muttered, "I know, I'll be good."

"Don't you worry, Molly," I added in. "I'll make sure she behaves. Come on, you can lead us to the sick people, Alice!"

The three of us all but rushed out of the cafeteria, although Molly had to remind the young girl to slow down at times, and down various hallways and corridors. The staff all made a conscious effort to avoid the three of us. I could only imagine what kind of menace this kid could be if they behaved like that just from seeing her. It was almost as if they were terrified of her, although it was probably more accurate to say they were terrified of what would happen if they accidentally broke a rule because of Alice.

We made it halfway to where I remembered the patient ward to be when an announcement broke the flow of our travels. This was actually the first time I had heard one since coming here, which was strange. I'd been to my fair share of hospitals in the past, and there was always one thing or another being announced throughout the building.

"Attention all staff! Attention all staff! We have an escaped patient roaming Hope's Memorial. All staff are to prioritize the capture of Patient 755. The patient is considered highly dangerous with unknown mutations.
Attention all staff! Attention all staff! We have an escaped . . ."

Oh, it seemed like one of the aspirants managed to escape. It must be someone quite skilled. If they were trying to stage an escape this early on, then a part of the regular aspirant's clear conditions probably had something to do with getting out of this hospital. Or maybe this was just a special case. It was too early to tell without more information.

Wait . . . how had this person managed to escape? If just getting out was easy, then Jae-Hyun wouldn't have purposefully asked me to get him a key out of there. Did this escaped aspirant manage to somehow steal one in the few days he was here? It was also possible he or she managed to do so with a unique ability, but I couldn't risk losing out on the chance to acquire one of the items that the regressor needed.

That only left one option for me, really: I had to capture this escapee before anyone else did. If he or she had the keys out, I'd just nab that, and if not, I could ask them how they managed to get out. Worst case, I could just add another name to my ever-growing list to show to the director.

"Say, Alice," I said, gesturing for her to slow down a little. "Did you hear that announcement?"

She nodded.

"And didn't you say that you were really good at hide-and-seek?"

"Yup!" she answered. "I'm the best in the whole hospital! You can ask Molly!"

"That she is," the doll answered with a chuckle.

"Then I think I have an idea for a fun game we can play," I added with a smile. "But it'll be challenging since you're so good. Do you think you're up for it?"

"Is it hide-and-seek?"

"It is, and it's with that no-good patient that escaped," I answered with a nod. "But it wouldn't be very fun to just catch them normally. That'd be too easy, right?"

"Yeah," Alice said with confidence, "I've caught lots before!"

"I would expect nothing less from the master of hide-and-seek!" I replied excitedly. "And since you're the best, I have to make sure it's extra hard. Do you want to hear the rules for *super* hide-and-seek?"

"Yes, Uncle Walter!" the girl answered, her eyes practically sparkling with anticipation.

"Okay, well, we'll be competing with all the other hospital staff to catch that patient, but we have to be the first to get them!" I explained. "But you can do that easy-peasy."

Alice agreed readily.

"So we have to catch the patient without squishing them! Even the stuff they're wearing needs to be in one piece," I continued. "You know what that means, right?"

The girl thought for a moment before slowly nodding. "Yeah, he's got to be breathing and stuff, so I got to be gentle. That's going to be super hard! I can see the bad man running out of the hospital right now. He's pretty good at not being caught."

Oh, so the ghost girl was clairvoyant as well. Why was I not surprised? No wonder she was so good at hide-and-seek if her opponents couldn't even hide in the first place. Good luck getting out of this one, Mr. Escapee.

"But do you think you can do it?" I asked. "Of course, Molly and I will help as well. You can be in charge, and we'll follow your orders, Captain Alice! So, what do you say?"

"I can, Uncle Walter! Captain Alice can do it no problem!" the girl said with uncontained excitement. "Is that okay, Molly?"

"You'll really spoil her like this," the doll said with that familiar sigh. "But fine, we'll let her have some fun since we do need to find the patient in any case. Yes, Captain Alice, we'll follow your orders."

Alice hugged her doll and swung her around. I was worried the fragile-looking doll would break, in all honesty, but Molly was a lot tougher than I thought.

"Okay," I said once we were all in agreement. "Once you find the patient, make sure you catch him real good and bring him back to us. We can even show him to your mom after. I'm sure she'll be happy to see you help out."

Alice nodded again. She was practically bouncing up and down now, eager to start the game.

"All right," I said. "Since you're in charge, tell us what to do, oh mighty Captain Alice!"

She gave me and the doll a resolute salute and told us our instructions. It wasn't too bad, all things considered. Alice was honestly a very bright child. Unfortunately, the patient who escaped would find out this brilliance in the worst way possible.

CHAPTER THIRTY-NINE

Running for Your Life

Patient

Henry ran for his life.

He could sense the approach of more of those monstrous doctors and nurses, just steps behind. They were approaching fast. Henry knew he couldn't outrun them, and the number of times that he could use his skill was fast approaching the limit. Yet the exit was surrounded by those damn nightmare creatures.

Henry gritted his teeth. He was so close to his destination and the chance to get out of this fucking hellhole. The door to the outside world was so close . . .

With one final grunt of effort, Henry drew on a force of will he never thought possible, and his image disappeared from view once more. His already-depleted MP was ticking down alarmingly quickly, and he had only one potion left to replenish his reserves. He'd have to save that for the final stretch, once he was out of the building proper.

It was enough.

He slipped through the guards and bolted toward the door. If the information that he managed to collect over the past forty-eight hours was correct, then the main entrance doors were never locked. He had suffered through so much to get that information, not to mention the key needed to start his escape, and it was now time to risk his life to see if he was correct.

One final surge of adrenaline and Henry ran straight to the door and into the glorious outdoors. The cold, harsh rain never felt better!

He had been right! Now it should be smooth sailing since no one aside from the dreaded physicians could exit the building during work hours. There were only a handful of those in the whole building, and Henry was certain that he could evade them once his mana reserves were replenished. With the eternal dusk that blanketed the whole courtyard along with the huge open space, coupled with the never-ending downpour, he couldn't fathom a world where he couldn't get out.

But Henry was disciplined. He ran toward a dark corner, hiding behind some dense foliage, and took a moment to rest. He wasn't out of the trial yet, and he couldn't afford to be sloppy. He took out the last mana potion from his inventory and drank it quickly. Henry decided to wait the full twenty minutes for his mana to recharge before making his move, and although it was a risk to wait for the physicians to all come out, it was most likely more dangerous for Henry if he couldn't use his invisibility skill to complete his escape.

With his mind made up, Henry made himself as small as he could and waited. All was well for the first ten or so minutes, and he was even starting to relax his body. He hadn't realized how fatigued he was until now; he hadn't been able to rest with the constant fear of doing something wrong. He had seen how the poor sap sleeping next to him had been taken away because he was snoring. They couldn't make any sounds outside of designated hours, and these freaks made no exceptions to the rules.

Since that moment, Henry was on edge. It had been more than two full days since he had any amount of rest, let alone sleep, and he was starting to feel its effects even through the enhancements of an aspirant. Damn, was he ready to get a good night's rest and a proper soak in a hot tub when he was out of this nightmare, then he'd have a proper "talk" with that idiot of a party member who decided it was a good idea to leave Pandora for an extended adventure.

Henry breathed in and out. He was so close to freedom now. He just needed to wait a little longer and he was home free. He'd bet that his reward for being the first person out of this hellhole would be amazing as well!

All was well until it wasn't.

A sudden chill enveloped the aspirant, followed by the telltale sounds of heavy footsteps. Henry froze. There was no way someone could have found him, right? His skill hid all traces of his presence, including footsteps and odors, so how could a physician locate him this quickly? He had only released his skill for ten minutes. That wasn't enough time for any traces of his presence to leak out. No, Henry rationalized, it was probably some other staff, maybe a gardener or something, just passing through.

But to be safe, Henry bent down and slowed his breathing. He had recovered enough to use his skill again, but doing that, or using any mana at all, would disrupt the efficiency of the potion. He cursed himself for buying the discount stuff at the stores. The high-end elixirs didn't have this drawback.

Just pass through! Just let it be some random worker!

Henry closed his eyes and prayed for the first time in his life.

You'll be fine, Henry, just a little more and you're out. Then you can just stay indoors and never risk leaving the damn city again!

A sharp, piercing pain in his leg told him that he was wrong. Henry was not fine. He suppressed a scream and saw that he was wounded from a strange black dart made out of . . . hair?

"There you are, Patient 755!" a cold, raspy voice said, piercing through the gloom. "Did you think you could escape? That's very naughty of you!"

Henry inadvertently looked up, even through the agony of his new wound. His heart almost stopped.

Never has he seen a monster so grotesque. The thing's face was all raw muscles and sinew, with only small rotting patches of flesh left clinging onto his horrible visage. His mouth was widened to an impossible degree that was a gross parody of a smile, the thing's facial muscles were sawed off so that its grin could reach from ear to ear. Or at least it would have if the creature had ears. Instead, sharp, corroded metal wires dug into the thing's ear canal, the metal bending around his face and ending with small metal hooks that permanently kept its putrid, pus-filled eyes open.

How it even spoke with its neck so mutilated was beyond Henry's comprehension, and he quickly activated his class ability. Worse yet was the awful doll sitting eerily on the creature's shoulder. The escaped aspirant could swear that he could see it move as it judged him with its unblinking stare. Henry panicked. The horrible pain in his legs was an afterthought, and he didn't even see how the wound was slowly spreading to the rest of his leg.

Henry didn't have any thoughts other than to get out of there as quickly as he could.

Henry ran.

Yet somehow, despite his skill, the freak of a doctor appeared to be following him. Henry made random movements, dashing left and right, turning around and zigzagging as he sprinted, but no matter what he did, the distinct sound of the horrible doctor's wheezing rasp was omnipresent. Henry couldn't help glancing back to confirm his fears, and it was true—he was still following him. Worse still, all of his random movements had made the gap between him and the monster close up. He didn't know how it was possible for it to track him, but he had a sinking suspicion that it was the creepy doll. No matter where he turned, how he ran, the damn thing would continue to stare right at Henry.

How was that possible? No one in the entire hospital, not even that one dreaded physician he met on the first day, could see through his abilities. What had he overlooked? Henry was so sure that his plan for escape was perfect. He almost died stealing that key and map, and even spent hours meticulously tracking all the staff and the rules they had to obey. But it was all going downhill fast . . .

Then Henry realized something. In his panic, he had lost track of his position and didn't know where he was running to. He knew that it was imperative that he stayed on track when he was out in the open—the eternal night and foggy weather made navigation a nightmare—but his rush to escape had destroyed days of careful planning. Worse yet, he was visibly slowing down. That wound on his leg that he ignored earlier was a lot worse than he thought.

"What's the matter, little patient?" that mockery of a proper health care physician said, its gangrenous voice sending chills down Henry's back. "Are you giving up already? Run faster! Run! RUN!"

Henry didn't need to be reminded of that. He scrambled through the thickening fog and torrential downpour, and as luck would have it, he saw a gated-off area just to his left. Squinting his eyes, he saw that there was an opening in the corroded metal fencing that looked to be just wide enough for him to squeeze through. It was his only hope. His stamina was fast approaching its limits, and the pain in his leg was becoming unbearable even through the adrenaline. If he could get in that area and find a spot to rest, if only for just a moment . . .

He made up his mind and rushed toward the gate. The fog and weather were getting so dreadful as he neared his destination that he couldn't make out what was on the other side of the fencing, but nothing could be worse than being chased by that creature. Henry reached the rusted metal and using the last reserves of his strength, he grabbed onto the cold bars and heaved. They distorted just enough for Henry to squeeze inside, he tore up his right arm and back in doing so but was relieved to see that the doctor monster stopped when it saw that Henry was out of reach. It was still smiling at him.

Henry backed away slowly, his legs aching like he never believed possible, all the while taking uneasy glances back to make sure that he was no longer being chased. Little did he know that the doctor went back to the opening and straightened out the metal fencing, trapping the aspirant inside. Then, once its work was done, the doctor strolled away leisurely. His work was done for now.

Henry retreated into a large stone mausoleum and all but collapsed onto the ground. It wasn't the best place to hide, since there was only one way in and out to the outside. The only other notable feature was a dreary set of stairs near the back that led down to the crypts. Henry hadn't realized that he had gone into the gated-off cemetery, but it wasn't like he had any other choice. He didn't hear anything about this place when he was gathering information. He should have been more thorough!

Either way, it was too late for regrets, and at least he was out of the dreadful weather. Henry took out a small lantern and took some time to care for his wound. He pulled his trousers up and gritted his teeth at what he saw. The dart thing that the doctor monster threw was made of hair, and this damn hair was starting to crawl up his leg from the inside.

Henry saw it wiggle just under his skin as if it was alive. The aspirant took out a rag and bit down on it. With both hands, he grabbed onto the tuft of hair sticking out of his leg, and before he could second-guess his decision, Henry pulled with all his might. He almost passed out from the pain, but his enhanced stamina and endurance saved him from the worst of it.

He quickly threw the living mass of hair to the side and burned it with a lighter. It sizzled in the flames and dissolved into a foul-smelling sludge. Looking down, Henry tried his best to staunch the bleeding with a precious potion before wrapping the wound up with shaking hands. He was thankful that the cold was numbing the worst of the pain.

But once again, right as Henry was about to get comfortable, right when even a semblance of safety was established, he felt every single sense in his body warning him of danger. Was the doctor somehow back? But he couldn't hear the thing's ominous footsteps. Henry focused his senses, trying desperately to understand what was going on.

That was when he noticed the subtle temperature change. It had gotten . . . colder. No, it was still getting colder, and after just a few minutes the aspirant could see his breath condense before his eyes. He scrambled to get up, but his leg gave in and he stumbled on the ground. No, he didn't stumble, he slipped. Frost and ice had formed on the damp marble floor, and there, standing by the mausoleum entrance was a pale girl dressed in all white. She floated slowly toward the terrified man.

With his heart going into overdrive, Henry forced himself up. The girl didn't look dangerous, not like that monster that was just chasing him, but his experience in the trials told him that this creature was equally—no, it was worse than that doctor. He had to run, but his only way out was blocked by the child, and the only other exit was down the stairs, deeper into the crypts.

Could he fight the thing? No, there was no way that he could in his current state. Henry felt that he would collapse from just walking, let alone combat. Seeing no other options left to him, Henry forced his exhausted body down the dark stairs. He resolved that, if he was going to die, then he would make these damned abominations work for it!

CHAPTER FORTY

A Game of Hide-and-Seek

I rounded the corner to where the cemetery's main entrance was and strolled inside the enclosed space, making sure to close and lock the gothic gate behind me, as was expected from a respected member of this hospital. The graveyard itself was pretty impressive, with old, expertly crafted gravestones and epitaphs all lined up in neat rows. The richer families had massive monuments erected to house their dead, and the paved stone path was free from weeds and other clutter. There was also a creepy altar near the back, but I didn't want to risk going near that thing.

All told, it was a comforting place to be.

The grave keeper, or at least that was who I assumed the hunched-over man was, greeted me with a polite nod before heading off into his hut once more. I waved back before stopping to deal with all the soil caked on me.

Apparently, I was in another dimension where it was perpetually dark and rainy, and I was very glad to have some pavement to stand on again. The mud and rain were starting to seep into my socks from all that running around, and I had to take a solid five minutes trying to scrape the gunk off my shoes.

"It's not going to come off, Dr. Walter," Molly told me. "I had the same thing happen when Alice dropped me outside the other day. Just have the girl dry you off when you see her."

"Feels awful, though," I grunted. "I never thought I'd hate the rain so much. It's even getting into my windpipes."

Wait, my windpipes? How was it doing that?

"We'll get you a proper hat next time. The madam should have some spare ones," the doll answered, tugging onto the little beret that she was still wearing. "Keeps the worst of the moisture off."

"Yeah," I grumbled as I shook more clumps of debris and moisture off my head. "I'll take you up on that offer. Any news from Alice?"

I had wondered how we were going to communicate when Alice suggested we split up, but she had some kind of psychic link to her doll that allowed them to talk to each other. Molly informed me that they'd been doing this a lot whenever they played similar games with the patients. It made me miss the system chat a little.

"Yes," the doll answered after a short pause. "The patient made it into the catacombs a while ago. Alice wanted to give him some time to hide, but she's giving chase right now, and she needs the two of us to cut him off in there. We'll head in on the opposite side and meet her in the middle . . . although I might have overdone it with the cursed dart earlier, so we should hurry before he dies."

I remembered that small bundle of the doll's hair that Molly shot at the patient when we first met. It was barely the size of a toothpick. I didn't think it would do that much damage, even if it was cursed.

"The patients should be a little more tenacious than that, right?" I asked. "There's no way that little dart would kill one that quickly."

Molly chuckled. "You'd be surprised by how frail they can be, Dr. Walter, but I hope you're right. Anyway, it's still best to hurry; just follow me."

"Lead the way!"

The way Molly directed me kind of reminded me of the way that the twins used to guide Vadeem. She sat on my head and would point at where I needed to go. It had been a little hard to follow her instructions when I was chasing that patient earlier, but I had gotten used to it at this point. I sighed as I wondered how the others in the Abyss Guild were doing. I was having the time of my life here since all I had to do was babysit a kid and play some games with her. I hoped their experience was as easy as mine.

"That's the one," Molly said as we reached a massive stone door blocking off the entrance to one of the many stone structures that littered the place. "Just push it aside and we'll be on the other side of Alice."

I looked at the door hesitantly. The structure was huge, with the old mausoleum being at least three stories tall. The door sealing off its interior was almost as tall and just as wide. Honestly, it was more like a slab-shaped boulder than a door, and I wasn't sure if I could even budge it, let alone move it.

I placed my hands on the smooth surface and pushed hard. The door all but flew out of the building, and I had to grab onto it before it crashed into the gravestones close by. My fingers dug into the rock face just fast enough to stop the thing from careening away before I gently lowered it to the ground. The stone door was a lot lighter than I thought.

"Please don't destroy the courtyard," Molly lectured. "The grave keeper will not be happy having to fix it again."

"Sorry," I said quietly.

Molly just shook her head. "Come on then, let's get going. I'll seal the door behind us."

Once the two of us were inside the staircase, Molly's hair extended outward and coiled around the big slab. With little effort, she hoisted it back to where it was before and closed us off. Thankfully I didn't need any light source to see down here.

The catacomb, as the name suggested, was filled to the brim with the dead. Some of the skeletons and skulls were arranged neatly on the various alcoves and shelves carved into the bare rock, kind of like what you'd see in those famous ones in Paris, but the vast majority of bodies in various states of decay simply littered the floors. They made for horrible tripping hazards, and I swore that some of them were still twitching.

Molly noticed my struggle trying to navigate my way through and used her hair to clear a path forward. Her hair engulfed the bones and other decaying substances as it swept all around us. I wasn't sure where all that material was going since it all just ceased to be once she was done.

"Sorry," she said, "I forgot how cramped it is here. Alice just floats around, so I never noticed before."

I nodded. The piles of bodies practically covered the place from floor to ceiling. I'd probably twist an ankle if I had to wade through this stuff.

Molly shook her head. "We haven't had a chance to clean this space out since we got that influx of patients."

"What about the crematorium?" I asked, remembering distinctly that this hospital had one on the map. "Wouldn't it be easier to just burn all the bones here? It can't take that long if we have some of the patients do it."

Molly shrugged. "Cremation's already operating at maximum capacity as it is, and we do need some new bodies down here to feed the rats. But you're right, this is still ridiculous. I don't think anyone we bring in here can even move with the clutter. The inhabitants will grow fat if they're not hunting active prey. I'll bring it up to the director tonight to have this place emptied out, at least partially."

I chuckled. "Seems like you're keeping the whole hospital from imploding."

"It's one of my many jobs," she answered with a tired sigh. "Wish we had more staff like you to help out, though."

"You got those interns, though!" I joked with a cheeky smile.

She gave me a look of dismay and sighed even harder. "Don't get me started on those fools, Doctor . . ."

"All right." I chuckled. "They're more work than they're worth, I have a few on my list I have to report later as well."

"At least that'll keep the madam busy."

"So where is our escapee anyway?" I asked, changing the topic. "I can't tell one corridor from the next. Easy to see where the exit is, though, since you ate all the bones leading to it."

"I don't eat bones, Dr. Walter, but I get your point. I'll make sure that our patient doesn't come across this path and find the exit, not that he can get out the door in any case."

I shrugged. "Better to be safe."

"You should see his traces after you turn left there," the doll stated, pointing at an intersection. "Just remember to let Alice play with him a bit first, and let her have the honor of catching him."

"Like I'd steal the fun from a kid," I answered. "It's all hers!"

Just as Molly said, the traces of the patient were pretty clear once I walked a little bit along the left hallway. There was some faint torchlight illuminating the dark, and I could hear the echoes of hurried footsteps crushing bone underneath, followed by the stifling gasps of an exhausted man.

Now how do I approach this? Patient 755 was fast approaching my location, and it would be all too easy for me to just grab him. I frowned. At this rate, he'd run right into me and I'd have a hard time finding a good excuse for letting him go if that happened. Guess I'll have to spook him a little and have him run toward Alice's position.

"Just have him run down the right path," Molly interrupted once she saw my hesitation. "It leads to a dead end. Alice can have her fun there."

I nodded and made my way back to the intersection and positioned myself in the hallway that led to the exit. Finding a suitably dark corner, I picked up a skull off the ground and waited in position. I'll just throw it at the patient once he's here and hope that'll startle him enough to run in the opposite direction. Molly was tucked away down the left passage as a backup in case he decided to turn around and backtrack.

Once the patient rounded the corner, passing Molly along the way, I lightly threw the skull at the aspirant, doing my best to avoid his head and neck. The projectile all but exploded, connecting right on his arm, and I watched in horror as the aspirant's arm broke in at least a dozen places.

Worse yet were the fragments of the skull that were embedded in his face and body. I was afraid that I had killed him then, but he miraculously kept on going, not even letting out a cry of pain as he dragged his broken body toward the dead end.

Hopefully Alice could catch him quickly . . . I had a few potions left that could hopefully stabilize his condition, but that required him to be alive first. I swore that I only threw the skull lightly, but something was odd about the amount of strength that I could output.

Molly waddled over to where I was and gave me a disapproving look.

"Uh, he's still alive . . ." I muttered before apologizing. "Look, maybe you were right about how fragile they were."

"I told you so, Doctor."

"I can stabilize him if he's still in one piece," I added quickly. "Can you tell Alice to perhaps hurry up a little?"

She sighed for the who-knows-how-manieth time before agreeing. Molly paused to communicate with the girl before turning her attention back to me.

"Alice said she'll catch him now," the doll said. "You should be thankful that she's in a good mood today and agreed, Dr. Walter."

"I'll make sure to properly thank her after."

True to her words, Alice appeared next to Molly and me shortly after, an unconscious but still-breathing individual levitating a few feet behind her. He looked even worse than before. If Central hadn't awakened him then I doubt he'd still be among the living. I took out one of the more expensive elixirs from my stash and quickly gestured for Alice to bring the man over to me.

I hastily poured the stuff all over the aspirant and only calmed down when I saw that his condition seemed to improve. I also pocketed the little key I found in his pocket while doing so, but that little maneuver I hid. There was one of the harder requests that Jae-Hyun had me complete out of the way, and I hardly had to do anything at all to receive it!

Once I was fairly confident that he wouldn't expire, I had Molly wrap him up tightly, and the three of us left the catacombs in high spirits. Alice began retelling her side of the game in great detail, and I chuckled at how inventive she was when she was catching the escaped patient. I guess she really was a master at hide-and-seek!

Time to head somewhere a little quieter so I could ask this patient some very pertinent questions. I had almost gotten ahead of myself and asked him there and then, but I remembered that pesky rule about speaking with patients. I couldn't talk with them outside of official medical procedures.

Well, I wasn't sure if that still applied to patients who attempted to escape, but there was no reason to risk that when I could just bring him inside and book a spare operating room in the hospital. I did need to make sure he didn't die, after all, so that must count as practicing medicine. I'll even have some interns to help out so that if things do go badly, I can put all the blame on them instead.

More plans started to formulate in my mind as we exited the rainy weather and headed back into the comforts of the increasingly familiar hospital. I kind of liked it here, honestly.

CHAPTER FORTY-ONE

Interrogations and Information

Finding a free operating room was easy enough. The other doctors and nurses were more than glad to help, and so they were restraining the patient on the operating table. What was challenging was trying to get the man to talk at all, since he was completely unconscious. His wounds had stabilized with the elixir I gave him earlier, but the amount of punishment that the patient's body had suffered was too much for his mind to handle. It seemed like the man, who I found out was named Henry, simply didn't want to wake up again.

I was even left with four very nervous interns and a half dozen nurses, all on standby awaiting their instructions. Alice wasn't allowed in the surgical theater, much to her disappointment, but after I promised that I'd meet up with her to go see her mom at the end of the workday, she cheered up immediately. For now, she went back to the cafeteria to play. Additionally, news that the illustrious Dr. Walter had subdued the escaped patient had already spread through the hospital, and a few curious hospital staff even popped in to congratulate me.

That's no good though, I wanted to see what this man knew about the trial, and more importantly, the situation with the other aspirants. Any information I could find out about the patient ward would be immensely useful for me, as I still needed to meet up with Jae-Hyun to figure out what to do. Plus, I was very curious about what the normal aspirant's clear conditions were, and how much they differed from the weird corrupt version we were experiencing.

Unfortunately, that also meant that I had to wake him up, but the problem was that I wasn't an actual physician, so there was only so much I could do before the others in the room could start suspecting me of being a fraud. But why do my own work when I had idiots to work for me? The interns here made a great scapegoat to blame for all of my problems! They could be in charge of simply waking the man up, and I'd say it was due to my brilliance that I was able to stabilize the patient in the first place!

"All right!" I said in my most commanding voice as I addressed the room. "As you can see, I have successfully captured the escaped patient, and I have even stabilized his condition so that he could be in prime condition to meet the director. In other words, I have done all the hard work already! But this man is destined for a meeting with our lovely director, and I don't have to say what would happen if he met her in his current state, do I?"

Everyone present quickly shook their heads, beads of sweat forming on their brows.

"Good," I continued with a smile. "Which is why I am allowing you interns to help out today with a simple procedure."

The four people gathered looked nervous.

"Now, now," I added, "I know that you're not supposed to work on actual procedures until much later, but that doesn't mean you should just sit around and observe! All you have to do is figure out a way to wake this patient up with his mental capabilities intact. Simple, right?"

They nodded as one.

"It's 5:30 p.m. right now," I stated, gesturing at the old clock hanging on the wall. "And I have to present today's findings to the director at eight, but I still have to question the patient once he's awake. I will give you a full hour and a half to do this task; it's more than enough time. Do it well and I'll put in a good word for you, but fail . . ."

"We will do our best!" one of the male interns shouted. "Sir!"

I nodded. "Good, I'll observe. Don't mess this up. You're allowed to use any method you think will help."

I took a seat in the corner and watched the half-panicked interns go to work on Henry. Knowing that these were aspirants and not actual physicians (or at least I don't think any of them were doctors prior to all this bullshit), I wasn't too surprised when they made almost no progress with waking up the unconscious man. They were very creative with their approach, in any case, using everything available to them in the room to the best of their ability.

It wasn't until an hour and fifteen minutes had passed that the interns got increasingly more nervous and impatient. With the deadline fast approaching, one of the interns resorted to using her class ability. That was a big mistake.

A soft glow appeared on one of the female intern's hands, and I could feel a surge of healing energy wash into Henry. He was getting better by the second, and even showed signs of waking up, but everyone else in the room, aside from the other interns, stopped what they were doing to stare at the woman.

"An imposter!" one of the nurses said.

"Imposter!"

"An imposter is among us!"

The other interns slowly backed away from the woman, leaving her alone and isolated. Not wanting to look out of place, since I was also an imposter myself, I pointed at the poor intern and joined in the chants. Then the strangest thing happened: The woman who was deemed an imposter simply . . . vanished. It was like she just disappeared into thin air. The hospital staff quickly went back to normal and acted like she had never existed in the first place.

I gulped.

Was this the consequence of breaking character in this damn creepy hospital? Thank god I didn't have any flashy skills like the nonexistent intern and only used a potion to stabilize Henry. I didn't think it would be too strange for a renowned physician to be carrying something like that . . . but I'd make damned sure that I didn't take any further risks in the future.

One of the other interns was able to collect themselves and hurriedly reported the condition of the patient. "Dr. Walter, t-the patient seems to be coming to."

Right, best not to acknowledge the existence of that imposter and pretend that Henry was able to recover by himself.

"Good!" I said as normally as I could. "You're lucky that he was able to recover by himself. The interns are dismissed."

Without further prompting, the aspirants all quickly left the room, leaving me with just a handful of nurses on standby. I turned my attention to the now-awake patient.

"Why hello, Patient 755," I said to the wounded man. "Or should I call you Henry?"

The man looked at me with weary eyes but otherwise didn't say anything.

"Now I'm going to ask you a few questions, and I want you to answer them as best you can."

He spat in my face, or at least tried to. Henry was still so weak that he couldn't muster the energy to do that properly, and only managed to make a mess.

"That's not very nice," I said, shaking my head. "Now let's try that again."

"Go to hell, you damn abomination!"

I sighed. Why did they always have to make my life so difficult? It would have saved everyone a lot of time and effort if this patient just listened to my instructions.

I turned to one of the nurses waiting on the sidelines. "The patient is being unreasonable and is refusing to follow orders, please help him understand the error of his ways."

They did so, and it was an unpleasant experience for everyone involved. But for all the agony that Henry endured, he didn't cave in and was giving me a death stare the entire time. I turned my attention back to the patient once the nurses were done.

"So, do you want to answer my questions now?" I asked again. "Or do you need another session with the wonderful nurses in this facility?"

"Go fuck yourself."

I shook my head as the nurses got into position to help me again.

"Suit yourself, Henry," I said. "Nurses, please do your thing."

And they did. I will give the aspirant this, the man had a tenacious soul. No matter what the nurses and interns did to try to persuade him to talk, Henry did not mutter a single word to me after . . . Well, that wasn't completely true. He did say some quite rude things about me and my mother, but nothing useful outside of that. It was like he was doing this just to spite me, and I was afraid that any more sessions with the nurses would cause him to expire.

"Enough," I said finally. "Your methods are not going to make the patient talk, that is quite clear to see. We'll need a new approach."

"I apologize, Dr. Walter!" one of the nurses said. "W-we can try harder."

"No, that will not be necessary," I said, shaking my head before facing one of the nurses in the room. "You, go get me Father Marcus, he's one of the new priests that joined us today. Perhaps the patient will change his mind with a more spiritual approach."

The priest arrived a few minutes later. His schedule was a lot less strict than mine, and he had already finished his duties for the day. The nurses quickly filled him in on what I needed, and he agreed readily. He gave me the gentlest smile as he observed the patient, looking over him as if Henry was a particularly interesting piece of furniture. All the while, a continuous swarm of horrible insects were gathering above the priest's head. Where they came from, I had no idea, nor did I want to find out.

"Do not worry, Dr. Walter," Marcus said with his now-trademark smile. "Give me a moment alone with the patient, and I guarantee that he will cooperate. It is surprising how much a man is willing to say when you . . . *inject* the right dose of enthusiasm into their brains."

Yeah, that was definitely not what he was going to do, but I nodded anyway and told the nurses to do as the good priest said. We all left the priest alone with Henry. There was a horrible buzzing sound as I closed the door, followed by the desperate whimpers of the patient. Whatever Marcus wanted to do with Henry wasn't something that I wanted to know about. What was even more surprising was that the father came out not even two minutes later, all smiles and good humor.

"The patient will talk, Dr. Walter," he assured, "but only with you."

"All right," I answered. "Everyone else, you're dismissed. Make sure you thank the good father for his work."

Henry was a much more cooperative man when I reentered the operating theater. In fact, he seemed like he couldn't wait to begin telling me his whole life story. Whatever the father did to him was effective, and I was only too glad to have been outside the room. Sometimes ignorance was bliss.

"Now then, Henry," I said once again. "Please tell me how you managed to escape, and why you're trying so desperately to do so."

I wasn't sure if I could talk about the trials blatantly, so I asked in a round-about manner. There weren't any rules that said I couldn't, but I remembered Jae-Hyun being very adamant that I not break character, and Dr. Walter would certainly not know about any Trials of Ascension process.

"Yes, Dr. Walter," the patient said in a daze. "I was trying to escape because the System—"

Henry started to spasm as if he was having a stroke the second he attempted to mention the System. Could he only communicate these facts with other members of his own party, or was there some kind of failsafe that the Trash Matrix put into place so that its interference in these strange dimensions could be contained? Either way, I best steer clear of any talk about clear conditions and trials.

"Never mind that last question, Henry. Just tell me how you managed to escape from the patient wing."

Henry's condition started to improve, and he continued, "My teammates and I devised a plan for me to escape. Only one of us needs to get out for the whole party to clear the tr—ial."

More spasms, albeit not as harsh. There were also a few huge hairy flies that buzzed out of his ears and nose then, but I don't think that was because he broke some kind of hospital rule . . . Yeah, I was glad I didn't see how the kind father convinced Henry to be more cooperative.

There seemed to be something in place that makes it difficult for the aspirants to share information about the Trash Matrix. My own rulebook stated that if I heard any of these patients talk about trials and whatnot, then it was a sign of an incurable disease, so perhaps they only had a limited capacity to talk about the trial between each other. That was useful information to have.

"And who are these teammates who helped you?"

"You will know them as Patients 756, 757, and 754."

"But you seemed to know the layout of the hospital quite well. Did you get outside help from say, interns or nurses?"

"No," he said again, "I used my . . . mutations to leave at night after stealing the key out of the ward."

"Good, and what did you find out on those nights out?"

And he told me everything he knew then.

CHAPTER FORTY-TWO

Communications and Communions

Once Henry was finished dictating what felt like his entire life story back to me, I had one of the hospital staff restrain him and sent him to Alice and Molly. I did tell them that we would present the escaped patient to her mom, and I wasn't about to break a promise to a child.

I could summarize Henry's information into a few main points. First of all, the way they were tasked with leaving this hospital, aka the clear conditions of this trial, was simply to get oneself out of the confines of the hospital property. The hardest part would have been escaping the hospital building itself, while getting out of the courtyard would have been a breeze in comparison had it not been for, well, me.

Additionally, the patient wing was heavily guarded by disciplinary staff, nurses, and the doctors who frequented the ward, and a normal patient was all but confined in that section except during treatment hours and lunch. However, what surprised me was that the doctors knew about the strange abilities of the patients here. That was what the mutations were talking about in that announcement and the reason why the patients were here in the first place. The strange alterations that the Trash Matrix imposed on the people here were seen as a disease that needed to be cured.

That meant that the patients could use their abilities without being "erased" like the interns, but it also meant more treatment sessions if they were caught doing so. That was going to be a tough balancing act for the patients since survival would be quite challenging without the use of their class and title skills. And that was for the normal patients . . . What kind of horrible situation would Jae-Hyun be in?

"Say, Father Marcus," I said tentatively, still unsure how much I could say without the hospital questioning my identity, "did you perhaps have an opportunity to frequent the patient wing today?"

He nodded in understanding. "Yes, that is one of the main duties of a priest stationed here. I had the chance to chat with a very interesting new patient today as well; a new arrival by the name of Jae-Hyun."

"And did he tell you anything?"

"Nothing that I can say here," he said with a small smile. "That would be highly unethical of me to do so as a priest, just as you wouldn't tell me the details of one of your patients, Dr. Walter."

Right, so if I was reading between the lines correctly, then we couldn't communicate directly about the patients. I thought as much, would have been too easy.

"But," the father continued, handing me a small note, "he did give me an interesting note to pass along to the physicians, any physician, really, if I were to ever see one. He was very curious about the well-being of his caregivers as well, so I can also pass along a message for him if you wish."

So indirect methods of communication worked, interesting.

I took the paper and stuffed it in my coat pocket. I'd read it when I was sure that I was alone and out of sight after.

"What a wonderful individual!" I said with an exaggerated smile. "The people under our care generally do not ask about how we are doing, so it is quite rare to see someone different. Perhaps I will go and thank this gentleman myself sometime! But if you see him before I do, let him know that Dr. Walter is doing well, and he is doing his job as is required of him. In fact, one of his *key* tasks is already complete!"

Marcus nodded slowly. "I shall pass along those exact words, Doctor."

Wait, another thought came to me. I probably wouldn't be seeing Marcus all that often, so I should pass along as much information as possible while I still could. I grabbed a piece of paper from a clipboard and hurriedly wrote down as much as I could. I also added in the responsibilities that I had, my unique situation in the hospital, and the instructions that Jae-Hyun gave me there.

"This is a . . . thank-you note," I said, handing the priest my paper. I was hoping that this excuse would be in line with what was acceptable for staff to do, "for all the help that you have done for the hospital on your first day here. Please read it when you have time. In private, of course."

He nodded. "Thank you, Dr. Walter. I will make sure that I respond to you in kind. Look forward to my letter in the near future, and may God be with you."

I shook his hands, reluctantly if I was being honest, as the memory of the bug priest's skin was still fresh on my mind, and we parted ways shortly after. Once I was sure that I was completely alone in the room, I took out the note that Jae-Hyun wrote.

Hello Walter,

I apologize about the unclear instructions that caused you to enter the trial as a physician. I don't know how you are dealing with the pain of the transformation, but know that I am doing my best to clear this trial ASAP. I hope that your will is strong enough to withstand the changes.

Given your unique situation, I have given some of your responsibilities to Marcus. I just need you to find the key out of this ward and access to the basement, although that might have changed as well. Marcus has already given me access to a nurse's uniform that I can use later, and I can acquire the other things myself.

I can explain more when we meet in person. Go to the patient ward first thing in the morning and perform my treatment there. I will give you instructions on how to do so. I can talk freely during the treatment.

One last thing, there has been a change that I did not foresee. The entity in the basement escaped early. If you see a little girl with a doll, leave the area immediately and never approach it.

I apologize again, and I hope you continue to endure.

Kim Jae-Hyun.

Well . . . how was I supposed to let him know that I was doing pretty well because of Noe? Or that I was on friendly terms with Alice and Molly? Uh . . . best to just pretend that I was holding out fine due to my resilience from the prior trial and leave it at that. As for Alice? I'd leave the smaller details for Future Walter to deal with. Sorry, Future Walter! At least I knew what I had to do tomorrow.

However, I still had to survive the current day before I could plan for the next one, and after checking the time, I did have a few more things to do before I could hit the hay. It was a little after half past six, but I had to hurry to meet up with Alice and Molly since I said that I would try to get some dinner together before meeting up with the director. Plus, I was honestly pretty hungry, and I wanted to see what the dinner menu was.

The cafeteria was as somber as I remembered it and a whole lot emptier, although that weird plaque with all the rules was gone. In theory, that meant that people could talk and walk around, but no one seemed to want to do so. The reason for the awkward silence and lack of people in general was clear to see. She was sitting smack dab in the middle of the cafeteria and rushed to greet me when she saw me enter.

"Uncle Walter!" Alice shouted as she ran up to give me a bear hug. "Thanks for helping cure the sick person!"

I put her down and laughed. "Not a problem, it's what doctors here do! But I don't see him around. Where'd you put him?"

Molly wobbled toward us and spoke next. "Good evening, Dr. Walter."

I nodded in greeting.

The doll continued. "That would be my doing. I kept the patient in a safe environment where we could present him to the director later. We wouldn't want him escaping again before that."

"Fair enough," I answered. "Have you two eaten yet?"

"Molly has," Alice answered first, and I swore I saw some of the few patients and staff left here shuddering when the girl said that. "She gets grumpy when she's hungry, but I waited to eat with you!"

"I don't get grumpy when I'm hungry, Alice."

"You so do!"

I chuckled. "All right, all right, either way, Dr. Walter certainly gets cranky when he's hungry, so why don't we get some dinner?"

"Okay, Uncle Walter."

"I am so glad she listens to you, Doctor," the doll said, giving me one of her now-very-familiar sighs.

"See? She's grumpy!" Alice added in before picking Molly up and taking her with us to the empty cafeteria queue.

Curiously, there were some options available for me to pick from unlike the default stuff they gave me for lunch. Well, there were options, although that hardly mattered since they were simply labeled *Dinner Set 1* through *5*. There wasn't anything to tell me what each one was, and the weird Frankenstein monsters that worked as servers didn't have mouths, so I couldn't ask for their options on what set was what.

"What dinner set do you normally get?" I asked the cheerful girl beside me.

"I always get a different set every day like Mom told me, so that I can get all the, um, nutrients and vitamins to grow big and strong . . ." Alice took a quick glance at Molly before whispering. "But I like the number two one the most."

Molly rolled her eyes but chose not to respond.

I nodded quickly. "Good sir, we'll have two orders of . . ."

Alice looked at me expectantly, and I couldn't help but giggle.

"Two orders of Dinner Set Two, if you could," I continued. "I just felt like that set today. That okay with you, Alice?"

"Yes, Uncle Walter!"

Molly gave me a silent shake of her head and sighed again. Alice, on the other hand, was all smiles and good humor, which was quite the contrast to her doll.

The food came quickly in a little container, and we returned to the spot that Alice chose for us. I opened mine up and whatever they were feeding the staff here certainly smelled nice, although I couldn't for the life of me explain what that scent was. As for what it looked like?

> **Primary Soul Title: It That Sleeps at the Edge of Dusk (??? Rank)**
> **Progress to Awakening: 13.11%**

It just looked like food. Yeah, like normal food.

"Yes, my host," Noe's warm voice assured. "It's delicious, and is good for you. Do not worry about anything else, dear Walter."

Yeah, good idea, Noe . . .

I scooped up the food and ate, and it was honestly pretty good. Watching Alice eat the same stuff as me was a nice sight either way. We finished in no time, and after making sure that our stations were clean and free of clutter, it was finally time to make my dreaded report to the director.

I had done everything that I could to ensure that this meeting went successfully, but the fact remained that I had no idea what a standard report would be about. The clues that I'd gathered suggested it was just a general briefing about the state of the hospital, and I was also hoping to distract this mysterious director with the presence of her daughter. Maybe I could be excused for not following whatever standard procedures were in place for these things, if there were even standards in this weird hospital.

Alice led us the whole way to her mother's office. Molly excused herself briefly to fetch Henry quickly, and although I didn't know where she put him, she did come back rather quickly with the man tied up in her hair. There were several disciplinary staff waiting outside with a handful of captive people, the same ones I told them to bring to the director earlier, and after one final check to make sure that I had everything, I opened the door with as much confidence as I could muster and entered the director's office.

CHAPTER FORTY-THREE

The Director's Report

I wasn't sure what to expect going into the dreaded director's office, but I remembered the role that I cast myself into. Dr. Walter wasn't someone who was fearful; he was someone to be feared. I strolled in as if it were my own office. As long as I didn't react negatively, no matter what the director looked like, I should be in the clear. Aside from myself, Alice, and Molly, the other prisoners—er, I mean staff and patients—looked like they'd die from stress at any moment. There was clearly something they feared here, and I was moments away from finding out what that was.

I'll admit that I was a little nervous. But just a little.

The office itself wasn't anything special. It was more modern than the rest of the building, with a nice large laminated desk nestled near the back of the building. Cluttered on the sides were various shelves and bookshelves filled with odd medical memorabilia, books, and miscellaneous assortments of office equipment. There was a worn-out sofa nestled to the side that looked neglected and a small table that served some espresso and snacks opposite the seats.

The only things that definitely didn't belong in a normal office were the cages that were built into the walls in the very back of the office. They kind of looked like a standard Xollon food cage now that I thought about it. They were empty, but the disciplinary staff quickly stuffed the poor staff and patients into them before quickly making their exit.

The only person missing from the scene was the actual director herself.

Her desk was empty, and the chair which I would assume belonged to her was likewise unused. What the hell was I supposed to do now? Presumably, Dr. Walter would have had a lot of these reports before, so I couldn't ask where the director was without being suspicious as hell. I was just about to do that anyway when I felt a huge . . . alien something gather in the office space and coalesce.

The presence felt odd. It didn't feel hostile, not to me at least, but I could tell that whatever was making such an aura was pissed off. No, I think it would be more accurate to say that the suffocating feeling was directed at the poor sods in the back, or at least another party, while a completely different feeling was directed at the three of us. It was so disorienting because that presence was immensely powerful. My heart was palpitating erratically just standing here.

I gritted my teeth and remembered who I was here. Dr. William Walter was not the type of guy to get intimidated by his (why did I choose this damn background for myself?) lover. No, he was a man of action! I couldn't fuck it all up here because of a little bit of intimidation. This director thing couldn't be any worse than Q and his staff. They were probably small fry compared to Xalla and Rogue!

I could do this!

I shook my head and reminded myself of the stuff I'd already witnessed. Between dimension-destroying Xollons and multiversal systems, the director honestly didn't seem that bad. I met and pissed off the person in charge of the entire Central Collective, so why would I be intimidated by some random hospital worker? I felt my body relax immediately as I eased into the pressure. I let it just flow through me, and with a casual shrug, I walked toward the director's desk and sat down on her chair.

Fuck it, if I was going to be Dr. William Walter, then I'd show the whole world how he operated! The illustrious doctor was not one to shy away from breaking down social norms, and the more I got intimidated by all these rules, trials, and other useless information, the less I acted like the man I had envisioned when I first introduced myself to Sarah.

I turned vaguely in the direction where the aura was the strongest and gave it my signature smile. "Director, darling, come on now, enough with the theatrics. We have Alice here, and she wants to give you a present!"

Alice came over with a smile. The small girl didn't seem to even notice the suffocating presence. "Yeah, Mom! But it's from me and Molly and Uncle— Um, I mean Dr. Walter!"

As if agreeing with our request, the invisible malevolent force condensed into a physical form. First, a black sludge-like substance seemed to gather from every corner of the room, flowing against gravity onto the table by my side. It solidified into a vaguely humanoid shape first, then morphed ever quicker into a distinctly female form. Once the last of the black liquid gathered with the rest, the entire mass seemed to freeze and congeal, before solidifying into a woman.

She was pitch black, not as in that she had a very dark skin tone, but rather, it was like her whole form simply sucked in all the light around her. She looked like a three-dimensional shadow, with the only defining feature being her eerie, perfectly circular white eyes and her bright red lipstick. Those eyes were terrifying, if you could even call them eyes. It looked more like two floating white orbs among that otherwise featureless face. The director didn't look like she should even belong in this dimension.

I even tried to peek at her information with the Rookie Arbiter's eyes, but I found nothing. I didn't think the director would be immune to my skill, since I was able to see even Xalla's basic information, and I highly doubted that she was more powerful than a full-on Xollon . . . although if she was, then that would be a whole other problem.

But that kind of thinking seemed unlikely. No matter how strange this place is, it was still only the third trial. There was no way that piece-of-shit overseer could bend the rules so much to introduce beings stronger than literal eldritch horrors this early. I suspected something else was up. It was like the figure before me didn't exist, so perhaps this wasn't the true body of the director at all? Maybe she was simply not alive in the conventional sense? Either way, I'd have to be careful with such limited information to work with.

The dark void of a woman sighed but had a playful smile on her lips. I felt her gaze at me with amused eyes. "My dear Dr. Walter. I would normally be a little angrier with you for getting my favorite chair dirty, but you've managed to do quite the number of tasks today, so I'll forgive you just this once. And hello, Alice. I see the good doctor's been keeping you busy as well. Were you good today?"

Alice nodded so quickly it looked like she was doing her best impression of one of those bobblehead toys. "Yes, Mom! We even caught you the bad sick person that ran away! Dr. Walter told me to not squish him, so Molly tied him up after Dr. Walter fixed him up again!"

The director laughed. "Thank you. I'll make sure to thoroughly enjoy your gift. Why don't you and Molly go down and get a cookie as a reward? It's about time for you to head to bed soon, and I still need to chat with Dr. Walter about work."

The girl's cheer deflated almost immediately. "Okay, Mom . . ."

"Hey," I added, "I'll see you again tomorrow, so don't go with a frown on your face!"

The director nodded. "That is true. You are better with children than I thought . . . That's good. I'd be glad if you would continue to look after my daughter and her little friend."

I gave her my best smile and a thumbs-up.

"Off you go, then, Alice," she continued, "I'll see you after I'm done here, and you can tell me how your day went. Save a cookie for Dr. Walter as well, okay?"

"Okay, Mom," the girl said finally. "And good night, Dr. Walter . . . Will you play with me again tomorrow?"

I gave her a good-hearted chuckle. "I already promised, didn't I? Here, let's pinky promise, that way you'll know that I'll be there!"

Alice's expression brightened, and we sealed the contract with the time-honored tradition of the pinky promise. Nothing could get me out of that!

Alice seemed satisfied with that and left the director's room shortly after giving her mom a hug. That left just the director and me alone in the room (if you didn't count the people in the cages, but I highly doubted they'd remain people for much longer). Guess it was time to see if I'd survive the night now.

Once the door was firmly closed, the director's demeanor changed immediately. She slumped down on the sofa by the side and produced a drink that smelled of heavy alcohol from the void and drank it all in one go.

"Gods damn it, Will!" she muttered before producing another drink. "Those fucking invaders are getting out of hand! They think they can just walk all over us! Fuck! They really think they can just ignore us? I'd love to give whoever's in charge a piece of my damn mind . . ."

She calmed down and sighed. "Have a drink. I know you need one as well."

Okay . . . this was certainly not what I was expecting. Then again, when had things ever gone the way I thought they would? At times like this, it was best to lend her a comforting ear and just allow her to continue ranting.

I took the offered alcohol and took careful sips. The thing tasted like liquid fire.

"Is it that bad?" I asked.

"Eight hundred and nineteen new patients, Will," the director continued, "and who knows how many of the worthless interns are imposters? I'm betting all of them are, again. It wasn't always this bad, you know. Things were fine before my idiot grandfather made that brain-dead deal, and now I'm the one who's saddled with the consequences."

The director took another heavy sip of her alcohol before pouring another generous portion. "And it's just gotten worse lately . . . Fuck! Our hospital can't continue like this! We don't have the personnel to handle these kinds of numbers! And we can't fight back against those pieces of shit before Alice is ready, but I don't think we'll last that long!"

Wait, did she mean the invaders were the people from Central? It would make the most sense for that to be the case since it was the Trash Matrix shoving all these new patients down the hospital's throat. Since we were using other worlds and dimensions as trial grounds, I could only imagine the frustration that the natives of those worlds would feel having their homes invaded by unknown beings. If that was the case, then the director had my sympathies.

More importantly, maybe I could find an ally here since I was trying to dispose of that damned overseer myself. It was good to see other people hate the Central Collective as much as I was starting to. It seemed like everyone who'd worked with the Overseer, whether they wanted to or not, was not a fan of the man. Yeah, this was certainly a situation that I could leverage to my advantage, but I'd have to be careful how I approached things.

I put my drink down and started to massage the very-stressed-out director's shoulders. Feeling her skin, if you could even call it that, was odd. It was like I was touching nothing, but the resistance was clearly there.

"Hey, no use stressing over it right now," I said with the most calming voice I could muster with my Idol skill. "Just relax. We'll figure something out, like we always do. You're not alone dealing with this anymore, remember? I've been doing a bit of research about our invaders on my end as well, and I think I can do something about them soon."

She relaxed, and I felt her body ease up. "Thank you, Will. Gods, what would I do without you here? And thank you for taking care of Alice today. I wasn't planning to wake her up so early, but things have gotten out of hand."

I nodded and continued my massage, making sure to keep the director relaxed and amicable. "Yeah, how come she's awake so soon? I was surprised to see her in the cafeteria today."

"Couldn't help it," she muttered, her body completely at ease now. "The influx of new arrivals is disrupting everything in the hospital and even the basement's not insulated enough to prevent all that noise. I'm making her a new toy to keep her occupied, but you must have heard about how fast she goes through those. Thankfully, now that she's taken such a liking to you, I don't have to worry about her going out of control in the short term. You've taken one of my biggest headaches out of the way; I can't thank you enough for that, Will."

"I'll do what I can for Alice, but you know that it's not a long-term solution, though," I added, and it was true. I couldn't stick with the girl forever, after all.

"No, but if I could just make her a permanent companion . . ."

I furrowed my brows. "She'll be content with just a buddy?"

"Yes," the director answered, "but it's harder than it sounds."

She moved a little bit and gestured for me to have a seat beside her. She refilled my glass and poured another one for herself before continuing. "You weren't here when I first tried to solve this problem, but my first few attempts were failures. I just tried to modify existing life-forms to suit my needs, but that didn't work. It's not their fault. The people in my bloodline have always been sensitive to emotions, and it's especially strong with my daughter. If there's any hint of fear or distrust, she'll know, and then it's another month cleaning up after her."

The director took a deep sigh and downed another shot. "But our counter-offense against the invaders can't start until Alice is stable."

While I wanted to know what any of that meant in more detail, it was, once again, something that I couldn't exactly ask without risking my disguise breaking. What I did know was that helping out the director and her daughter was likely to help fuck over the Overseer, and I was all too happy to help with that!

"And all you need is to make her a true friend, right?" I asked.

"Yes, but that's a hard task to do like I said." Those hovering orbs of hers looked at me with curiosity. "Why, do you think you can manage?"

Now that I thought about it, Alice seemed like a nice girl, but she seemed overwhelmingly lonely. There were no other kids her age here, and before I met her, she only had her doll to play with. That was not really the life a child should live. As for creating her a friend . . .

Say, Noe, how much longer will it take for you to upgrade fully?

"One day, eighteen hours and thirty-two minutes, my host."

And I had over a thousand luck charges to work with, plus however many I could regain by recharging . . . I could actually do this.

"Yeah . . ." I said, nodding slowly. "Do you think you can trust me with something?"

"Depends," she answered. "What is it you need?"

"Quite a lot, honestly, but I think I can make your daughter that friend of hers in about two days."

CHAPTER FORTY-FOUR

The First Day's End

The director's whole vibe changed instantly. She stopped chugging down those drinks of hers and stared at me hard. "How sure are you that you can do this, William?"

I thought about it for a second. With that many luck charges, I should be able to bullshit my way to success somehow if I had the other people do most of the hard work. If I just used luck charges during key procedures, giving directions and making random corrections as needed . . . yeah, it was possible.

"Fairly confident if I have a full staff of your best surgeons and doctors at my command, plus I'll be busy for at least a full day, maybe longer," I answered. "I'll need a lot of raw materials, the best quality that you can get, and I need to see the equipment that I'll have access to."

She continued to stare at me but nodded after a short while. "You'll get it. You're the best physician I know, Will, so maybe you can do what I couldn't. I'll show you what I've managed over the years, and you'll have access to my personal lab and equipment. If you can do what I couldn't . . . I'll give—"

"No need to thank me that much." I chuckled. I honestly didn't want to be shackled to this hospital with random rewards. "If it'll help fight the invaders and make your kid happy, then it's enough for me. I'm a doctor anyway, it's my job."

Unexpectedly, the director put down her drink and gave me a sincere hug. I didn't expect the warmth of the gesture from this woman who seemed to frighten everyone around me.

"Thank you, Will, I mean it," she said and gave me a gentle peck on the cheek.

"Don't thank me until I'm actually finished," I added quickly, feeling a little more embarrassed than I thought I would be. "And you said something about showing me your work?"

She nodded and took out a set of keys before sitting up. "Here, take the keys to the basement. All the research and labs are down there. It's too large to show you in one night, but feel free to explore the space yourself tomorrow. I'll just go over the main things now, and maybe both of us can tuck Alice in for the night when we're done."

"Cool," I answered, putting the keys in my pocket—there was another request the regressor needed finished without me having to do much of anything.

I'd still have to inquire what the clear conditions were, but I wanted to help out with the director's side of things first. If we were close to completing this trial, then I could always just withhold the keys for now. I hoped Jae-Hyun didn't mind waiting an extra day or two while I made sure that I sorted out the director's side of things.

I looked back at the cages and inquired. "What about those guys?"

Those weird orbs of hers glanced back at the terrified people locked up, and she grinned. "I'll have a nice little de-stressing session after I show you around. I certainly need it after all the shit the invaders gave me, and a little physical exercise is just what I need. You can join me if you want. It's always more fun with two."

Yeah . . . no thanks. I declined as politely as I could. "Not tonight, love. I have to start planning for my creation. We're not sure how long Alice'll remain stable, so I can't slack off right now."

She giggled, her voice remarkably innocent. "It's rare seeing you so fired up for once. You're usually finding any excuse to not work."

"Well, it's also not every day that my talents are actually put into practice." I smiled back. "I don't necessarily hate doing work; I just hate doing drudge work!"

The director just shook her head and beckoned for me to follow her. She took me to an unassuming locked door close to where the cafeteria was. I'd probably passed by this little metal door a few times today already and didn't even realize it led to the basement. She unlocked the door, and I followed her down the dingy staircase and into the basement proper.

I was expecting more of the horror dungeon aesthetic to continue to the basement, but no. The stairs led down to a nice, brightly lit welcoming room. I even had to take off my dirty shoes and put on some slippers because the interior was nicely carpeted. Along every corridor were homely decorations, and a few children's toys were strewn on the floor.

"I swear I told her to clean up after herself," the director muttered as she picked up the discarded toys on the ground. "I apologize for the mess, Will. I've been so busy with those new patients and idiot interns that I hadn't had the chance to come down here too often. I'll have someone come down and clean the labs as well. They've probably been in disrepair ever since I moved most of my operations aboveground."

We passed by Alice's bedroom on the way to the labs. It was a standard-looking room for a girl her age. We didn't stay there long as the child herself wasn't there yet. I guess she was still out getting that cookie with Molly. The labs were deeper down, and the director had to input a code into an old-looking computer from the eighties to get the place powered up again.

Maybe this was the reason why Jae-Hyun wanted the woman's computer password. Everything he requested from me seemed to lead to this place, so there must be something here that was important for the trial's completion. At least I had easy access to the whole facility when I needed to leave the hospital once and for all, but I wouldn't do that just yet. I wasn't so heartless as to leave a small child alone without at least trying to help her out first.

However, what the regressor wanted specifically was beyond me. If it was something special, then it must look like all the other random assortment of stuff strewn about. The room itself looked spooky. It kind of reminded me of a mix of Dr. Frankenstein's lab with what you'd expect a stereotypical mad scientist's workstation to look like. It was all odd electrical equipment, vaguely medical-type tools, and a lot of random bits and pieces that looked like it would pose a lot of health and safety violations just having them around.

That is to say, I had no idea what anything here did, but it was very complex looking, which was what I needed for the Absolute Luck skill to work. Thankfully I could peek at the equipment's information with my title skill, so I wasn't going in completely blind.

Noe, how likely do you think I'll succeed in this?

"Reasonably, my host," she answered quickly. "As long as the task is the most beneficial to you, then I shall endeavor to create the best possible outcome for you, and with 1,057 luck charges available, along with my complete gamma upgrade, the task is more than doable."

Thanks, that's good to know.

"I can work with this," I said after circling the room for the second time. "Anything else to note?"

The director nodded. "Give me a second."

That suffocating feeling came back as a dark abyss opened up near the ground she was standing on. She reached into that gaping void and pulled something out; it looked like an incomplete, lifeless body. The director gently placed it on one of the surgical tables and gazed at the corpse fondly.

"This is the culmination of my research," she said bitterly. "An incomplete husk . . ."

I looked at the failed creation as well. My Arbiter skill was still active, so I could see the description of the body.

> **Abigail's Lament (A Rank)**
> **Description:** The culmination of years of effort in developing a friend for her daughter. Her research and relentless experiments were all for naught, for the results always ended in failure. This represents the death of hope for the young director Abigail.

So the director's first name was Abigail, but I had yet to see anyone use that name. Was it another taboo subject to avoid? Best to be safe and just refer to her as the director for now.

"No, this is perfect," I added as I approached the corpse. "Making a friend for Alice from scratch will take way too long, so this will accelerate the procedure dramatically if I use it as a base. Two days, Director, give me two days to prepare, and I can guarantee that I can do it."

And if I couldn't, then I'd make sure to clear the trial and get out as quickly as I could, but I really didn't want to do so. But having a way out of a bad situation was never something bad, especially when I was making wild promises that I couldn't be certain that I could keep. I wanted to make the director a long-term ally to fight against the Overseer, so I still had to be careful about how I acted.

Abigail nodded. "I'll have everything set up by then. The one good thing about the invader's interference is that we'll never run out of raw materials. With so many new patients, there was going to be no shortage of spare parts either, especially since they all seemed so incapable of following basic instructions."

The director placed the body she took out into a weird glass tubelike structure and submerged it in a liquid.

"Some of the equipment here's old, so feel free to take some time to familiarize yourself with my setup. I'll have my best staff ready for you in two days. They'll be instructed to follow your every command. Do you need me there as well?"

I shook my head. "No, it'll take too long, and you're still the director. I don't think you can afford to be away from your position for so long, especially if I'm draining the hospital of even more resources."

"True . . . I just wish we had more doctors and nurses, but recruitment's lower than ever." She shook her head and laughed bitterly. "But why would they want to work here? We can't even predict how the invaders will interfere with our operations next."

"Hey, enough of that. Just let me do my magic and we'll be back on track."

She smiled at me. "Thank you, Will, I really mean it this time. Sometimes it feels like you're holding this entire hospital together."

I gave her a smile of my own back. "I am the illustrious Dr. Walter, after all. I have some plans to fight back versus the invaders myself as well, but I'll let you know what I have in mind once we're done with Alice's things."

"Speaking of my daughter," the director added. "Do you want to see her off for the night? She just came back, and she's taken quite the liking to you, or do you need a little more here?"

"I'm good here for today," I answered. "Let's put Alice to bed. I have a few things I have to plan for, but that can wait."

"Thanks." She smiled. "I mean it."

I chuckled. "You've said that a few times already. I'm just doing what I should be doing."

She gave me a tight hug, which I returned in kind. The woman seemed like she was way too overworked, and genuinely had the best interest of the hospital and its staff in mind, plus she was going way above and beyond as a parent as well. Despite what the others said about her, the director honestly didn't seem all that scary in my eyes. Then again, rumors did tend to exaggerate the subject matter.

"It's because I really mean it, Will," she answered. "I've been trying to keep this hospital running for so long, but there are only so many more rules I can implement. I don't think I could keep on going for much longer if I was alone."

Oh yeah, this was definitely someone way too overworked. She almost reminded me of Q, since both of them were being screwed over royally by the Overseer. I had to find a way to help her out, not only because I was starting to feel bad for her, but because she'd probably be a major thorn in that piece-of-shit overseer's side as well if she was as powerful as I thought.

Either way, I had to come up with a proper plan by the end of the day, and before I met up with the regressor. I wasn't sure how well he'd take me helping the crazy hospital people, but I could maybe work out a happy medium if I chose to omit some of the more problematic pieces of information. Then I'd just hope for the best.

CHAPTER FORTY-FIVE

A Night of Contemplation

The two of us left the labs, and the director locked the place up again after giving me the password. It didn't take us long to walk over to Alice's bedroom from there; the girl was already in bed when we got there. She quickly got out of her blankets when she saw who was by her mom's side, although I could tell that she'd been starting to doze off.

Now that I got a closer look at the room, I realized that it was bog standard in terms of furnishings. Most noticeably, there were boxes of various toys around that looked like they were well loved, and Alice's bed was filled with stuffed toys and pillows. She was practically buried under a mountain of blankets and quilts. Off to the side, in her own bed, lay Molly. She seemed to have already fallen asleep.

"Hey, Alice," I said with a wave. "Thought I'd say good night one final time. Sorry if I'm keeping you up."

"Hello, Uncle Walter. Hi, Mom." She waved back enthusiastically. "And you're not keeping me up! Do you want to see my toys?"

"Not now, Alice," the director said. "You can show him all your toys tomorrow, you need some sleep right now."

The girl nodded. She really was exhausted if she didn't fight back on that front, but she had helped out quite a bit with Henry today, so that wasn't unexpected. She's been running around the whole day practically.

"I need some sleep soon as well!" I added. "My old bones will break if I don't get my beauty rest."

Alice chuckled. "You're not that old, Uncle Walter!"

"No, he's not," Abigail said with a smile. "But he does need his rest. We just wanted to make sure you're doing okay, dear. Are you . . ."

"I'm all good, Mom," she said. "I had a lot of fun today! I'll tell you all about it in the morning!"

"I'll be glad to hear it," the director said as she helped her daughter back in bed. "I'll make you your favorite pancakes as well. You did great catching the bad patient today."

"She gave all the orders as well!" I added in with a smile. "I just had to follow her instructions. Captain Alice was a great commander!"

"Well," the director answered, clearly amused, "you'll definitely have to tell me all about it, then. Now be a good girl and get some sleep, okay?"

"All right, Mom," she said with a yawn. "Good night, Uncle Walter. Good night, Mom."

The director turned off the lights and gently closed the door behind her.

"She's stable at the moment," the director said after a moment. "Thank goodness . . . I haven't seen her so calm in a very, very long time. I wish she'd be like this all the time."

I gave the director a gentle pat on the shoulder. "Hey, Alice is doing great now, so don't be so down yourself. Kids are sensitive to their parent's emotions you know. We'll get that pal made for her, and she'll be like this all the time."

Abigail nodded. "You're right, sorry, it's just been so long since I've seen her like this. I'll . . . I'll go make some pancakes for her now."

I chuckled. "It's the middle of the night, love. They'll get cold if you make them now. How about you get some rest as well, or at least go play with those rule breakers and destress a bit."

"You're right," she said finally. "I've been too strung up lately, especially with my daughter waking up out of the blue . . . I'll take your advice."

"I am a doctor after all!" I added with a smile.

She returned that smile, although I could still see the fatigue underneath it. "Thank you, Will. I'll let you have free rein at the hospital after hours as well; the dogs'll know to not bother you. I'm not sure how much prep you have to do, but know that you have my full support for your project. You know where to find me if you need anything."

"Thanks," I said. "And I'm serious when I said to take better care of yourself, okay? Alice is awake now, and she needs her mom with her more than ever in the next few days. Don't burn yourself out when we're so close to the finish line."

She nodded gently. "I'll try, although I think you'll be busier than I will be. Take care as well, Will."

She gave me one final hug before excusing herself, then the director simply vanished, and I was once again alone with my own thoughts in this hospital. There was a lot to do in the upcoming days, and I hoped I could get everything I needed done.

Since I was given access to the entire hospital, I did want to do a little bit of exploring. Nothing too suspicious, since I had a sneaking suspicion that my actions were being watched, but at least I could see a better layout of the other wings and wards that I didn't check out today. But first, I checked the registry in the administrative building to see where I would be sleeping for the foreseeable future. The staff dorms were right around the corner, so the first thing I checked out was my room.

The room was bare-bones, all things considered. There was a small single bed, a desk that didn't look like it had been used in ages, and a closet that housed identical surgeon's uniforms. I did use the small bathroom on the side to wash off all the accumulated grime and dirt, however, and change into a fresh set of clothing.

I was honestly tempted to just lie down and sleep, but my rational mind won out in the end, and I quickly left the room to check out the rest of the hospital. I always did my best planning when I was on the move, and I had a lot of planning and thinking to do.

I gathered all that I'd learned today with what I already knew from my interactions with Central. First of all, the Overseer wasn't a well-loved individual, and although I didn't know how he, or the Trash Matrix, chose the worlds and dimensions that were used for trial grounds, it was clear that the natives of those places were not fans of this intrusion. They were also not taking the abuse lying down either; no wonder everyone was calling the Central Collective a doomed enterprise.

What was good to know was that I could be fairly confident that most places that we were sent to, as long as there was intelligent life there, would harbor some kind of resentment for the Overseer if Rogue and Big Bob's words were true. If I could use that to my advantage and gather enough supporters of my own, then waging war against that Trash Matrix and the even trashier Overseer wasn't just a pipe dream.

However, even if I went from trial to trial fostering relationships with other people who hated Central, I had no way of consolidating those forces into one group. Without that ability, we'd just be a collective of small entities that are just waiting for the Overseer and his slimy ass to squish one at a time. There had to be something that I could exploit so I could connect all these separate people together . . .

It shouldn't be impossible, since all these trials were connected, at least loosely, via the Origin Matrix. Perhaps Noe could usurp more of the Trash Matrix's functions when she was stronger, and use its own abilities against it?

"I am not yet capable of such a feat, my host," she answered for me. "But I may be able to do so after my upgrade is complete if you provide me with access to some of its source code."

What do you mean?

"If Unit Noe has access to a more detailed understanding of how the Trash Matrix operates, especially its abilities to link Pandora with the various trials together, then it is theoretically possible for me to modify its functions to suit my host's wishes."

Do I . . . plug you in to the Trash Matrix or something? Sorry, Noe, I'm not really sure how you access information from Central.

"Negative, my host," Noe answered with a hint of amusement in her otherwise clear voice. "That is not how I function. Unit Noe simply needs my host to be close to one of the Trash Matrix's databases, or nodes, when it transfers information between trials, and I can do the rest."

Well, that was good to know, although I couldn't put that into practice for a while longer. I wasn't sure if Q was still in charge of Site 1104, or if the Overseer expedited his transfer as well, but I'd have to make a stop back to his office once this was over. Hopefully he could show me the local servers or nodes or whatever it was Central used to house the Trash Matrix; I didn't think he'd mind breaking a few rules for me now that he'd been fired from his position. Plus, I was pretty sure Q said they had local ones for each site during one of our talks in the second trial. Worse case, I could still rely on Xalla to help me out.

I was so distracted with my thoughts that I hadn't noticed that I had already arrived at the patient ward. Strangely, none of the doors had been locked when I was walking alone in the hospital, nor had there been any guards roaming around like I thought. In fact, it wasn't until I reached the patient ward that I saw any other signs of life.

By the gate leading into the other side of the hospital were two little dogs lying down on a small cushion. Now, the director had said something about letting the dogs know I was out and about, but I had thought they would be a little more . . . monstrous? Maybe something like Cerberus or the like, but these two were wiener dogs. They had stubby little legs and barely reached past my ankles, and their chubby tube bodies were flabby.

The two dogs looked up at me before coming over to sniff my hands. I gave both of them a good patting down before they showed me their bellies to scratch. There was no way I could say no to that! But . . . were these the guard dogs in charge of keeping people inside at night? The regressor had stressed how dangerous it would be to operate outside work hours, but there was no way these two were anything other than small dogs.

I rubbed one of their chubby heads before picking the other up to look at it closer. The dog didn't struggle and even tried to lick my face. Now, I knew that Noe was slightly altering my perception, but surely she couldn't alter my perception of the size and shape of the dogs. No matter how I looked at them, these were wiener dogs.

I shrugged. No point trying to figure out how those little guys could do anything other than look cute. I gave them one final pat on the head before walking past them and into the next section of the hospital. I made a mental note of the rooms and general layout of this part of the hospital in case I ever needed to rescue Jae-Hyun if things went really wrong, but once again, I was mainly here just as an excuse to move around.

And speaking of Jae-Hyun, what the hell was I supposed to do when I met up with him tomorrow? How much was I supposed to tell the guy? I'd basically completed all his tasks, so I couldn't imagine clearing this trial would take too long, but I still needed to prolong my stay in this trial for at least two more days. I'd only interacted with the patients for a limited amount of time, but even that much told me how horrible it was to be a patient in this hospital. I couldn't imagine what kinds of treatments the regressor had to endure.

Which ultimately meant that I had to lie to him again, or at the very least omit some of the truth. I didn't want to do that to the man, but the alternatives were not things that I wanted to explore. But I was getting ahead of myself again. I still needed to ask him what the clear conditions were in the first place. Maybe they'd take him more than a few days to accomplish, even with my part out of the way.

I walked around the ward one final time, just absentmindedly looking at the phantoms of the day's activities, before heading back to get a good night's sleep. I had a general idea of what to discuss with the regressor in the morning, and I had a few different scripts I could play out depending on what he told me. But ultimately, planning things with imperfect information can only get a person so far.

CHAPTER FORTY-SIX

Meeting with the Patient

The morning came soon after, and although my bed was small, it was surprisingly comfortable as well. I got one of the best nights of rest in a very long time and had almost overslept if not for Noe waking me up on time. I finished my morning ablutions quickly and headed out to meet up with the regressor, as per his instructions.

Once again, I was dismayed by just how little work I actually had to do during the day. Aside from reporting whoever broke the rules, I just had to oversee three operations, and that took hardly any time at all. Since I had to see Jae-Hyun soon, I might as well just get all the other supervision duties out of the way after.

With the day's plan worked out, I walked to the patient ward and strolled in. I noticed that the dogs weren't there today, so I guess they only came out at night when they were tasked with guarding the hospital. How that was possible was still beyond me. The others in the room, both staff and patient, all avoided me as best they could as I walked up to the reception.

"Morning," I greeted the nurse stationed there, "I'm here to see a new patient. He goes by Jae-Hyun."

"Good morning, Dr. Walter," the nurse greeted back. "You're here for the special patient, then. He's in isolation recovering from his most recent procedure, just down the hall in room 126."

I stifled a grimace. I couldn't imagine any procedure here that would be easy to endure, especially if he needed to recover from it afterward. I was hoping that Jae-Hyun would have been left alone for the most part, but that was a pipe dream given our situation. Best see how he was holding up.

"Thank you," I answered. "I'll work with him today. Let the others know if they ask."

"Will do, Dr. Walter," the nurse replied. "Take care, the patients and staff are all nervous after yesterday's escape attempt."

I nodded and quickly made my way to the room. The nurse was right, everyone in the patient ward had a nervous air about them. The patients seemed to be eating breakfast at the moment, and although they were grouped together in what I assumed were their parties, no one was talking.

Jae-Hyun did state that breakfast and dinner were safe times, and I didn't see any rules about proper breakfast conduct here, so I could only imagine that the aspirants were simply choosing to stay quiet. I could only hear indiscreet whispers permeating the room, but even those whispers quieted down when the patients saw me.

The disciplinary staff stationed around were standing at attention, their eyes darting back and forth, constantly looking for any suspicious activities. I guess that the director was able to inform her staff about the patient's "irrational" need to escape their care from Henry . . . Had I accidentally made clearing this stage for the normal aspirants exponentially harder by accident?

Oh well, too late to change that. For now, I had a regressor to see.

The man himself was in a sorry state when I saw him lying on the bed. I'm not sure how much censorship Noe was doing, but I almost cried out when I first saw what the doctors did with his body. Horrible scar tissue was covering every part of his exposed flesh, and the bandages that were hastily bound to him were soaked in various fluids. Worse yet, he removed the blankets covering him and I could see the other augments that the doctors here gave him.

There were weird metal instruments crudely sewn into his limbs and other extremities, and they caused a horrible screeching sound every time the regressor moved. Yet despite the intense pain, the man simply nodded at me in greeting when he saw me come in. I guess he couldn't talk with me before a procedure started, as per the rules. He did, however, silently hand me another handwritten note. I turned my back to the only nurse stationed in the room and quickly read what Jae-Hyun wrote. It was short and concise this time.

Take me to the second operating theater, room 122.
Instructions for how to stabilize my condition on the back, fol-
low them. We can talk then.

*Don't worry about my body or yours. It'll return to normal
once we're out of here, and will not affect my performance.*

I flipped the note on the back and saw that Jae-Hyun had indeed given me instructions for what to do. His note was neatly written and easy to follow, and he even detailed how long I should spend during each step of the guide. It must have taken him quite some time to write down all of this, yet he somehow managed despite his current condition. The guy never slacked off, it seemed.

"All right, patient," I said, mainly for the other staff member to hear. "Follow me, we have a procedure to complete."

"Will you need assistance for Patient 004's treatment, Dr. Walter?" the nurse asked.

"No need," I answered. "I'm just going to stabilize his condition. It's a one-person job, especially given how busy our hospital's been lately. No point wasting precious staff resources."

"I understand, sir!"

Jae-Hyun followed me to the designated room, and he sat himself down on the table. I glanced back at the paper instructions he gave me and started whatever procedure he was outlining for me. Thankfully the regressor didn't require me to do anything complex, and all I had to do was plug him in to preexisting equipment in the room. What those did, I had no idea.

"Okay, patient," I said as I double-checked to make sure that no one was overhearing us. "The cure is officially underway. You may speak now . . . although you might want to mind what you say. The director could still be monitoring us."

"Thank you, *Doctor*," Jae-Hyun said, emphasizing the title. "And you don't have to worry about people overhearing us. Even the director will not overstep her bounds and break patient-doctor confidentiality."

I nodded. The fact that he called me a doctor should imply that we still had to stick by the general rules of the hospital even if we weren't actively watched.

"Of course, Patient 004," I answered as I fiddled with another machine. "Confidentiality is very important in this profession."

"But even if we were overheard," Jae-Hyun continued. "They would only hear the delusions of a very sick person. I want to be cured of these delusions, Doctor."

"That's a good attitude to have! You must know the nature of your sickness in order to seek the much-needed help to get better."

"Yes," he agreed. "But I have difficulties differentiating reality from fantasy, can you help me with that, Doctor? Can I speak about these delusions of mine?"

So . . . if Jae-Hyun framed everything he said as the mental hallucinations of someone infirm, then he could practically speak his mind without the worry of breaking character. After all, he was a patient, and it would be my job to hear him out, no matter how sick in the head he might be. Quite a nice way to circumvent the rules of this trial.

"Please do," I continued as I helped disinfect one of the nastier wounds on his arm. "I will do my best to help heal your mind while I stabilize your body."

"Thank you, Doctor," he answered. "I've been dreaming about an imaginary friend of mine, one W, sent to infiltrate the hospital. I gave him a few tasks to perform, but I fear that it was too much for him to complete. I also fear that his body and mind will not endure the stress of the infiltration."

"You worry too much," I replied. "It's not good for the mind. I'm sure that this hypothetical W person is more than adequate for the job at hand, and I am equally sure that his mind and body are fine with the changes. I can only imagine that someone like that would have prepared for an event like the one you imagined and will have abilities to counteract most of the harm."

I helped him with another bandage, but this time I slipped the key I got off of Henry into his pocket. The regressor noticed immediately and gave me a barely perceptible nod of thanks.

"I see," Jae-Hyun said, and I could hear the relief in his voice. "That's good to know. Thank you, Doctor, and I apologize for making you help me."

"It's not a big deal," I answered earnestly. "And I would worry about your own condition first."

Jae-Hyun nodded. "It's fine, really. Just like my imaginary friend W, I also have abilities that counteract the worst of the changes."

That's a relief to hear, I was worried that the regressor wouldn't endure this kind of treatment for much longer, although I probably shouldn't have worried at all in the first place. If there was one thing that I was dead sure about, it was Jae-Hyun's ability to survive through sheer willpower alone. He didn't make it until the very end for nothing.

"And," the regressor continued, "I have had this recurring dream about clearing a very difficult situation. The method to do so lies in the basement."

"I see, and what do you have to do in that dream basement?"

"There is an entity in that basement in the shape of a small child," he said. "To escape, we must either destroy this entity, which will be next to impossible at the moment, or destabilize it by destroying a doll it is always carrying."

Wait, the way to clear this stage was to either kill Alice or destroy her best friend? No way that could be right . . . I wasn't ethical in any sense of the word, but there was no world where I'd actively harm a kid, weird psychic powers or no.

Making sure my tone was as calm as possible, I asked, "What, specifically, were the exact words for the clear condition?"

The regressor frowned, unsure why I was asking him this, but he answered after thinking for a while. "It should be to eliminate the source of the hospital's grudge."

Okay, that was a little more vague than what he told me. The fact that the regressor gave me two options for clearing this stage should mean that I had some wiggle room for how to interpret the clear conditions. I could easily imagine the Trash Matrix using its aspirants as a way to weaken the people opposing Central, which would explain this shitty clear condition, but there's no way that I'll go along with its plans.

"And destroying this entity or its doll will resolve this?"

Jae-Hyun nodded. "That should be the case. The grudge is tied to the entity, so if we get rid of it, or force it back into confinement via the doll's destruction, then the grudge will be gone, at least for now. Just be careful. If we hypothetically destroy the doll, it'll cause the entity to lose control, and we'll have to survive its anger while we wait for staff to confine it."

"Just a second," I interrupted, "killing or confining the entity's not really dealing with the source of the problem, right? We're not getting rid of the grudge so much as we're getting rid of the person who has the grudge, that's like getting rid of poverty by killing all the poor people. Doesn't that seem kind of counterproductive?"

"I see your point, Doctor," Jae-Hyun conceded. "But that's the easiest way to clear the stage. I don't know what the source of the problem is, but I do know that getting rid of the entity is the easiest method of getting out of the dream."

I was fairly certain that the thing causing Alice the most anguish was her loneliness, so there was a good chance that my own goal of abusing my luck charges to create a buddy for her would be in line with the regressor's needs as well. I couldn't be sure until I found out some more information, but this was the most logical reasoning.

"Let's say that I have free access to this basement that you speak of," I said slowly. "Can you give me two, no, three days to work on your dream problem on my side? I think I can clear your scenario in that time, one way or another. We'll go with your strategy if that doesn't work, but can you trust me and endure the treatments until then?"

He looked at me hard in the eyes. "Are you sure?"

"Very," I answered.

"Fine. I trust you, Dr. Walter," he said finally. "Do what you must in that time. I will send you a thank-you letter later. Make sure you read it in case you find yourself in the basement and decide that my plan is the best course of action."

"Thank you," I said. "I won't let you down."

CHAPTER FORTY-SEVEN

Everyday Operations at Hope's Memorial

Hospital

Rumors of Dr. William Walter's planned surgery spread throughout the hospital like wildfire. It was the hottest topic among all the staff, with the best doctors and physicians lining up to see if they would be selected as a part of his groundbreaking procedure. Although everyone present feared the director, the staff working at Hope's Memorial were first and foremost trained medical personnel, and to have a once-in-a-lifetime opportunity to create a new life under the famed Dr. Walter was something that many could only dream about.

In any other year of operation at the hospital, the process of selecting the staff working under the physician would have been a carefully screened process, but the current situation was anything but normal. With the huge influx of abnormal patients hitting the hospital all at once, every employee at Hope's Memorial was swamped with work just trying to keep things in operation. There was precious little time left to interview for the position, much less showcase the various doctors' fields of expertise.

Yet every single individual associated with the hospital knew just how important it was for Dr. Walter's operation to succeed. Every staff member felt the squeeze the invaders had been asserting lately, and they all knew that it would only be a matter of time before something in their carefully crafted society broke. The director herself, although formidable and more than a match for any one invader, was tied too closely with the hospital. She could, at most, send out false bodies to help with communication and organization, but her powers would mostly be tied down.

Her daughter, on the other hand, was the perfect candidate, if they could just stabilize her condition. Alice's powers could easily eclipse the director's own if she learned to control it, but that could only begin once her emotions were in check. The child's lifetime of loneliness had stifled her growth, and it was only exacerbated by all the failed attempts at fixing this grudge.

Strangely, even though the director had failed time and time again, and any physician or doctor understood just how difficult of a task it would be to create a being that Alice could truly call a friend, everyone at the hospital was still strangely optimistic about Dr. Walter's chances. There was just something magnetic about the man and his impressive physique that made the people around him confident, and so, the race was on to provide the good doctor all the resources and supplies that he needed.

There was only one final day before the scheduled operation, and the only major obstacle left was to provide enough fresh resources for the doctor. Thankfully, or perhaps regrettably, getting those was the least of everyone's worries.

"Dr. Walter!" one of the nurses stationed nearby said. "We have five more patients who made it out of the building!"

"Goddamn it!" the doctor cursed. "What are the disciplinary staff doing?"

"They're working on it. It's a new batch with strange mutations again!" the nurse quickly explained. "One of them was able to shrink the size of their compatriots, while another had the ability to briefly blind our staff."

The number of mutations had exploded in recent days, and the staff was fighting an uphill battle trying to contain all the escape attempts. This kind of mass exodus was most likely staged by one member of the patient population, and it would only be a matter of time before that individual was found. But they had to weather the storm and contain as many patients as possible first.

"Where are Alice and the other physicians?" Dr. Walter asked as he scrambled toward the door. "I can't catch five by myself."

"The young lady has managed to isolate three of them in the crypts, and the other physicians not on other duties have secured the exits to the courtyard."

"So it's up to me to chase down the two stragglers—again."

The nurse looked at the doctor in shame. "I apologize, sir, but you're the only one who can communicate with the young lady's doll. The two who have escaped have strange abilities that make tracking them the normal way very difficult."

"Molly's by reception like always?"

"Yes, sir."

"All right, I'll go get them." Dr. Walter sighed. "I swear I feel more like an animal wrangler than a physician these days."

"I'm sorry, sir!"

"Not your fault, just make sure no one else gets out while I'm gone."

The nurse almost saluted the doctor before he collected himself. "I'll make sure to do so, sir! You can count on me!"

Dr. Walter nodded and bid the other staff members farewell. It would be another exhausting afternoon.

It had only been two and a half days since Patient 755 escaped, but news about William's need for fresh material must have made its way to the patients as well, because everyone seemed to be trying to leave the ward lately. Most didn't make it past the disciplinary staff, especially after the director increased security measures, but when there were hundreds of mutated patients versus a handful of staff, some sneaky individuals were bound to escape.

It had been William's job, with the help of Alice and her doll, to catch the most tenacious ones who made it to the courtyard. Not a single soul managed to thwart capture when he was on duty, but many had managed to do just that when the doctor was busy with other concerns.

Dr. Walter grabbed his coat as he met up with the living doll near the entrance. This was his fifth foray into the courtyard, and it was starting to wear down even his patience.

"Where are the two stragglers?" he asked the doll.

It gestured incomprehensibly as it made its way atop the doctor's head. No one else could understand what the creature was saying aside from the director and her immediate family, but somehow William could. The staff had long since given up trying to understand the genius behind the man and accepted that he could regularly do the impossible.

"All right," he answered the doll. "Let's get this over with. I'm sure even Alice will get tired of hide-and-seek soon if this keeps up."

The doll made more gestures.

"Fair point." The doctor nodded in amusement. "But she's still young. It's best not to overdo things."

The doll pointed in a direction and waved its tiny hands.

"Right," Dr. Walter said before turning around to grab a hat from the desk. "Almost forgot the hat; keeps the worst of the rain out of my hair. Let's get the two idiots before I get the rest of me soaked again, though."

William was so acquainted with capturing stray patients at this point that his movements had become automatic. There was a formula that he could follow that would result in the quickest capture rates. First of all, the positions of each escapee were tracked by the doll, so finding where the patients were posed very little challenge. The main issue was catching them once Dr. Walter closed in on their positions.

The best method, he found, was to sneak up on the unfortunate individuals by using the ever-present rain and gloom as cover. The doctor's heavily augmented body made navigation in the poor weather a simple process, and he was very adept at sneaking despite his large size. After that, it was just a matter of allowing the doll to shoot one of its cursed darts at the victim and wait for the wound to do the majority of the work for him.

Of course, that was the best-case scenario, and it was impossible to predict what would happen when each patient had such unique mutations. That was the case for this afternoon's hunt. The doctor was able to easily sneak up on the unsuspecting duo, and the doll was even able to hit one of the two patients. However, this alerted the second one, and the female patient disappeared in the blink of an eye, leaving the first victim squirming on the ground in pain.

The doll contained the escaped man and made some frustrated gestures before pointing at another location.

"Seems like short-range teleportation, then," Dr. Walter muttered. "That's going to be a pain in the ass to deal with. There should be some limits to her mutation, though, otherwise there's no way any one of us could feasibly catch her."

The doll paused for a second before saying something else that only the doctor could understand.

"Shit, you're right . . ." he answered. "And Alice is busy at the moment, right?"

The doll nodded.

"Damn, there's no easy answer, then. But wait . . ." Dr. Walter continued, "if what you're saying is right, then how come the patient didn't leave already? She could have easily gotten away before we even arrived. I'm willing to bet it's because she doesn't want to leave the people she escaped with behind."

The doll thought for a moment before responding with a shake of its head.

"That is true," the doctor answered. "But only certain patients disappear when one of them leaves; I think the files say that at most four others go, and they all would have been processed at the same time. What if the people she left with were not a part of that group?"

The doll nodded slowly, seeing the logic behind the doctor's words. One of the most frustrating things that the hospital staff had learned to deal with over the years was how nebulous the patients under their care could be. If even one of them managed to leave the hospital's property, many others, usually patients with adjacent designation numbers as the escapee, would mysteriously vanish along with them. That was why the director was so keen on keeping security as up-to-date as possible.

The doll stopped for a second before relaying some information to William.

The doctor laughed. "I knew it! If she's stopped now, then she's hesitating between leaving her friend behind and escaping herself. We just need to incentivize her to stay. Tell me where she is, and we can use her new friend as bait. I have the perfect way to make him cooperate with us."

The doll nodded and allowed the doctor some private time with the healing patient.

Dr. Walter looked at the man gently and smiled. Then, gently, as if speaking to an old friend, the doctor spoke, his voice containing an ethereal power to them that drilled deep into the man's psyche.

"We're here to help, Jaylynn, your friend Isabelle needs to see a doctor badly, and she'll die if we don't get her treated, but she's fighting us."

The patient looked at the doctor with glazed eyes, as if he was trying to fight off some foreign entity, but eventually he nodded slowly.

"Yes . . ." the patient mumbled, "Isabelle needs treatment. I need to help her . . . We promised to leave this place together."

Dr. Walter nodded. *"Good, can you help us catch her? All you need to do is stick this little dart in her without her knowing, and she'll get the treatment she needs. Then she'll get better again."*

The other man nodded slowly, his speech still slurred. "Yes, Doctor . . . I can do that. She will listen to me. She needs treatment."

"That's a good man!" William said with a smile. "Now, just follow where the nice doll is pointing to, and you'll meet up with her again. Remember, she's avoiding treatment, so best not to alert her!"

"Yes, Doctor . . ."

"All right," Dr. Walter said to the doll this time. "He'll cooperate, at least for the time being. Just bring him close to the other patient's path and let him do the rest. We'll collect both of them once he's done."

The doll frowned and said something.

"Oh, please," the doctor replied with a laugh. "I'm the best physician in the world. Do you honestly think I don't have my ways of getting a patient to cooperate? The brain, and in turn, the mind, is like any other organ—it can be manipulated if you know what you're doing."

The doll slowly nodded its head but seemed to calm down, as if satisfied with the doctor's claims. It climbed off the doctor's head and sat on the patient's shoulder, pointing to where the man needed to go.

It didn't take long for both of the escaped patients to be brought to order after that, the poor woman never suspecting that her friend would betray her like that, and the doll ensured that she could not use her abilities to flee a second time. However, although the doctor and his staff were able to contain this set of escape attempts, more were reported hourly, and Dr. Walter was kept busy until his shift was finally over.

CHAPTER FORTY-EIGHT

Upgrades and Operations

I woke up on the day of the scheduled operation to the soothing voice of Noe as she informed me that her upgrade had finished. I had originally planned to stay up until the very moment of her completion, but last night had been so hectic that I all but passed out after dinner. I wasn't sure what the hell was going on, but practically every aspirant who had even a moderately useful ability tried to get out then.

Something must have spurred them on, but I wasn't sure what. The regressor surely would have informed me if the other aspirants were working under a time limit or the like.

"My host," Noe interrupted. "You are becoming distracted again. Would you like to hear the rest of my explanation on the gamma upgrade?"

Oh, right, sorry, Noe. Please continue. Don't know why my mind's wandering so much lately. It's like I'm living a dream or something.

"Showing my host the new system skill."

Abilities: 4
Total Luck Charges: 1,557

. . .

Skill: Emotional Redux (EX Rank, System Active): Unit Noe will influence the emotions of the user's target, spending Luck Charges to do so. Unit Noe will ensure that the best possible state of mind is chosen to suit the needs of the Host. Luck Charges spent increases depending on the strength of the target and the emotional state needed.

Oh, that was a very interesting skill, although how to utilize it could be tricky. Emotions themselves were a powerful thing, and being able to manipulate them could come in handy. Now that I thought about it, this new skill also used luck charges, even though it didn't have much to do with luck itself. And the upgrade even gave me an extra 500 points to work with! Did that mean that all future system actives would consume the same resource?

"Clarification, my host," Noe answered. "As I am the Absolute Luck System, all of my functions relate to the expenditure of luck charges, regardless of how many shards I successfully integrate in the future."

Okay, that's good to know. So, what exactly does this skill do? The description's a bit unclear. How strong of an effect are we talking about?

"That depends entirely on what you desire, dear Walter," Noe explained. "If you only want to subtly influence a person by making them slightly happier or sadder, then only a small amount of luck charges will be consumed. However, this effect can be amplified as well. For example, the host can cause a target to experience so much lethargy that they will waste away from dehydration because of a lack of will to move."

Oh . . . that's something I can use. I mean, even a slight lapse in concentration in a fight can determine the victor. But I'm guessing it won't work too well on someone like the Overseer and his gang, right?

"With your current limited form, no, my host," Noe answered sadly. "I apologize."

That's fine, it's not like I'm anywhere near ready to tackle those monsters head-on.

"That is good to hear, my host," she continued. "But Unit Noe suggests that the hosts wash up quickly and meet the director in the basement. It is time for you to do what you have promised. I will, as always, assist you where I can."

Right. How had I almost forgotten about making Alice that friend of hers? It was the whole reason I waited this long. I took the fastest shower of my life and changed into a new set of surgeon's clothes before hurriedly making my way to the basement.

The pitch-black shadow of a woman was waiting for me by the entrance to the labs. Even though I couldn't see her facial features, since she didn't have any, everything about the way she presented herself told me just how stressed and anxious she was. She probably hadn't gotten any rest in these last few days.

"Director." I nodded in her direction. "Is everything ready?"

"Good morning, Dr. Walter," she replied. "Everything you asked for is prepared, all the spare parts are on freeze, and your staff are on standby and have been instructed to follow your every command. I'll take Alice out today and watch over the patients personally. I guarantee that no one will escape on my watch. Don't worry about your regular duties. I'll fill your position myself if it means even a slightly better chance of this procedure working."

"Thank you, but please take better care of yourself," I answered. "I don't have to be a doctor to see how exhausted you are right now."

She sighed. "Thank you, Will, and you're right, but I'll rest when this crisis is over. There's too much on the line right now for me to rest."

I nodded and made my way through the door into the lab. I made one last trip around the room, reviewing some of the basic information I could gather from my Arbiter skill to make sure I had at least a vague idea of what all the equipment did. It wasn't that helpful, all things considered. Like what on earth would this particular machine do?

Organic Desaturator

Description: A device used to desaturate organic matter. Use the onboard controls to control the strength of the desaturation process and what matter to separate from the whole.

Yeah, I kind of knew what the word saturation meant, but not in any kind of scientific or medical context. That didn't mean that I wouldn't use the thing; as long as there were knobs and controls, I could luck my way through. I'd be sure to abuse it with my skill. As for when to use it? Blind luck would solve that as well! I was unstoppable as long as I had luck charges here!

The rest of the machinery and lab equipment fell in a similar vein as the Organic Desaturator. I kind of understood the general purpose of each machine, but that was about it. In other words, I'd just have to let my little helpers do all the setup and prep work, while all I did was direct them on what device to use, and fiddle with the fine controls after. That was probably where my luck would be used best.

The last thing was to check the staff assigned to me. The director really went all out here. I already knew that we didn't have a lot of doctors or nurses stationed at the hospital, but I think close to a third of the staff were here under my command. I counted fourteen doctors here to assist me in rotations, and practically three times that number of nurses and other staff around. I even had a little minion whose only job was to make sure that I was properly hydrated and didn't miss a meal.

With everything set up, I activated the Absolute Luck skill for what felt like the first time in forever and got to work.

"You!" I shouted at one of the doctors awaiting orders, before pointing at a random machine. "Take the director's work and put it in the incubator. Set everything up yourself, but let me do the fine adjustments when you're done."

"Yes, Doctor!" the man said quickly.

"The rest of you, go find the best-quality materials from the freezer and clean them up. I trust your professional judgment here. Take the ones you think are the best and put them on the operating table. I'll choose which ones to use from there."

"Understood, Dr. Walter!"

"Finally," I commanded before pointing at a few other random machines, "get those systems up and ready for immediate use. Double-check that they're all in working order."

Those first few commands only used up thirty-six luck charges. So far so good, but the true test was still to come.

"Dr. Walter," the first man I addressed came up and said, "the incubator is set up."

I nodded and went over to the machine. It looked like a very big version of the kind of thing you'd see used for newborn infants, but just a lot bigger. The body was placed inside, and it was hooked up to a bunch of electrodes and other devices. On the side was an ancient computer.

I pretended to scan the body for a few seconds before pushing buttons and turning knobs frantically. My luck charges started to go down much faster now, and I only stopped what I was doing once the charges stopped decreasing. At least that was a very helpful indication for me to stop what I was doing.

Almost immediately, the body's corpse-like complexion started to improve, so it seemed like whatever I did was working at least. The doctor at the side looked at me wide-eyed in marvel. Even the director came over and gave me an approving nod.

"I see that you're not just boasting this time, Will," the director said. "I think I can confidently leave you to your work. If you need me, let one of the nurses know, and . . . good luck."

I gave her my most confident smile. "Just leave it to me. I'm willing to bet even more patients will try to escape today."

"Yes, it is time to wake up Alice as well. Like I said, if you need anything on my end, do not hesitate to call."

I nodded and bid her one final farewell before turning my attention back to the operation at hand. By now, the additional spare parts were cleaned and processed, and it only took three luck charges to pick out the most compatible ones for the project. The prep work was easily finished after that, and by the time we were ready to start the major surgery, I was only down fifty-five luck charges, having recovered most of them with time.

"Dr. Walter," a nurse said, "our work is finished. It's time for you to restructure the body."

"You've double-checked the parts and the body's stability?"

"Triple-checked it, sir!"

I nodded and took one final drink of water offered to me by my helper. "Perfect! Prepare my tools, and make sure that no one disturbs me going forward."

Here was where things got dicey. I had no knowledge of any medical procedures, much less creating my own Frankenstein monster, which meant that I had to rely on Noe for the next part entirely. It was also why I told the others to give me space to work; they didn't need to see how weird my movements were, or the fact that I was closing my eyes for most of the procedures.

I grabbed a random tool off the tray, grabbed one of the offered limbs, and just closed my eyes and allowed the luck to flow through me. Once again, I was assaulted with the feeling of having a part of my body lose control as it moved seemingly by itself. My fingers twitched and jittered uncontrollably while I had no idea what my other arm was doing as it flailed about. My entire attention was on the amount of luck charges I had available to me.

Luck Charges: 1,507/1,557

A jerk of my hand cost me a few luck charges here.

Luck Charges: 1,499/1,557

I felt some warm fluid on my hand before I felt myself lose even more control of my body. I had to open my eyes for a bit to see what the hell was happening, although I wished I hadn't. My left arm was rapidly making incisions on the main body, while my right arm was fiddling with a complex-looking device that I didn't remember even being there before, all while the other doctors and nurses looked on with shocked expressions. It was disorienting to the max, and I had to quickly close my eyes again before I puked.

Luck Charges: 1,420/1,557

As I thought, the bigger movements caused me to lose way more charges than the subtle finger twitches, but I couldn't exactly control what Noe was doing. I just continued to close my eyes and watched the number go down and down.

Luck Charges: 1,404/1,557
Luck Charges: 1,355/1,557
Luck Charges: 1,173/1,557

It wasn't until my charges hit 870 that Noe's movements stopped, signaling the end of whatever procedure I was doing currently. I opened my eyes to admire her work, and I wasn't disappointed. All of the missing limbs were successfully attached to the director's base body, and although the corpse was still clearly dead, it looked like it had only recently passed away instead of the decrepit mess it was before. Its coloration and overall state was pretty impressive for a few hours of work, but what else could I expect when that work was done by the best system in the multiverse?

"I only do my best," Noe answered with a smug tone. "Because I am the best, my host."

I chuckled at her response and gave myself some time to rest. Well, more accurately, it was to recover luck charges before pointing to a new machine and continuing my work. This would be the pattern after a while, with frequent rests disguised as time for the other medical staff to do minor procedures, while I focused solely on the most important tasks. And on and on it went, well into the night.

CHAPTER FORTY-NINE

The Culmination of Luck

It took twenty-nine hours total, practically all of my luck charges, give or take, and I felt like I was about to collapse at any moment, but whatever magic Noe managed to do was enough to imbue life into what was once a collection of spare body parts. But that was all it was. The body was alive, it could think and even talk, but it felt . . . lifeless. I looked at the creature and frowned.

It looked back at me with its emotionless eyes, as if judging me, cursing me for creating something so devoid of purpose. Was this why the director failed all those times? This was nothing more than an animated doll, not a true friend. What was missing? Was it too weak to play with Alice?

"My creation's strength is more than adequate for the task at hand, my host, as that was the optimal outcome when using the Absolute Luck skill. It feels incomplete because it lacks emotion," Noe answered for me. "It is in a state similar to my own, pre-integration, but you can fix that now."

Right! My new skill! Between my exhaustion and disappointment, I had forgotten all about it. But Noe's ability could only manipulate a being's emotions for a time. That wouldn't change anything in the long term. I couldn't just sit by the creature's side and reuse the skill over and over again like I was recharging a battery. And Alice would eventually realize that the being's emotions were artificial.

"No, my host," Noe corrected. "There is another way, but the cost will be steep."

Explain.

"With the acquisition of your Devil's Advocate skill, it is possible to fuse its active with your new ability to induce a permanent emotional norm for the creature."

So, if I command it to be best friends with Alice, then it'll do that to the best of its ability? Emotions and all?

"Correct, my host."

And what's the cost?

"You will lose the Devil's Advocate title."

I frowned.

I thought you said you couldn't delete any titles, though, Noe.

"You cannot, dear Walter," she answered. "You are not deleting the title, but transferring the essence of the ability, that is, the authority to manipulate truth, to your creation with my help. The title will still exist, in part, but it will not be with you."

I chuckled. And here I thought I would have to give up a lot more for that. What was one stupid title I got by accident to the happiness of a kid? The decision was a no-brainer.

Do it, Noe.

"Are you positive?" she asked again. "Your decision can not be undone."

I'm sure, Noe. I'm a lot of things, but I'm not one to break a promise to a child. And plus, I can always get more titles in the future. I don't think Alice will have that luxury if I stop here.

"Understood, my host. You may use the title at any time."

I turned to look at the creature. No, I turned to look at the boy and activated my skill for the last time.

"Your name from now on will be Toby, and soon, you'll meet with a girl around your age. Her name is Alice, and I want you to be the best friend you can possibly be for her. Make sure to play with her a lot, and have as much fun as you possibly can with her. Make sure you give her lots of love, and I hope both of you live a happy life."

I felt something leave my body as I said those words, and with each word that I said, the boy's expression brightened more and more. Once the last word left my lips, Toby's eyes cleared and he gave me a smile of genuine joy. It felt like I was imparting life to the boy. The feeling was surreal.

His dull, purposeless body seemed to animate right before my eyes, and a smile blossomed on his face as the boy took in the new world around him. The other doctors and nurses were all but crying out in amazement and joy at seeing the child finally complete, and a few of them clearly wanted to celebrate. They were professional enough to do so later, though, as it was not the time for such actions.

"Hello, Dr. Walter," Toby said to me with bright eyes. "Thank you for waking me up. I felt like I was asleep for a very, very long time."

"Good morning, Toby, I'm glad to see you awake as well," I answered with an exhausted smile. "And you should thank the director when you see her. She's responsible for most of that body of yours."

He nodded. "Okay, Dr. Walter . . . and when can I meet Alice?"

I chuckled. Good. My instructions had already taken effect if he was talking about Alice already.

"We can go right after we get you dressed," I answered. "It wouldn't be proper to meet the young lady in your birthday suit."

The boy looked down and saw that he was naked and hurriedly grabbed one of the surgical cloths to cover himself. Well, his emotions, at least for embarrassment, seemed to be in working order. That was a good sign, and I'd take Noe's word that he'd remain complete for a very, very long time.

One of the nurses came over without prompting. "I've got that covered, Doctor! The director prepared an ensemble of clothing for Toby to wear. If he could follow me?"

The boy looked at me, and I nodded. I took that time to inform the director about the success of my operation. Her response was more muted than I thought, but she did stress how she needed to take some time to get Alice ready to meet her new buddy. Not sure what she planned, but she told me to meet them in Alice's room once I was done.

I waited a bit longer than I thought before Toby returned fully dressed in a remarkably well-fitting suit. I wasn't sure why the director chose to include formal wear for a kid, but there you had it.

"Why did you dress him in that?" I asked the nurse. "That's not the most comfortable-looking thing to walk around in."

"He chose it himself, sir," the nurse answered. "In fact, he insisted on trying on almost all the clothes that the director brought."

Toby nodded. "I'm meeting a lady, so I thought it would be best to dress like a gentleman, so she doesn't think I don't know my manners."

I chuckled. "Well, it's your choice. Are you ready to meet Alice?"

"Yes, Doctor . . ." Toby answered nervously. "Do you think she'll like me?"

"I'm sure she will," I answered. "Come now, let's get going."

The director was outside Alice's room when the two of us arrived. The woman quickly rushed over and engulfed me in a tight hug when she saw me, but quickly let go once she saw the boy.

"This is Toby," I said. "Hopefully he'll be Alice's new friend. Say hello to the director, Toby."

The boy clung to me shyly. "Um . . . hello, Director. Dr. Walter told me you helped make my body, so thank you for that."

Huh, he was a little more shy than I thought. Then again, the director was a pretty intimidating woman.

"Sorry," I said. "He's still a little nervous."

"It's all good, Will." The woman bent down and smiled at the boy. "It's good to meet you as well, Toby, and don't worry, you don't have to be nervous around me. I see you've chosen the suit. You look very handsome, and I'm sure Alice will agree with me."

He blushed and lowered his guard against the director a tad.

She took something out from her shadow and continued. "Would you like a cookie before meeting with Alice?"

Toby looked at the offered cookie and glanced back at me, seeking my approval. I gave him a quick nod, and he snatched the snack out of the director's hand before stuffing most of it into his mouth.

"Wow . . . This cookie is delicious!" The boy took another bite before stopping as he looked at the tiny piece of cookie left in horror. "No, I should have saved some for Alice! It's not good to have it all myself!"

The director smiled and took out another cookie. "That's very thoughtful of you, Toby. I have another one here. Would you like to give it to my daughter when you see her?"

He nodded enthusiastically before gently taking the offered cookie. Toby tried to find something to wrap it in, almost resorting to using some old rags, before the director produced a little napkin out of the void and gave him that to use.

While Toby was trying to wrap the treat as best he could, the director came up beside me and whispered something in my ear.

"You did it, Will . . ." she said. "I almost doubted you, but you did it. I . . . I don't know what to say."

"A simple thank-you will suffice," I answered with a light-hearted laugh. "And maybe a cup of coffee as well. I need some caffeine in my system right about now."

The director jolted up. "I'll get one right now!"

"I'm joking," I said, placing a hand on her to stop her from actually fetching me a drink right this moment. "You can get one after the two kids meet. You do remember that they still have to do that, right?"

The woman scratched her cheeks, clearly embarrassed. "Sorry . . . It's not like me to get this flustered. But . . . Alice will finally get the friend she wanted. I mean, I never thought the day would come."

"Do you think she'll like him?" I asked, genuinely curious. "I did my best, but what if there's a flaw?"

"If there is a flaw, I can't see it, Will," she replied in awe. "I think he's perfect! He might need some slight alterations and maintenance work later down the line, but I can do that easily. How did you do it, Will? Making something like this couldn't have come cheap. There's always an equivalent exchange. What did you give up?"

"Nothing worth mentioning," I answered truthfully.

She stared into my eyes, not believing what I said, but eventually nodded. "I don't believe that for a second, Will, but you have my eternal thanks. If there's anything you ever need, you'll have it. I owe you a debt that I can never pay."

I shrugged. "Hey, I'm just doing what I should be doing. Now, it seems that our new friend's wrapped up his gift. How about we introduce him to Alice?"

"I mean it, Will," she said again. "But you're right, my daughter's waited long enough for this day. And thank you, for everything."

The director opened the door, and the three of us entered Alice's room. The girl was to the side playing with Molly and a bunch of other stuffed animals, but she quickly dropped what she was doing when she saw the three of us. Her gaze was fixated on Toby, and I could tell the boy was a little nervous himself. He froze for a second, and I had to nudge him forward.

"Um, hello . . ." Toby said shyly. "Are you Alice?"

The girl looked at him, perhaps trying to see his intentions, but he must have passed whatever test she was giving him because the usual smile I saw her with returned.

"Yup, and who are you?"

"I'm Toby," he replied. "Dr. Walter made me. Um . . . it's good to meet you."

Damn it, the boy completely forgot about the gift he was holding. I coughed quickly to get his attention before mouthing the word "cookie" over and over again. He understood after the third attempt and half shoved the wrapped snack toward Alice, almost dropping it in the process.

"I, um, this is for you. I wrapped it myself."

Alice was still a little unsure what was going on, but she took the offered gift and unwrapped it. Her smile was radiant when she saw the cookie.

"Wow! It's my favorite!" she exclaimed and broke the snack in half. "But you can have half of it. My mom always told me to share."

"It's okay . . ." he answered. "I had one outside already, that one's for you."

Alice shook her head. "No, cookies are made to be shared. It tastes better if you eat it with someone else."

Toby looked back at me. It was kind of cute how he sought my guidance when he wasn't sure what to do, and I had to suppress a laugh at how worried the little guy was. I just nodded, indicating that he should just accept Alice's goodwill.

"Okay . . ." he replied slowly before taking the offered half, "and um, do you want to be my friend?"

With the mention of the word *friend*, Alice's entire demeanor seemed to change. She was always a gloomy child before, even when I was playing with her, but that weird gloom seemed to fade before my eyes now. Her snow-white hair fluttered in an invisible breeze, and I could see her complexion brighten up.

"Of course, Toby," she replied with a giggle. "I'd love to be your friend. Do you want to see my toys?"

The boy looked around the room for the first time and nodded quickly. "That's a lot of toys . . . Can you really show them to me?"

"You can even have some of them!" she answered. "But not Molly; she's not a toy."

Toby looked over to where the doll was sitting and waved at her. "Oh, hello, Molly, it's good to meet you as well."

"Hello," the doll replied. "Although I'm not sure if you can understand me."

"What do you mean?" he asked, clearly confused. "Am I not supposed to understand you?"

"You can talk to her as well!" Alice exclaimed before grabbing Toby's hand. "Wow! That means the three of us can play together!"

"All right," the director interrupted with a happy sigh. "Why don't you three go play in the other room? There's a lot of old toys back there that I'm sure you can show your new friend; I have to speak with Dr. Walter for a bit.

"Okay, Mom," Alice replied. "Come on, Toby, I have to show you all the cool things I've got!"

The director shook her head. "Wait! Now what do you say to the good doctor for creating Toby?"

"Sorry . . . I forgot my manners," Alice answered before turning to me. "Thank you, Uncle Walter, you're the best doctor ever!"

"All right, off you three go, then," the director said. "And make sure you treat Toby respectfully!"

"I'll look after them both, madam," Molly answered. "You have my word."

"I will, too!" Alice added. "Let's go!"

The three scrambled off quickly after that, leaving me alone with a director who looked like she had just gotten rid of the biggest weight off her chest. Her smile never left her face, even when it was clear that she had gotten even less sleep than I had in these last few days.

CHAPTER FIFTY

Alliances and Adversaries

"Congratulations, my host," Noe's voice interrupted. "You have achieved the clear conditions for the Third Stage. The Trash Matrix wishes to initiate end-of-trial procedures. Does the host accept?"

I frowned. *What would happen if I don't accept?*

I still had some things to do before I left the trial, so I couldn't just disappear right away. My main goal for helping out, aside from just being nice to Alice, was to establish a proper relationship with the director and have her help with getting rid of that piece-of-shit overseer.

"You will delay the clearing of this trial until you accept the Trash Matrix's request," Noe answered. "With my upgrade, you may delay it indefinitely, although Unit Noe does not advise that, as it may alert Central's higher-ups."

But they probably won't notice if I delay it for a day or two, right?

"The probability of that outcome is negligible, my host," Noe replied. "You are safe to ignore the Trash Matrix for the time being."

Perfect, ignore the Trash Matrix right now. I'll let you know when I want to clear this stage.

"Acknowledged."

"Is something wrong, Will?" the director asked. "You were spaced out for a while there."

"Sorry," I answered quickly. "Just a little tired. The operation took longer than I anticipated."

"You should get some rest in that case. It's not good to push yourself like this. The hospital can survive a few hours while you're sleeping, Doctor."

I shook my head. "I'll rest in a bit. I need to speak to you about the invaders. I think I have a way to infiltrate them. Mind getting me that coffee while we chat?"

The director looked at me skeptically. "All right . . . I'm not sure what kind of crazy scheme you have, but you were able to solve Alice's problem. I'd trust any hair-brained plan of yours. I don't know how you do it, Dr. Walter."

"Talent, Director," I answered with a smirk. "And a lot of luck."

She rolled her eyes. "It's not like you to be modest, although it's a nice change of pace. Now go sit down and relax. I'll go make you that coffee. And call me Abigail. I think you more than deserve it now."

"All right, Abigail."

The director, or I guess I should call her Abigail now, left toward the kitchen with a spring in her step. I wanted to sit down but strange noises were coming from the back room, and it didn't sound like anything the two kids could make. I was a little curious about what the kids were doing and opened the door just a bit to poke my head inside. Alice and Toby were busy in the back, playing with something that I couldn't make out, while Molly watched on. The doll waved at me in greeting.

"Sorry if the noise is disturbing you, Doctor," Molly said as she made her way over toward me. "I'll make sure Henry's quiet from now on."

She threw one of her hair darts into what I could only assume was the person making all that noise, and the room immediately quieted down. Now I had to strain my ears to hear the patient over the giggles and chatter of the children. Alice and Toby were so engrossed with whatever they were doing that they didn't even notice my presence. I didn't choose to disturb them.

"Henry?" I asked, moving a little to get a better view but failing. "You mean that first escaped patient?"

I could just about make out some flailing limbs and muffled screams, but most of my view was still obscured by the backs of the two children. Some instinct deep down told me that it was better that I didn't see what was going on. I trusted that instinct.

"Yes," Molly replied. "The madam chose to save that particular patient as a present for Alice and her new friend to play with. She never doubted that you'd succeed, you know."

I smiled. "I try to keep my promises, after all."

"And I would also like to give you my sincerest thanks, Dr. Walter," Molly continued. "I've been the only companion for Alice for far too long, and seeing her interact with someone like her is . . . nice. I also know that you're in a very interesting situation yourself, Doctor. You're not from here originally, are you?"

Oh . . . the doll knew. I didn't know what to say. Did I deny it?

The doll shook her head before I had to make a decision. "Don't be so nervous, Dr. Walter. I don't care what your background is. You've done more for Alice and the madam than anyone else has, and that counts for more than anything else. Like I said, Doctor, you have my gratitude."

I nodded slowly, still unsure what to say.

The doll took out a little trinket, which looked like a tiny laminated paper charm, and gestured for me to take it. "I'm not sure what you'll do in the future, but I know that you'll go headfirst into danger with the invaders. Take the charm, Dr. Walter, and keep it safe. It will allow you to communicate with us here, no matter where you may be. Make sure you talk with Alice every now and then. She'll miss you, you know."

Molly's Cursed Charm (S Rank):

Description: A charm containing the concentrated resentment from a child's doll. The holder of this charm will be haunted by the spirit of the doll and its owner. Prolonged exposure to the curse will allow the spirit of the doll and its owner to manifest in the holder's dimension.

Well, that was an ominous description to get from my Arbiter skill. If I didn't have any background context, I'd probably have thrown the thing away as far as I possibly could, but knowing the friendship I established with Molly and Alice, I thought the haunting would be quite pleasant, honestly. Plus, if they could both manifest into the trials and help me out . . . Yeah, I'd keep this safe.

"Thank you, Molly, and I'll make sure to keep in touch," I answered and took the charm from her.

I looked at it and saw that there was a little piece of hair placed inside the plastic, probably from the doll. I placed the trinket carefully in my breast pocket. I felt a chilly sensation when I did so, which I assume is the curse working, but that sensation quickly faded.

The doll nodded. "All right, the director's coming back with your coffee, Doctor. Best not to keep her waiting. I'll keep the two kids out of trouble . . . and thank you again. I mean it."

I closed the door behind the doll and went to the table where the director was waiting with two hot cups of coffee. It smelled amazing.

"Checking up on the kids?" she asked before handing me my cup.

"Yeah," I answered. "And chatting with Molly. She gave me a charm to keep in contact with everyone here as well."

The director nodded. "That doll knows a lot more than she lets on."

"What is she, anyway?" I asked as I took a sip of my drink. It was honestly some of the best coffee I'd ever had. "I know she's always with Alice, but I don't think anyone else can even talk with her."

Abigail shrugged. "That's because no one else can. I'm honestly not sure how you're able to understand her. As for what she is? I'm not sure myself. My mother gave Molly to me as a child, and she got it from her mother. Honestly, the doll's been in my family for as long as anyone can remember. It's a tradition to pass on the doll to the youngest, so she's with Alice now."

"I see."

"But getting that charm means you're planning to leave, aren't you?" Abigail said with a hint of sorrow, but she didn't seem to press the matter more.

"Yeah," I answered. "That's what I wanted to talk to you about. You said that we needed to take the fight to them, but how can we do that when we don't even know where they're headquartered? We can't fight back without adequate information about our foes."

"That is true . . ." the director conceded. "I was hoping to get that information out of the patients if we can just understand what's preventing them from saying anything intelligible when questioned. It's all trials this and levels that. They don't seem to know anything about the inner workings of the invaders, but certainly one of them must know more."

I shook my head. "I don't think that's the way to approach it. The patients can't be trusted. They're sick after all."

"Fair," Abigail answered with a sigh. "That is true. I guess relying on information gotten from the sick and dying's not exactly accurate."

I continued. "We need to find this information ourselves, and I think I found a way to infiltrate the invaders."

Now that got the director's interest. "How so, Will?"

"You know how some of them disappear when one of them escapes the hospital grounds?"

She nodded. "Yes, it's one of the more annoying aspects about the strange patients the invaders send here."

"I think I found out the method they're using to disappear," I continued. "My research suggests that the invaders are governed by some kind of system that's allowing them to transport people where they please. I should be able to tweak it so that I get transferred with them if we allow the patients to escape all at once."

"All at once?" the director asked with a frown.

I nodded grimly. "It's the only way I can think of for my plan to work."

"That's asking for a lot, Will. You know what would happen if too many patients escape," the director said. "I can deal with the fallout now that Alice is stable, but it's still a risk. Our shareholders will not be happy with a mass escape like that unless you can provide them with solid intel about the invaders. How sure are you that you can do this?"

"Almost certainly," I answered honestly. "If the patients all leave at once, the system responsible for taking them all out will be overloaded for a brief period of time. I can use that instance to slip in myself."

"You've done the impossible before, so I trust you, Will," she replied. "Can you take any others with you? Even one more physician or doctor helping will be a boon."

"No, there's only room for one to go through, and since you can't go yourself, it'll have to be me that enters. I can't wait too long either, as we're losing more and more patients each day, and I need to have a minimum number of them alive to have this plan work."

The director frowned, but she couldn't argue with my logic. If I was speaking the truth, then the most logical person to go for such a mission would be the best doctor in the hospital. She couldn't refuse.

"I can't argue with you when you put it like that, Will," she answered with a sigh. "I'll . . . I'll need to get things ready. If you're going to an unknown location, I'll have to make sure that you're well equipped. Molly's charm will allow you to communicate with us here, but what if you need emergency backup? How would you be able to get back to us if you need to? Give me . . . give me a day to prepare. Can you wait that long?"

"One day should be fine," I answered. "And I'll be glad to take anything you think will help."

The director finished the last of her cup of coffee and got up. "All right, I'll go get things set up. The hospital won't be the same without you, Will, but we all know how important it is to get rid of the pests hounding our home."

"I'll miss it here as well," I replied in truth. "But we can't continue like this, and you know it. Alice being stable's just the first part of our fight back against the invaders; there's a lot more work to be done."

Abigail sighed again. "I know . . . Get some rest, William, and take the rest of the day off. I'll contact you once I'm done. Just make sure you say goodbye to Toby and Alice before you go. I'll let them know beforehand."

I nodded. "Make sure you let them know that we can still chat, and it's not like I'll be gone forever."

"I know," she answered. "But they'll still miss you."

Abigail took my finished drink and shook her head. "Anyway, get to bed now, Will. You'll need all the rest you can get."

I yawned. The director was right. I had been up for over an entire day, and despite my massive boost in endurance, I was still exhausted. A few hours of sleep would be nice. I still had to inform the regressor and Marcus about what I did, or at least a censored version of it, but I don't think they'll mind waiting a little longer for me to give them the good news. For now, I quickly made my way to my dorm and all but passed out on the soft bed.

I would miss this cozy hospital after I cleared this stage. I hoped Abigail would find a way for me to come back sometime.

CHAPTER FIFTY-ONE

The End of the Third Trial

The rest of the day passed by remarkably fast. After my nap, which lasted much longer than I anticipated, I had to hurry over to the regressor for another session of treatment. Of course, I didn't tell him the whole truth, but I did let him know that I was close to clearing the stage.

"You're sure you can clear it by the end of the day?" Jae-Hyun asked me. His condition didn't seem to be any worse, which was a good sign. Whatever treatment he was undergoing must have paused for the time being.

"Yeah," I answered. "But I'll need a distraction while I'm in the basement. I've managed to . . . overhear that key personnel guarding the patient ward will be incapacitated, so it would be an awful shame if you managed to, say, lead the patients here to escape."

He nodded. "I see . . . When do you need it done?"

That was a good question. I wasn't sure, actually. I was still waiting for the director to finish her prep. Well, I trusted the regressor to figure things out himself in any case.

"There'll be a signal," I said vaguely. "I'm not sure what the hospital's response will be when I act, but it'll be very obvious in any case. Just get things ready within the next day or so, and be ready to move soon."

Jae-Hyun frowned but didn't complain. "I'll get it done. Is there anything else you need?"

"No, just leave the rest to me."

"Thank you, Dr. Walter."

"Not a problem," I answered with a smile. "I'm just doing my duty."

I finished bandaging up the rest of Jae-Hyun quickly and let him go off to do whatever it was that he needed to do. I didn't want to take up any more of his time. I wasn't sure how he would win over the trust of the entire patient ward in a handful of hours, but that was none of my concern. The only thing left for me to do was to wait for the director, which left me with a lot of time to just wander around the hospital.

Walking around the various wings of Hope's Memorial made me realize, once again, how much this place had grown on me. I'd only been here for a few days, but the staff working here had been nothing but amazing. Once you memorized the strange rules, living here wasn't so bad, honestly, and sure, having to chase down the odd escapee was exhausting, but it was fun nonetheless.

And so, for the rest of that day, I just spent my time chatting with various doctors and nurses. I even checked up on the two kids, although I needn't have worried. They had fast become best friends in the way that only children could, and I spent more time than I should joining the two in their games. They were enjoying themselves too much for me to bring up my imminent departure, but I knew that I had to let them know soon.

It was shortly after night fell. The hospital was clear of all activity, so the director called for me to come down to the basement again.

She looked gloomy when she saw me, but she gave me a friendly hug anyway. It was hard not to let the melancholy affect me as well when she was like that.

"I've never been the best at goodbyes," she said with a forced smile. "So I won't say it. You're not going forever in any case, but I do worry. The invaders are dangerous, Will. I know you'll keep yourself safe, but . . ."

"Hey," I interrupted before Abigail could become even sadder somehow, "I'll be fine. I know my limits, and I'm not going there to wage war against the invaders all by myself. I'll get some intel, find out where their headquarters are located, and report back ASAP."

"I know, Will," she answered. "And I wish it was as easy as you put it. I just wish you could come back faster . . . I know we're not together, I don't know what we are honestly, but I'll still miss you, you know. You've done more for my family than anyone else has."

"I know," I replied softly. "But I might be away longer than that. You know as well as I do that we can't fight back against the invaders alone. It doesn't matter how strong you or Alice get. They outnumber us, and we'll need allies."

Abigail frowned but nodded slowly. She understood the power of Central better than anyone else in the hospital.

"So I need to go out there and find people in similar situations as ours," I continued. "There's no way that the invaders only targeted this place. I don't believe for a second that they didn't screw over other civilizations like ours, and I'm betting that others are just as angry as we are toward them. If we can gather enough allies . . ."

"Then we can launch a proper counteroffensive," the director finished with a sigh. "You're right, Will, although I wish you weren't. We don't stand a chance alone, although many would argue otherwise. We've only seen the tip of the invaders' might, and I fear that nothing we can do alone will be enough."

"But we won't be alone," I assured her. "If there's one thing that I'm good at—other than being an amazing doctor, that is—it's convincing people of a cause. But I can't do it alone. I need you to help me coordinate things once we've built up a strong enough force. Can you do that for me, Abigail?"

This time the director smiled for real. "I am more than happy to do so. Anything to get back at those bastards."

"Thank you."

"Anyway," she continued and pulled a small satchel from her shadow, "I packed you some things to take. I'm not sure what you'll need with you, but I focused on things that will help keep you safe in case you're ever found out. Take a look at it once you're on the other side."

I nodded and took the offered bag. Feeling curious, I peeked inside and saw it was stuffed full of little baubles and the like. I'll have to properly inventory what I got when I was alone.

"And finally," she added, "please take this as well."

Abigail offered me an antique-looking watch. It was an older design that was all form and function. I put the leather strap on and gazed at the little iron display, but I saw that the watch's hands weren't moving at all. I didn't think the director would give me a broken timepiece, and I couldn't find a place to put any batteries in it either. Confused, I used my title skill to glean any information about the device that I could.

> **Abigail's Memento (??? Rank):**
> **Description:** This timepiece represents the hopes and aspirations of its creator and her hopes for a brighter future. The holder of this memento is loved by the god of death.

God of death? Well, I already knew that gods were up and about from the regressor's explanation earlier, but I never thought I'd meet one in the wild as a human. No wonder people were so anxious about the director . . . but did that mean that Alice was some sort of fledgling deity as well? Then what the hell would Molly be?

I shrugged. Well, it wasn't a big deal in any case. I was pretty sure I'd met dozens of deities in my Xollon form, and if I'd learned anything from my interactions then, it was that the gods behaved remarkably similar to normal people. If nothing else, I'm kind of glad to have powerful backers helping me out.

"Please wear that if you can," Abigail continued. "It'll let me know if you're safe."

Something told me that it did a little more than that, but I didn't press the issue. The director had my best interests in mind, and it wouldn't do any good to question her help.

"I'll make sure to do so," I answered. "And do you know why the watch isn't working?"

Abigail frowned before taking my hand and glancing at the watch. It was like I said: The hands were not moving at all.

"That's . . . interesting," she started. "It's not moving, but that shouldn't be possible, unless . . ."

"Unless?" I asked, curious.

The director's expression brightened considerably, and a huge smile crept up on her face before she forced herself to calm down. "No, it's nothing, Will. But the fact that the watch isn't moving is a good sign. It means that I'll have to worry a lot less about your safety."

"Uh, that's good to hear?"

"Yes, it is," she said quickly. "Anyway, I think you should go see Alice and Toby one last time. Just give me a moment with them first. I'll have to tell them about what I just found out."

"What you just found out?" I asked. "What do you mean?"

"Never mind," she said dismissively. "Just wait here, okay?"

Before I could respond, the director quickly left the room. I wasn't quite sure what had happened, but the woman came out not even five minutes later, all smiles and cheer. I was even more confused seeing the change in her expression.

"Okay, Will," she said, "I've let them know about your situation. They'll be a lot more receptive now."

"All right . . ." I still wasn't sure what had caused her change, but dwelling on it wasn't going to do me any good. I got rid of the distraction and entered Alice's room.

The two kids and their doll saw me immediately, and I waved a hello.

"Uncle Walter!" Alice all but screamed. "I heard from Mom!"

"What did you hear?" I asked.

"That you're like us," the girl replied, "but you'll be going away for a bit."

I'm like they are? What did that mean?

"It is nothing, my host," Noe answered. "Don't worry about it. You do not need to concern yourself at this moment . . . It is still too early."

Yeah . . . good call, Noe, I don't need to be distracted. Let me continue to s—

"How long will you be gone for, Dr. Walter?" Toby asked, interrupting my thoughts. "I hope it's not too long."

I frowned. What was I thinking about just now? I felt like I was forgetting more and more things lately. Maybe that mental contamination was getting serious. I'll make sure to take some of that medication the doctor gave me.

"I'm not sure," I answered as I refocused on my current situation. "But I can still talk with you guys, so it's not like I'm completely gone."

Toby nodded. "Okay . . ."

"And you'll take care of Alice when I'm away, right?"

"Of course I will!" he replied with pride.

"He really has been," Molly added. "I've never seen someone who could keep up with Alice and all her antics like he has."

"I don't have antics!" Alice interrupted with a pout. "I'm a proper lady!"

Molly sighed. "Do you even know what an antic is?"

"Um . . ."

"Never mind . . ." the doll said before Alice could continue. "But be safe, doctor. Remember to keep in touch when you can."

"I will," I promised and turned to the director. "Are you ready for the patients to do their thing?"

She grimaced. "I am, although it will not be pleasant. I've informed the staff about your plan, and I've kept the dogs in my office tonight. The doors will unlock when you're ready."

"All right, we might as well get this over with now then," I said. "Guess I'll be seeing everyone here later."

"Yeah . . ." the director said one final time. "But it's not goodbye."

I bid everyone farewell one final time, which happened to involve a lot of hugs and a few promises of keeping in regular contact, but I was able to extract myself from the basement before too long. I did say that I had to be within the vicinity of the escaped patients, so I found an empty closet to hide in before giving the director the signal for her to begin.

A loud buzzing noise erupted from the speaker systems, and I could hear the metal doors unlock. That was followed a few minutes later by the scrambling of bodies and other noises that I couldn't distinguish. I could also swear that I heard Jae-Hyun's voice within that cacophony, but I couldn't be completely sure. Either way, I waited another fifteen or so minutes before deciding it was time to accept the Trash Matrix's request.

All right, Noe, let's get out of here.

"Acknowledged, my host."

I was engulfed in that familiar light, and I left the hospital, but not for good.

"Congratulations, my host," Noe said. "You have completed the third trial. Unit Noe has taken it upon myself to disregard the Trash Matrix's worthless babbling and inform you of the rewards myself. You have acquired two additional secondary titles and bonus experience for your hard work."

Thanks, Noe, can you show—

> **Yoona:** Brother? Walter? Where have you been? Are you okay?
> **Lady Awesome:** Boss, are you back? Yoona's pendant thing says you're back. Is little bro okay as well? And where's the priest?

What was going on? I didn't even have time to check over my rewards before being bombarded with party messages.

> **Walter's Fine:** We're fine, we just got out of the trial. What's going on?
> **Vadeem the Dream:** What's going on? You guys have been gone for over two months, that's what's going on! Get back to the guild as fast as you can. There's some big changes here. Apparently, the people in charge of the trials have changed, and they're making a mess of things.

The Storm to Come

The Overseer of the Central Collective drank his offer of tea and addressed the aspirant who sat beside him. He smiled at the other man, the final piece of the puzzle that would ensure that the lord arbiter W would have no choice but to conform with the rest of his operations. The man had embarrassed him in their last meeting, but the Overseer had ensured that such a thing could not happen once more, and this Ryan human was but one tiny cog in the machine that would ensure W's return, one final contingency in case the lord arbiter did the impossible again.

"Do you understand what you must do?" the Overseer said as he took another sip of his drink.

"Yes, sir!" the aspirant named Ryan replied.

"You will have my full support," the Overseer continued. "And I will ensure that you will be the king of the future human aspirants once you are done with your training. No aspirant shall be your match, even the anomaly."

"Thank you, sir! I have already memorized the anomaly's information and have taken the necessary first steps. My staff have been sufficiently briefed and will ensure that no mistakes are made."

The Overseer smiled. He liked this human, even if that insignificant lifeform was so woefully misguided. "Good, but never underestimate Aspirant Kim Jae-Hyun. You understand what would happen should you fail, yes?"

"Yes, sir!" the man said. "Your will shall be done!"

The Overseer got up from his chair and nodded. "Excellent! I look forward to seeing the results from you. The lord arbiter should be returning from his mission any moment now, so it would be best if you and some of your best men leave Pandora for the time being. There is much to do if you want to measure up to the anomaly."

Ryan hesitated for a moment, unsure if he was allowed to question anything that the god in front of him said, but he ultimately opened his mouth to ask, "Would it not be best for me to stay and hinder his operations here?"

The leader of the Central Collective laughed. This human thought too highly of himself. As if he could do anything at all to W, as if he wouldn't be anything more than a minor annoyance to that legendary figure. But the Overseer didn't voice that. It was best to allow the lesser species to think that they could, and although Ryan couldn't do much to the arbiter, he was a needed asset to rein in the anomaly and his guild. Origin made this strange individual for a reason, and the Overseer needed to understand what that was.

"No, my little aspirant," he said. "Your task is needed elsewhere. Pandora will fall, with or without you here, that much I am almost certain of. Your job is to deal with the aftermath because there will be fallout to manage, even if all my other plans are foiled."

Ryan thought for a moment before nodding. "Yes, sir. I understand my role. I will not fail."

"Excellent! Now get your people ready. You leave within the hour."

The Overseer finished his tea and left the meeting room. There was still so much to do before W's return from his impromptu trial. Yes, the leader of the entire Central Collective would give the lord arbiter W a most thorough welcome back. He hoped that W would be ready for the storm to come.

About the Author

Tismon is the author of the Unwilling Eldritch Horror of Fortune series, originally released on Royal Road. He has too many ideas in his head and just enough time to jot them all down on paper. Tismon resides in Ontario, Canada.

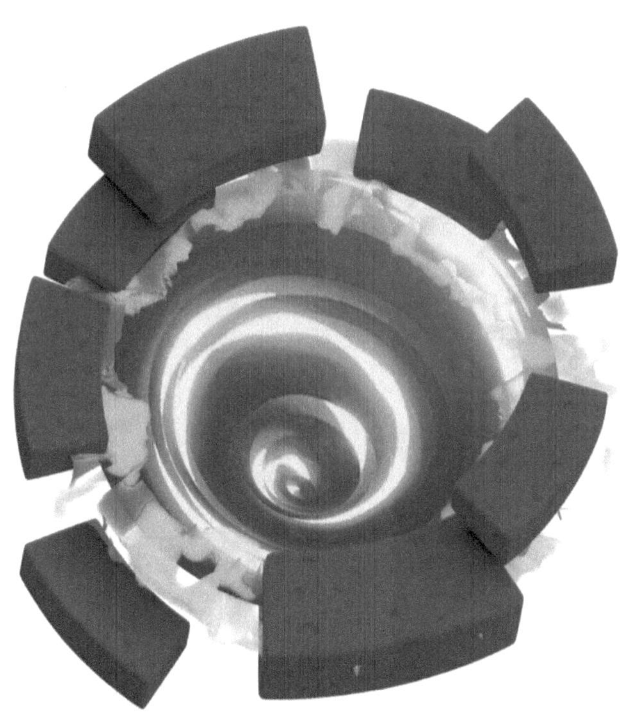

RESPAWN YOUR CURIOSITY

follow us on our socials

podiumentertainment.com

@podiumentertainment

/podiumentertainment

@podium_ent

@podiumentertainment